Tom Holt was born in London in 1961. At Oxford he studied bar billiards, ancient Greek agriculture and the care and feeding of small, temperamental Japanese motorcycle engines; interests which led him, perhaps inevitably, to qualify as a solicitor and emigrate to Somerset, where he specialised in death and taxes for seven years before going straight in 1995. Now a full-time writer, he lives in Chard, Somerset, with his wife, one daughter and the unmistakable scent of blood, wafting in on the breeze from the local meat-packing plant.

Find out more about Tom Holt and other Orbit authors by registering for the free monthly newsletter at www.orbitbooks.co.uk

VALHALLA

Tom Holt

www.orbitbooks.co.uk

An *Orbit* Book

First published in Great Britain by Orbit 2000
This edition published by Orbit 2001
Reprinted 2002

Copyright © 2000 by Tom Holt

The moral right of the author has been asserted.

A CIP catalogue record for this book
is available from the British Library.

ISBN 1 84149 042 3

Typeset in Plantin by M Rules
Printed and bound by
Clays Ltd, St Ives plc

Orbit
An imprint of
Time Warner Books UK
Brettenham House
Lancaster Place
London WC2E 7EN

For Mary Q and the Brain in Aspic:
gallant Knights of the Salamander,
churchwardens of the last, best Valhalla;
and for Fang the Dog, as always.

CHAPTER ONE

'**O**h look,' observed Napoleon. 'There's a speck of dust.' Because of the marvellous acoustics in the vast, crowded amphitheatre, his muttered observation rolled through the rows of seats and out across the stage like summer thunder. Nobody moved or spoke for a very long time.

'Coo,' said Genghis Khan eventually. 'So there is.'

A week passed uneventfully. Far away, above, outside, the latest minor war sputtered ambitiously as it swept through a medium-sized town (*Hundreds feared dead*, the newspaper men typed, big soppy grins on their faces) and drops of blood froze as they sank into the snow. But this was a better place, a peaceful place. No war here.

'Are you sure it's a speck of dust?' quavered a frail little voice somewhere near the back.

'Shut *up*, Attila, I'm trying to concentrate.'

In the middle of the stage stood The Wall: a plain brick wall some seventeen feet high, painted white. From the far end of the auditorium it looked so tiny that the men squashed together on the back row had to use massively powerful binoculars to see it at all.

'That's not a speck of dust,' said Frederick the Great, adjusting the eyepieces. 'That's a gnat.'

'Rubbish,' replied Ulysses S. Grant, a thousand rows further down. 'That's dust, I'm telling ya.'

'You reckon?'

'Yeah.'

Two more weeks passed. The latest minor war fizzled out into wussy peace talks, and at the back of the auditorium a door opened and the usher discreetly escorted a few new arrivals to their seats.

'Welcome,' he whispered.

'Thank you,' replied one of the new arrivals. 'Um, where is this?'

The usher smiled pleasantly. 'Valhalla,' he said.

The new arrivals sat down, and the usher issued each of them with a warm rug, a thermos flask and a pair of incredibly sophisticated binoculars. 'Enjoy,' he added, and withdrew.

A month slipped by; after which, one of the newbies managed to summon up enough courage to tap his neighbour gently on the sleeve.

'Excuse me.'

'Piss off, I'm trying to concentrate.'

'Sorry.'

A fortnight later, he tried again. 'Sorry to bother you,' he said, 'but—'

'*Now* what?'

The newbie took a deep breath. 'Excuse me,' he said, 'but what are you all looking at?'

'The Wall, of course,' replied the old hand, tucking the rug closer around his knees. 'Now keep quiet, for God's sake. We're just getting to the interesting bit.'

'Ah,' said the newbie; and for the next ten days he stared hard at the Wall through his state-of-the-art Zeiss lenses. The newbie was an intelligent man, and observant – well, you didn't get to be second-in-command of the entire Air Force without being pretty damn observant. 'I don't get it,' he whispered.

'Christ,' hissed his neighbour angrily (and thanks to the excellent acoustics, he shared the remark with the whole audience). 'Don't you ever stop talking?'

The newbie was a master tactician. 'I'll gladly shut up,' he replied, 'if you tell me what you're all staring at.'

The old hand sighed. 'The paint, of course.'

'The paint?'

'On the wall.'

Far away, above, outside, another minor war cautiously nuzzled its way into the world, like a snowdrop blossoming. 'But that's crazy,' muttered the newbie. 'Watching paint dry: what kind of eternal reward is that for a lifetime of service and a glorious death in battle?'

'Reward?' The old hand looked at him oddly. 'You fool, this is *Valhalla*.'

'Val-halla,' Carol repeated, rolling the syllables round her tongue and savouring them. 'Sounds cool.'

Her friend gave her a contemptuous look. 'Cool,' she repeated. 'A great big place full of dead guys fighting. Sounds to me like somebody needs to get a life real bad.'

The young man propped his elbows on the bar and shrugged. 'You're entitled to your opinion,' he said. 'All I'm saying is, that was how they saw it. They *liked* fighting and killing. Their motto was, who needs to get a life when you can take one instead?'

The girl dried a glass thoughtfully. 'Tell me more about the – what did you say they were called? Valkyries?'

The young man nodded. 'Literally translated,' he said, licking beer-froth out of his moustache, 'it means *choosers of the slain*. Like, they got to decide who was worthy of going to Odin and who wasn't.'

'That's what they did?'

'You bet,' said the young man. 'And then they escorted the souls of the heroes to Valhalla, where they brought them these huge jugs of ale and stuff.'

'Driving cabs and clearing up after dead guys,' sniffed the cynical friend. 'It gets better. In my neighbourhood, most of that Valkyrie stuff gets done by Puerto Ricans.'

'Ignore her,' said the girl. 'I think it sounds—' She paused, searching for the right word. 'Glorious,' she decided. 'It sounds glorious.'

The young man finished his beer. 'Well,' he said, 'I gotta go. It was real nice meeting you.'

'You're leaving?' the girl said.

'Yes.'

'Oh.'

The young man left; and not long after that the bar closed and it was time for her to go home. *Choosers of the slain*, she thought, as she unlocked the massively secured door of her apartment. *That's got a ring to it. That's what I call a job description.*

She played back her messages – boring, dull, mundane, obscene phone call, boring – got undressed, climbed into bed and clicked off the light. In the darkness, the image lingered: a high, vast roof of massive beams dimly visible through the smoke of a great orange fire glowing in a long hearth that ran the whole length of the enormous, crowded hall, with tables and benches crammed with bearded warriors on either side; at one end, a raised dais, a high table in the shadows where a looming presence sits and watches; noise and thundering laughter, wooden platters and horn mugs banged on the tabletop, not quite drowning out the strange, compelling music of the old blind harper in the far corner—

(*Jesus! I don't know spit about Viking interior design. Where in my mind is all this weird stuff coming from? Or did I die in my sleep and get sent to California?*)

She woke up, her eyes open, and listened: nothing, except (far away, below, outside) the blaring of car horns, a few shouts – angry, confused, drunk, stoned – two people having a loud argument in one of the apartments down the hall, distant synthetic music. *Must've seen it on TV or some movie,* she rationalised sleepily. *Wasn't there that thing with Kirk Douglas and Tony Curtis?* She lay back and listened to the noises, strangely comforting in their familiarity. They lulled her to sleep like the babble of a mountain brook or the patter of spring rain on thatch.

—Back to the smoky, echoing hall, where she slammed down a froth-slopping mug of ale in front of a huge man who looked like he was drowning in his own beard. She barked out, 'Okay, what'll it be?'

The bearded man looked at the slab of rune-inscribed wood in his hands. 'May I to be having the double roast ox on rye?' he said. 'Extra onions. However, please to hold the olive.'

Out of nowhere, a heavily laden platter appeared in her right hand. (*Of course: all the food and drink are magic here.*) She put it down on the table, skilfully avoided an enormous wandering hand, muttered 'Have a nice day,' and hobbled – goddamn uncomfortable high-heeled boots – down the line of benches to fill another order. Her armour (why was she wearing *armour?*) was hot and slimy with ambient cooking grease. She could feel *things* snooping about in her hair. Another wandering paw probed her defences and this time managed to slip past; she cracked it across the knuckles with the edge of her tray.

You don't have to be dead to work here, but it helps.

'Of course,' laughed a flaxen-bearded, red-nosed giant, grabbing her wrist and pulling her toward him. 'Valholl.'

She was too startled to do anything except stare at him. 'Excuse me?' she said.

'Valholl. Val-hall-a.' He grinned, revealing a mouthful of yellow stumps that would have revolted one of those small birds who live by picking rotting meat out from between the teeth of crocodiles. 'Hadn't you for yourself it been working out? This the afterlife not for dead heroes is. This the afterlife for uppity cocktail waitresses.'

And then, of course, she woke up. As her eyes opened, she could feel relief flooding through her – for a brief, terrifying moment she'd actually believed that she'd died and ended up in that ghastly, horrific place. The light filled her eyes, warm and mellow. She yawned gratefully, stretched out her arms, and felt something.

A beard.

Eeek, she thought; and then, *It must have been a better night than I thought I remembered.* She blinked through the yellow dazzle of sunlight and propped herself up on one elbow.

Beside her in the bed – you could just about call a pile of mangy furs and smelly blankets a bed – was a large, naked, sleeping, unhygienic-looking Norseman.

Oh shit, she thought. *Valhalla.*

All the comforts, all the excitement, all the fun: everything the original had, in fact, except the need to die first.

That, at least, was the theory.

At the end of the table there was a crash, and someone swore. Howard leaned forward enough to be able to see round Veronica's knee-thick elbow and quickly identified the source of the disturbance. Dennis had tried to get up from the table, forgotten that he was still wearing his chain mail, been pulled off balance by the weight, and fallen over. He was now lying on his back like a silver beetle, waving his arms and legs in the air in a futile attempt to get up again.

It can't have been like this, Howard thought. *For all that our props and costumes and armour are near-as-dammit authentic, we must be missing something. People back then didn't just fall over, surely? Someone – Chaucer, or a saga-writer or somebody – would have mentioned it.*

'Help him up, someone, for pity's sake,' Veronica sighed. 'Just lying there, he's making the place look untidy.'

'Nah,' replied Fat Tony, his mouth full of spit-roast Sainsbury's ox. 'Falling over and writhing about in the straw is period. Definitely period. He should be drunk, of course, or dying of ergotism, but the effect's the same. Leave him be.'

The helping hands that had been reaching out to the fallen man quickly withdrew. Fat Tony was the duly elected Authenticity Cop for the War-Band of Sigurd Bloodtooth (Smethwick chapter) and on matters of what was and wasn't in period, his word was law. Why this should be, nobody was quite sure. Fat Tony was no historian: he'd joined the War-Band so as to be able to bash people with bits of metal without being arrested. Maybe it was because Fat Tony was big, and tended to find expression for his magnitude in belting people who disagreed with him. God, yes; there had been the time when the visiting British Museum lecturer had pointed out to Fat Tony that an outfit consisting of a home-spun cloak, baggy cross-gartered trousers, woollen tunic, stainless-steel mailshirt and Reeboks contained at least one gross anachronism. Afterwards, when the lecturer was fit enough to be discharged, they'd had to take him from the hospital to the station in a wheelbarrow.

'More ale!' someone thundered up at the top end of the table. 'Ale! Ale!'

'All right, hold your water,' a female voice replied. 'I'll be with you in a jiff.'

Or maybe, Howard reflected, shoving a chunk of utterly authentic pork fat on to the edge of his trencher, maybe this is *exactly* how it was, and the only misapprehension is on the part of those who equate Valhalla with *Heaven*. For all he knew, the Norse afterlife for people who didn't come to a bad end after a lifetime of killing and bullying was really rather pleasant: quiet and peaceful in a Laura Ashley sort of way, with books and bone china teacups and asparagus quiche and big handmade teddy bears . . .

'Pass the mustard.'

Howard clicked out of his daydream and shoved the mustard pot down the table. Mustard wasn't period, but Fat Tony wouldn't eat boiled pork without it, so the Colmans pot was hidden inside an utterly authentic Norse drinking vessel, made out of what Howard devoutly hoped was a synthetic skull provided by Roddy the medical student. You lifted back the top jaw to reveal the mustard. The spoon stuck out through the left eye socket.

Having rejected the rest of his allocation of boiled pork, Howard poked about on his plate for something to eat. The only thing he recognised after a thorough excavation was a leek, and he spent a frustrating minute or so trying to find some way of transferring this to his face using only the permitted period utensil, a whacking great knife that looked like the sort of thing Captain Ahab would have used for cutting up whales. One of these days, he knew, he was going to slit open his own tongue like an envelope with the bloody thing. Whether that was likely to be worse than Fat Tony's ordained punishment for eating with a fork during a banquet ('Gosh,' someone had said when he'd first announced it. 'But are you sure it'd fit in there?') he wasn't sure and certainly didn't want to find out.

'You look miserable,' said the man next to him. Howard moved his head forty degrees to the right and caught a glimpse of Martin the mortgage adviser in the narrow interstice between helmet and beard. 'Have some more ale, cheer yourself up.'

Howard sighed impatiently. 'It's not ale,' he said. 'It's Tesco's own-brand lager. Not,' he added quickly, 'that I mind. Not in the least. It may not be authentic but at least it hasn't got plankton living in it, like it would have done back then.'

'Please yourself,' Martin replied cheerfully, sloshing yellow fizz into his horn mug. 'Nikki's driving, so I'm all right.'

Now that's the Society all over, Howard reflected. *Killing, maiming, plundering, carousing and ravishing non-stop from half-past seven Friday night till teatime Sunday, but none of them would ever dream of breaking the law. That's what makes it all a farce, not because someone shows up with a zip fly or a cloak the wrong shade of indigo. Modern people in primitive clothes are just modern people who look silly.* He'd joined the Society because he hated being modern, because he was painfully and perpetually aware that he'd been born out of his time—

''Scuse me,' someone a bit further down the table said. 'Oh God, did it land in your lap?'

'Yes.'

'Christ. Sorry. Look, it *will* come out. Most of it.'

—not because he was a slob or a nutcase who believed that it was all right to behave like a wild animal and blame it on History. Even in the real Valhalla, surely, people didn't go around doing – *that* – and then carry on blithely stuffing and swilling as if nothing had happened. It was wrong and unfair to assume that people in history were like that; on a par with saying that people who live in council houses wash their socks in the bog and pee in the sink.

'You're right,' said the bloke on his left. 'It wasn't quite like this. For one thing, the wall hangings are the wrong colour.'

'Of course this isn't like the genuine Valhalla. For one thing, Valhalla wasn't a galvanised steel barn seventy-five yards from the northbound carriageway of the M5. For another thing,' Howard added with a slight scowl, 'there *was* no real Valhalla. Even the real Valhalla wasn't real.'

The bloke on the left – Howard couldn't remember having seen him before – shook his head. 'You reckon,' he said.

Howard nodded. 'Yeah,' he said, 'I do. Likewise, I don't hang up a stocking for Santa any more, and I don't believe in the Tooth Fairy. I've even heard a rumour that it isn't really the stork who brings babies.'

'So my son assures me,' the stranger replied, 'though I

prefer to keep an open mind on the issue. True, it doesn't bring babies round where I live, but maybe that's because it's got enough sense to realise that if it landed for more than half a second, some bugger would steal its wing-feathers. Don't you want that bit of pork fat? No? Mind if I—?'

'Go ahead,' Howard replied. 'You aren't from round here, then?'

The stranger dipped his head by way of confirmation. 'Just passing through,' he said. 'On business, you know.'

'Ah,' Howard said. Then, to make conversation, he added, 'What line of work are you in, then?'

'Personnel,' the stranger replied. 'Executive recruitment. I'm what they call a headhunter.'

'Right.' There was something in the way he'd said *head-hunter* that Howard didn't like. He couldn't quite put his finger on it, except that it brought to his mind a mental image of a violin-maker rattling a spoon against a saucer and calling out 'Here, kitty, kitty!' He impaled another short section of leek, but it toppled off the point of his dagger and landed in his lap. 'Must be an interesting job,' he added.

The stranger shrugged his unusually broad shoulders. 'Not really,' he said. 'I mean, a job's always a job, whether you're a shelf-stacker in the Co-Op or a Hollywood director; it still comes down to rolling out of bed on a cold winter morning and *knowing* your day's not your own. That said, I'd rather do my job than most others.'

'Good money?' Howard ventured, wondering why he was bothering with this conversation. 'Promising career structure? Opportunities for travel?'

'Perks,' the stranger replied. 'Well, perk singular. But one hell of a big one.'

'Really?'

The man grinned. 'Oh yes. You don't believe me, do you?'

Howard shook his head. 'Not at all,' he said. 'Truth is, I don't know the first thing about head— about executive recruitment. Obviously you do, so I'm happy to take your word for it.'

'Listen,' the man said, 'never take anyone's word for anything. Golden rule of life, that is. No, I've made a pretty sweeping claim, so let me prove it to you.'

'Oh,' Howard said. 'Well, all right, then.'

'Good. Now, watch carefully.'

So saying, the stranger took the large, sharp knife out of Howard's hand and drew it across his own jugular vein with a swift, firm movement. Then, quickly, he clamped his own hand across the cut. Howard stared in horror; he could see little beads of blood welling out from between the man's clasped fingers.

The man was counting.

'Five,' he said. 'Six.' He removed his hand, revealing a deep gash and a thick slush of blood that appeared to be trickling *upwards*, back into the wound. 'Had to put my hand there,' he explained, 'else there'd have been a spurt of blood like a burst water-main. You'd have been soaked to the skin, and I'd never have got it all back in again. Now, do you agree that's one hell of a perk?'

The thin smear of blood that had been messing up the blade of Howard's dagger turned to a fine mist and sprayed itself neatly into the rapidly closing wound. The stranger leaned forward and used the knife to spear another gobbet of pork fat. 'And the money's not bad,' he went on, 'not marvellous but not bad. Only,' he added, 'there's nowhere to spend it except in the Company shop. No, the immortality's got to be the main thing about this business. Once you've got eternal life, everything else just sort of gets left behind; you grow out of caring about anything else, like kids grow out of playing at being soldiers.'

He handed the knife back to Howard, who took it point first. 'Eeek,' he exclaimed and came within an inch of dropping it on his toe.

'Anyway,' the stranger said, his mouth full of pork fat. 'Now then, is that proof or would you rather I took off something bigger – let me see, bigger, bigger. Well now, what about my head? Might be a bit messy, but I defy you to stay sceptical.'

'*For God's sake*,' Howard hissed. 'Look, who are you? CIA?'

The stranger frowned. 'Isn't that the big chain store where you buy those rather old-fashioned shirts?' he said. 'If it is, I'm insulted. Do I look like I stand behind a till all day?'

'Please,' Howard groaned, quickly sneaking a look to see if anybody else was watching. 'I believe you, really I do. I'll believe anything; just stop cutting yourself up like a self-propelled bacon-slicer.'

'Whatever you say,' the man replied. 'Well, then, ready when you are.'

Howard would have got up and made a run for it if his legs hadn't turned to spaghetti. 'Ready? What for?'

'The journey, of course.' The man was holding his own knife now. 'It's a longish haul, so if you want to take a quick pee before we set off—'

'Set off? Where?'

The man smiled agreeably; then, as he quickly shoved out the hand with the knife in it and buried the full length of the blade in Howard's heart, added, 'Where do you think, silly? Valhalla, of course.'

The four horsemen reined in their ghastly steeds, lowered their weapons and waited anxiously. The Great Beast curled up at their feet and started washing itself with its tongue. Behind them, the back-projection of burning cities and erupting volcanoes faded into white. On the ground, brimstone hissed as it cooled.

'That's it?' said the man with the cigar.

The rider of the pale horse assured him that was it, and his face fell; he looked like he'd been expecting a more animated response. But the man with the cigar looked, if anything, slightly bored.

'You've got something,' he said. 'Definitely you've got something. But to be honest with you, and unless I'm really, savagely honest I don't see how I can help you guys – to be brutally, viciously honest, I don't really see you people in comedy.'

The look of disappointment on the four horsemen's faces would have melted most hearts; it was like watching a bunch of six-year-olds being told that Christmas had just been cancelled. But the man with the cigar had a heart that not even an oxyacetylene flame would melt. Rumour had it, in fact, that this had been proved by experiment on a number of occasions.

'If I were you,' the man went on, 'I'd stick to what you know. Doing the End of the World, I can get you all the gigs you want – well, one gig, guaranteed. But comedy, you've got to work on it. Lighten up a little. Lose the Beast. Till then,' he added, relighting the cigar on a puddle of molten lava, 'don't give up the Doomsday job. I'll call you, okay?'

The horsemen nodded and trooped out, with the Beast trotting at their heels like Jurassic Park's answer to a Yorkshire terrier. When they'd gone, the man shook his head sadly and sat down behind his desk. On the window above it was written

LIN KORTRIGHT
SUPERNATURAL AGENCY

only backwards.

The telephone rang. Kortright scowled at it and frowned. He wasn't really in the mood for listening patiently to the neurotic witterings of some of his clients, and he was tempted to let the answering machine pick up the messages while he put his feet up on the desk and tried to get his head together.

On the other hand, a significant proportion of his client base was made up of gods of one sort or another; pretending you aren't in when the guy on the other end of the line is all-seeing and omniscient isn't the best way to foster a close working relationship. He sighed, picked up the phone and tucked it in the slot between shoulder and jaw.

'Hey, Zeus,' Kortright said, as his face reverted to its default smile. 'This is great, I was just about to call . . . Yes, I spoke to the Disney people, I . . . No. Basically, Zee, the bottom line is no, nada, forget it. Why? *Why?* Well, it's very simple, my friend, you *can't* sue Disney, they got better lawyers than you do, they can afford better lawyers . . . Hey, don't give me that, man. I mean, you may be God Almighty, but they're the fucking *Disney Corporation* . . . Yes, okay. Yes, I'll talk to them again. There must be some way to sort this out to our mutual advantage. Yeah, you bet. Of course I'm here for you, Zee, that's my entire purpose in life, you know that. Lunch? Well, actually, lunch is kinda hard for me this week—'

Suddenly his desk was covered in plates of food. An ice-cold magnum of champagne landed in his lap, making him wince sharply.

'—Except,' he continued smoothly, 'Wednesday, Thursday, Friday or Saturday. No, nothing I can't put off. All right then, Friday. Yeah, you too, Zee. It's been great talking. Ciao.'

The line went dead, and Kortright put the receiver back with a muted snarl. Then he pushed his chair back as far away from the desk as it would go, took a stopwatch from his vest pocket and started the countdown. Precisely five minutes later (over the hill, perhaps, but Zeus was still one hell of a special-effects man) the desk shook, the receiver was jolted out of its cradle and leaped like a friendly dolphin, sputtering with fat blue sparks. One minute later by Kortright's watch, the firework display stopped, and he was able to flip the receiver back into its rest using the long, massively insulated hard plastic pipe he always kept handy for just such an emergency. Then, albeit reluctantly, he used the pipe to switch on the answering machine, at least until the receiver had cooled down enough to touch.

He used the unexpected respite period for some power thinking; and what he thought about was the big deal, the once-in-a-lifetime-even-if-you're-immortal deal that was now so close to being closed that he could almost reach out and brush his fingertips against it. The Valhalla™ deal.

It had started, the way everything starts, with a phone call; and, to begin with, Kortright had had his work cut out taking it seriously, for all that it was, when you thought about it long enough, a viable (not to mention brilliant) concept – the universe of time and space's first privately run, free-market afterlife. Once you got past the sniggering stage, it made sense: a specially designed, up-to-date, consumer-choice-driven, fee-paying Hereafter for wealthy, discriminating clients who wanted more than the traditional afterlives that the world's religions could offer. It was, looked at from the right angle, an idea whose time had come, in a world where monolithic State monopolies were going down like dinosaurs at the start of an ice age. After all, once you'd dumped all the mystical trash, what was the difference between a heaven and a retirement park? One was life after death, the other was life before it, that was all.

The consortium behind the idea were businessmen, which was of course an advantage. By the time they had established contact with him, they'd already worked out the basic quantum astrotheology needed to make the idea technically viable, acquired all the rights to the name 'Valhalla' and trademarked them. That was as far as they were qualified to go. Being sensible men of commerce, they'd stopped there and called in an expert to advise them. Being men of wisdom and vision, they'd hired the best and made him an offer he couldn't refuse. The choice had been his, between a flat $10,000,000,000,000,000,000,000,000,000,000 fee and 0.00001 per cent of gross turnover. It had taken Kortright less than half a nanosecond to make up his mind. Whatever else he might be, he was no cheapskate. He'd taken the percentage, and now all he needed to do was come up with the package. It would be that simple—

On his desk scratch pad, several days previously, he'd written the one big question:

WHAT DO PEOPLE WANT OUT OF DEATH?

– and under it, a coral reef of jottings was beginning to form as he'd turned the proposition over and over in his incredibly powerful mind. But it was one of those things where the more you thought about it, the more complicated it became, and the increasing complexity showed up visibly in the geological strata of his notes.

The first layer was nice and straightforward:

- *Fun*
- *Relaxation*
- *Oneness with the cosmos*
- *Beach babes and margaritas round the pool*
- *A closer walk with Thee*
- *You wanna go where everybody knows your name*

Then the doubts had started to creep in:

- *? Catering for special dietary requirements*
- *? Disabled access; ramps for wheelchairs*
- *? One man's meat; some guys just aren't into beach babes*

– which had led to the first quantum leap into complexity: separate facilities for different interest groups, ethnic groups, cultural and philosophical mindsets, and socio-economic alignments. (What market are we targeting? Has anybody done any solid market research on this? What are we looking to build here: Plato's Republic, Disneyland or Reno?) This had led him inexorably into the first of his El Dorado hunts, the quest for the universal common denominator. Rephrase the original question:

WHAT DOES *EVERYBODY* WANT OUT
OF DEATH?

Unfortunately, there was only one possible answer to that. Namely –

TO AVOID IT.

All right, he'd thought, maybe this is the answer in disguise. Try this: what everybody wants out of death is immortality.

Back to the scratch pad; having to write very small indeed now, to fit it all in:

– *Okay, define immortality. Immortality is not dying.*
– *Fine; but how do you know you're not dying? How do you know you simply haven't died yet?*
– *Immortality isn't enough; you have to know you're immortal, else you'll just worry.*
– *Define death.*
– *No, that sucks. Define life. Life is what you lose when you die.*
– *So, if you're constantly dying but at the same time still staying alive, you know you're immortal.*
– *Valhalla.*

– which was precisely where Kortright had started from. Next he'd pulled down his original list of suggestions and tried a little elucidatory annotation:

- *Fun: fun is activities, games. Such as playing, swordfighting, paintball. Beating the shit out of people is fun, provided you don't get arrested next day.*
- *Relaxation: relaxation is an absence of stress. Stress is worry. Okay, so if you know you're immortal and no matter how many times you get your head cut off in a battle, it'll always grow back and be good as new, what's to worry about? On the other hand, it sounds unpleasantly like* Groundhog Day. *Needs work.*
- *Oneness with the cosmos: what exactly does this mean? Screw it.*
- *Beach babes and margaritas round the pool: well, no problem at all about what that means. Substitute Valkyries and horns of ale round a roaring fire, makes no odds. Subtlety isn't really at a premium in this scenario.*
- *A closer walk with Thee: guys will want to feel that the experience has significance, some kind of meaning, otherwise it's just non-stop party-party-party, no challenge, no sense of achievement. I guess we need a doctrine or dream of some kind.*
- *You wanna go where everybody knows your name. Indeed: community, a sense of belonging. Brand loyalty. Otherwise, a thousand years down the line, they'll all start slipping quietly away and defecting to Mithraism or some such shit.*

When he'd finished writing that, he'd felt rather good about it. There was a certain specious consistency, as if he'd discovered something that was actually true. This feeling lasted just as long as it took to visualise himself pitching the idea of a wooden shed where people bash each other with swords to a consortium of the universe's richest and most influential life forms. At this point, he'd found himself stopping and thinking hard, and realised he'd bitten through and swallowed the top half of his pencil.

Now, nearly a week later, he was sitting staring at a scratch pad that only had enough space left on it for one word. Lin

Kortright had been in the business long enough to know the value of signs and portents (hell, some of his best friends were signs and portents); if there was only space for one word, then that one word would be the answer. Unfortunately, every time he glanced across at the window ledge and caught sight of Mr Webster's extremely fat book, he had to face the fact that he was spoilt for choice.

One word.

All that money.

One lousy little word.

The phone rang. Not the still-incandescent one on his desk; his mobile. He flicked it open and tucked it under his ear.

'Julie? *Julie?* What's come over you, doll? You know better than calling me at the office. Yes, yes, I know, but hey, I'm in a meeting. I'm in a meeting *right now* with some pretty fucking important gods, and— Yes, look, all right, I'm sorry, but talking right now is really out of the question— Carol? Who the hell's Carol? Oh, right, that Carol, no, I hadn't forgotten we've got a daughter. But listen, honey, this really isn't the time, because—'

And then there was a moment when everything stopped.

When it slowly began to move again, Lin Kortright lowered his voice and said, 'Christ's sake, Julie, she can't be. Not Carol. I mean, how can Carol be *dead*, for crying out loud? She's only twenty-four. No, no, there's got to be some mistake, you can't . . . All right. All *right*, you stay there, I'm on my way. No, I'm not going to accept this, Julie. It so happens I know some pretty damn influential guys in the death business and— Julie? *Julie?* Oh, for fuck's sake.'

He folded the mobile away and stowed it in its shoulder holster. On his desk the scratch pad seemed to grin up at him, its two square centimetres of blank space taunting him. At least he knew what the one word was now, but he didn't write it in. Instead he tore off the sheet and started a new one.

On it he wrote:

WHAT DO *I* WANT OUT OF DEATH?

– and under that:

I WANT MY KID BACK, YOU BASTARD.

He stood up and reached for his overcoat (it could be cold in Cleveland at this time of year); then he stopped, turned back and scrawled a line through 'YOU BASTARD'. Above it, he wrote:

PLEASE.

Just as he was walking out through the door, the phone rang again. Instinctively he picked it up, yelped as the hot surface burned his fingers, whipped the handkerchief out of his top pocket and wrapped it round the receiver.

'Mr Kawaguchi? Hey, Toshi-san, this is unreal, I was just about to call you. Yes, I swear to God, my fingertips were actually in contact with the numbers at the *precise moment*— Yeah, sure, Toshi, but first there's this favour I want to ask— Yeah, sure it's about the project.' Kortright pulled out a chair and folded himself into it, still talking fast. 'Toshi, I have here a proposition that's going to be so much to our mutual advantage you simply won't believe— Yeah, listen, it's market research. Well, I'm coming to that, Toshi-san. What makes this market research different is—' Kortright paused for a moment, closed his eyes and took a deep breath. 'The difference is,' he said, 'I got someone on the inside.'

CHAPTER TWO

Howard opened his eyes.

'Where—?' he said. Then something exploded a few yards away, and the force of the blast picked him up and threw him through the air. He landed heavily, painfully, on his back, unable to move, as chunks of masonry the size of fists and footballs sleeted down all round him and on him; their impact was like a succession of express-delivery punches from the reigning heavyweight champion. Just when he thought it was clear at last, a flying roof tile smacked against the side of his head, temporarily blinding him with pain, shock and fear. It was the next thing to incredible that he was still alive after that.

He still couldn't move; worse, he couldn't feel his feet or his legs. Did that mean his back was broken?

Not far away he could hear a repetitive thudding noise. It was like the sound of machine-guns that you heard every night on the TV news, except that it was much, much louder; he could feel the vibration pulsating through the ground beneath him. (*Figures: they have to tone the sound down for TV;*

if it was this loud they'd get complaints. Not about the war, of course, just the antisocial noise levels.) Another explosion, also quite painfully close. He realised that he had drastic burns all down one side of his face and body. By rights he ought to be dead.

No. Hold that. By rights I shouldn't be dead at all. Shouldn't even be here, because this isn't Smethwick.

This can't *be Smethwick. Surely.*

Another explosion erupted a few hundred yards away, reducing a large building to flying rubble. Just before it ceased to exist, Howard recognised it as the Fire Station—

Which means this must be Stony Lane, and that crossroads over there is the intersection with Green Lane. Hey, my cousin Trevor lives in that – that pile of disintegrated rubble over there. This is *Smethwick.*

War? In the West Midlands? How the hell could there be war in Smethwick? Unless West Bromwich had finally invaded, or diplomatic efforts to resolve the vexed question of the sovereignty of Chad Valley had finally broken down . . . Impossible. Out of the question. War only happened abroad, in hot, foreign countries where people didn't know any better.

(A deafening *whump!* and a tremor like the earth shuddering; to judge by the direction of the blast, a Scud missile had just taken out the public library.)

Just enough sensation had returned to Howard's left arm to enable him to lift it, and he saw that instead of his utterly authentic reproduction chain mail (lovingly hand-crafted by himself using two pairs of pliers and approximately sixty thousand 8mm split-spring washers) he was wearing some sort of camouflage jacket, the kind that smells of camphor and costs you twenty-quid in an army-surplus shop. The little he could see of it, just about from cuff to elbow, was filthy with brick dust, smoke and blood. *Crazy,* he thought. *The last thing I can remember is sitting round the table in the mead hall, feasting on roast ox. How the hell can I suddenly be—?*

'In Valhalla.'

He tried to turn his head, but it wouldn't budge. The voice, however, was familiar. It was the last voice he could remember hearing before— well, before this happened, whatever 'this' was. It was, in fact, the voice of the nutcase who'd stabbed him with a knife.

'Hey,' he wailed. 'Get away from me.'

'Or?' The voice laughed. 'Or what? You'll call the police? Loosen up, will you? You're supposed to be enjoying yourself.'

'*Enjoying*—' The rest of what he'd been going to say was lost in a bout of agonising coughing. He could taste blood, trickling down over his lower lip.

'Of course,' said the voice. 'This is Valhalla. This is where heroes go when they die gloriously in battle. Here, for ever, they fight all day and feast all night, and at dawn the next day the dead stand up reborn and start up where they left off. Just as well for you, that,' the voice added, 'because otherwise you'd be a complete write-off.'

Howard could hear something gurgling in his own throat. He couldn't speak.

'I mean,' the voice went on, 'broken neck, broken back, two lungs punctured by shrapnel, skull smashed in four places, catastrophic internal bleeding from multiple bullet wounds; my friend, all the king's horses *and* Hawkeye Pierce and BeeJay *and* the tech team from *Bionic Man* couldn't put you back together again. Still, tomorrow's another day.'

With a last frantic effort and the final few cubic centimetres of air left in his shredded lungs, Howard managed to croak, 'What the fuck do you mean, Valhalla?'

The voice clicked its notional tongue. 'Oh, come on,' it said reprovingly. 'Isn't this what you always wanted? Only this isn't the silly pretend dressing-up-basket version; this is the real thing. You wanted total uncompromising authenticity? You got it. Jesus, and here was me thinking you'd be grateful.'

Another shell (or missile or whatever was causing the explosions) went off a few yards away. Howard watched the whizzing fragment of razor-edged steel casing all the way, from so high up in the sky that it was hardly visible, right down to the moment when it became too close to focus on and buried itself four inches deep in his forehead.

'Brought up to date, of course,' the voice went on. 'After all, the Vikings envisaged it in modern dress – modern by their standards, that is. They didn't dress up in bearskins and woad and pretend they were living hundreds of years earlier than they actually were, and neither should you. This is Valhalla with the benefit of modern cutting-edge technology; no pun intended, of course,' it added, as the blood stopped oozing out of the wound in Howard's forehead. 'Well, there you go,' it went on. 'Your heart's stopped beating, so I'd better be on my way. See you tomorrow, I expect.'

Don't leave me. He watched a pair of army boots walking away from him, until sight failed and he was left alone in darkness and pain, no longer even able to hear or feel the explosions. *This isn't Smethwick,* he tried to tell himself. *This is just a bad dream.*

This is Valhalla.

'First,' said Big Olga, 'we are to be the lavatories cleaning. This a job distasteful is, but to be doing it must someone.'

She handed Carol a wooden bucket, a bunch of thorn twigs bound together with a strip of rawhide, and a shovel.

'Excuse me?' Carol said.

'To be cleaning. Hastily.'

Carol took a step backwards, shaking her head. 'I'm sorry,' she said, 'but I think there's been, like, a mistake. I don't live here. This is not my home. And that,' she added, letting the bucket, thorn brush and shovel fall noisily to the floor, 'is not my job.'

Big Olga sighed; then, with a movement too fast for Carol's eyes to follow, she grabbed Carol by the back hair and lifted her off the ground. 'To be cleaning,' she said, slowly, like a native English speaker in a foreign land. 'Hastily. To be a Valkyrie is this what it is.'

Then she let go, and Carol found herself on her hands and knees on the floor, which was damp and covered in extremely smelly, mouldy rushes. 'All right, already,' she mumbled. 'To be cleaning, I'm on to it. And then,' she added, as she got up again, 'I'm going straight to the US embassy, and they're gonna send the Air Force to nuke your butt to hell. You got that?'

'*Youess?*' Big Olga frowned at her curiously. 'And what is meaning *nooke* and *butt?*'

Carol opened her mouth, but nothing came out. *My God. This crazy woman has never heard of the United States. Where is this?*

'Ah, come on,' she said nervously. 'Quit fooling around; you're beginning to scare me. We're in Arizona and this is one of those survivalist camp places, right? And you're all militia nuts, or religious freaks. Hey, I can handle that, it's okay. Just don't look at me like you've never heard of America.'

Big Olga's puzzled look relaxed into a contemptuous smirk. 'Ach,' she said. 'Amerikan.'

'That's right,' Carol said. 'Hey, thank God for that, you had me worried there.'

'Skyfather,' Big Olga continued. 'Skyfather he us instructs, when to here are Amerikans to be Valkyries coming, them this to be telling. I for a moment thinking, to recollect exact words.' She frowned, and the sight of her vast eyebrows being drawn together put Carol in mind of frontiersmen dragging their wagons into a circle. 'Skyfather, his message: *You in Kansas any more are not.* What is meaning,' she went on, 'me it beats, but is of Skyfather the word, for damn you good enough. Lavatories.' She scooped up the bucket, the brush and the shovel, dropped them on Carol's toes and clumped out of the door into the driving snow.

Carol looked round. Daylight was pouring in through the smoke-holes in the roof, seeping across the floor in puddles, but there were parts of this hall that would never see the light, let alone a damp cloth or the business end of a vacuum cleaner. The ugly wooden furniture was liberally draped with discarded animal pelts, bones and sleeping Vikings; the roar of their snoring was like a great waterfall, or the inside of a giant lumber mill. There were enormous dogs curled up in the cold ashes of the long fire, and dirty crockery everywhere. Carol shook herself. Had to be some kind of loony religious sect, Heaven's Gate or neo-pagan: no rocket launchers or AK-47s to be seen, which was something, but plenty of nastily genuine-looking swords, axes, daggers stuck in tables; all superfluous, since the smell alone was enough to stun. *Think, think; these fruitcakes like to hole up out in the desert somewhere. (Desert? Too damn cold for the desert, and when she opened the door, didn't I see snow?) Or at any rate in the wilderness, miles from anywhere.* Alternatives, then, were stealing a jeep and hoping she could make her own way back to civilisation, or finding a telephone, radio, whatever – except she hadn't a clue where she was, so how could she tell them where to come and fetch her from? Snow; could be Maine, Vermont, Canada, maybe even Alaska. Unless someone had these geeks on file and knew exactly where to look, she'd be asking them to scour a sizeable proportion of the planet's surface. Asking that of a government that can't even be relied on to deliver a letter was probably a bit too much.

She sat down on a bench, having first removed from it a half-eaten rabbit leg and a pair of wolfskin underpants. There was a third alternative, one that couldn't possibly be true: that she had died and gone to Valhalla, and all this was *real*. She felt ill at the very thought and had to put out a hand to stop herself falling off the bench; then, when she'd reset her internal gyros, she wiped whatever-it-was off her hand on the only semi-clean surface available, which was regrettably the skirt of this outlandish get-up they'd put on her. One thing was for sure: whoever and wherever, this costume had been designed by a man. Necklines like this one, in sub-zero temperatures; no way . . .

Yeah, but if I died, what did I die from? I'm not ill. People my age don't just die in their sleep. Okay, there's murder, or suicide, or a massive OD, or the building collapses; something like that I'd have noticed, surely. You must know it if you're dead. Mustn't you? Can you really die without realising?

She thought about that for a moment. Then she pinched her arm. *Ouch. There, you see? Alive.*

Or after-alive.

Presumably the woman knew; the one who'd dragged her out of bed and introduced herself as Big Olga. Surely she knew if she was alive or not. And all these Vikings: well, they seemed pretty much alive. Nobody snored like that when they were dead.

Valhalla. The afterlife for uppity cocktail waitresses. In the absence of decisive proof, it'd have to be a question of belief. Unfortunately, she believed. Because nobody from the twenty-first century, no matter how deluded or deranged, could ever possibly choose to live like *this*. Logic could gnaw holes in that line of argument in no time flat, no doubt about it. But logic, like a second-hand Lada, would only take you so far. The more she saw of this place and its inhabitants, the easier she found it to believe.

On a nearby bench, a Viking groaned and stirred. There was no way of knowing whether this was a Viking she'd already encountered or a new one; irrelevant, anyway, since they all looked pretty well identical: shaggy, grubby, greasy and lank, like an unwashed sheepdog but with absolutely none of the charm. They were so alike, in fact, they could all be brothers. Twins, even—

Or something else. Began with C. For some reason, Carol couldn't remember the word.

'Ale,' groaned the Viking. 'Of the that bit me dog in haste a hair. Very over am I hung, alas!' He dragged himself round and flumped onto the table, his head lolling across his enormous forearms. 'Also, for the love of Odin, a pastry Danske.'

Carol waited for a few seconds before replying. 'Excuse me,' she said. 'You talking to me?'

'Ya, ya. You Valkyrie, ya? To be hurriedly ale bringing. Of my head the anguish!'

Carol folded her arms. 'First, I got some questions. Where is this?'

'Valholl. With ale what that has to do?'

'Valhalla; I see.' She was frowning now. The more intelligent of her colleagues in the bar had taken that frown as a cue to go collect glasses from distant outlying tables. 'And you are?'

'Ragnar Earwax. In life being a great hero I was.'

'Really? Where I come from, there's a lot of guys that look like you sleeping in cardboard boxes under road bridges. Okay, Mr Earwax, I want you to do something for me.'

The Viking lifted his head an inch or so. 'Talking not good is. Ale I am needing, not chittering-chatter.'

'One little thing, Mr Earwax; then maybe you get your ale. Say something for me in Viking.'

'Chittering-chatter,' growled the Viking, 'and double Deutsch. Of this the point what?'

Carol shook her head. 'Go on, say something in Norwegian.'

'Was?'

'Norsk. Svensk. Dansk. Islensk. Anything. Ask me for ale in Islensk and you can have the whole goddamn barrel.'

The Viking looked at her pitifully. 'Was is *Islensk*?' he asked.

'You can't, can you? All you can talk is this funny-broken-English shit. You haven't got a language of your own; you can only talk what I'm supposed to be expected to hear.'

'For talking is Valholl not,' grumbled the Viking evasively. 'For fighting and drinking is Valholl, and so fit for heroes.'

Carol took a step closer; the Viking squirmed away. 'You aren't real, are you?' she said. 'You're some kind of lousy hologram or back-projection. You're a goddamn *prop*.'

She reached out, grabbed a handful of his copious beard, and yanked hard. The Viking yowled, slipped off the bench and crashed to the floor, leaving her holding a dozen or so long blond hairs. The Viking, meanwhile, had grabbed hold of her ankle and was trying to bite it, so she jabbed her toe into his mouth. He howled again and scuttled under the table like a crab.

'My big brother,' he whined, 'on you to be telling.'

'You haven't got a big brother, you freak!' Carol yelled. 'You aren't human, you're a—' She froze. She couldn't think of the word that began with C. 'Pain in the ass,' she concluded, so as not to leave the sentence incomplete. 'Ah for Christ's sake, come out of there.'

'Yours to be up.'

She aimed a sharp kick at the only bit of the Viking that wasn't protected by the table, namely his right heel. He yelped, and quickly drew it back out of harm's way. 'Out!' she commanded. 'I want answers, and I want them—'

Then someone hit her with a beer-jug, knocking her out cold.

'In the old days, of course,' droned the voice next to him, 'before the latest round of cuts, we had proper Dulux brilliant white gloss, not this cheap own-brand stuff. Now Dulux, there's a brand you can really *watch*, you know? Why, I spent the whole of the fifteenth century just following this one minute little run forming on the bottom left-hand corner. This modern non-drip rubbish—'

Attila the Hun closed his eyes, just for a moment. He didn't want to; the last time he'd let his attention wander, somewhere in the seventeen-eighties, he'd missed the event of the century: a gnat landing on the Wall and getting its feet stuck. But his neighbour's voice was so amazingly dull, so entrancingly soporific, it'd have taken reinforced steel joists to keep his eyelids from closing . . .

It wasn't always like this.

'—was always my favourite bit, just about when it wasn't *dry*; you couldn't in all honesty say dry exactly, more sort of squidgy-tacky so if you prod it with your finger you can feel the wet stuff deep down moving under the dry skin—'

Once there had been the open steppes, the thudding of hooves, the whistle of arrows descending, the screech of the sword against the steel chape of the scabbard. But no paint. Must've been pretty damn boring with no paint.

'—and when you've been here as long as I have, you'll get to the stage where you can actually see when it reaches that precise point where if you were to press into it with your thumbnail it'd be hard, not soft, though of course it depends on how thick the coat was to begin with; I mean, if they put on a decent undercoat to start with it changes everything—'

Behind his eyes he could see it now: the moment when the line had faltered at Chalons, when Aetius's Gothic infantry had held up, in spite of their catastrophic losses, and refused to give ground any further; that point where his wave had broken, and gradually started to recede. Funny, he thought, on that whole vast, gaudy battlefield there hadn't been a single newly painted surface, not so much as a skirting board or a windowsill; but at the time he'd actually thought it was mildly interesting, almost as if something important had been happening. Of course, he knew better now, but at the time—

He sat up and opened his eyes. 'How long have I been here?' he asked.

'—plastic emulsion, which I wouldn't give you the pickings of my teeth for. What did you just say?'

Attila blinked. 'I asked you if you knew how long I'd been here.'

His neighbour nodded, his eyes still fixed on the distant white glow. 'I thought that's what you said. Aren't you feeling well, then?'

'I'm fine, thanks. Why do you ask?'

'Because of what you said just now,' his neighbour replied. 'Some crazy nonsense or other, I couldn't make head nor tail of it. Hello, it's off again. Here, can you see? About fifteen feet west of the centre; if you look really closely you can just make out that tiny pucker where a drip will some day form. Now if you really concentrate, and I mean *really* concentrate, then in about sixty years' time—'

'Bloody hell,' Attila said, standing up. 'My army. My kingdom. Dammit, my whole empire—'

His neighbour's eyes were still fixed on the wall; he was watching Attila's extraordinary behaviour with the trailing edge of his peripheral vision only. But his peripheral vision was giving Attila one hell of a funny look.

'Where do you think you're going?' his neighbour hissed.

'I can't stay here,' Attila protested. 'This is wrong. Out there, the world—'

A hand descended on his shoulder, pushing him back into his seat. He tried to struggle, but all his strength, those exceptional resources of muscle and sinew that had allowed him to draw a hundred-and-twenty-pound composite horn bow with no more effort than if he'd been wiping a runny nose, had somehow evaporated. His knees buckled, and his backside and the base of his spine jarred as they made contact with the hard, cold stone.

'Let me out!' he tried to yell, but the words came out in a little quavery whisper.

'Sit still,' said a low, deep voice behind his ear. 'Watch the nice paint.'

'But I don't want to watch the frigging paint,' he twittered.

'Do you know who I am? Do you? Then I'll tell you. I'm
A—'

'Well?'

Attila made a funny queeping noise at the back of his
throat. 'I can't remember,' he croaked.

'That's the spirit, son. Keep it up. Watch the nice paint.'

'But—' He got no further. Suddenly he needed all his
strength and determination just to breathe in. That was something a person could easily forget to do, breathing. And then
where would a person be?

'My name.' The sound of his voice was as faint as the wind
rustling in a single blade of short grass. 'Somebody tell me.
I've forgotten.'

'Don't need a name to watch the nice paint. Go on, look.
Otherwise you might miss something.'

'Wouldn't want that,' Attila murmured drowsily.
'Doanwannamissnuvvernat.'

'You're getting it. Sit tight, now. Remember, watch the nice
paint.'

The grip on his shoulder relaxed, but Attila didn't move or
speak. Instead he yawned, and his eyelids slid shut like a pair
of those automatic doors you get in supermarkets. Then he
stayed absolutely still and quiet for a week, just to make sure
the nasty man with the big heavy hand had really gone.

'I'm Attila,' he said softly. 'Attila the Scourge of God, king
of the Hun nation, and bugger me, did you see that, the drip's
fallen off. Bloody hell, I've been tracking that drip since the
Kaiser was a lad, and now I've missed it.'

'Serves you right,' said his neighbour unsympathetically.
'That's the trouble with you young people today, you just
won't sit still.'

Attila stared at the Wall. But it was somehow different now;
it was as if someone had rigged up an old Super-8 home-
movie outfit and was projecting a film on it. There he was –
Bloody hell, look at me, I'm on the Wall – galloping full tilt

across a corpse-strewn plain on a small, wiry black pony, while behind him a hundred thousand warriors whooped and yelled and hollered and *somehow didn't leave dirty hoofmarks in the paint . . .*

He stood up again. His knees were still weak; but the rug had slipped off them, and as soon as he was free of its unspeakably oppressive weight he immediately felt stronger, fitter.

'Oww,' he wailed, and sat down.

'Now what?'

'Pins and needles,' Attila whimpered. 'In both feet. Ow.'

'Huh. What do you expect, standing up suddenly when you've been sat there for fifteen hundred years.'

On the wall he saw himself again; a dirty bloody mess, four arrows sticking in his back as he crawled painfully through the mud, dragging himself by the elbows. That looked like it was even more painful than pins and needles. But the Attila on the screen didn't seem particularly bothered; he was elbowing along at one hell of a lick, swift as a thoroughbred tortoise, faster than a speeding glacier. Oh, if only he could have been that Attila, instead of this one.

You were, once. Now pull yourself together and start walking.

'But the paint,' he said aloud. 'I can't leave now, it's nearly dry. Come on, what's the rush? A few more hundred years won't hurt, and I'd hate to miss the end.'

Now.

'But suppose that Attila wasn't a nice person?' he objected. 'Why, I don't know the first thing about him. For all I know, he might have been dishonest. Maybe even violent,' he added, with a refined shudder. 'I can't actually remember anything at all, but I'm prepared to wager that my mother told me never to be reincarnated into the bodies of strange men.'

Wimp.

'Sticks and stones may break my bones but names . . .' Attila hesitated in mid-quote. 'Where am I?' he asked his neighbour; but the man had his hands clamped over his ears and his eye rammed up so close to the eyepiece of his telescope that the flabby skin of his brows and cheeks actually enclosed the metal. 'Be like that,' he said, trying not to let the hurt show in his voice.

'I thought I told you to sit still.' It was Him again, the nasty man; and there was his heavy hand, pushing him down. 'Why can't you just stay put and watch the nice paint like everybody else?'

'I don't *want* to watch the nice paint,' Attila screamed. 'I think the nice paint is *boring*.'

The hand on his shoulder was tightening, the thumb digging into the hollow between the muscle and the collarbone. It hurt. Attila couldn't remember having felt pain before. It wasn't nice. 'Don't start,' said the nasty man. 'And don't talk like that about the nice paint.'

'It's not nice paint. It's boring. Boring, boring, boring.'

Thwack! The nasty man slapped him across the cheek. Attila felt his eyes become hot and wet, and his throat was convulsing. The detached part of his mind that dealt with cataloguing and analysing new experiences made a log entry tentatively attributing these symptoms to fear, distress and unhappiness. 'Boring, boring, *boring!*' he squealed. 'I don't want to watch the boring paint. I want to go—'

Home.

Home. Where's that?

What a particularly fatuous question, coming from the leader of a tribe of nomadic raiders. Home is where the heart is; usually still quivering and nailed to a tree.

'I won't tell you again,' warned the nasty man. 'Calm down, or you'll end up where the bad boys go.'

I am Attila, the Scourge of God— A little fragment of a forgotten reflex surfaced in his unconscious mind, and he grabbed the nasty man's wrist, flipped him neatly over his shoulder and threw him six rows forward. There was a grisly sounding crunch as the nasty man landed. 'Yes!' Attila exclaimed. 'Ouch,' he added, as his muscles filed a formal complaint about the unexpected violent exertion. 'Where on earth did I learn to do that?'

Nobody answered. His neighbours on both sides had edged away from him; they were still concentrating like crazy on the paint, as if he didn't exist. He half-rose from his seat, completely undecided about what to do next. More scraps of half-digested memory were floating into his mind; bizarre, horrid stuff about burning churches and savage hand-to-hand fighting. (*Gee, those big sharp knives! A person could cut himself on one of those.*) But somehow, by some incredible effort of will, he wasn't looking at the paint.

'Run!'

He swivelled round to see who'd spoken, and saw a man standing in the ninth row up; a funny-looking man with long, droopy moustaches and a peculiar round fur hat with a steel peak. 'Run,' the man repeated. 'Go on, get out of here before they come and get you. Run, Attila, run!'

Attila stared at him. 'Where am I?' he asked. 'Where is this?'

'Valhalla,' the man replied. 'But for pity's sake don't tell them I told you. I'll get a thousand years in the blindfold just for talking to you.'

The blindfold – he remembered. Here, in Valhalla, if you were naughty they blindfolded you so you couldn't see the paint; instead you had to listen to the radio commentary over itchy earphones, a millennium of 'Looks like it's still wet; yup, not dry yet, what do you think, Bob?' 'Well, David, I'd say it's definitely still on the wet side.' It wasn't an experience you'd ever choose to repeat.

'Don't listen to him.' There was another nasty man behind him, another cruel, harsh hand on his shoulder. 'He's just making trouble, and he'll be punished. Besides, where could you possibly go? You're dead.'

Attila sagged; he could feel all the vitality ebbing out of him, like air leaking from a punctured rubber ring. 'Am I?'

'Of course. You died and were sent to Valhalla. That's why you can't remember who you were. We take all that stuff away. Believe me, it's for your own good.'

'Really?'

'Of course. If you had even the slightest notion of who you used to be, it'd burn you up. It'd be a far worse punishment than any blindfold.' The voice laughed harshly. 'In your case especially. For God's sake, you used to be Attila the Hun!'

Attila closed his eyes. For a while, all he could see was the Wall, white paint slowly drying on the insides of his eyes. He decided to ignore it, and found that he could.

'I don't care,' he said. 'Whoever I was – *am*, dammit – I have to find out. And no big *bully*,' he added, repeating his earlier over-the-shoulder manoeuvre with just enough power to bring the other nasty man sprawling across his knees, 'is going to tell me I'm not allowed to know. So,' he went on, gripping the nasty man's throat in both hands, 'I suggest you tell me.'

Then Attila noticed; or at least, he remembered. The nasty man's face was achingly familiar. Didn't he once have a face that looked like that?

'Correct,' whispered the nasty man hoarsely, through a painfully constricted windpipe. 'What keeps you here is you. It's the most efficient system and brilliantly cost-effective.'

His neighbour on his left took one hand away from his ear to adjust the focus on his Stargazer Magnum 3 astronomer's telescope, then hurriedly clamped it back. 'That's Hirohito,' the nasty man said, 'former Emperor of Japan. He's got enough sense to realise that the last thing in the universe he'd ever want to know is who he was. And compared to you,' the nasty man added nastily, 'he was a sweetie.'

'If I strangle you, will it be suicide? Let's find out.'

'You can't leave,' said the nasty man. 'And you can't kill me. Because you're dead. Dead people don't go anywhere when they die, not even if they do it bravely in battle. The story that they end up in Pittsburgh,' he added, 'is just a silly rumour.'

'I don't believe you,' Attila replied, increasing the pressure. 'And even if you're right, what have I got to lose?'

The nasty man's face was starting to turn blue. 'There's always the *risk* you'll find yourself in Pittsburgh,' he croaked. 'Six weeks there, you'll be really sorry you left. At least here, there's paint.'

Attila scowled. 'Shut up and die,' he growled.

'How can I, I'm dead alre—'

The nasty man wriggled convulsively, then stopped moving. Attila stared at him for a moment, then let go and stood up, looked round. Nobody was looking at him. The paint, he noticed, was still wet.

He remembered who he was.

'Wow,' he said. 'Way to go.' At the back of the auditorium, no more than a mile from where he was standing, he could see a little door. Something told him that if he went through that door, he would find himself in Somewhere Else.

'Hey.' He nudged his neighbour in the ribs with his toe. 'Save my seat for me, will you? I'm just popping out for a while.' He grinned. 'I may be gone for some time.'

CHAPTER THREE

'Conflict of interests?' said Lin Kortright, casually. 'What a strange idea.'

They looked at him and said nothing. A little dribble of sweat ran discreetly down past Kortright's ear and drained away into the gap between his neck and his collar. One of the distinguishing marks of a really first-class agent is never sweating where it shows.

'On the contrary,' he went on. 'I want you to look on this as a really unique opportunity. For both of us.'

'You already said that once,' said the small, frail Japanese man. 'You didn't say why.'

Kortright spread his hands wide. 'Sorry,' he replied, 'I didn't want to insult your intelligence explaining something so goddamn obvious. Okay; you guys want to open an afterlife service that's gonna appeal to the consumer. You think this is a new idea? Come on, will you? This concept's been around since Adam complained about the first shooting pains in his chest. It's never gotten off the ground because nobody knows what the consumer actually wants; because nobody ever got to ask one. Now, out of the blue, we got that opportunity. If I were you, Mr Kawaguchi, I'd start measuring Europe for new curtains, because when this deal goes through you're gonna be able to buy it out of petty cash.'

Mr Kawaguchi shook his head; a tiny, precise movement. 'I still don't follow, Mr Kortright,' he said. 'I fail to see how your unfortunate bereavement is going to make it possible for you to contact the dead. Sad to say, you can no longer ask your daughter anything. She's dead.'

Lin Kortright put on a smile that could have bridged the Grand Canyon. 'Because,' he said, 'you're going to help me bring her back to life. Soon as she's back, we can start doing some really detailed market research; you know, did you find the service in the underworld (a) excellent (b) satisfactory (c) poor? Did the staff do everything they could to make you welcome? Were the towels clean? Mr Kawaguchi, Carol's my daughter; commercial-opportunity awareness runs through her DNA the way the Mississippi runs through Dixie. I'll bet you that right now she's negotiating with King Pluto for a topside franchise for a chain of Hades Fried Asphodel restaurants.'

Mr Kawaguchi stared at him again; then he pulled the immaculately folded handkerchief from his top pocket and handed it to Kortright without a word. Kortright slumped a little, took it and wiped the sweat off his forehead.

'Distressing though your sad loss must be, Mr Kortright,' said Mr Kawaguchi, 'I must ask you not to allow it to cloud your professional judgement. I should regret having to cancel our agreement.'

'But . . .'

Lin Kortright stopped there. Until he'd met Mr Kawaguchi, he'd firmly believed there wasn't a person or a thing this side of Andromeda he couldn't negotiate with to the point where he could not only sell them the Golden Gate bridge, he could make them pay extra for postage and packing. Mr Kawaguchi was different. Compared to him, a brick wall was an elderly widow from out of town holding a shopping bag full of banknotes and stopping drunks and street crazies to ask them for investment advice.

Still. Desperate situations and all that.

'You want to cancel, Toshi-san, you go right ahead.' When it came to saying the lines like he meant them, Lin Kortright was a legend in his own breakfast meeting, a man who not only called bluffs but had a whole string of them chasing after him Pied Piper fashion with their tails wagging. So; though both of them knew he was bluffing, Mr Kawaguchi's stone face wobbled just a little and, in the split second before Kortright threw himself to the ground and started blubbering, he shook his head a second time and said, 'I believe cancellation would suit neither of our interests.' It was as if God had suddenly winked at Adam and said, 'Gee, why didn't you tell me you liked apples?'

'I agree,' Lin Kortright said. 'So why don't we work together on this and do each other a favour?'

'I'm listening,' said Mr Kawaguchi. 'Tell me what you have in mind.'

'Simple. You use your anti-thanaton displacement beam to create a purpose-built afterlife for my Carol, and shift her across into it. Then all you gotta do is reverse the polarities and hey presto, there she'll be.'

Mr Kawaguchi tilted his head twenty degrees to the left so he could confer with two of his associates. 'I fear you misunderstand the technology,' he said. 'The anti-thanaton field can create a pocket in the Great Unknown where certain specified conditions prevail; where, for example, all the client's wishes can appear to come true. If the client wants clouds and harps, we can provide them; likewise sherbet and houris, milk and honey, even perfect enlightenment. This is not a problem. But reversing the polarities would simply cancel the effects of the field; all you would bring back to this continuum is what already exists here of the dear departed. Nothing.'

Kortright nodded slowly. He'd been in this position before. Usually, it was the point in a contract negotiation where the guy on the other side, having produced as evidence that he had no more money to offer his bank statements, an inventory of his furniture and clothes and a formal valuation of what his dead body might be expected to fetch at auction, started opening his veins to prove he hadn't hidden any secret assets in his bloodstream. And every time, Lin Kortright had found a way to squeeze out just one more per cent, because nothing – *nothing* – is ever final. 'All right,' he said, 'here's the deal. We create an afterlife that's so like this life, nobody could ever tell the difference. Then your technical guys find a way to drill a hole or dig a tunnel – don't let them tell you there isn't a way, there'll be a way – and we bring her out. Like, meet me halfway. *Believe*, Toshi-san; that's how we do things in my business. We believe. And belief moves mountains; man, with enough belief, we could move 'em so much we could train them to deliver pizza. Just belief, that's all.'

Mr Kawaguchi raised an immaculately trimmed eyebrow. 'Belief, Mr Kortright?'

'Yeah,' Kortright replied. 'Belief. Some deadbeat walks into my office, he's got no talent, no personality, no charisma; hell, sometimes I find out I've been using their ears as ashtrays for a month before I even notice they're there. But then I *believe*. I look at this guy and I believe he's got what it takes, I believe he's gonna be the next major property. I have faith, I generate faith and that faith *makes things happen*. That's why I'm the best goddamn supernatural agent the universe has ever known, Mr Kawaguchi; all the gods there ever were, all the dragons and elves and saints and djinns and rakshasas, crop circles, unexplained lights in the sky, sightings of Elvis Presley, prophecies of Nostradamus – you bring 'em here, I'll believe in them. And once I believe, you'll believe too. And you'll take out your pen and start writing cheques.'

Mr Kawaguchi was still and silent. For a horrible moment he'd felt himself believing too, without having the faintest idea what it was he was believing in. 'You believe in my company's anti-thanaton beam, Mr Kortright? You believe it can bring people back from the dead?'

'Believe? I can make little kiddies hang out stockings for it on Christmas Eve. All you've got to do is give me something to believe in.'

Slowly, Mr Kawaguchi shook his head, fifteen degrees either side. 'I wish I shared your faith, Mr Kortright,' he said. 'But I don't. Thank you for your time, but we no longer require your services.' He stood up, and suddenly all his associates were standing too, though Lin Kortright was sure he hadn't seen them move. 'If you submit an invoice in due course, I'll tell my accounts department to believe it's been paid. Good afternoon.'

When they'd gone, their helicopter shredding clouds twenty thousand feet above the Cleveland skyline, Lin Kortright sat down at his desk and let his head roll forward against his hands. He wasn't beaten. He didn't understand the meaning of the word defeat and, like most Americans, encountering a word he didn't understand just prompted him to talk louder. On the other hand, he had to admit, he'd been bullshitting, making it up as he went along. All that crap about faith and belief—

'Excuse me.'

He looked up. Sitting on the opposite side of the desk, in the client's chair, was a little thin guy, a weedy little creep with thin sandy hair and enormous spectacles.

'Hey,' Kortright said. 'How did you get in here?'

'Faith,' the little guy replied.

Lin Kortright though for a moment; then he picked up a heavy cut-glass paperweight shaped like a human heart (a

Thanksgiving gift from Quetzalcoatl), took careful aim and threw hard. The little guy ducked just in time.

'Don't be like that,' he said.

'Who are you?' Kortright snarled. 'No, don't bother telling me, I don't want to know. Get out. And on your way, tell whoever let you in that he's fired.'

'But, Mr Kortright,' said the weedy little guy, 'you let me in yourself. Well, you called me in, anyhow. You sent for me.'

Kortright's brow furrowed. 'I did? I don't think so. I think I'd remember it if I ever got that sad.'

'You did too,' said the little guy. 'Don't you remember? Just now, when you were telling that man about faith and belief. You believed in me and – heck, here I am. Mr Kortright, you *created* me.'

A vision flicked across Kortright's mind, of the end result of the Frankenstein story as acted out by the Marx Brothers. 'Get outa here,' he said. 'Go on, shoo. I'm busy.'

'But, Mr Kortright, you did. You had faith. You believed, and I heard you.' The little guy hitched his face into a winning smile. 'I heard your prayer and, well, here I am.'

Kortright's hand was just closing on the desk stapler – not as aerodynamic as the paperweight, but almost as heavy – when something clicked into place in his mind. He looked up and studied the little guy carefully. 'God?' he asked.

The little guy nodded. 'Bless you, my child,' he replied.

Lin Kortright took a moment to organise his thoughts. 'Okay,' he said. 'Okay, suppose for a moment I'm buying what you're telling me. Lord,' he added. 'Just what in God's name kind of a god do you think you are?'

The little guy beamed at him happily. 'I'm the god of a guy who really knows what gods are like,' he said. 'I'm the god of Lin Kortright.'

At which point, he leaned back in his chair, overbalanced and toppled to the floor, crashing into the waste-paper basket and knocking over a standard lamp and a filing cabinet in the process. 'Sorry,' he said.

Lin Kortright stared at him with a curious blend of awe and loathing. 'Okay,' he said wearily. 'This time, I *believe*.'

The little guy looked pleased, but surprised. 'You do?' he said. 'That's great. Why?'

Kortright smiled sadly. 'Because every time a god comes in here and sits in that chair and says "Hey, I'm a god, I also do children's parties and bar mitzvahs"—' Kortright shook his head. 'I'll tell you something. To me, they always look like you.'

The little guy laughed happily. 'Isn't that amazing?' he said.

'Yeah,' Kortright said wearily. 'Look at me. I'm amazed.'

On a street corner stood a little man.

He was somewhere between sixty and seventy, white-haired, and dressed in respectable, slightly shabby clothes that were obviously his best – a somewhat shiny blazer with a badge on the breast pocket, carefully ironed white shirt with a frayed collar, crisply creased grey flannel trousers with thin knees, ancient but brilliantly polished black shoes and an antique regimental tie. Hanging from a string round his neck was a plastic tray, and in his hand was a collecting tin. He peered at the world nervously through thick-lensed, utilitarian-framed spectacles. He had cut himself, very slightly, shaving.

Every ninety seconds or so he would shake the tin, producing a noise known to Zen masters the world over as the sound of one coin clunking. One brisk, rather severe shake, as if anything more flamboyant would embarrass him, followed by ninety seconds of perfect stillness.

A stout middle-aged lady, the sort who can generally be relied on to fling largesse to the masses for any cause that doesn't actively endorse drug trafficking or boiling down small children to make glue, stopped and then approached him, her hand already inside her handbag groping for her purse. She stopped, looked into the tray, looked up sharply at the little man and walked away, terribly quickly. The little man seemed embarrassed, but not surprised.

Five or six rattles of the tin later, two nuns came round the corner, saw the tin and the tray (presumably the man too, but not necessarily: military authorities spend millions every year on disguising secret installations when all they really have to do is make them look unimportant and ever so slightly sad, like this little man) and stopped to investigate. One nun fumbled for loose change, while the other bobbed her head down to look into the tray; then she straightened up sharply, as if she'd got an electric shock, slapped the little man hard across the face, and stalked off, with her sister-in-Christ scuttling nervously behind. The little man sighed, dabbed a tiny smear of blood from the corner of his mouth, and solemnly shook his tin.

It wasn't the busiest of street corners; it was ten minutes before anybody else came along, and the next passer-by was a seven-foot-tall-and-broad-to-match biker, with the shoulders of a wildebeest and a ginger beard that brushed softly against his Death's Head belt-buckle. He walked on, then stopped and turned back; something quite unexpected had registered in his peripheral vision, drawing him ineluctably towards the tray. He inspected its contents, grinned evilly, muttered 'Cool' under his breath and squashed a ten-pound note through the slot in the top of the tin. The little man picked a small ornament out of the tray and with visible distaste hooked its shiny pin into the oily leather of the biker's jacket, just below the shoulder. The biker looked at him, shuddered involuntarily and stalked off, craning his neck as he went to admire his new trophy.

Clunk; ninety seconds; clunk; ninety seconds; clunk. A small boy was standing on tiptoe, trying to peer into the tray.

The little man lifted it out of his reach and sighed, 'Push off, son.'

'But I wanna buy a flag,' the boy protested.

'Well, you can't. Now get lost.'

'But it's charity,' the boy replied plaintively. 'My mum says it's good to give to charity.'

'Go away.'

'It's my own money. I was going to spend it down the arcade, but I'd rather buy a flag.'

'Clear off, before I smack you one.'

The boy trailed away, muttering; and the little man glanced down at his watch, visibly willing the hands to move faster through his allotted shift. No sooner had he gone than a policeman walked up. The little man looked at him guiltily.

'Excuse me, sir,' said the policeman, 'but can I see your permit?'

The little man shuffled his feet. 'I haven't got one,' he said.

The policeman looked sad but stern. 'Then I'm going to have to ask you to move on,' he said. 'We've had complaints, you see, and— Bloody hell!'

He'd caught sight of the little badges in the tray. They were small and crisply moulded out of gold- and red-coloured plastic, and vividly depicted a still-beating human heart impaled to the trunk of a broad tree by a thin-bladed dagger. The text printed on the side of the tray read:

VALHALLA FLAG DAY
Please Give Generously To Help Those Whose Fight
Still Goes On By
Wearing Their Heart On Your Sleeve

'That's *disgusting*,' said the policeman. 'Right, I'm arresting you under the provisions of the Public Order—'

And then he stopped speaking; not to mention moving, or breathing. The little man wasn't doing much, just looking at him in a particularly sad and self-conscious way, but his gaze's effect made Darth Vader's lung-paralysing scowl look like a cheerful smile from a four-year-old. Seconds later the policeman dropped to his knees, then sprawled on the ground, then vanished altogether, leaving behind nothing but a small patch of oily liquid and a faintly distasteful smell.

'Trouble?'

The little man turned his head and saw a smartly-dressed young woman in a grey business suit. He shook his head. 'No, not really,' he said.

'Taken anything?'

The little man nodded. 'More than all of last year already,' he said, with no apparent satisfaction. 'Never ceases to amaze me what people will give money to, provided they think it's for charity.'

'More fool them,' the young woman replied briskly. 'All right, Skyfather, I'll take over now.'

'Good,' said the little man with feeling. 'I feel such a fool standing here.' He extricated himself awkwardly from the strap of the tray. 'There's some very strange people about, you know,' he added with a shake of his head. 'Very strange indeed. It makes me realise how— well, *normal* our lot are. By comparison, I mean.'

The young woman smiled thinly. 'Homicidal lunatics,' she said. 'Bloodthirsty megalomaniacs. Psychotics. Sociopaths. Yes, reasonably normal for *Homo sapiens*. Did you know, by the way, that *Homo sapiens* is Latin for "man the wise"? I never realised anthropologists had such a sick sense of humour.' She looked down and dabbed at the oily puddle with the toe of her black court shoe. 'Policeman?' she said. The little man nodded. 'Oh well,' she said. 'That's your good deed for the day, then. Last year, I got two Jehovah's Witnesses and a traffic warden.'

The little man frowned. 'It's not a game, you know,' he

said; then, relaxing the frown a little, added, '*Two* Jehovahs? That's a free go.'

'On a triple points day, too,' replied the young woman smugly. 'Now I just need a journalist for House.'

The little man shuffled away – he had a slight limp in his right leg – and took a turning into a narrow, dark alley. After a moment fishing about behind some dustbins he hauled out a couple of black plastic sacks and a battered old cardboard suitcase. He slipped off his blazer and tie, folded them neatly into the case, laid a couple of sheets of tissue paper over them and closed the case up; then from the sacks he produced a shiny coat of steel chain mail, a close-fitting gilded helmet with a mask that covered his face, and a broad circular shield of gold-plated steel. With the air of a sewage worker getting kitted up before climbing down a manhole, he pulled these on, adjusted the chinstrap of the helmet, clasped a broad belt round his waist, folded the plastic sacks and packed them securely behind the handgrip of his shield. From nowhere, swooping low out of the shadow of the tall buildings that flanked the alley, came two oversize coal-black, ruby-eyed ravens. One perched on the man's shoulder; the other one carried on past him, pitched on a burst dustbin bag and started poking about with its beak.

'Hugin,' the little man snapped. 'Leave! Dirty! Honestly, from the way you carry on, anyone'd think I never fed you.'

The raven waggled its wings resentfully and flapped up to join its mate, just as a man in a boiler suit and a flat cap came marching down the alley, wheeling a barrow full of breeze-blocks. He stopped in his tracks and opened his mouth to say something; but before he could, the little man cleared his throat.

'Excuse me,' he said, 'but is this the right way for the Opera House?'

The man with the wheelbarrow relaxed a little and started giving directions, for which the little man thanked him politely. When he'd passed out of sight, the little man drew something black and shiny from a special pocket in the inside of his shield and pressed something on it.

'Odin to bridge,' he said. 'One to beam up.'

He vanished in a cloud of foul yellow smoke, and a moment later was standing in the dark, smelly wooden long-house where Carol Kortright had arrived the previous day. In fact, she was the angry-looking young woman who confronted him before he'd even had a chance to take his helmet off.

'You're Skyfather, right?' she said.

He nodded. 'That's one of the things they call me,' he replied. 'And before you say anything, yes, it's one of the politer ones. My real name is Odin.'

'Whatever,' Carol replied impatiently. 'But you're the guy who runs this joint, right?'

Odin dipped his head. 'I run it,' he said. '"Right" is a matter of opinion.'

Carol scowled away the feeble attempt at humour. 'Then you're the guy who's going to send me back,' she said. 'Look, I don't want an apology, I may not even sue. Just send me home and maybe we can forget—'

'I'm terribly sorry,' Odin said. 'But that's out of the question. You see, I'm just the officer in charge, not much more than a glorified janitor, really. If you've got a complaint, you'll have to take it up with the proper authorities.'

Carol made a visible show of keeping her temper. 'All right,' she said, 'how do I go about doing that?'

Behind his steel-and-gold mask, Odin smiled ruefully. 'I honestly haven't the faintest idea. If you ever find out, do please tell me, I'd be ever so pleased to know. You see, I don't even know who they are.'

The sharp hissing noise could easily have been a fight to the death between two very large sidewinders; in fact it was Carol, drawing her breath in sharply. 'Bullshit,' she said. 'Of course you know.'

'Do I? Oh confound it, you'll have to excuse me while I take this damned helmet off. I suffer from mild claustrophobia, would you believe, but still I have to wear the wretched thing; it's part of the uniform.' He ducked out of the helmet and dumped it on a nearby table. 'Sorry about that,' he said, smoothing back his thin hair. 'Here's a valuable tip for you: never work for a mythology with a strict dress code. Now, where were we? Oh yes. You were having difficulty believing me when I said I don't know who's actually in charge here.'

'You got it,' Carol replied.

Odin clicked his tongue. 'I don't blame you for being sceptical,' he said, 'but it's true. Look at it this way; the bar you used to work in.'

'Yeah? What about it?'

Odin scratched his ear. 'Naturally, you know who owns it.'

Carol frowned a little. 'Sure,' she said. 'It's part of a nation-wide chain.'

'Exactly. And that chain's part of a holding company that's part of the leisure and catering division of a corporation that's a wholly owned subsidiary of a group of companies whose shares are quoted on Wall Street; thirty per cent of those shares are owned by another multinational group, another thirty per cent belongs to various insurance companies—'

'All right,' Carol interrupted. 'But that's different. That's humans. Mortals. This has got to be different, right?'

'Oh yes,' Odin answered. 'Very different. For one thing, all those companies and corporations are efficiently managed and properly run by people who know what they're doing. That's a *big* difference. The Valhalla Group isn't like that at all.'

'Wait a minute.' Carol held up her hand. 'Valhalla *Group*? You mean there's more than one of these places?'

Odin nodded. 'In roughly the same way as there's more than one star in the sky, yes. Would you mind awfully not leaning on my suitcase, by the way? It's rather old and fragile, and I simply can't afford a new one.'

One of the ravens hopped off his shoulder and started pecking at a derelict sausage it had spotted under the table. Carol ignored it. 'What do you mean, can't afford? Aren't you some kind of god?'

Odin seemed a little offended by that, and it showed in his tone as he replied, 'Yes, of course. And you're some kind of human. But you were working in – pardon me – a grubby little bar.' He indicated the hall with a slight nod of his head. 'And I work here.'

'Oh,' Carol replied, a little ashamed of herself. 'I didn't—'

'Here,' Odin went on, 'and other places. As you so rightly guessed, there's more than one. But, sadly,' he went on, 'only one of me. And only one salary, too. Divided equally between all my various personae, it doesn't run to expensive luxury items like new suitcases.'

Carol straightened up quickly. 'I'm sorry,' she said. 'Really I am. It sounds lousy. But,' she continued with an effort, 'I can't help that, it's between you and your bosses. Come on, you must report to somebody. And I want to talk to him, whoever he is.'

Odin nodded gravely. 'Be my guest,' he said. 'Hugin, sit up straight. Young lady would like to talk to you.'

The large, rather scruffy raven on Odin's shoulder stopped pecking his collar and turned its beak towards Carol. 'Ark,' it said.

'Excuse me?' Carol murmured. 'You report to a goddamn *bird*?'

'That's right. I make my report to Hugin here, he flies off with it and comes back with my orders. When,' he added sourly, 'he doesn't go wandering off nibbling roadkills, that is. The administration of ten thousand afterlives ground to a halt once, just because he got himself shut in somebody's garage.'

Carol sat down on the table. 'You know,' she said, after a long silence, 'I believe you. I mean, that's just the sort of lousy, feckless way things would be run.'

'Explains a lot about life in general,' Odin replied sadly. 'I'll tell you another thing; I've been doing this job for, what, two thousand years? Something like that. And you know what I trained as? Assistant librarian. But,' he continued mournfully, 'as luck would have it, I got assigned to Personnel as an archivist, and Valhalla comes under Personnel; so, when they were roaming round with handcuffs and a big sack looking for someone for this job, guess who didn't get out of the way quick enough.' He smiled heartbreakingly. 'Out the back, just past the lost-property office and the slops bins, I converted one of the outbuildings into a really rather good little library. Dewey-decimal system, paid for all the books myself. Spent hours glueing on the little pockets you put the tickets in. Apart from me, the only time anyone's ever been in there was when Eirik Bloodaxe was hiding out from Hrolf Kraki and Sigurd Fafnisbana. He figured it was the last place anybody would ever think of looking.'

Carol bit her lip. 'That's awful,' she said. 'Seriously, I think it sucks, the whole thing. But even so, there has to be some way I can lodge an appeal. I mean, the way you describe it, there must be mistakes happening practically every day.'

Odin laughed. 'Don't get me wrong, please,' he said. 'Just because it's a bad system doesn't necessarily mean it doesn't mostly work most of the time. And in your case, it worked just fine. This is the Valhalla for female ancillary workers in the catering sector whose aspirations don't conform to the generally prevailing norm.'

'Uppity cocktail waitresses?'

'That's what I just said,' Odin replied, 'but without the derogatory language. You're here because you used to work in a bar, and you died.'

Carol frowned. 'I wanted to talk to someone about that. I didn't die.'

Odin sighed. 'Oh dear, this is very awkward. I know it's bound to be terribly traumatic for you, and believe me, I do sympathise; someone your age, young and attractive, with her whole life before her, it's little short of tragic. But you died, and that's all there is to it. Sorry, but as we say in the trade, if you're afraid of the dark, stay out of the coffin.'

'So I died,' Carol said angrily. 'What of?'

'I beg your pardon?'

'I said, what of? You're not trying to tell me I suddenly just stopped, like a gas station watch.'

'Well, of course you died of something,' Odin said. 'You really want to know?'

'Yes. Is that unreasonable?'

'No, I suppose not. Munin, here please.' The other raven hopped back up on to Odin's shoulder; the bird was the size of a small turkey and almost completely featherbare in places. 'Munin is old Norse for Memory,' Odin explained. 'Other people have a database, or at the very least a filing cabinet. I have a large black scavenger.'

The raven stuck its beak into Odin's ear – he didn't so much as wince – and said something like 'Ark ark'. Odin nodded, and the bird went back to what it had been doing, which was nobody's business but its own. 'According to Munin,' Odin said, 'the cause of death was a catastrophic brain haemorrhage resulting from a freak blood-clot – an extremely rare condition for someone your age, statistically you'd be more likely to die of a septic panda-bite, but invariably and immediately fatal. If it's any consolation you just went to sleep and didn't wake up: you never felt a thing.'

Carol growled. 'I know I didn't,' she said. 'That's what's pissing me off. Sorry, but I just don't believe you. I want to see some evidence.'

Odin scratched his head. 'You do? How depressingly morbid. Still, if that's what it takes to make you happy.'

He snapped his fingers; and on the table next to her was a long, narrow shape under a blanket, something more or less her size and shape. Before she could stop him, Odin leaned across and lifted the blanket.

'As you can see,' he said, 'they did a very thorough autopsy. I don't know if you can see it with the naked eye, but that little varmint there – just there, look . . .'

Dead people can't vomit. Fact. Ask Carol. They can try – vigorously – but nothing actually comes out. 'Please,' she said, when she could speak again, 'put it away. I believe you.'

'Sure?' Odin asked solicitously. 'Take all the time you need, please. I want you to be absolutely happy about this.'

'Mmmmggh.'

Odin flicked the cloth back and snapped his fingers again. The corpse stayed where it was, to his obvious disappointment. 'Damn,' he said. 'Loose connection somewhere, I expect. I'll try again later. Anyway, here's a unique opportunity for you to make some sort of witty remark along the lines of "over my dead body". Right, try again. You know, if this was an overdue book rather than a dead body, I'd have no trouble at all knowing how to deal with it.'

He snapped again, and the body vanished, leaving nothing behind except a slight smear on the tabletop and a strong smell of preservatives. 'That was *gross*,' Carol said.

'Really? But it was your body. You used to *live* in it. Whatever its shortcomings you must have loved it once, or else you wouldn't have spent all that money buying it food, or wrapping it up in expensive clothes. I suppose it's a bit like leftover scraps; however nice the food was, it's all unappetising and yucky once it's gone cold and been scraped into the bin. What you might call the Doctor Jekyll and Mr Formaldehyde syndrome.'

'But I didn't do anything.' Carol looked up at him piti-fully. 'I didn't kill anybody or go around stealing or setting fire to buildings. What am I being punished for?'

Odin shook his head. 'Nothing,' he said. 'No such things as punishments and rewards up here. It was just your time, and this is where you were meant to go. It's been painstakingly handcrafted to suit your own personal needs and require-ments, you know. Oh, that reminds me; you're not a vegetarian, are you? No nut allergies or religious food taboos? If you do have anything like that, please make sure I know about it early, so I can tell the kitchen staff. In a ideal world, of course, all that stuff'd be on the file. Now, if you'll excuse me. I think it's terribly important to make new arrivals feel at home and give a really personal service, but I do have other things I should be seeing to. I can't be in two places at once, you know. Well, that's not strictly true, I *am* in a damn sight more than two places all the time, but that just makes it all worse. Cheer up,' he added, as he picked up his helmet and his various other bits and pieces. 'You'll fit in eventually, as the coalface said to the flower.'

He walked away, leaving Carol staring after him. He went about five yards, then turned back.

'Actually,' he said, 'strictly off the record, if after you've given it a fair trial and all and you still don't like it here—'

'Like now, for instance.'

'—Say in a hundred years or so, or let's not be too hasty, let's say a thousand, there is something you might be able to do that'd make the powers-that-be a little bit more inclined to listen to what you've got to say. Not that I'm promising any-thing, you understand, and whatever you do, you mustn't say I told you this. I'm trusting you, so please don't let me down.'

'Yes, yes, all right. What is it?'

'Ask them for a job.'

Carol blinked. 'A *job*? You must be crazy. I got a job. It's a life I need to get.'

Odin grinned uncharacteristically, the broad grin of someone springing an elaborate verbal trap. 'Quite,' he said. 'That's why you're here.'

For a moment, Carol had a strong urge to hit him, but she decided against it. 'That's cheap,' she said. 'If I've been brought here – *killed*, dammit, and brought here – just so you can make your goddamn jokes, then I promise you there's going to be trouble.'

Odin shook his head. 'Calm down,' he said. 'It's not a joke. Well, obviously not, because an essential ingredient in jokes is being funny, and it wasn't, much. But really, that's why you ended up here. Think about your life; go on.'

'Okay.' Carol closed her eyes and contorted her face into a pantomime of concentration. 'I'm thinking. All right, I've thought. Now what?'

'Didn't take long, did it?'

'So what?' Carol replied with a shrug. 'It was a simple life—'

'More than just simple. It was *nothing*. Get up, go to work, come home, go to bed.'

'So I worked hard.'

'All right, you worked hard. Diligently. You were an employer's dream of a cocktail waitress. You devoted your entire life to picking up empty glasses and putting down full ones for the benefit of a lot of basically sad people, with occasional time out to daydream about lost Mayan cities, strange visitors from distant galaxies, genies in bottles and, finally, Valhalla. Remind me, what was your degree from MIT in?'

'Electronics.' Carol scowled. 'Fine,' she said. 'I admit it. In fairness to myself, I should have carved myself out a significant career, rather than dropping out. Then I could have got up in the morning, gone to work, come home, gone to bed, slept and earned *lots of money*. Big deal.'

'I don't make the rules,' Odin said. 'You didn't get a life, so you got an afterlife. Now I'm giving you some good advice. If you ever want to get out of here, get a job. Do something useful. People who make themselves useful don't fit in around here. If you really try hard, you might just get thrown out. And that's all the help I can give you. I shouldn't even have told you that, but what the hell. The thought of sharing Eternity with you in this mood isn't a cheerful one.'

'Okay.' Carol looked down at the floor. 'Can you do just one more thing for me? Please?'

'I'm going to regret this,' Odin said. 'What is it?'

'Get a message through to my mom and dad. *Please*,' she added urgently, as Odin opened his lips to refuse. 'I know, it's against regulations and you'll get in all kinds of trouble and probably it breaks the Prime Directive and undermines the fabric of space/time. But – well, it's not so much my mother: we weren't close but we were kind of friends. But Dad and I had this big fight when I said I wasn't going to take the really cool job with MacroSoft he pulled all those strings to get for me – like, he's a control freak. I guess it goes with what he does; he's an agent, you know, finding people work in films and TV and commercials and such. Anyway, I want him to know I love him, and I miss him, even if he is an asshole.'

'That's so touching,' Odin replied sourly. 'Look, this isn't like mortality, you don't have a right to a lawyer and a phone call. Millions and millions of people die; if we did requests, we'd never get any work done.'

'Please?'

Odin nodded. 'All right,' he said. 'Though it's completely against my better judgement. Not to mention the fact that I've got a brontosaurus tibia to pick with your father.'

Carol frowned. 'You have?'

'Sure,' Odin replied grimly. 'Who do you think got me this crummy job in the first place?'

CHAPTER FOUR

'On your feet,' said the sergeant. 'Come on, jump to it. You're making the battlefield look untidy.'

Howard groaned. 'Leave me alone,' he muttered. 'Please.'

The sergeant grunted and kicked him in the ribs. 'I said on your feet,' he said. 'You deaf or something?'

'Last time I looked I hadn't got any feet,' Howard moaned. 'There was this mortar bomb, you see, and—'

'Really?' The sergeant jumped in the air and landed on Howard's ankle. The pain was—

But he'd proved his point. 'They're back,' Howard said, once he was through screaming. 'My feet, they're there again. How did that happen?'

'This is Valhalla, stupid,' the sergeant said. 'Now get up and get fell in, or I'll kick your arse from here to Brierley Hill.'

Howard stood up, wobbled as he tried to put his weight on his bruised ankle, and grabbed hold of something to steady himself. The 'something' proved to be the wall of the house that, late yesterday afternoon, had been blown to pieces, one of which had landed on him and caved in his skull.

'Getting the hang of it now, are we?' said the sergeant unpleasantly. 'Penny finally dropped? Little light bulb finally lit and hovering above your head?'

Howard nodded. 'We die, but then we come back to life again. And the scenery, too.'

'We call it the Reset Button,' the sergeant said. 'All the pain without the nasty long-term effects. Decaff warfare.'

Howard rubbed his aching ribs. 'That ought to make me feel better, I suppose,' he said. 'Presumably, then, after a while you sort of tune out the pain and stop noticing it.'

The sergeant shook his head. 'Don't make me laugh,' he said. 'And if you think you know something about pain, you just wait till you're pinned down in a burning building. The pain carries on till the last bit of you turns to ash. In fact, it hurts so much there's weeks we have trouble getting volunteers for burning-building duty.'

Howard stared at him. 'People *volunteer*?' he stuttered.

'Sure they do.' The sergeant patted him on the shoulder. 'You see, son, once you've been here a while you'll get the point. The worst pain of all is the boredom.'

Before Howard could reply to that, a missile screamed overhead and the whole street disappeared in a cloud of smoke, dust and cinders. Something, probably displaced masonry of some description, hit Howard between the shoulders and catapulted him into the middle of the road, just as a machine-gun started tearing up the tarmac like an invisible pneumatic drill. Without hanging around to see if he'd been hit, he scrambled and crawled for cover and snuggled hedgehog-fashion behind a shattered residue of brickwork. The machine-gun stopped firing, but some instinct made him stay where he was; five seconds later, the instinct earned the gratitude of the rest of Howard and the right to wear a smug grin as a sniper's bullet ricocheted off a jagged corner of brick about a sixteenth of an inch above his head.

'Well?' said a voice from under the fallen masonry. 'You just going to crouch there all day, or are you going to fight back?'

'That depends,' Howard replied. 'Will it do any good?'

'What do you mean?' the sergeant queried, puzzled.

'Will I be able to escape? Will it be safer?'

'Oh, for crying out loud.' The machine-gun opened up on the masonry heap, sending flattened bullets and knife-edged breeze-block chips spitting out in all directions. 'Haven't you got it yet? You aren't here to be *safe*. You're here to be *dangerous*.'

'But that's crazy,' Howard said, while the machine-gun reduced the fallen blocks and bricks to gravel and dust. 'What about survival instincts, self-preservation? They're part of every living thing's DNA.'

'The key word there is "living",' the sergeant said. 'And you ain't. Immortal, yes. Alive, no. Now deal with it, and get fighting.'

Another explosion lifted the debris into the air and rearranged it, uncovering the sergeant's body. What with one thing and another, it looked like the sort of jigsaw you'd expect to find given away free with the *Butcher's Gazette*. 'No,' Howard said firmly. 'Now, what're you going to do about it?'

'Remember it, next time we can't find a volunteer for the burning-house scenario. And that's a promise. About the only thing around here that never gets shot off or blown up is the memory. And I can prove it, too; go on, ask me something. Ask me who was the losing team in the 1974 FA Cup final.'

'I'll fight,' Howard said wretchedly. 'Anything to get away from the sound of your voice. What do I fight with, exactly?'

'The choice is yours,' the sergeant said. 'We got guns, grenades, rockets, bazookas, bayonets, axes, flame-throwers – you name it. Weapons R Us.'

'Wonderful,' Howard sighed. 'And where do you go to get some?'

'Easy. Find someone who's got what you want, stove his head in with a lump of rock, help yourself. Here, can you fly a helicopter gunship?'

'No.'

'Doesn't matter. After all, the worst thing that can happen to you is you crash it.'

'Fine. And how do I know which side is us and which is the enemy?'

'Don't talk soft, son. We don't bother with sides. Where's the point?'

The machine-gun stopped firing, and Howard jumped to his feet and ran. A line of bullet holes followed him all the way across the street to the burnt-out jeep he'd selected as cover. He huddled under it until he got his breath back, then set off again. Ten seconds later, the jeep was hit by a mortar bomb and blown into piranha confetti; by then, however, Howard was cowering at the bottom of a shell-crater. The next leg of his journey landed him behind a toppled wall. No sooner had he dropped down, breathing heavily through his nose, than he realised he wasn't alone; there was another man there with him, trying to unblock a jammed machine-gun.

'Hello,' said the man cheerfully, and lashed out with a length of broken gaspipe. 'Turned out quite mild again, hasn't it?'

Howard managed to avoid the blow but tripped on a stray breeze-block and ended up on his backside in the mud. The other man stood over him and raised the gaspipe; then he toppled forward, riddled with bullet holes.

'But the forecast says rain later,' he croaked; then he died.

Howard allowed himself a moment to get over the feelings of numb terror; then he grabbed the machine-gun and ducked down out of the way of the next spate of gunfire. He was kneeling on the dead man.

'Some time after lunch,' the dead man added. 'Intermittent showers followed by sunny intervals.'

Without waiting to see if the coast was clear, Howard jumped up and sprinted away, the jammed machine-gun tucked under his arm. The blast from a nearby shellburst lifted him up and hurled him into a pile of rubble, the hot gases roasting half the skin off his face as it did so. He landed right on top of a dead body.

'Morning,' said the body. 'You didn't happen to catch the weather forecast, did you?'

'Rain after lunch, sunny intervals,' Howard replied. 'Do you know how to unjam a machine-gun?'

'Pulling back sharply on the cocking handle usually does the trick,' the corpse said. 'Failing that, you're looking at stripping it right down. Here, take mine instead if you like.'

Howard noticed that there was another machine-gun, bigger and blacker and shinier, under the dead man's left leg. 'Thanks,' Howard said.

'You're welcome.'

Behind the next burnt-out building shell Howard came to, he found two men still alive and on their feet, grappling with each other over an RPG7. He pointed the machine-gun at them and blew them both into mincemeat.

'Snow forecast for Tuesday,' one of them remarked, though after what Howard had done to him with the M-60, it was difficult to imagine what he said it with.

'They said the same thing last week,' remarked the other one scornfully. 'Sometimes I think they just make it up as they go along.'

Howard looked at his handiwork and shuddered. 'The weather,' he said. 'Is that all you people talk about here?'

'Yes,' the dead men replied together.

Howard thought about that for a moment. 'Figures,' he said. 'And why not, after all?'

'See you tomorrow,' they called out after him as he dashed

into the street, the machine-gun in his hands spitting out bullets and spent cases. 'Light showers, turning into heavy rain around teatime.'

After a few hours of this sort of thing, Howard was almost beginning to enjoy himself. Before he lost count he reckoned he'd killed seventy-four men, and by a succession of miracles that ought to have set back the study of probability theory about a hundred years, his own injuries were confined to a few minor scrapes and bruises. He'd single-handedly wiped out the four platoons guarding the junction of the High Street and Cooper's Lane, defended the Warley College of Technology against greatly superior forces and driven them back into the Victoria Park boating lake, and left the Council Offices looking like a sequence that Tarantino had cut from the final version of one of his films as being just a trifle excessive; he only stopped, in fact, when he couldn't find anyone else to kill. He felt like a cross between James Bond and an American postman. It was scary, but— well, fun.

'Bet you're glad you came now, aren't you?'

He whirled round, aimed from the hip and pulled the trigger. Clunk, no bang-bang-bang; he let the machine-gun fall from his hands and brought up the 9mm Ingram that hung round his neck on a strap. That appeared to have jammed, too, so he let it drop and reached for his grenade belt. It was empty, which was odd; there'd been at least five left after he finished mopping up round the Council Offices.

'Remember me?'

He realised he hadn't looked at the man, except fleetingly as a silhouetted target. 'You,' he said, as he recognised the bastard who'd stabbed him at the ox roast and sent him here in the first place.

The man nodded. 'Me,' he said. 'Oh, by the way, none of the guns and bombs seem to work when I'm around, so if you want to get your own back, you'll have to use something with no significant moving parts, like a rock or a bit of old stick.'

'Like this?' Howard snarled, brandishing a jagged strip of scrap steel.

'Ideal,' the man replied.

Howard lunged forward, aiming a vicious slash at the man's head. He blocked it with his forearm – there should have been a thin spray of blood as the metal cut him to the bone, but there wasn't – pulled the strip out of Howard's hands and threw it away. 'Pathetic,' he said. 'A dying Teletubby could do better than that.'

Howard grunted like a bull rhino and snatched up a lump of shattered breeze-block. Yesterday he could barely have lifted it; now he hurled it like a man throwing a rubber ball for his dog. It bounced off the man's forehead without apparent effect.

'Sticks and stones won't break my bones,' the man said, sounding bored. 'You could try some really barbed repartee, if you like.'

'Arsehole.'

The man considered this. 'No,' he said, 'sorry, doesn't cut it. You'd better stick to the physical stuff, I reckon.'

Howard stooped, picked up a discarded bayonet, and lunged with it. The man fended him off with the tip of his little finger, then flicked him on the nose, the way you flick a screwed-up ball of paper across a table. Howard flew through the air and landed in a painful, complicated heap on a pile of twisted aluminium window frames and broken glass. When he held his hand up, it was streaming blood.

'Your go,' the man said.

Howard tried again, this time with a long-handled fire-axe that just happened to be handy. Instead of simply lashing out, he cunningly feinted a blow to the man's head and then brought the blade whirling down on his left ankle. The handle snapped, and the axehead whizzed past his own ear.

'You may find there's something of a pattern emerging,' the man said. 'Let's see, silver bullets are out, so how about a sharpened stake through the heart? That always seems to do the job on *Buffy the Vampire Slayer*.'

By a remarkable coincidence, there was a sharp-ended wooden tent peg lying a couple of inches from Howard's feet. He collected it deftly, sprang forward and drove it into the man's chest on the left side. It broke.

'It was just a suggestion,' the man said apologetically. 'One more step in an ongoing process of, no pun intended, elimination. I know; since a benign Providence has seen fit to bless you with a working flame-thrower – there, look, just behind you; and gosh, there's the user's manual, open at the right page, too.'

The curtain of fire from the flame-thrower vaporised the wooden door frame the man was leaning against, melted the hinges and turned the door into fine white ash. The man used the blaze to light a cigarette.

'Terribly bad for you, these,' he remarked. 'My children don't approve; they keep saying I should take more care of myself.' He blew smoke in Howard's face, and the gust swept him off his feet and dumped him in a pile of burst dustbin-bags. 'That's a thought,' he said, 'why don't you try chemical weapons? By some million-to-one chance, there's a nearly full cylinder of mustard gas just behind that fallen rafter.'

Howard shook his head and slumped to his knees. 'I give in,' he said.

'Can't do that, I'm afraid,' the man replied with a sympathetic grimace. 'Got to keep trying until either you succeed or the sun sets. Rules is rules.'

Howard scowled. 'And if I don't?'

'Then this happens.' The man tipped the ash from his cigarette and inclined his head just a little. At once every nerve in Howard's body started to shriek with pain. 'Normally I'd be inclined to say that this hurts me more than it hurts you, but I sense you aren't in the mood for light-hearted wordplay. If it's the legal aspect of using the mustard gas that's bothering you, then try something else: you don't have to use it. Again, it was just a suggestion.'

By a supreme effort of will, Howard managed to break free from the paralysing effect of the pain just long enough to pick up a small stone and lob it gently. The man ducked, and the pain stopped as abruptly as it had started. 'Good boy,' he said. 'Like I always say, it's the thought that counts.'

Howard slid full-length on the ground, his face in the dust. 'Who are you?' he said.

'My name is Odin,' the man replied.

Howard lifted his head. 'Odin,' he repeated. 'Like the god?'

'Very like,' Odin replied with a smile. 'I expect this is the crowning moment of your existence, actually getting to meet the god you and your enthusiastic re-enacter chums spent so much time and energy honouring. Not to mention money,' he added. 'I don't suppose all that gear comes cheap.'

'Mostly we make it ourselves,' Howard mumbled.

'Out of empty Fairy Liquid bottles and sticky-backed plastic? Oh well. Blessed are the cheapskates, for they shall see God and still have change out of a fiver. Anyway, don't let me stop you savouring the moment.'

Howard spat out a mouthful of brick dust. 'You killed me,' he said bitterly. 'I never did you any harm, and you—'

'Didn't you? Well, matter of opinion, I suppose. If you ask me, keeping me hanging around in this dimension when all the other pagan gods have long since fallen into disuse and gone off to run bars in the Algarve or start their own production companies strikes me as ill-mannered, to say the least. When I think of Jupiter and Baal and Zoroaster lounging beside the pool in their pyjamas while I still have to turf myself out of bed at half past five every morning, I don't mind admitting I feel a little bit put upon, at times. Still, one has one's duty to one's public, and the show must go on.'

Howard stared at him. 'But we didn't *believe* in you,' he said. 'Perish the thought. I mean, it was only *fun*.'

'Fun.' Odin's brows drew together like two shrubberies fighting to the death. 'Best part of a thousand years of unpaid overtime, and you tell me you didn't actually believe, it was just for fun. Oh dear. Does the concept of consideration for others have any meaning whatsoever in your nasty little mindset?'

'I – I'm sorry.'

'And what about all this?' Odin continued. 'All the work I've put into getting this place ready for you, making sure everything's just the way you want it. I suppose you're going to tell me you'd have preferred something quieter in eggshell blue?'

Howard had great difficulty regaining control of his lower jaw, which had swung open like the lid of a broken suitcase. 'For me?' he said.

'All for you. Every last brick, blade of grass and razor-edged fragment of shell casing, lovingly handcrafted in perfect detail, just so that you can experience killing and mayhem in all their multifaceted splendour.'

'But I don't *want*—' Howard wailed. Odin cut him off short with a horrible scowl.

'Talk about your serpent's tooth,' he sighed. 'And please, don't insult my intelligence. Every weekend, fifty-two weeks of the year, devoted to playing at fighting; obviously this is what you wanted. No question about it.'

'No!' Howard cried. 'You've got it all wrong. I only joined the club to make new friends and meet girls.'

Odin raised one shaggy eyebrow. 'Girls?' he repeated.

Howard nodded. 'Girls,' he said. 'You know, young women. You see, all my life I never had the knack; and then a friend of mine from work – well, not a friend, exactly, I never had any of them either – he took me along to a club night and there were quite a lot of girls there, and they seemed a bit different, like they were drinking beer and wearing lots of leather and chain mail and stuff, and I thought I might stand a better chance.'

'I see,' Odin said. 'And did you?'

'No. They used to stare at me and then giggle, just like they all do. But at least some people talked to me after I'd been going regularly for a year or so, and I hadn't got anything else to do, so I stayed. But all the fighting and stuff was never my cup of tea. The only bit I ever really liked was the embroidery.'

'Embroidery?'

'Yes. If you want to be really authentic, you embroider wall hangings for the clubhouse, using genuine period motifs and organically dyed vegetable fibres. I quite enjoyed that. Well, mostly it was boring, but when you'd finished one it gave you a real sense of achievement.'

'Right.' Odin gave him a look of pure scorn. 'Embroidery. Not the pure love of battle or deeply held religious beliefs. Originally, if I understand you correctly, the vague hope of getting your leg over. It was just something to kill time at the weekends and a passing infatuation with cross-stitch.' He shook his head. 'Honestly. You people.'

Howard put his face in his hands. 'I'm sorry,' he said. 'That's the story of my life, really. All I ever do is cause trouble.'

'Yes,' Odin said. 'You do. Well, I really wish you'd thought of doing evening classes or amateur dramatics instead; it'd have saved us both an eternity of boredom and misery. Too late now, though. Anyway,' he added, as the world around them suddenly fell into shadow, 'bright and early tomorrow morning, remember, it's your turn for the burning-buildings shift.'

'Oh.'

'Well, tough. Like I said, this Valhalla is expressly designed to enable you to sample every aspect of the death-in-battle experience, and burning slowly to death is an essential part of it. And you had your day's victory today, so you can't grumble.'

'My day's victory?' A thought occurred to Howard; not a nice one. 'Are you telling me that I killed all those people and survived all those explosions just because it was my *turn*? Like, I didn't have anything to do with it?'

Odin laughed unkindly. 'What do you think?' he said. 'Do you seriously believe a total loser like you could last five seconds in a battle unless the script was a hundred and ten per cent on your side? That was a whole century's worth of good luck you just used up in one day. I thought at the time you were being a bit extravagant with it, but I didn't want to spoil it, not when you were obviously having such a good time. Well, it seemed obvious. Apparently it wasn't.'

Odin turned to go. 'Wait,' Howard shouted, 'there's been a mistake, obviously. Isn't there anything at all we can do about it? For both our sakes,' he added imploringly.

'No.'

'But surely—'

Odin frowned. 'Look, son, this isn't a week's free trial, this is Death. You've dug your grave and now you must lie in it. Oops, almost forgot.' With a movement that was too quick for Howard to follow, Odin swept up a discarded Kalashnikov and emptied its magazine into him, starting with the feet and working his way methodically up to the top of Howard's head. 'Just in time,' the god said as the sun dipped below the horizon. 'House rule: nobody on their feet at lights out except me. And now I've got to go round tidying up and putting everything back together; don't suppose I'll see my bed much before four-thirty a.m. If you think you've got it rough, just you try rebuilding war-torn Smethwick every night for a thousand years.'

Howard called out after Odin as he walked away; but Howard's lower jaw had been completely shot away, and his throat was like a colander. His last conscious thought, before slipping away into the abyss of pain, was a vague but devout wish that he'd done as his cousin Steve had suggested and joined the St John's Ambulance instead. He might have ended up in some similar heap of shit – with his luck, he was beginning to see that as inevitable – but at least he'd have had the basic grounding in anatomy to be able to put himself together again.

He opened the door—

('Hey!' exclaimed Shaka, former King of the Zulus, responsible for the death of a million human beings at a time when the cutting edge, no pun intended, of killing technology was a long wooden stick with a knob on the end. 'Look, everyone, there's a brush mark in the top left corner that's just starting to smooth out!')

—slipped through and closed the door behind him, quiet as a little mouse.

It was dark, and he couldn't see the paint. His first reaction was blind, paralysing fear; he froze, like a rabbit caught in oncoming headlights. Memories were edging back, sure enough – battles mostly, and the bloody sack of towns and villages, the sweetly disgusting smell of blood soaking into dust, the orange light of burning thatch visible five miles away against a starless night sky. But one of them concerned a little skinny boy lying in a carved wooden cot in a dark tent, awake when everyone else was asleep, staring in fascinated terror at the black silhouette of an edge of the tent-flap that (he was convinced) moved every time he took his eyes off it, a tiny twitch visible only on the furthest edge of his peripheral vision, jerky and extremely fast like the movements of a spider . . . *You aren't afraid of the dark*, his father used to say, *don't be such a girl*; and his brother, cruel and spiteful Bleda, made fun of his fears and played horrid tricks on him, creeping up behind him and pretending to be monsters—

'Help,' Attila whispered. 'Mummy.'

—But that wasn't even his memory, because Mummy had died or gone away or been left behind when he was still only a tiny baby, and the King's son had been nursemaided by scarred and calloused warriors, weaned from mare's milk on to yoghurt and *kvass* when other children his age still hung from their mothers' breasts; it was inviolable tradition that the King's son should be reared from the very first as a warrior, untainted by any feminine contact, kept out of the way of anything that might weaken or dilute a warrior's devotion to his craft. Which raised the question: if not my Mummy, then whose?

'Mummy,' he repeated nevertheless. 'Mum-*meee*!'

Suddenly there was light, an explosion, a great flood of searingly white illumination, apparently radiating from a curious glass knob hanging from the ceiling by a string. In all the places he'd been, from the snow-blinding steppes to the brilliant midsummer sun of the Mediterranean, he'd never seen pure white light before.

'Shut up,' said a voice.

Attila lifted his head. He was in a solid structure, a bricks-and-stones house like the ones the Romans used; he recognised walls, floor, ceiling, door frame. In the door frame was a huge woman, the size of one of the mountain ogres in the campfire tales of his childhood. She was wearing a long white gown that reached down to her bare feet, and her hair cascaded about her shoulders like a golden waterfall.

'Shut up, you miserable little snot,' she growled. 'It's four o'clock in the bloody morning.'

Another thing about the room that caught Attila's attention was the decorations. Someone had gone to the trouble of pasting some kind of parchment or (what did they call that stuff that burnt so well? Papyrus? Paper?) paper all over the walls, from top to bottom, covered with a profusion of little paintings of what looked like animals. Yes, they were definitely supposed to be animals: that was meant to be a bear, and that was a donkey, that was an Indian tiger (he'd seen one in a cage once, in the amphitheatre at Ravenna) and that was a small pig standing on its hind legs. But the paintings were all in a most peculiar style, and furthermore the animals were wearing human clothes; the bear had a red jacket, the pig wore a stripy tunic, the old grey donkey had its tail attached to its body with a nail. It was all quite bizarre and disturbing, like the weird animal spirits who were supposed to guide the tribe's shamans on their wandering between the worlds. Was this a shaman's tent, perhaps? Who was the giant woman?

Whoever she was, she was standing over him, her hands on her hips, glowering down at him with furious hatred in her eyes. He tried to shrink away, but the pillows (Pillows? He was in a bed; a ludicrously wide, soft bed, with flowery sheets and a padded quilt. Even Honorius, the mighty Roman Emperor of the West, never swaddled himself in such ridiculous luxury as this) got in the way.

'Well?' snarled the woman. 'What's the matter this time?'

'I was frightened,' Attila said, in a little tiny voice. 'I thought I saw something moving.'

The woman sighed impatiently. 'Don't be so silly,' she said, her voice softening just a little. 'You're a big boy now; big boys aren't afraid of the dark.' She reached out and grabbed something— Eeek! It was a wolf, grey and cruel, with huge round glassy eyes; no, it wasn't, it was furry cloth stuffed with wool and made to look like a wolf. What kind of sick mind would come up with an idea like that? 'Here,' the woman said, 'you cuddle up with Mister Dog and go to sleep, and I don't want to hear another sound out of you till morning. Understood?'

Dear God, Attila realised with a feeling of sick horror, *I'm a child. How in Hell's name did that happen? This is—*

'Mummy?' he asked tentatively.

'Well?'

'You're my mummy?'

The woman's face hardened again; Attila observed that she had the yellow hair and pale white skin of the Goths. 'Oh for crying out loud, don't start. I've got to be up at half-six to get your father's breakfast; I haven't got time to play silly games. Go to sleep *now* or you'll be sorry.'

The woman stretched out her hand towards the wall beside the door, and suddenly the white light was completely gone; no sunset afterglow, no red gleam of dying embers in the hearth – white light that appeared and vanished as quickly and completely as opening or shutting one's eyes. What kind of devilish sorcerers had he fallen among this time?

'Sweet dreams,' the woman said; and he heard a click, some sort of mechanism, like the sprung latches of the Romans' siege engines, one of the most ominous sounds he could ever remember having heard. Maybe the terrible woman had set up such a device, one of those giant mechanical crossbows that hurled three-foot arrows, rigged to shoot if he tried to get out of the bed. It was just the sort of diabolical cruelty you'd expect from a Goth and, since the last time he'd heard of them they'd just struck an alliance against him with the Roman Aetius, that would account for where they'd got the siege engine. And they were so clever, those Roman engineers; it would only take the slightest movement, a sneeze, a cough, to trip the gossamer-fine wires and release the locking catch; and the next thing he'd feel would be an arrow the size of a young pine tree pinning him to the wall.

Attila kept perfectly still.

The important thing, he told himself, was to keep his mind from dwelling on the mortal danger that was probably less than a hair's breadth away from him. Instead, think of something else; anything. So he made himself think back to the great and glorious deeds of his youth and manhood, which were just starting to flood back into his memory in full, sharp detail, like soldiers reporting for duty after a long and riotous spell of leave. He pictured himself standing before the smashed gates of Aquileia, watching as his grinning troopers dragged away the Roman women by their hair. In his mind's eye he savoured once again the abject terror of Leo, the Pope of Rome, as he grovelled before the conqueror's sandalwood throne in his lurid silk robes of office, now stained and spattered with mud. His imagination swept him up on the wings of eagles and let him soar over the battlefield of Chalons, where his horse-archers shot down the great lumbering Gothic knights by the score on every pass, then wheeled away on their swift Steppes ponies, and *Oh no, I need to go wee-wee, I need to go wee-wee NOW!*

He thought of the monstrous engine of death, lurking in the shadows like a giant spider, surrounded by the lethal threads of its web. Sure enough, he desperately wanted to go wee-wee, wanted it more than he'd ever wanted anything in his whole life. But with that hateful contraption out there waiting to pounce, he was just going to have to cross his legs and—

Can't. Must go wee-wee. Oh well.

He squirmed. Somehow, he couldn't seem to find his way back to those memories any more; great conquerors, a voice inside his head seemed to be saying, don't wet their beds in the night, so it stands to reason that you aren't a great conqueror and these aren't your memories. Access denied; go away. He shivered, wondering what sort of ghastly mess he'd got himself into. Lying in the dark wasn't much better than sitting watching the nice paint; in fact, it was considerably worse, because he'd been clean and dry watching the nice paint, and he hadn't had a Roman *arcuballista* aimed at his heart the whole time. At least he'd had a few shreds of dignity left, watching the nice paint. This, on the other hand, wasn't nice at all.

I can't stay here for ever, he told himself. *Sooner or later I've got to move. Maybe if I was to start to sit up, and then quickly hurl myself sideways, perhaps then I'd fool the machine and the arrow would miss. Unless they anticipated that, of course. Sounds far-fetched, but a lot of good men ended up dead through underestimating Roman artillery engineers.*

True enough. On the other hand, it was worth bearing in mind exactly who won that particular war, who burnt whose cities to the ground, and so forth. If he'd had a defeatist attitude like that back in the fifth century, chances were the Hunnish nation would still be trudging through the high passes of the Caucasus, eating stale yoghurt round a fire of dried horse-turds. Stands to reason: a man who can conquer half the known world can probably figure out a way of getting out of a piddle-soaked bed without getting shot.

All right, then. If V is the vector in flight of the arrow, and T is the time elapsed between release and impact, find the coefficient of X where X equals the angle relative to V through which the target Y must fall during the time T so that Y is greater than E, the margin of aiming error expressed as an angle relative to the vertical . . .

Piece of cake. Odd, he reflected, how things work out. Little had he suspected when he decided on pure impulse to spare the life of that Greek mathematician from Aquileia that, years later, all that gibberish he'd taught him would finally come in useful. He double-checked the calculations, knocked off a couple of decimal points in the interests of practicality, braced for impact and launched himself shoulder first at the floor.

He hit something that wasn't the ground, and there was a deafening crunch. At first he assumed it was the *arcuballista* bolt smashing through the headboard and burying itself deep in the wall; on reflection, however, he realised that it hadn't been that kind of noise at all. This was more a sort of brittle grinding noise, like the sound of someone trampling on shards of thin pottery. The point, in any event, was of academic interest only; the priority was to get clear of the bedroom before—

'What the hell do you think you're doing?'

If anything, the light seemed whiter and harsher than before; and *she* was back, the fierce Gothic warrior princess, with an even more blood-curdling look on her milk-white face. He wanted to shout defiance, death to the whole treacherous Gothic nation and victory to the feathered-skull banners of the Huns; what actually came out was, 'Sorry.'

'Look at you,' the woman thundered, 'falling out of bed at your age.' She stepped closer, touched the mattress with a fingertip and said 'Oh *God*.' Interestingly, there wasn't so much as a trace of a siege engine to be seen anywhere in the room.

She reached out, took hold of the lobe of his ear between thumb and forefinger and applied force, lifting him clear of the wreckage of an MFI flat-pack bedside table and a shattered table lamp. 'Just look what you've done, you bloody little brat,' she said. 'You wait till your father hears about this.'

Having no choice in the matter, Attila followed his captive ear. He had a feeling it was going to be a long day.

CHAPTER FIVE

'You can call me God if it helps you relate to me better,' said the god, carefully fastening his seat belt. 'But most people call me Willard.'

'Willard,' Kortright repeated. 'Don't like it.'

'Oh.' The god peered at him anxiously through his thick spectacles. 'You think it's wrong for me?'

Kortright sighed. 'It's dead right for *you*,' he replied, 'just all wrong for a god. Trust me, I know these things. I been around gods since— gee, I don't know when.' A thought struck him. 'You know, I really don't have a clue how long I've been in this business. Do you?'

Willard shook his head.

'You should know, dammit, you're supposed to be a god. I mean,' Kortright added, spotting a gap in the traffic and aiming the car at it, 'look at you.'

'I'm the way you see me,' Willard said, slightly hurt. 'Made me in your own image and all.'

'Sure.' Kortright gestured expansively, taking both hands off the wheel to do so. Willard winced and gripped his seat belt tightly. 'You know and I know what you're like. But a god – well, gods are meant to look and act a certain way. And you don't.'

'Is that good or bad?'

'Bad,' Kortright said firmly, as he whisked the car past a carnivorous Yellow Cab with at least one hundredth of an inch to spare. 'In the looks department, you're a definite non-starter. Small and weedy simply isn't acceptable; you should be tall, broad-shouldered, deep-chested, the whole matinée-idol thing. Like Kirk Douglas. A strong chin is very god. You aren't god at all, chinwise; like, you make up in quantity what you lack in quality. Basically, it's all a matter of image. I mean, there's latitude, don't get me wrong, none of it's what you might call graven in tablets of stone. A new look is good, it helps build up that all-important brand loyalty. But it's got to be god. If it ain't god it ain't good, and that's all there is to it.'

'I see,' Willard said thoughtfully. 'So we've established I'm not an idol or a graven image. I'd have thought that came under the heading of making progress, wouldn't you?'

Kortright stood on the brakes and swung the wheel hard to avoid a pedestrian. 'Hey,' he said, 'all I'm doing here is giving you the benefit of all my years in the business. Save your god-damn wit for the customers.'

'Sorry,' the god said remorsefully. 'But picking on me because I'm not cute-looking in tights isn't fair. Really it isn't.'

Kortright shrugged. 'All's fair in love and theology,' he said, 'it's one of the rules of this business. But I guess it's not so important in your case – the appearance thing, I mean. After all, you're here to help me, not so I can find you work. Just as well, really, because I hate failures.'

'Excuse me.'

'Yeah?'

'Would you mind keeping your eyes on the road, please?' Willard said nervously. 'I don't like to sound critical at all, but we nearly had an accident back there.'

'So what's that to you?' Kortright said. 'You're a god. Talking of which, can't you do anything about this traffic? I'll miss my flight if this goes on much longer.'

'Do what?' Willard asked.

Kortright waved his hands impatiently. 'I don't know, do I? You're the god, supposedly. Whatever happened to all-knowing and omnipotent?'

'With all due respect, I never said I was all-knowing or omnipotent,' Willard replied meekly. 'That's just your assumptions. I'm the god of Lin Kortright, remember.'

'Yeah, but still. If you can't do normal god stuff, then how in hell are you going to help me get my daughter back?'

'I don't know,' Willard answered. 'I was hoping you were going to think of something.'

Kortright made a rude noise. 'Not omniscient, not all-powerful, looks like Woody Allen on a bad hair day; man, what kind of god are you?'

'The kind of god you deserve,' Willard said quietly. 'That's what you get. Didn't you know? I'd have thought you'd have realised that years ago, you being a big theological agent and all.'

Kortright looked thoughtful for a moment. 'I never thought of it that way,' he said. 'But who knows, you may well be right. Makes a lot of sense.'

'You don't really need a god, you see,' Willard went on. 'Not the way most people do. I mean, if I was what you'd call a proper god – thunderbolts and fiery thrones and stuff – you'd know it was all basically fake, because you know how it's all really done. No point trying to impress you.'

'Okay, okay. You made your point. If that's how it works, that's how it works. Is there *anything* you can do? Type? Keep the books? Hey, maybe you can make sense of Windows 95.'

Willard shook his head. 'I don't think any of us can do that,' he said. 'But, honest, there's tons of really cool stuff I can do. Real god stuff, too.'

'Such as?'

Willard thought for a moment. 'I can forgive,' he said. 'To forgive's divine, isn't it? I read that somewhere, I'm sure. For a start, I can forgive you for the way you drive.'

Kortright gave him a sour look. 'You think you can do any better, pal, you just slide across into the driver's seat and carry on.'

'I can't. I'm sorry. I don't even know how to drive a car.'

'Enough of this telling me what you can't do,' Kortright growled. 'Come on, show me something you can. One thing's all it'll take.'

'All right.' Willard took a deep breath. 'For a start, I can do this.'

Suddenly and without any preliminary manoeuvres, Kortright began to cry. It started with deep, convulsive sniffles, followed by streams of tears that rolled down his cheeks like herds of migrating lemmings cascading off a cliff, followed by resonant, deep-throated bawling. 'Please,' Kortright blubbed, 'stop it. Stop it now. Oh, it's so *sad*.'

'Or this,' Willard said.

Now Kortright started to laugh, building from a snigger to a chuckle to a giggle to a full-bodied, filmed-before-a-live-audience roar. 'Hey,' Kortright guffawed, 'for Chrissakes, this is killing me. You want that I should have a stroke and die?'

'Sorry.'

Immediately the laughter stopped. 'I'm your god, you see,' Willard explained. 'I can make *you* do most anything, it's just other people I have a problem with. Other people, and things.'

'Great,' Kortright said bitterly. 'And just how's that going to help me rescue Carol?'

'It won't,' Willard said apologetically. 'Won't do you any good at all. Excuse me saying this, but I really don't know where you get this idea from that I'm here to help you.'

Kortright nearly hit a water hydrant. 'Are you saying you aren't?'

Willard shook his head. ''Fraid not,' he replied. 'And that's a real shame because, basically, your Carol's a good kid; she might have made something of her life if she'd had the chance.'

'You aren't here to help,' Kortright said, bemused. 'So what are you here for, then?'

Willard shrugged his thin, narrow shoulders. 'Beats me,' he said. 'You're the one who summoned me, remember. I took it for granted you had a reason.'

'Well, are you capable of helping me? At all?'

'I'm pretty good at filing,' Willard said hopefully. 'Show me a big pile of papers and a filing cabinet and I'll show you some pretty neat god stuff. Divided into subject groups, alphabetical and date order within each group; I could make your office routines up to ten per cent more efficient. Wouldn't that be a real help?'

'No,' Kortright answered sourly. 'I got a really good system as it is. I just wait till the letters on the bottom of the pile have been there long enough to turn into coal, then sell the open-cast mining rights and take a week's vacation.'

'Shrewd stuff,' Willard said in admiration. 'You must be awfully clever to think up something like that.'

Kortright glanced down at the clock on the dashboard and swore. 'This lousy traffic,' he said. 'I missed the damn plane already. Jeez, I got enough to worry about as it is. That's my trouble, I spread myself too thin. They say to me, delegate, Lin, delegate; but this is a kinda personal-service, one-to-one business. What I really need is fifty more of me.'

Willard cleared his throat. 'I'll make a note of that,' he said. 'And maybe there's other ways I can help, too.'

'You think so?' Kortright said, looking up hopefully.

'Would you like me to try?'

Kortright nodded; and at that precise moment, his phone buzzed. 'Kortright here. Yeah, just on my— Oh. But just a . . . Well, if you feel that way I guess there's no more to be said. Yeah, and you too, asshole.' He snapped the phone shut. 'Can you believe it?' he cried furiously. 'That was that creep Knaussgarten in DC.'

'The guy you're on your way to see?'

'Yeah,' Kortright said. 'He calls me and says, have I left yet? So I say no, and he says, that's cool, he can save me a trip, because the deal's off. No reason, just the deal's off. How d'you like that?'

Willard nodded. 'You see?' he said. 'I knew I'd be able to help.'

Kortright looked at him apprehensively. 'What have you done?' he demanded.

'Well, you were worried about being late for your meeting,' Willard explained. 'I figured that if you didn't have a meeting to go to, it'd save you a lot of harmful stress and worry. Now you can take the rest of the day off, maybe go and play golf or something.'

There was a long silence, as Kortright pulled over and stopped the engine. 'You know how long I've been setting up this deal?' he said. 'Only five years. Five fucking *years* of my *life*, down the tubes because you figure I could use a day off. Tell me something, are you the kind of god it's okay to crucify?'

Willard blinked at him. 'But surely,' he said, 'you can't afford the time for that kind of thing right now. Shouldn't you be concentrating on working out a plan for getting your daughter back? Tell me to mind my own business if you like, but maybe you should kind of, you know, take a step back from your life and prioritise. Just a thought,' he added quietly. 'My two cents' worth, and all.'

Kortright turned the car through a hundred and eighty degrees, right under the wheels of an oncoming truck. But the truck driver managed to scream to a halt just in time, so that was all right. 'Your two cents' worth,' Kortright repeated. 'You just cost me five and a half million dollars.'

'Money isn't everything, though,' Willard said cheerfully. 'There's more to your work than just making money, surely.'

'You bet. Like in this deal, I was this close to placing this really talented, promising river goddess with a major delta, and it'd have been really cool, because so far she hasn't got the breaks because she's a Vietnamese disabled single parent.' He sighed. 'And now I guess she'll have to go back to irrigating rice paddies. Life sucks, you know?'

'I expect she'll forgive you,' Willard said reassuringly. 'It's what gods do best.'

'Really?' Kortright shrugged. 'Is that so? In my experience, which is only the result of I don't know how many thousand years of working closely with gods every day of my life so why should I know anything about it, what gods do best is tracking down guys who've offended them in some way and then dropping a skyful of white-hot, nail-studded horseshit on them from somewhere up above the ozone layer. I dunno, maybe we hang out with different types of gods.'

Willard shook his head. 'I don't think so,' he said. 'What you just described sounds to me like an integral part of the forgiveness process.' He smiled; suddenly, unexpectedly, savagely. 'That's the part we gods call getting even first.'

'This,' gibbered a distraught Viking, pointing a trembling finger. '*This!* Is what, sake of God?'

Carol followed his line of sight. 'You mean on the table there?'

'*Ja, ja.* Loudly to be out crying, is damn well what?'

Carol smirked. 'It's a bunch of flowers. It looks nice. It makes the place look cheerful.'

The Viking whimpered, and made the sign of Thor's hammer across his forehead. 'If seeing that, our foes are thinking what? That we a consignment of— *elves?*'

'Nice try,' Carol said, 'but I think you meant "fairies". And no, they won't. And if they do, who cares? They're nothing but a bunch of macho muscleheads anyhow.'

Little red spots of rage burned in the Viking's eyes. 'Our foes to insult, how dare you?' he stuttered. 'Sacred their honour is, for you not to be impugning. Headstrong wench, for shame!' He looked like he had a lot more to say; but then he caught sight of something else and squeaked in horror. 'The table! The table! Haunted!'

'Haunted?'

'Haunted! *Draugr es i hus!* Its face, there in the table to be seeing!' He snatched a short-handled axe from his belt and raised it over his head, ready to strike.

Carol looked at the table. 'You idiot,' she said. 'That's your reflection. I cleaned all that crap off the table and polished it, and now you can see your reflection in it.'

Slowly he lowered the axe. 'Clean?'

'Yeah,' Carol said with a sigh. 'As in, centuries of grease and sticky dried ale and dust and dirt and shit scraped off. Took me hours. Calling this place a pigsty is demeaning to pigs.'

'Fool wench,' the Viking sobbed. 'Is not dirt, is *patina*! Is to nourish and preserve of the wood the vital natural oils! Ruined it is, ruined!'

'Bull. It was filthy. And talk about unhygienic.'

The Viking shook his head. 'Here is of hygiene no need,' he explained, tears welling up in his eyes. 'To catch disease, to fall ill, to die, is so what? Tomorrow is to be reborn. But of genuine antique bench the thousand-year-old patina, if gone, is forever.'

'Tough,' Carol said, folding her arms. 'Jesus, you people! And put that axe away before you do somebody an injury. No, wait, I got a better idea. Right, go to the kitchen—'

'Kitchen? Is where?'

Carol furrowed her brows. 'Say,' she said, 'how long you been here anyway?'

'Me to search.' The Viking shrugged. 'A thousand year? Two?'

'A thousand years, maybe two. And still you don't know where the kitchen is? Per-lease!'

'Not to be knowing!' the Viking protested. 'Is for warriors not the kitchen, for only wenches. There of a wench the place is. Of a warrior— *oww!*' He looked at her, bewildered. 'To be hitting me with wooden dish, why?'

'Go in the kitchen,' Carol repeated icily. 'Take your goddamn axe with you. On the table you'll find a chopping block and a big pile of onions.'

'Fie! Fie! To be cooking? Is of wenches the— see, see, I go. The wooden dish, kindly to be lowering.'

'Out! Shoo!'

The Viking retreated, walking backwards. 'A warrior to be striking of good wenches the way is not. Not is fair, since back honourably warriors to be striking cannot. About you Odin to be telling!'

'Go ahead, tell Odin,' Carol replied with a shrug. 'See if I care.'

'Eeek!' The Viking gave her one last incredulous stare, then bolted through the doorway. A little later, Carol heard the sound of an axehead being buried inches deep in an elm chopping block, accompanied by blood-curdling yells of *Sla, sla! Odin!* She smiled contentedly, then looked around for some other, equally aggravating things to do.

She looked up at the raised dais at the end of the hall, on which stood the high table and the great carved throne of the Lord of the Ravens. It was largely made out of bones: four substantial femurs for the legs, two tibias for the arms, a split ribcage for the back and so forth; the seat was rather cleverly made up of three thigh bones cut down and dovetailed together, bringing into Carol's mind a charming image of a little old man in a brown apron with thick spectacles and a pencil tucked behind his ear, painstakingly filing, sanding and fitting, then dabbing a little French polish on to a soft cloth, while his mug of coffee went cold – quite probably the coffee mug had GRANDPA written on it, but her mind's eye couldn't quite manage that degree of resolution. Anyhow; she saw what she had to do, and the thought brought a big, wicked grin to her face.

It took a long time – there was a lot of work involved, and Carol hadn't actually done anything like this since she was a little girl, and she'd hated it back then and hadn't paid proper attention; but time didn't work the same way here, probably for the same reason that New York subway passes aren't valid on the Orient Express. In any event, she found the materials (amazing, the stuff that was hidden away in the huge chests and trunks tucked under the tables), set to work and, before she knew it, the job was done. She put it in place and stood back to admire her handiwork; at which point, another Viking strolled in from the battlefield, carrying his left hand in his right. He walked straight past her, stopped, and did a double take.

'Is different, something,' he said.

Carol nodded. 'You bet,' she said.

The Viking looked round carefully. 'Definitely is different something. Is worse different.'

'Matter of opinion. I think it's cute.'

The Viking looked round a second time; then a third; then he saw it.

'Aagh!' he said. 'Is doing this who?'

'Me,' Carol replied. 'With my little hatchet. You like it?'

The Viking shivered and let his left hand drop to the floor with a *thunk*. 'I hope you're going to pick that up,' Carol said sternly. 'Where's the point of me working myself half to death getting this joint tidy if you guys are just gonna come in here and leave bits of yourselves scattered all over the floor?' The Viking wasn't listening. He was staring, as if he was Macbeth and not only was Banquo's ghost sitting in Macbeth's favourite chair but also filling his spectral pockets with Macbeth's best Havana cigars.

'Is *horrible*,' he muttered. 'Is what?'

'We call 'em loose covers,' Carol replied. 'Hey, get a load of that embroidery, will you?'

The Viking looked more closely and made a small, mournful queeping noise. 'Is *animals*,' he said.

'You bet. Puppies and lambs and kittens and little cuddly fawns – did you ever see *Bambi*? No, guess not. Anyhow, it's a good likeness, and all done from memory.'

'Animals!'

'Dear little fuzzy animals,' Carol amended. 'Unfortunately I ran out of pink, so some of the dear little baby bunnies had to be white instead; but I think they work okay. What do you think?'

'Blasphemy,' the Viking groaned. 'On of Skyfather the throne, to be embroidering white rabbits. The thigh bones you scarcely can be seeing.'

'You don't think he'll be pleased, then?'

The Viking spun round and gave her a look that would have curdled mercury. 'Pleased is unlikely. Angry is likely. Angry to be trampling mountains and of the Earth the crust with his spear to be piercing entirely is possible.'

'Great,' Carol said. 'Way to go. Wait till you see the matching table-napkins.'

The Viking went an alarming shade of green and started backing away from the chair. He backed so far, he fell off the dais. If he noticed, it was only on a subconscious level.

'On of Skyfather the throne!' he repeated. 'Is it for trouble you are asking?'

'Yes.'

'Madness! Madness! Of this shall Odin be hearing!' The Viking scrambled to his feet, grabbed his severed hand, tucked it hastily down the front of his mail shirt and groped his way to the door, knocking over a bench in the process.

'Pink!' he whispered, in a tone of voice that reminded Carol of the dying Kurtz in *Heart of Darkness*.

'Tell him it was Carol Kortright; that's Kortright with a K, and Carol is C-A-R-O-L. I hate it when people get my name wrong.'

When he'd gone, Carol set about finding her next project. All this stereotypical female domesticity grated on her at the quantum level, and the ease with which she'd part remembered, part assimilated needlework and embroidery alarmed her. She forced herself to think of her own apartment – it was hard, the mental picture was already fading to sepia, drifting into unreality and legend – and made herself conduct a virtual tour of inspection: the sink, full of unwashed mugs and plates, the kitchen floor, which crunched when you walked on it, the unhoovered carpet, the undusted surfaces, the single unplumped cushion that had been there when she arrived, the matter/antimatter clash of the dark green curtains with the duck-egg blue walls – no hint of domesticity there, no pandering to the ancient lie. The woman who had single-handedly built that monument to Not Giving A Damn—

—had a pretty similar outlook to these poor Vikings whose brains she was so mercilessly jangling. Dammit, polishing tables and making loose covers were the kind of things her *mother* would do. Query, she thought: is it really worth saving your life if it costs you your soul? It was, of course, the age-old dilemma of the soldier, the guerrilla, the freedom fighter: in order to win, you must lose the very thing you're fighting for. If she cleaned and polished and tidied and decorated her way out of Valhalla, what sort of person would she have become if she ever really did get back home? Maybe – it was a scary thought, but she had to deal with it before it went septic and slowly poisoned everything – maybe she really did belong here, among the period equivalent of empty styrofoam pizza boxes and a floor covered with screwed-up balls of paper that had been shied at the bin but missed. There was a certain degree of logic to it; after all, if she'd been happy enough selling herself short in life, working as a waitress in a crummy bar when she could have been doing something worthwhile, then why shouldn't she be equally content doing the same thing in death?

'Oh yes.' The voice snapped her out of it. 'Oh, that's a definite improvement.' Odin was running his hand across the newly polished tabletop. 'Just make sure you keep it that way, now you've got it looking so nice. Of course, that would mean spending Eternity on your hands and knees with a scrubbing-brush and a duster, doing menial chores like some dumb *hausfrau*; still, if that's what you really want, you got it. It'd be in character.'

'Shut up,' she snapped.

'Oh, and this is *sensational*,' Odin went on, looking down at the embroidered covers on his throne. 'You really did all this yourself? Quite the little nest-builder.'

Carol scowled at him. 'You were the one who said it was my best chance of getting out of this lousy joint,' she said.

'Your interpretation,' Odin replied, with a dismissive wave of his hand. 'I may have inadvertently dropped something that might be construed as a hint, but what you do with it's your own affair. Just because you've got the wrong end of the stick doesn't entitle you to go bashing me with it.' He traced the outline of a particularly cuddly embroidered puppy with the tip of his index finger. 'You're going to have to tell me how you did this exquisite Florentine cross-stitch,' he went on. 'Whenever I try, it never seems to come out right.'

'Just a damn minute,' Carol interrupted. '*You* do embroidery?'

Odin nodded, and the great bronze wings on his helmet cast sprawling shadows across the floor. 'And why not?' he said. 'You see, I believe in making the most of my own potential, even if it leads me in unexpected directions. Tsk,' he added, prodding at the table top. 'You missed a bit.'

Howard had a dream. He dreamed that he'd died and gone to Heaven.

In this dream, he was sitting on a slightly rickety swivel chair in front of a desk, on top of which sat a VDU and a telephone. He wasn't alone; the huge room he was sitting in was full of similar desks, computers and telephones, all being operated by remarkably similar people. Like him, the men were dressed in white C&A shirts, cheerful polyester ties and Marks & Spencer suits; the women showed a degree more variety, preferring variations on the standard modes offered by Primark and Richards. What they weren't wearing, not a single one of them, was battledress, DPM camouflage or Kevlar body armour.

I was right, Howard said to himself. *This is Heaven.*

Nor were they trying to kill each other, not even a little bit. Instead, they spoke into the telephones and pressed keys on the keyboards in front of them, often at the same time. He strained his ears to overhear what they were saying, but the words were indistinct; all he could pick up were tantalising fragments, words and phrases like *lunch* and *Saturday* and *So I said*, and a strange, intoxicating subvocal noise that at first he didn't recognise, until with a sharp pang of loss and regret he realised it was laughter.

This is Work, Howard remembered. *This is The Office.*

And still nobody threw a grenade or opened fire with an Uzi; and this struck Howard as odd, because surely that's what people did, or at least they did where he came from. Or did they? He frowned, and his memory seemed to jump out of phase. It was possible that once upon a time he'd lived in Heaven himself, back in the days before the Fall and the theft of the apple from the Tree of the Knowledge of Good and Evil. Somewhere in his head there were memories of that time, but it seemed probable that when he'd been expelled from Heaven, those parts of his mind had been sealed off so that the memories wouldn't plague him and drive him into melancholy. If he was right, there really had once been a whole different world or dimension called The Office, and the people who lived and worked in it hardly ever stabbed or shot each other or hosed each other down with flame-throwers, unless of course the Office they worked in was the US Postal Service. And as if that wasn't weird and wonderful enough, this heaven was reserved for the living . . .

He looked up; something was going on. Two women and a man had got up from their desks and were going round the room handing out slices of cake. *Food*, Howard remembered. *I think I used to like food. You ate it.* The cake-distributors were smiling and chatting; *Happy birthday*, someone said, and one of the women replied, *Thank you*; that sounded like conversation, the practice of talking to other people about subjects other than matters of immediate strategic concern, troop movements or the weather. Large gobbets of recollected data were flooding back now; birthday was the anniversary of the day you arrived in Heaven, and on your birthday other people in The Office gave you pieces of folded cardboard with pictures and lewd or insulting inscriptions as an expression of their esteem; by way of reciprocation, you produced a cake you'd bought or created and handed out slices to everyone in The Office. It was all part of Being Nice and All Getting Along, which was how the people here interacted with each other, the Heavenly equivalent of kicking in a door and emptying the clip of your M-16 at anything that moved.

Different, Howard mused. *Too early to judge whether it's better, but certainly different.*

The cake-givers delivered a slice at the desk on his left, and then the one on his right, and then moved on. He watched his neighbours eating the cake; fingers compressing the squidgy fabric of the sponge, jaws opening wide to get around the broad wedge, cream and jam squeezing out of the sides as the bite was taken, dribbling and oozing over fingers and dropping messily on desks and papers. He realised that they'd passed him by, overlooking him as if he wasn't there, and at that moment he understood that he wasn't yet a member of Heaven, just a visitor or observer; that would account for his screen being blank and his telephone silent. Howard felt his throat tighten and his eyes become uncomfortable, and instinctively he groped for his gas mask. But the cause of these symptoms, he knew as he rummaged, wasn't CS gas or some deadly nerve agent; it was one of the emotions, called 'sorrow' if he remembered correctly. Where he came from there was no sorrow, presumably because in order to feel sorrow you needed to have something to contrast it with. Sorrow in Valhalla would be as pointless as rain on the sea.

Time passed; how quickly Howard didn't know, since the things by which he gauged the passing of time (the ten o'clock rocket strike; the noon bombardment; the three o'clock mortar barrage) didn't seem to happen here. In some respects time passed slowly, since he had nothing to do, but after a while he stopped trying to gauge it, and then it seemed to slip past, because suddenly people were standing up, putting on jackets and coats, switching off screens, walking through doors; the people were leaving Heaven. That struck Howard as incredible. Nobody was chasing them out or forcing them to leave at gunpoint; they were walking out of Heaven quite happily – cheerfully, some of them, as if they really wanted to go. An illusion, obviously; a brave face put on the Fall of Man. But they managed to make it look thoroughly convincing.

When they'd all gone, Howard sat for a while in the darkness (they'd turned off the lights) and relished the lack of explosions for a subjective hour or so. He was listening with rapt attention to the sound silence makes when it isn't being interrupted by the booming of distant howitzers when another dribble of memory dropped into his mind. Heaven, he seemed to remember hearing somewhere, wasn't just The Office; The Office was just one of several component parts of the continuum. There was also Commuting, not to mention Home and The Shops, plus a vague and shadowy recollection of something called Evenings and Weekends.

It was a gamble – what if he'd got it wrong, and walking through the door landed him back in Valhalla, among the landmines and chlorine gas? Wouldn't it be better to stay here, where he knew it was safe? Given time, he might even be able to figure out how to operate the computers (*Can't be difficult, after all; they're designed to be convenient and easy to use*) and do some Work. On the other hand, he had a fanciful notion that the other parts of Heaven were sometimes even better than The Office. He owed it to himself to find out. Slowly, and feeling rather as Columbus would have felt if the first thing he'd seen on the beach at Hispaniola had been a finger-post pointing west and inscribed THIS WAY TO THE SHEER DROP, he felt his way to the door, opened it and found himself at the top of a staircase.

Howard knew all about staircases. If you went down, you ran into the enemy patrol. If you went up, you were the enemy patrol that the other guy ran into. In either case, the result was a maximum of ten seconds of fierce combat, until either everybody had shot everybody else or some bright spark threw a grenade that reduced the whole stairwell to matchwood. The only place in a building more dangerous than a staircase, in fact, was the lift.

Not, apparently, in Heaven. Howard made it to the bottom of the staircase without having to dodge a single bullet or grapple with a single black-balaclava'd intruder. The next thing he knew, he was in a street; a familiar place, bustling with civilians – New Street, in the heart of war-untorn Birmingham. From here, the blessed denizens of Heaven caught trains that carried them home, like sweet chariots.

One of them would take him to Rolfe Street station in Smethwick, which was just twenty minutes' walk from Home.

Home. Smethwick on my mind. Ich bin ein Schmethwicker. For a moment his sense of balance failed him and he reeled as he contemplated the sheer geographical extent of his life in Heaven, a place so vast that you needed a train to get from one end of it to the other. In Valhalla, geography was circumscribed by the distance you could reasonably expect to get without being shot or blown up first; on average, something between seventy-five yards and a mile and a half. Once, he knew, he'd managed to get all the way from Stanhope Road to Alma Street unscathed except for the loss of one arm. He'd felt like General Sherman marching from Atlanta to the sea, and when he'd finally trodden on a mine and dissolved in the usual fine red spray he'd actually felt relief at the thought that his massive overdraft of borrowed time wasn't going to get any bigger. In Heaven, however – well, to continue the metaphor he'd used earlier, in theory you could go as far as West Bromwich and still not fall off the edge. The thought was amazing, if a little agoraphobic. One thing you had to say in favour of Valhalla: it was small and compact, and it didn't matter if you got lost. If you did somehow manage to lose your way, you simply asked the next person you killed for directions.

Smethwick. To boldly go where no armoured division has gone before.

It would have been nice. Unfortunately, that was the moment when the guard at the ticket barrier hauled out a Stechkin from the depths of his little booth and opened up at point-blank range. 'A cloudy start to the day,' he yelled as he jerked out the empty magazine and replaced it with a full one, 'with gale-force winds expected from the north-east. The pollen count—'

Howard sat up. The guard was nowhere to be seen, though the pile of empty 9mm cartridge cases suggested he hadn't been just a figment of the imagination. It was morning in Valhalla, one minute after dawn, same as usual. Having rolled sideways into the cover of a burnt-out armoured personnel carrier, Howard looked round to establish where he was. The few floating bubbles that were all that remained of his dream gave him the crazy notion that he wasn't in Smethwick any more; but dreams lie. He was in Rolfe Street, and the pile of rubble away to his left was the remains of the railway station. No yellow brick road, no pearly gates, no New Street; just the earth-shaking *whump* of the battery of 105mm guns in Brook Street and the scream of falling mortar shells. Back to real life with a vengeance.

CHAPTER SIX

Attila the Hun collapsed on his bed, sobbing hysterically. He wasn't quite sure why; in fact, he could think of quite a few good reasons why he *shouldn't* be behaving this way, among them the deeply ingrained rule that barbarian warlords don't cry; and if they do, it's not simply because they've been told to tidy their room. Tell a barbarian warlord to tidy his room and he'll either do it or he'll have you torn apart by wild horses; he won't suddenly burst into tears, bolt upstairs and hide under the duvet, hugging his teddy. And yet, Attila reflected, here he was, driven by some apparently irresistible instinct, which knew that screaming and howling would make Mummy give in, eventually, and the room would stay agreeably untidy till about the same time tomorrow, when they'd have to go through this whole performance again.

That sounded familiar, somehow: a battle fought every day for ever, with nothing changing, the combatants simply starting again from the same positions, without either lasting victory or permanent defeat. He frowned, trying to pin down the elusive memory, but it wouldn't stay still long enough.

The door flew open, and Mummy loomed at him. He was shocked. This was against the rules of the war, which stated that once he'd flounced upstairs to sob, he should be left alone and allowed to regroup until bathtime. Not that he minded, not one little bit; he'd just have liked an opportunity to place it on record that he hadn't been the one to violate the rules of engagement.

'I've had enough, do you hear me?' Mummy thundered. 'Now get this pigsty cleared up, or else I'm going to put the whole lot out for the dustmen. Understood?'

All right, said his inner voice with a hint of relish, *I can relate to this. You want to escalate, that's fine by me. And here's a word of advice, lady; with that face, don't ever play* n'g'chuk *for money.*

What he said out loud, however, was 'Waaaaaaaaaaaaaa-muhuhuhu,' very loudly and with appropriate commentaries in body language: drumming fists and feet on the bed, bouncing up and down, turning up the tear volume from steady-stream to cascade mode. In his time, Attila had called the bluffs of emperors, kings and provincial governors. This ought to be a piece of—

Ouch! That hurt!

'And you'll get another smack if you don't start tidying up *this instant,*' Mummy added savagely. 'I mean it. If that's all you understand, that's what you'll get.'

Go on, we can take it. What are you waiting for? But those confounded instincts weren't obeying him. To his horror and disgust, Attila realised that this no-good body was afraid of pain and was refusing his direct orders. Worse; he was off the bed and on the floor, grabbing handfuls of Lego and stuffing them back in the plastic bucket. *Coward!* he fulminated, but his body wasn't listening. Dammit, she'd won.

So this is defeat, Attila mused, *I always wondered what it would feel like. Can't say I like it a whole lot. Winning is so much nicer.*

When he'd finished tidying it was bathtime; culture shock registering 10.9 on the Richter scale. Not that the old Attila had never got wet. Far from it. He could remember days and nights of unspeakable discomfort as the caravan trudged and squelched through snow and driving rain, the water streaming down the inside of his saturated clothes. He'd always put up with it – no choice in the matter – but it stuck in his memory as one of the most wretched things he'd ever experienced. Here, for some bizarre reason, they got wet on purpose; these people, with their amazing watertight roofs, had even built a special room just for getting wet in. Perverts, the lot of them. The really disturbing thing was that this body he was stuck in seemed to enjoy it. The rubber duck helped, of course (between his inner voice and the towel rail, the rubber duck was way cool, totally neat; if you squeezed its tummy, it went *waak waak*, just like a real duck.) But that wasn't enough to account for a fundamental reversal of all his most deeply seated preconceptions. Maybe it was the bubbles. They were way cool too, of course. In fact, they were *amazing*.

And after bathtime, bed. Attila lay in the dark, struggling to reconcile it all, but he couldn't. All he could be sure of was that he'd gone from one bad place to another. He was no more himself here than he had been back in the great big auditorium where he'd sat watching the paint. If there was a difference, it lay in the fact that, in Valhalla, at least he hadn't been able to remember what it had been like to be himself, Attila the Scourge of God (on reflection, quite possibly an unfortunate choice of epithet for someone now experiencing an afterlife situation). He thought of what they'd told him, just before he'd escaped; the sort of people who end up in Valhalla don't want to be reminded of what they used to be. Not so, not so; all his life he had wanted to be the very best barbarian warlord he could be, and by and large he'd managed to live up to those principles. He'd burned churches, sacked towns, destroyed millennia of cultural heritage, all with no thought of self, no pointless agonising about *Is this what I really want to do with my life?* That sort of question was irrelevant to the son of the chief of the war-band; chief's sons didn't sneak out of the yurt at dead of night and run away to become accountants. *It's a matter of duty, obligation, accepting one's place in the fabric of barbarian society.* Not, of course, that he'd have chosen a different life even if he'd had the option. At least, he didn't think he would have; since the issue hadn't ever occurred to him before, he hadn't given it any thought.

'Perhaps you should.'

Barbarian warriors aren't afraid of things that go bump in the night; it'd be utterly counter-productive, like having a vampire who fainted at the sight of blood. Six-year-old children, however, follow a different set of programming protocols.

'Eeek!'

'Ssh.' The voice was calm, soothing and infuriatingly familiar. 'You'll wake your mother and she'll be cross. Major-league cross. You think you were a holy terror when you devastated the Veneto? You ain't seen nothing.'

To his shame and annoyance, Attila found he'd instinctively buried his head under the bedclothes. 'Who are you?' he asked, in a pathetic little trembly voice.

'Who, me? Attila, I am thy father's spirit, doomed for a certain term to walk the night, and for the day confin'd to fast in fires till the foul crimes— no, hang about, that's not right, look, is today Tuesday?'

'Tuesday?'

'Sorry,' said the voice. 'My mistake, I should have realised. It can't be Tuesday, because this is Nottingham. I'll be perfectly honest with you, ever since my daughter gave me that electronic personal organiser thing I've been all over the place. You try and find out which appointment you're supposed to be doing and all it'll tell you is the time in Rio de Janeiro.'

Cautiously, Attila poked his head up above the blankets. Things that wittered on and on and on in the night weren't quite so scary, somehow. 'What are you doing here?' he said.

'Huh,' replied the voice testily, 'don't get me started on that one, puh-*lease*. By rights I shouldn't even be here, because properly speaking this is 5633423's night on and I should just be on standby, but he calls in with this real tear-jerker about a flat tyre and a sick nephew in Addis Ababa – well, it may be true for all I know, but I wouldn't bet my dinner money on that, if you know what I mean—' The voice stopped, then started again. 'Oh, I see, you mean, what's the purpose of this visit? What's behind it all? Was that what you meant?'

'Yes.'

'Sorry. You know, I'm not a hundred per cent with-it this evening. Right then. Is your name Scrooge?'

Attila blinked. 'Huh?'

'Scrooge,' the voice repeated, 'Ebenezer Scrooge. It's not, is it? Right, that's fine, that's useful data because it helps me narrow it down a little bit more. Okay, so I'm *not* the Ghost of Christmas Present – you know,' the voice continued, 'I have real trouble with that one, real difficulties keeping a straight face, because every time I've got to say it, you know, in the big sonorous voice *like that*, I get this mental image of a parcel in coloured paper with a bow on top walking through a wall with its head under its arm. Hang on, we're getting there. You're Brad, right?'

'Brad?'

'Brad Wilson, aged six and two months, formerly Attila the Hun? The only person ever to escape from Valhalla and live to tell the tale? Please say you are, because otherwise my supervisor's going to play war and I just couldn't face . . .'

'Yes,' Attila said. 'Or at least, I used to be Attila. I don't know anything about any Brad whatever-you-said.'

The voice sighed with relief. 'That's all right, then,' he said. 'Now then, if you're six I'm assuming you can write your name, so if you'd just care to sign here and here—'

'Write?' Attila sounded shocked. 'I can't write.'

'Ah. Are you sure about that? Because unless I get these waivers signed, our legal boys are going to very stroppy indeed and I'll give you three guesses whose nose is going to get used as a bootwipe—'

'Of course I can't write,' Attila interrupted. 'Writing's for cissies. *Romans* write. We don't.'

There was a brief silence. 'Excuse me saying this,' the voice resumed, 'but you really aren't quite up to speed on this, are you?'

'No,' Attila replied.

'Figures. Look, here's a pen.' Attila felt something being thrust into his hand. 'And here's the clipboard.' Something grabbed his hand – something that was cold as ice and hard as steel – and pressed it against a flat surface. 'Now try writing your name: B. Wilson. Go on, you'll surprise yourself.'

Attila felt his hand move, describing a complex evolution of movements that drew the pen across the surface of the clipboard. 'Hey,' he said, 'I'm writing. How the hell did I do that?'

'Thank you.' The clipboard was pulled away, and the pen flicked out from between his fingers. 'All right, now we've got that out of the way, we can make a start. My name is Odin.'

'Odin,' Attila repeated. 'I've heard of you.'

'I'll bet,' the voice replied. 'Actually, of course, I'm not Odin, just as the man in the red dressing gown and white cotton wool with the pillow up his jumper in Debenhams isn't really Father Christmas; let's say I'm *an* Odin. Really, I'm from an agency.'

'An agency.'

'Yes, but don't think about that. Forget I said it. Thinking about it'll just get in the way of your suspension of disbelief, and that'll make things harder for both of us. So for all practical purposes I'm Odin, okay?'

'Whatever you say,' Attila replied. 'Are you real?'

'Good question, very good question,' Odin replied. 'And I'm not going to answer it, not because it isn't a perfectly valid point to raise at this juncture, but simply because if we get sidetracked into peripheral issues like that, I'm still going to be here when your mum comes in to wake you up for school. Which reminds me,' he added, 'this has to be Sunday, not Tuesday. Hellfire, if this is Sunday and I'm here, where the devil is Tuesday?'

'What are you talking about?'

'What? Oh, don't mind me. Look, here's the deal. I'm Odin, right, and just for argument's sake let's assume I'm real. Now, my job is running Valhalla. You know, the big theatre place with the wet paint.'

'I know where that is,' Attila replied.

'Okay; and you've just escaped from there, and now you find yourself imprisoned – that's not too strong a word, is it? – imprisoned, in the body of a six-year-old boy living in a remote and distant land, fifteen hundred and something years after your death. In other words,' Odin went on, 'somehow, and we're still not absolutely sure how, you beat the system. You made it. You escaped. You're the first human ever to come back from the dead and get a new life. Congratulations.'

Attila furrowed his brows. 'Thank you,' he said.

'That's all right. And really, you have to believe me when I say absolutely no hard feelings, okay? I can say that, you see, because really I'm not the real Odin. I mean, if I was *the* Odin, the one you made a complete and utter arse out of, do you think we'd be chatting away like this? No way, by now you'd be in more pieces than a de luxe three-day jigsaw. Come to think of it, maybe that's why I'm here and not the regular Odin. That'd make sense, wouldn't it?'

'Would it? It'd be the first thing you've said that does.'

'Actually,' Odin said coldly, 'that was a rather hurtful thing to say. May I suggest that you stop using me as an emotional punchbag if you want me to help you?'

'Sorry, sorry. Can you really help me?' Attila asked hopefully. 'All I want is to know what's going on.'

The voice chuckled. 'That's all you want, is it? I'll pretend I didn't hear you say that. Now then, cards on table. Because of the embarrassment you've caused us – when I say "us", you understand, really I mean "them", because of course I'm not "us", I'm just filling in for "us" – because of all that, we're treating your escape from Valhalla as a death.'

'Death,' Attila repeated. 'Go on.'

'Which means,' Odin said, 'that we're looking on this as an afterlife. Which it is, of course,' he added, 'it's a life after death, so we're really playing it absolutely true-blue down the middle, and categorically no question of a cover-up. That's in case you get asked any questions by the media, all right?'

'Fine by me,' Attila said. 'Is that likely?'

'No. Now then, the question you're really bursting to ask is, what's in it for me? That's "me" meaning "you", of course, not "me" meaning "me", because the *me* me is just, like, this guy from an agency. Let's rephrase that, shall we? What's in it for you?'

'All right. So what *is* in it for me?'

'Need you ask? Isn't it obvious? You've got a whole new life in front of you, all but six years of it. And, believe me, you wouldn't want those six years, you're better off without them; all that potty training and learning to eat with a spoon. No, basically you're just nicely run in, all set and ready to go. The world is yours and everything that's in it. Enjoy.'

'But this is *awful*,' Attila protested. 'I'm Attila the Scourge of God, and I'm marooned in this rotten little kid's body with a right Nazi for a Mummy. If I don't eat all my disgusting dinner I get sent to bed and as far as I can tell this body's brain is convinced there's a huge scaly monster hiding in the toilet cistern, which means I daren't go for a pee in the night even if I'm about to explode. This whole thing sucks. I want out.'

Odin tutted reproachfully. 'You say that now,' he said. 'And that's because it's early days yet, there's bound to be a few teething troubles—'

'And that's another thing,' Attila interrupted. 'According to this body's memory files, every time one of my teeth comes out, Mummy puts it under my pillow and this *thing* comes creeping up in the middle of the night to fetch it. That's horrible.'

'But,' Odin went on, 'in due course you'll realise that you've been given the kind of lucky break that most dead people can only dream about. Just think, will you? A whole new stab at life. And in your case especially, that must be really thrilling.'

Attila frowned. 'Why in my case?'

'Oh, come on,' the voice replied patronisingly. 'Use your head, won't you? Last time round, you were Attila the ruddy *Hun*. One of the five most hated and despised figures in history.'

Attila sat bolt upright. 'That's not true,' he blurted out. 'It can't be. I was a hero.'

'Uh-huh.' Odin sighed. 'If you don't believe me, I suggest you check yourself out in any reliable reference book. You'll have to wait a few years, of course, because right now your reading skills are at the Here-are-Peter-and-Jane level.'

'Read? Don't say I do that as well.'

'Just about. Anyway, you take it from me, Attila the Hun – utter scumbag, according to the consensus of human opinion. Right up there on every historian's Most Unwanted list. Not,' Odin added, 'that you can really be blamed for what you turned into. After all, it wasn't your choice.'

Attila thumped his pillow angrily. 'Yes, it was,' he said.

'No, no, no. You think it was, but it wasn't. When you

were – well, your age, I guess, maybe a few years older – what you really wanted to be when you grew up was an aqueduct designer.'

'I did?'

'Oh yes. Really, really wanted. But your father, of course, he wouldn't hear of it. No, he went straight into that No-son-of-mine mode of his, kept banging on about duty and obligation and thirty generations of looters and pillagers turning in their graves. You held out for much longer than anyone expected, but you had to give in.'

'Really?' Attila said, pleased. 'How long was that, then?'

'Twenty minutes. And that was good going. They reckoned that another forty-five seconds and he'd have cut you in half and fed you to the dogs. Anyway, that's how you came to be who you were, Attila the Scourge of God and all that garbage. Basic survival instinct, pure and simple. So you see, you never really had a life of your own; your life was just a continuation of your old man's, just like his was, and so on back for centuries. Think about that, will you? One life, repeated over and over again, endlessly recurring; the same patterns, the same basic events, and every time you die, you go back to the beginning disguised as your own kid.'

'Valhalla,' Attila said quietly.

'Well spotted,' Odin said with approval. 'In other words, a pretty raw deal; you got your eternal punishment before you'd even had a chance to do the sins, except of course that in a sense the eternal punishment *was* doing the sins. Neat system, and as far as the powers that be were concerned, a tremendous saving on employer's national insurance contributions. No, of all the mean stunts I ever heard about (and this is me talking now, you understand) sending someone to Valhalla while they're still alive must be about as low as you can get.'

Attila thought about it for a long time. 'All right,' he said. 'So this is my second chance. What if I still want to be me?

Grow up into another barbarian warlord, I mean? Is that allowed?'

'Ah.' The voice sounded doubtful. 'Problem there. You see, barbarianism sort of got done away with, quite a few centuries ago, along with slavery and the plague and a whole lot of other cool stuff. No, that's not strictly true; actually, there's a lot more barbarians per head of population now than ever before, a hell of a lot more. But where back in your day they were outside the gates, these days they're the ones on the inside.'

'Huh?' Attila scowled with bewilderment.

'It's sad,' Odin said, 'but true. You want to see barbarians these days, you go out – when you're older, of course, I keep forgetting that – you go out on a Saturday night when the pubs are closing, or go to a football match, or hire a video. That's the problem; you can't keep the barbarians out when they're already in.'

'Willard,' muttered Lin Kortright, as the barman collected the empty glasses, 'what are we doing here?'

'Rescuing Carol,' replied the god, checking his fly as he returned from the men's room. 'That's what you want, isn't it?'

Kortright nodded. 'You bet.'

'And designing a perfect afterlife for Mr Kawaguchi? That's next on the order of business, isn't it?'

'Yeah.' Kortright tapped the ash from his cigar on to the floor. 'But how's sitting in this crummy bar going to help?'

'Ah.' Willard fanned away the smoke ostentatiously. 'I wish you wouldn't do that,' he said. 'According to the latest surveys, passive smoking—'

'Why in hell's name should a god worry about passive smoking?'

Willard sighed. 'We're sitting in this crummy bar because it's necessary. Think.'

'I've thought. I still don't get it. Explain.'

'All right,' Willard replied. 'But I'm disappointed, truly I am. Someone like you shouldn't need me to tell you these things. First, if we want to rescue Carol, we've got to go to where she is, right?'

Kortright looked doubtful. 'Do we? Okay, we do. You're the boss.'

'Good. We have to go where she is. Valhalla.'

'Valhalla? What's she doing in Valhalla, for pity's sake?'

Willard closed his eyes for a moment. 'Wiping tables,' he replied. 'Clearing away empty glasses. Clearing away *full* glasses; but that's just because she's deliberately trying to be aggravating. I guess that's the old Kortright genes shining through.'

'All right,' Kortright said, slightly dazed. 'Suppose I accept she really is in Valhalla. And you're saying we've got to go there too?'

Willard nodded. 'Only way,' he confirmed.

'You're *sure* she's in Valhalla? I thought she wasn't, like, qualified. Hell, I should know something about the place, I've been there often enough.'

'So you have,' Willard agreed. 'But only on business. What you've seen is the front office; we need to get through to the shop floor. Only one way to do that.'

'What, you mean we've got to— Jesus, Willard, where do you think you're going?'

Willard, who'd got up from the table, beamed at him. 'Valhalla,' he replied. 'You coming or staying?'

'Willard, you really don't want to talk to those guys,' Kortright muttered, as his personal deity started to stroll across the room. 'Willard, this isn't a good—'

But it was too late. Already, Willard had tugged a man by his sleeve and said something that could only lead—

(It wasn't just any crummy bar. It was a New York Trekkies bar. The man whose sleeve Willard had just tugged was wearing the uniform of a Klingon admiral, and Kortright just managed to make out the words, 'My friend and I were just talking and we think you guys look like a load of—' before the roaring started.)

—to violence, in one of its most basic and efficient forms. Willard sailed through the bar's plate-glass window like a discus from the hand of an East German gold medallist, and a moment later Lin Kortright—

('Well,' Willard said, 'here we are. Death in battle gets you there every time.')

—was standing on a stage in front of a faded velvet curtain, looking out over two dozen small round tables and a bar. There were fifteen or so people at the tables, half of them looking up at the stage, the other half engrossed in conversation or eating.

'*Valhalla?*' Kortright whispered.

'You bet.' He couldn't see where Willard's voice was coming from; in the wings somewhere, presumably. 'Go on, then, do your stuff.'

Kortright felt his tongue seize in his mouth like an overheated piston. 'I . . .' he managed to croak. Two or three more of the customers turned and stared at him. He turned back to Willard. 'What the fuck is this, Willard?' he demanded hoarsely.

'It's an audition, Lin. You should know that by now, you've been to enough of them. This is an audition, I'm your agent. Now go out there and sock it to 'em.'

'Um—' Kortright said. He felt like a boffin in a big electronics company who'd just finished perfecting the ultimate foolproof lie detector and suddenly finds himself strapped down in his own chair with his own electrodes shoved up his nose while his immediate superiors sit round him in a circle and question him in minute detail about his latest expense account.

'You,' a voice called out from the darkness. 'Get on with it, will ya? We got other people to see.'

Kortright tried to speak but his voice appeared to have been repossessed by the finance company. He opened and closed his mouth a couple of times but nothing happened.

'Jeez,' said a voice, 'another friggin' amateur. All right, get this bum outa here.'

(*Hey, that's my line. Maybe that's the line I ought to be saying. For God's sake, someone, what's my goddamn line?*)

'Willard?' he whispered.

'Right here.'

Kortright looked round. Willard was standing right next to him. 'What am I supposed to say?'

'I don't know, Lyndon. You're the talent, I'm just your agent. Shouldn't you have prepared all this before we came here?'

'But—'

Willard sighed. 'I'm disappointed in you, Lyndon. Here you are, the biggest audition of your sad little life, and you haven't even taken the trouble to read the fucking script. You know, it'd serve you right if I just walked away and left you standing here.'

'No!' Kortright grabbed at him but somehow he wasn't there to be grabbed. He swung himself round, stared out at the darkened auditorium and said, 'Nowisthewinterofour-discontentmadeglorioussummer—'

'You.'

'Yes? I mean, yes, sir?'

'What in God's name do you think you're doing?'

Kortright stared into the darkness, trying to get a fix on where the voice was coming from. Was this how it felt for all those poor fools who stood up in front of him? Nasty thought.

'Auditioning,' he said.

'Right. So why are you reciting fucking Shakespeare?'

'I . . .' Good point. Why *was* he reciting Shakespeare? 'It's all I could think of,' he replied.

'Idiot. Look, man, we aren't casting Richard the goddamn

Third, okay? We're casting Lin Kortright. And son, I've seen enough to know that, frankly, you ain't got it. Now get outa here.'

'Lin *Kortright*?'

'Yeah. As in *The Tragedy of Lin Kortright*. As in probably the greatest, the most harrowing and cathartic tragedy ever written. You heard of it, boy? Or don't they have books where you come from?'

Somehow, Lin Kortright couldn't bring himself to turn his back on that darkness; instead he walked backwards, feeling the curtain gather round him, until he was through and the folds closed in front of his face. 'Willard?' he whispered.

'Here, Lyndon.'

Kortright let go the breath he'd been hoarding, like petrol in a *Mad Max* movie, for the last forty seconds. 'Where were you?'

'Right behind you,' the little god replied. 'Hiding.'

'Willard,' Kortright said, 'where is this place?'

'Valhalla. I already told you. Don't you recognise it?'

'No.'

A look of amazement spread across Willard's face like ink soaking into blotting paper. 'Really? That's strange.'

'All right, already, it's strange. Are you *sure*—?'

Willard nodded. 'Sure I'm sure. It's a place where there's guys dying the death every day and then getting up and going on to do it all over again. Like,' he pointed out, 'you've gotta do in less than an hour. If I were in your shoes, Lyndon Milhous Kortright, I'd go write myself some lines, quickly.'

'Lines?' Kortright stared at him as if he'd been asked for a gas giant in custard. 'What the hell do I—?'

'You're auditioning, you need lines,' Willard replied.

'But I don't know what the damn lines are.'

Willard shook his head. 'Don't talk dumb,' he said. 'You're auditioning for the part of *you*. Of course you know what the lines are.'

Kortright shook himself hard. 'Look, you said we were going to find Carol. Where is she?'

'In Valhalla, stupid. Where else would a dead person be?'

'So where is she? I don't see her. Is she out front waiting on the tables, or what?'

'No. Look, if it helps, why not write the lines on the back of your hand? It's crummy as hell, but it's got to be better than going out there and just standing with your mouth shut, like you're the President denying responsibility.'

'But how can this be Valhalla?' Kortright demanded. 'Shit, Willard, I know Valhalla, I've been there. Where's the guys with swords? Where's the Vikings?'

Willard shrugged his thin shoulders. 'Don't ask me,' he said, 'I don't follow baseball. All right, here's an easy one for you. Absolutely no way you can fail to get a laugh with this one. What did the chief of police say when he raided the whorehouse?'

Commandments, Kortright muttered to himself. *Thou shalt not bounce the Lord thy God off the walls like a squash ball.* No, doesn't ring a bell. So, if it isn't forbidden it must be okay. 'Listen, you asshole,' he snarled, picking the god up by his ears and holding him a foot off the ground, 'where the hell is my daughter?'

'You see?' Willard squeaked, his feet swinging backwards and forwards. 'I was sure you'd know that one.'

Your attention, please.

Nobody paid any attention. They never do.

Thank you for flying Valhalla Atlantic. The stewardess will now demonstrate the safety procedures to be followed in the event of an emergency. Please refer to the safety leaflet which you will find in the pocket of the seat in front of you.

Nobody looked up. The stewardess took her place in the middle of the aisle. As nobody watched, she pointed out the emergency doors, swinging her arms like a gym teacher. With nobody to see her, she mimed the approved method of putting on the lifejacket, tightening the straps, blowing the cute little whistle. Unobserved, she acted out the last few desperate moments of life in the freezing waters of the North Atlantic: the frantic scrabbling at the sides of the already overloaded life raft; the agony in the arms and legs as cold and exhaustion slowly drain away the energy and the will to live; the bubbling gasp as the head ducks under the water for the first time; the slow relaxation into acceptance and death; the head, bobbing just below the surface of the water; the gradual, graceful drift to the bottom of the sea.

Thank you for your attention. The aircraft will crash into the sea in precisely two minutes.

The plume of spray thrown up as the plane hit the water rose high into the air, then fell like rain. Inside, in the back row of the passenger compartment, a smartly dressed middle-aged man with a flamboyant black moustache put down his magazine, looked out of the window and saw a shoal of fish.

Fish?

Fish, flying?

Flying fish?

Not at forty thousand feet, surely; and besides, why has the sky suddenly gone all green and murky? And why has the plane slowed down? Flying low over Los Angeles, perhaps?

As the nose of the airliner hit the ocean floor and nuzzled its way down through countless levels of grot and crap (imagine what you'd get if you forgot to clean out the goldfish tank for seven hundred million years) until it jarred and crumpled on the primeval rock, the smartly dressed man quickly ran through the possible alternatives in his mind. He hit on the right one and recognised it for what it was just in time to be able to laugh quietly at the irony of it all before water flooded the main cabin and everybody drowned. *What a way to go, eh?* he mused. *This time, and I'm not ashamed to say it, I really am out of my depth.*

So perished The Immortal Vincenzo, without any question the greatest practitioner of the art of escapology the world has ever seen. His obituaries, in twenty-seven languages, praised his effortless skill, his impeccable calm, his dazzling showmanship. Grief-stricken colleagues confided to sympathetic microphones on five continents their debt to the man who'd pioneered such bewildering stunts as the plunge from a high clifftop while sealed in a nuclear-waste-specification concrete block into the maw of an active volcano. (Old hat now, of course, but when Vinnie did it for the very first time the whole profession sat up and took notice.) There were even some who smiled enigmatically at the interviewer's assertion that, this time, The Immortal Vincenzo had finally cashed his cheque. 'You reckon?' they said. 'Lady, you never knew Vinnie'; and went on to imply that a true artist like Vincent Ehrlich would only have died to the same extent that very rich men pay their income tax in full. One close associate ventured to say that if they were to show him Vinnie's severed head, screwed to the floor with a tungsten steel bolt, he'd still make a point of checking his wallet was still there before leaving the room. A publicity stunt, others said confidently, a great way to promote his new show on UPN, though possibly a bit rough on the other two hundred and six passengers.

Vinnie Ehrlich, on the other hand, accepted his death with impressive fortitude. (*Past life flash in front of his eyes? Nah. Never had that, and just as well. In his line of work, he'd have ended up seeing more repeats than a BBC viewer.*) Given time to rehearse, work it all out and practise the moves, he'd have had a chance. As it was, this time they had him cold, and he didn't begrudge it to them. As the cold salt water began to seep through the ruptures in the aircraft's outer membranes and fill the cabin, slow but sure like the pouring of draught Guinness, he sat in his seat with his arms folded on his lap, while all around him was chaos, shrieking, thrashing, despair and disorder. By the time the water had glugged all the way up to the back row of seats and was swilling around his neck, things had quietened down somewhat. He closed his eyes and waited, feeling rather like the most overdue library book in the history of the universe.

A few minutes later, he opened them again. The water level wasn't rising any more, and he appeared to be in a tiny pocket of air, his head and shoulders poking up through the meniscus. Against all the odds (and where'd he heard *that* before?) he was still very much alive.

Force of habit? Professional courtesy?

He wriggled across to the end of the row, took a deep breath and put his head under the water, allowing himself to slide down the aisle on his backside, until the effect of flotation slowed him down and he hung in the water a foot or so below the surface. Peering round through the gloom (some of the cabin lights were still, miraculously, working) he could make out a few drowned bodies, some copies of the in-flight magazine slowly drifting downwards as their pages waterlogged, and the in-flight movie still silently flickering across the miniature screen set into the back of one solitary seat.

Seen it, he muttered to himself, and bobbed back up into his private atmosphere for a change of air. It was, of course, ludicrous to imagine that he could possibly escape from this. The whole essence of the escapologist's art is recognising what's possible and what isn't, and this one was a definite 'isn't'; all he'd achieve would be to mar an otherwise perfect record with a first-and-last failure. On the other hand, it'd be interesting, as a matter of pure research, to see just how far he could get before the referee blew the whistle. Not out of the plane, for sure; definitely not out of the plane and up to the surface. But given a good deal of luck and his highly developed ability to hold his breath underwater, he might just be able to get to the emergency door and find the handle.

You're crazy, muttered his inner voice. *Not to mention unprofessional. First rule of the business: don't work unless you're getting paid.*

'Oh, be quiet,' he replied aloud. 'I'm doing this for the good of my health.'

He took the deepest breath he could manage and dived, speculating as he went about what could have stopped the water coming in. A freak air-bubble, preserved by some fortuitous balance of external and internal pressures? Improbable, to say the least, and the same was true of such far-fetched hypotheses as displaced submarine boulders dropping into place so as to block the hole, and frogmen with a ginormous bicycle-repair kit. No; it had been done so neatly and the timing had been so perfect that he found it hard to believe it wasn't somehow being done on purpose. Thinking about it, that might explain why he'd been given a seat in the very back row, or how come enough of the lights were still working to give him a chance of finding his way about. True, that sounded uncomfortably like paranoia, but there was a lot to be said for being paranoid and alive as opposed to entirely rational, well-adjusted and dead. Besides, who'd do such a thing – crash an entire airliner full of people into the sea, just to find out whether Vinnie Ehrlich could improvise?

He was by the door now, exploring in the gloom with his fingers for the release catch. Absolutely no chance of finding it before his lungs gave up, but it all helped to pass the time. Now then; here was something with the right feel for it. *Let's try pushing up first, then down.*

(All right; but what if this was all in order to discredit him in the eyes of the profession? Didn't they have gadgets that record the dying moments of aircraft? What if the purpose of all of this was to show his peers the spectacle of The Immortal Vincenzo taking the ghost of a chance he'd been offered, and failing? Obviously you'd have to be pretty sick to do such a thing, but . . . Well, there was his ex-wife, for one thing. No matter how many welded-shut safes at the bottom of flooded mine shafts he'd managed to get out of over the years, the greatest and most rewarding escape of his entire life had been divorcing Becky Ehrlich, formerly Becky Stein, best known to the public as Vanishing Velma from Valparaiso; a hell of an escapologist, but about as easy to get along with as a hand-grenade sandwich, and vindictive – compared to Becky, elephants write their names on the soles of their feet and have macramé handkerchiefs.)

The door opened a crack, but no more; there were quite a few million tons of Atlantic Ocean pushing on the outside, and just Vinnie Ehrlich on the opposing team. This was, in fact, as good a place as any to give it his best and start inhaling water; but then a mental image of Becky floated into his mind, arms folded and lips pursed, and he hurled himself against the door so hard that he felt something go *sproing* in his shoulder. Never mind; he'd widened the crack between door and frame, more than enough for the Vinnie Ehrlich who (so the hype went) had to walk very carefully indeed along the sidewalk for fear of falling down between the slats of drain-covers. One highly successful impersonation of toothpaste leaving a tube later, and he was outside, thrashing about in open water, suddenly eyeball to eyeball with—

Becky?

Close, but no cigar; it was, in fact, a fully grown hammerhead shark, its bizarrely transverse snout delicately sampling the smear of blood from the slight cut on Vinnie's wrist like a stockbroker savouring a fine claret. Easy mistake to make, though.

Problems, problems. Bracing his foot against the side of the fuselage, he pushed off and scooted under the shark's chin until he could reach out and grab a fin. The shark, startled by this, instinctively flicked its massive tail (another similarity), propelling itself through the water like a young torpedo hearing the school bell. Vinnie clung on with one hand and with the other began tickling the shark's armpit. He had no idea whether sharks were ticklish or not, but he'd known the technique work on his Uncle Maury's springer spaniel, compared to which this shark was the proverbial woolly lamb.

Add to the sum of human knowledge this rare jewel: sharks, when tickled on their tummies, swim upwards in an attempt to get away from the source of the aggravation. Although handicapped by the human being clinging to its starboard fin the shark made good time, almost but not quite fast enough to start Vinnie worrying about the bends. As it neared the surface, it accelerated, and the faster it went, the more vigorously Vinnie tickled, with the result that when the shark broke through into the upper air and immediately collided with the side of a large ship (the *Market Forces*, three days out of Reykjavik with a cargo of vacuum-sealed cod fillets in parsley sauce) it dealt itself such a ferocious blow on the head that it left a small but perceptible mark in the hull.

Jammy, muttered the Immortal Vincenzo to himself as he bobbed up and down like the last apple left in the barrel and waited for the pains in his chest to subside to mere agony, *but still perfectly legitimate; and any slight edge I might have had because this ship was conveniently here's more than made up for by that entirely uncalled-for and gratuitous shark*. Not a serious problem in itself, as it had turned out, but scary – dammit, it had her eyes and the same firm set of the jaw. For a moment there he'd thought he was in real trouble.

CHAPTER SEVEN

'Strike,' repeated the Viking, nodding vigorously. 'We are knowing what is strike. Is hitting, ja?'

Carol sucked air in through her teeth. 'Not that kind of strike,' she said. 'Maybe it's after your time. A strike is where you guys refuse to do any more work until management agrees to your demands.' She hesitated and played back that last sentence in her mind, scanning for long, difficult words. 'I'll put that another way,' she said. 'You tell Odin, no more fighting till he gives you what you want. Okay?'

Twelve benchfuls of puzzled Vikings stared at her as if her ears had just burst into flower. True, she hadn't expected miracles; she'd had enough difficulty when she was alive trying to organise the workers back at the bar, and at least they hadn't kept bashing each other with axes while she was talking. But some tiny spark of comprehension, one tiny hint that they had the faintest idea what she was talking about; too much to hope for? Apparently.

'Excuse,' called out a huge, hairy Viking on the end of the

eighth row. 'Is unclear. You to be saying, no fighting but that Odin to be granting our wishes, ja?'

Carol nodded gratefully. 'You got it,' she said.

'But wrong is. Our wishes only to be fighting, already that we have. And you to be saying, *not* fighting. Is—' The Viking frowned, searching for the right word. 'Is counter-intuitive,' he said. 'Your idea, my French excuse, to be sucking.'

With the palm of her hand Carol rubbed her elbow where she'd banged it on the edge of the table. 'Excuse me,' she said, 'but I don't think so. You reckon what you want is to fight all day; well, I say that's what they *want* you to think.'

'Ja,' the Viking replied, smiling happily. 'They are wanting, and we. Everybody to be happy.'

'Oh, come *on*,' Carol yelled. 'That's bullshit, and you know it. All right, you tell me something. What are you all fighting *for*?'

Bemused silence; then the big hairy Viking said, 'Excuse?'

'Well, you must be fighting about something. Anybody know what?'

The big hairy Viking shook his head. 'Just to fight, is all. To be slashing, and heads splitting. Is – is *cool*.'

'No, it *isn't*.' Carol closed her eyes for a moment and opened them again. 'Are you really trying to tell me that beating up on each other is the most fun you guys could possibly have? More fun than, say, sex or booze or chocolate or watching a good movie?'

'Ja.'

'These truths to be self-evident,' added a long, thin Viking somewhere in the middle, 'death, killing and the pursuiting after happiness.'

Quite unexpectedly, inspiration lit a pilot light in Carol's mind. 'Okay,' she said, 'if that's what you want, that's what you want. You guys really want to fight, yes?'

'Ja.'

'And you've spent all your lives being good Vikings just so you can go to Valhalla and fight all day long?'

'You are betting.'

'In fact,' Carol continued cautiously, 'you all worked so hard, you earned the right to fight, didn't you? Well? Am I right?'

'A mouthful you are saying, ja.'

Carol had a general idea where this was leading; she hoped the details would sort themselves out along the way. 'And now you're here,' she said, 'you fight all day, then sleep, then start again in the morning. Correct?'

'Ja.'

'So.' She paused and did a quick sum on her fingers. 'Let's say you do twelve hours' fighting, eight hours' sleep, four hours' boozing, waking up, eating and stuff. That sound about right?'

Sundry Vikings nodded, their beards waggling. 'On the head, the nail,' said one.

'So what that really means is, you work your guts out—' (unfortunate choice of words) 'to earn the right to fight in Valhalla, but when you actually get here, half the time you ain't fighting at all; you're vegging out or eating or putting your pants on.' She stopped and let the point sink in. 'Odin's swindling you, people,' she said. 'You're being ripped off. Think about it; you're dead, guys, you don't *need* sleep or food. That's all good quality fighting time going to waste – time *you've* earned with your sweat and blood, and you ain't getting what you paid for. I ask you, people, is that right? Well, is it?'

Stunned silence; then a soft undercurrent of muttering.

'A point to be having,' one of them said. 'To be eating and drinking is good, to be fighting better. And of sleep, the use what is?'

'How cheap the skate,' grumbled another. 'Our dues having been paid, short Warfather is changing us.'

Ah, thought Carol. 'You're damned right he is,' she said,

clenching her fists. 'And now I want you to ask yourselves, *why* is he doing this?'

More bafflement; thinking came as easily to these guys as playing the harpsichord to a cement mixer. 'All the war to himself to be keeping?' a fat, red-haired Viking hazarded. 'And us half the time none to be getting?'

They didn't like the sound of that; brows were furrowing like big furry glaciers, and they were muttering ominously in Old Norse, a language ideally suited to the purpose. 'An unfairness!' roared a short, thick-necked character at the front. 'Death! Death!' His colleagues started shaking their fists in agreement. Carol held up a hand for silence.

'Fine,' she said. 'So what're you gonna do about it?'

None of them had an answer to that one. Carol counted to five under her breath, then smiled encouragingly.

'Here's what you want to do,' she said. 'Nothing.'

Blank faces. 'Excuse?'

'Nothing,' Carol repeated. 'Don't fight. Don't carouse. Don't do anything. Just sit around all day, or stay in bed. Hell, if everybody joins in, we could bring this place to its knees in a day or so.'

A particularly bewildered-looking Viking on the far left stood up. 'To be explaining,' he said. 'In order to be more fighting, not to be fighting at all?'

'You got the idea,' Carol said firmly. 'You just wait and see, you'll have Odin crawling to you, begging you to get out there and beat the shit out of each other. And you'll just sit there like big dumb blocks of wood and do *nothing*. It'll drive him nuts.'

'Us similarly,' sighed a Viking doubtfully. 'Not to be fighting at all; in Valholl?'

Carol shook her head. 'I ain't saying it's gonna be easy,' she said. 'No way. It'll hurt like hell. It'll be—' (inspiration again) 'it'll be a real *battle*. Because this is the only way you guys can really *fight* for what's due to you.'

'By not fighting, to fight?' the doubtful Viking queried. 'Like mud the clarity.'

'To be silent, Thorgrim,' the big hairy Viking snapped. 'Of the wench the wisdom to be heeding. To be fighting,' he said solemnly, 'is without a fight to be giving in.'

'Thou dog!'

'Ruffian!'

'Guys,' Carol interrupted, as the two Vikings leapt up and drew their swords, '*guys*. Cool it, will you? Can't you see you're playing right into their hands? This is exactly the way they want you to react.'

'It is?' The two Vikings looked at each other. 'Of us the gullibility!'

'You bet.' Carol grinned. 'If you start fighting, it'll mean you've given up the fight. Whereas, by not fighting, you'll be fighting *them*, and fighting's what you're here for. So,' she added, taking a deep breath, 'if you want to fight for the right to fight, then don't fight, right?'

That one worried a lot of them. 'Excuse?' said one. 'Past me once more to be running?'

The big hairy Viking turned round in his seat. 'To be explaining,' he said. 'Of to be fighting the right to fight for, by not fighting is best to accomplish. Better?'

'Ja,' replied the other, relieved. 'But that in the first place, why could she not be saying?'

'Herself clearly to express, trouble is she having,' the big hairy one whispered. 'In life our advantages maybe not having had. The form, to be mocking, is bad.'

Carol clambered up on to the table and stood with her hands on her hips. 'Okay, guys,' she said. 'Are you with me?'

Beards waggled right across the rows.

'Then let's go to it,' she shouted. 'And remember, Vikings sedated can never be placated. You have nothing to fight except fighting itself.'

'Excuse?'

She left them, grimly sitting, sitting with every fibre of their being, and wandered through into the kitchen; where she found Odin, tossing a salad.

'Didn't you know?' he said, looking up. 'I'm a vegetarian.'

Carol ignored him. 'I guess you heard all that?' she said.

Odin nodded. 'You realise this is war,' he said.

'You started it,' Carol said. 'Hell, you even dropped the hint.'

'I know.' Odin smiled at her fondly. 'I wanted to start a war – after all, this *is* Valhalla, picking fights is what we're here for. And it was all getting so darn cosy.' He reached up for the dried basil. 'You know,' he said, 'I'm really pleased to see how quickly you've got into the spirit of things. We'll make a Valkyrie of you yet.'

It came to him, just as he was being crushed to death under the tracks of a Challenger tank—

(Something of a collector's item, as ways to die go. So far, from memory, he'd been:

- shot: 37 times
- blown up: by (a) artillery fire: 21 times
              (b) landmines: 14 times
              (c) booby-traps: 7 times
              (d) grenades: 2 times
- stabbed: 18 times
- gassed: 14 times
- hit by shrapnel: 11 times
- crushed under falling masonry: 9 times
- strangled: 7 times
- burnt to death: 6 times
- hurled off ledges: 6 times
- impaled on railings: 5 times

—but this was only the second time he'd been run over by a tank; and on the previous occasion it had been a mouldy old

T-34, not a shiny new Challenger. It reminded him of collecting bubblegum cards as a boy. After three years of assiduous collecting, he'd ended up with forty-nine spare Bobby Charltons and never did manage to find a George Best. Would it be possible, he wondered, to swap deaths with his fellow inmates to make up the set?)

—that there was one obvious way to break the cycle and get home free. All he had to do was not die.

It stood to reason, he assured himself, as his life's blood drained away into the dust. At the end of the day there had to be at least one man left standing, otherwise who killed the last-but-one? And when there was only one left, what happened to him? If he was allowed to go, at last there'd be some sort of sense to the whole ghastly business; something to fight *for*, an objective to strive towards, even if it wasn't terribly realistic to expect to be able to attain it any time soon. First he'd have to study advanced fighting techniques (he hadn't noticed many signs saying GROSVENOR ACADEMY OF FIGHTING around the place, but opportunities for picking it up as one went along were all around him), then he'd have to keep persevering until finally the day came and he made it. It could take a year, or five, or a thousand; but eventually he'd have served his time, learned whatever lesson it was he was supposed to learn here, and it'd be over.

Piece of cake, really. And with any luck, the hard crunchy bit in the middle of this piece of cake would turn out to be a file.

At one minute past dawn the trumpets sounded and the dead were raised; and Howard came roaring out of the traps like a greyhound who'd been promised forty per cent of the gross, paid in dog biscuits. Instead of trudging wearily down the street trailing his rifle after him, he bounded diligently from shell-hole to bombed-out shop frontage to abandoned jeep, shooting on sight anything not substantial enough to take cover behind, watching, listening, paying the strictest attention. If he got wasted again this time, it surely wouldn't be for want of trying.

It settled down into a long, hard day. To begin with, it was all ambushes and street-fighting, and for some reason he handled it all extremely well. Howard made every shot count, and he fired plenty of them – unusually good marksmanship for a man who'd earned the nickname Vlad the Impaler when he'd played for a pub darts team, thanks to his unfortunate habit of missing the board completely every third shot or so and dropping the errant dart neatly among the customers standing at the bar. In fact it was downright bizarre. His hand-eye coordination was usually so poor that it was rumoured to have been studied by a Civil Service research team; yet here he was, swatting down the opposition like flies all around him. *My turn?* he speculated as he swung the .50-calibre Browning machine-gun up to waist height and opened fire, mincing an ambush up fine. *Maybe each one of us here gets to have a good day like this, once every thousand centuries. That would certainly fit in* (he mused, as he sidestepped a Rapier missile and ducked under a strand of virtually invisible monofilament wire stretched throat-high between two posts) *with my last-one-gets-to-leave theory. It's even possible that they're deliberately making this easy for me.*

By just after teatime, Howard had wiped out every sentient being between Rabone Lane and Beechfield Road, survived a tactical nuclear strike on the Harry Mitchell recreation centre and single-handedly sunk a Trident submarine on the Victoria Park boating lake, armed with nothing but his bare hands, a set of Chinese spanners and a long piece of string. After he'd paused for a breather and eaten a Penguin biscuit he'd found miraculously unharmed among the glowing cinders and melted paving stones of the Hales Lane cricket pavilion, he looked around for new opponents, but there didn't seem to be any. The nuke had something to do with that, he was sure; and now he came to think of it, before he'd taken out the sub, it had been shelling the surrounding area for several hours with phosphor bombs, which in context was a very helpful act on its part. It was possible that he was already the last living creature in the war zone (assuming that the zone was basically confined to central Smethwick; if it continued up into Sandwell, he had a busy afternoon ahead of him). In any event, he was well on his way.

Five hours of fruitless wandering later (he hadn't seen the streets this empty since last Cup Final day) Howard found himself standing in front of the blackened shell of a building he recognised as the Constance Avenue post office in West Bromwich, just as the sun began to dip below the horizon like a huge fiery orange digestive biscuit dunked in an infinity of inky black tea. The last recognisable life form he'd encountered had been a small rat, which he'd surprised as it tried to cross the B4169 opposite Smethwick West railway station. He'd nailed it stone cold dead with the fourth shot from his M-16, just in case. He'd walked all the way from Smethwick to West Brom and nobody had tried to do him any injury whatsoever (further evidence to fuel his growing conviction that this couldn't be the real Smethwick). *Surely*, he told himself, *I've done enough. I've survived a whole day without getting killed in the slightest. Can I go now, please?*

'Sorry.'

He swung round and, on instinct, squeezed the trigger; but the pin clicked on an empty chamber. He dropped the rifle and dropped his hand to his belt, groping for the machete that had been there ten minutes ago but wasn't now.

'It's all right,' Odin said, raising above his head the hand that wasn't holding the bag of chips he'd been scoffing. 'I'm not going to hurt you. Now all you've got to do is kill me, remember, and you're out of here. Till then, though, you're mine.'

Howard remembered, all right: bullets, cold steel, wooden stakes had all bounced off the bastard like a bankrupt's cheques. 'We've been through all that,' he said. 'And what you said then,' he added, 'was that I had to keep trying till I killed you or the sun sets. Nothing about succeeding. After all, how can I kill you? If you're really Odin, aren't you some kind of god?'

'My, what a sharp memory you've got,' Odin answered with his mouth full. 'Chapter and verse, all off pat; quite the shop steward, aren't we?' He glanced up at the sky, where the last slice of sunset was boiling away into the night. 'You're absolutely right, of course,' he said. 'All you've got to do is make a reasonable attempt at knocking me off within the next, let's see, forty seconds, and you're free to go, back to your drab, mundane little life in peace-torn Smethwick. So? What're you waiting for?'

With a deep growl that frothed up from the bottom of his throat, Howard stooped to pick up a heavy spar of roof timber to use as a club. As he did so, however, the pile of fallen masonry that the spar had been supporting fell on him. He almost managed to jump clear, but a steel girder fell across his leg, pinning him to the ground and making it impossible for him to move.

'Well?' Odin asked politely, studying his watch. 'Here I am. You've still just about got time for one savage, albeit inaccurate swipe – no, sorry, I tell a lie. Time's up. What happened? You had a change of heart or something? Sudden change of role models, delete Rambo and replace with Gandhi? Charming sentiment, but the timing could have been better.'

'Bastard,' Howard said.

'Sorry?'

'I said "bastard",' Howard repeated, tugging helplessly at the girder. 'You knew that was going to happen. Probably you made it happen. This whole thing was a rotten cheat.'

Odin raised both eyebrows. 'I'm wounded,' he replied. 'Actually, if only you'd said that a few seconds earlier you'd be home in front of the telly right now, watching *EastEnders*, because a verbal wound's quite valid after seven p.m. on a Wednesday. So you see, I wasn't cheating, because you still could have won. Ah well,' he added, as the rest of the wall fell on Howard's head, spreading it like marmalade, 'better luck next time.'

'Mrghrmph.'

'Didn't quite catch that,' Odin said, walking away. 'Actually, I'm very pleased with the progress you're making. The way you massacred the crew of that submarine – vintage stuff. I might even consider nominating you for an Arnie. Anyway,' he added, waving without turning round, 'ten out of ten for persistence. You remind me of Robert the Bruce's spider.'

In spite of everything, Howard couldn't help feeling just the slightest little surge of pride. 'What, you mean I'm indomitable?'

'Hm.'

'Whatever the odds,' Howard went on, 'you know I'll never give up trying; every time I fall down I'll just pick myself up and give it another go, over and over again until the job's done? That sort of thing?'

Odin shook his head. 'Not quite,' he said. 'I mean you're a nasty little crawling thing who's going to spend the rest of his life not getting anywhere. Have a nice day.'

The inner barbarian; that, as far as his six-year-old cognitive skills had been able to make sense of it, was what Odin had been hinting at.

The bell rang for playtime, and all the other little boys and girls in Attila's class jumped up from their desks and hurtled out into the playground. Attila didn't join them immediately. He suspected it was something to do with being new to this body; he didn't seem to have mastered the fine points of controlling it, which made him perceptibly slower and clumsier than the rest of them. He was also, he'd noticed with annoyance, a good inch shorter than average, but that wasn't a new problem. Back in the good old days when he'd been a Hun, he'd quickly got used to all the Westerners – Romans, Goths, Vandals, Franks and the like – towering over his short, compact Central Asian nomad's frame, but when it came to the crunch (or the slash, or the *tchunk!* or the *chokk-thud-aaaargh!*) it hadn't proved to be an insurmountable handicap. Also, as if to compensate, what he lacked in height he made up for in weight. Few if any nomads of the steppes ever managed to hack and slash their way to a sufficient level of prosperity to acquire more than an ounce or two of surplus fat, whereas he had the sort of tummy on him that he'd only ever seen on the children of great khans.

As he got up, he noticed the teacher was looking at him oddly. Attila was thoroughly used to furtive sideways glances from women, signifying either lust or abject terror, but this didn't seem like either of those. It was— damn it, he knew this one, that strange, abstruse Roman emotion that his people had never quite managed to get the hang of. P-something. Ah yes, that was it. Pity. The woman teacher looked at him as if she was *sorry* for him. Now why on earth would that be?

'Brad,' she said, and even now it took him a moment to associate that peculiar name with himself. 'Aren't you going outside to play with the other children? It's a beautiful day.'

He glanced out of the window; couldn't see for the life of him what was so all-fire wonderful about it. Hot sun, cloudless sky, the sort of weather that turns the meat rancid and encourages the horseflies. 'Yes, miss,' he said meekly.

'Off you go, then,' the teacher said, patting him on the head. 'Play nicely.'

The barbarian within, he reflected, as he walked slowly down the corridor. It was an intriguing concept, at once contradictory and maddeningly seductive; the idea that one should strive to be the best barbarian one can in the circumstances in which one happens to find oneself – because we can't all lead hordes or sack cities, there aren't enough of either to go round, but we can do our very best to cherish and preserve the guiding principles of barbarism in our hearts, even if it's just in trivial everyday things, like making time each day to pull a cat's tail or drop some litter.

Or, Attila said to himself brightly, pick on someone smaller and weaker than ourselves. No shortage of raw materials here, he noticed, looking round the playground; the problem would be deciding where to start. So many pigtails, so little time.

While he was standing in the doorway, trying to decide between stealing the little blonde girl's pink bunny pencil case or pulling the extravagantly long hair of the little girl with the Barbie™ lunch box, he noticed that the bright sunlight he'd been deploring earlier no longer seemed to be such a problem. He looked up and saw that standing between him and the sun were two boys; late sixes, possibly early sevens. They were staring at him and grinning.

'Hey, you,' said one of them. 'Fat boy.'

Attila's eyebrows narrowed. 'You talking to me?' he said.

'Yeah.'

Oh joy, Attila thought. *I haven't smashed a skull or prised open a ribcage in— oh, I don't know how long. This is going to be such fun.* 'Are you calling me fat?' he asked, assuming the hapless infant had intended the term as an insult, though where he came from it was what you called your clan chief to his face if you were a brown-noser.

'Yeah,' said the boy. ''Cos you are.'

'Fat as a *pig*,' added his companion, much to Attila's delight. In his previous life, his record had been four suckling babes spitted on one lance, but he was out of practice and he knew it. *Start with two and then work your way up slowly.*

'Come over here and say that,' he replied.

After that, things didn't quite go as he'd anticipated. He was just winding himself up for a really bloodcurdling yell when he realised he was lying on his back, with one boy sitting

on his chest, pinning down his arms, and the other one banging his head against the playground tarmac. *No matter,* he
said to himself, *been in worse situations before, like that time in
Kamchatka when the Uzgars nearly trapped us in that narrow
pass.* Nearly but not quite, which was why nobody since had
ever heard of the Uzgars. He tried to do that really rather neat
wriggle-and-jump manoeuvre he'd learned from the Frankish
hostages, but somehow it didn't work. A rapid diagnostic scan
revealed that the source of the malfunction was an acute lack
of physical strength. The boys were bigger than he was, and
all his skill and experience couldn't make up for that. He was
helpless.

Not *fair* . . .

'Fat,' the boy on head-bumping duty was chanting in his
ear. 'Fat fat fat fat fat *fat.*'

For some reason the persistent repetition was unbearable,
worse even than the pain of having his head slammed down
on a hard surface. 'Stop it,' he wailed, but that just made the
boy slam harder and chant louder. *This is ridiculous,* he told
himself, *what kind of a fight do you call this? Obviously I can't
beat an enemy I'm not strong enough to deal with, so where the
hell's the point?* 'Stop it,' he repeated, 'you're hurting.' Why had
he said that? It was true, but so what? Attila the Hun had
always treated pain as a kind of speed limit, a theoretical barrier to be ignored except in cases of immediate and extreme
danger. His problem was the humiliation and helplessness,
not the pain; but instead of saying *You're showing me up* or
You're cheating, he'd said, 'You're hurting me.' damn silly thing
to say, of course; tantamount to saying, 'It's working fine,
lads, keep it up.'

'Fat,' the boy was chanting. 'You're *fat,* you're *fat,* you're
fat, you're . . .'

'Stop it!' That was the teacher's voice, shrill and horrified.
The two boys scrambled off him and turned to face her. *Now,*
Attila realised, *now's my chance – punch to the kidneys to drop*

'em, then a few kicks to the head, stamp on their windpipes to finish off. But he couldn't even get up; he was too weak to move and he was having some kind of trouble with his breathing, because his breath was coming in jerky sobs—

—Because he was crying. *Dammit*, Attila roared in his mind, *this is ridiculous, I don't cry, I didn't cry when the Clan Snow-Leopard captured me and dipped me in a vat of boiling tallow; stop it, whoever's doing this to me, it's not fair, it's not—*

The teacher was shouting at the two boys. Attila could hear the disgust in her voice, as if she'd witnessed something unspeakably obscene and revolting (odd; hadn't she ever seen a fight before? Where had she been all her life?) and he could see the boys standing listlessly in front of her. It was almost as if he could hear what they were thinking – they were bored by the silly lecture, they were ashamed of themselves for being so careless that they let a silly old grown-up creep up on them like that, they were worried about what was going to happen to them – would she keep them in after school, would she tell their mums? – and they were angry, because it wasn't fair that they should get caught like this when all they'd been doing was having some fun. All that was easily read from the droop of their heads and the slouch of their shoulders, though Attila could've guessed what was going through their minds even if he'd had his eyes shut. He'd have thought exactly the same thing in their place, obviously. (Because being careless was the only thing they'd done wrong, and the rest of it *wasn't* fair on them. Certainly all that stuff the teacher was spouting about how wicked it is to bully the little ones was pure, unadulterated garbage.)

Eventually the teacher stopped her babbling and sent the boys away. 'Are you all right?' she said, her voice dripping with such a superfluity of concern that Attila had to swallow hard to avoid throwing up.

'Y-yes,' Attila snuffled – *sob, grizzle, sniffle, whimper; for pity's sake, man, get a grip!* 'Yes, I – boohoohoo!'

Kind, gentle hands that he wanted to rip off and snap over his knee like dead twigs helped him up and brushed the dust off him. 'I know,' the teacher was saying, 'they're just great big stupid bullies, and as soon as we've got you sorted out I'm going straight to Mr Thompson's office and he'll write a strong letter to their mummies and daddies—'

Oh for shame! A strong letter! You stupid cow, that's no way to treat an enemy; even a dishonourable enemy deserves better than that. 'Yes, Miss,' he heard himself say – *spirits of our ancestors rot that insipid simpering voice!* – 'Thank you, miss. I feel *much* better now.' *Hellfire and buggery, get a load of that crumpled little smile, that heart-melting look of trust and hero-worship; my hero, my preserver! You snivelling little crawler . . .*

'And if they ever do anything to you again,' the nauseating bitch was saying, 'you come straight to me and tell me. Promise?'

'I promise,' said Attila's voice solemnly, while Attila's soul screamed and drummed its heels.

'They only do it because you're a bit small for your age, and a bit— well, chubby,' the bitch went on. 'They're cowardly bullies who wouldn't dare pick on someone their own size.'

'Yes, miss.'

'Now then.' She was kneeling down and smiling at him reassuringly with those huge round cow eyes. (*You still a virgin, miss? Well, of course you are, I mean, a bloke'd have to be so desperate . . .*) 'You promise me you'll be a brave little soldier.' She was dabbing at his face with a Kleenex, dammit. Among the rocky slopes of Central Anatolia he'd built cairns with the skulls of men who'd insulted him less. 'There's the bell. Come on, time for sums. And as a treat, you can hand out the exercise books.'

Seething inside like a supercharged volcano, Attila the Hun toddled beside her, his tiny moist hand slipped trustingly into hers, while in the back of his mind, hurling itself against the bars like a caged lion, the inner barbarian screamed for blood.

During sums (waste of his time; he knew sums already. You couldn't feed and clothe a hundred thousand people as they marched from Central Asia to France without being able to do sums) he thought long and hard about what had happened and what Odin had told him. He could see the way he was supposed to take; a whole new life, taking advantage of everything this strange new world had to offer if only he'd put aside what remained of himself, if only he'd surrender and go quietly. But not to be himself any more – it was worse than that; he was being asked to become the opposite of himself, to join the enemy, the other side—

—who had, of course, ultimately won, as shown by the fact that this society was as it was; civilisation had survived him, healed over him as if he'd never been there, and now he was being told to change sides. It was like telling him to stop being a horse eating the grass and start being the grass, on the grounds that the horse eventually dies but the grass never stops growing, eventually grows up between the horse's bones. *Swizzle*, thought Attila, *not fair. I don't want to be the grass. I don't want to be the good guy.*

Which means, I guess, I don't want to win.

He stopped at that point and thought about it. Sure, he'd lost and they'd won. But what was the point of winning if you couldn't win and still be you? If winning made you lose the thing you'd been fighting for? Where on earth would be the point in doing that?

Nah, he thought. *Stuff that. Don't want to win.*

Winning's for losers.

CHAPTER EIGHT

Sometimes he tried, really hard. Sometimes he just went through the motions, saying the lines without hearing them. Sometimes he didn't bother at all, and stood in the spotlight surrounded by darkness like a dilapidated barn in a hailstorm. It didn't seem to make any difference what he did; thirty seconds or so into the audition, the unseen voices told him they'd let him know, and he shuffled off the way he'd come, feeling as if he'd just been born and his mother was staring at him in the midwife's arms and demanding to see the manager. The only variable was the tune Willard hummed while he was getting cleaned up; it was either 'No Business Like Show Business', 'That's Entertainment', 'Make 'Em Laugh' or 'Be A Clown'. Kortright had never liked any of them much.

'Next night on your dressing room they'll— hi there, Lin, how'd it go?' Willard put down the magazine he'd been reading and looked up. 'Did you get it?'

'As if you cared, you jerk.' Kortright flopped into his chair, which always seemed to be on the point of giving way but never did – was this also the Valhalla for chairs, he wondered? Did chairs that betrayed their trust and collapsed under someone's weight end up here, to spend the rest of eternity groaning and flexing and never quite falling to bits? – and mopped blood from his cheek with a hank of cotton wool. 'If you were any kind of real god, you'd get me out of this dump.'

Willard chuckled. 'You should hear yourself,' he said cheerfully. 'Better yet, you should talk to yourself.'

'I might just do that. Probably my only chance of talking to somebody sane around here.'

'Oh, funny.' Willard's jolly smile shapeshifted into a scowl without any apparent movement of the muscles of his face. 'You're damned lucky to be here at all, Lyndon. After all, what are you? Are you a god? No. Are you a hero? No. Personified force of nature? Dragon? No. Mermaid? No. Werewolf? No. Man, you aren't even a goddamn prophet. You'd be nothing without me. If it wasn't for me putting my butt on the line for you, you know where you'd be? Probably you'd be guardian spirit of a small rock somewhere in the Shinto heaven, or following round after Cerberus with a poop-scooper. But no, I saw you right, I got you Valhalla, I even got you the big one, the chance to audition for *Lin-fucking-Kortright*, because I care about my people, Lyndon, I really *care*. And this is all the thanks—'

Kortright stared. 'I see what you mean,' he said quietly. 'Say, Willard, do I really talk like that to clients?'

Willard nodded. 'And that's to the ones you like, the ones who've actually got talent. To the others, well, sometimes you can be a bitty-bit brusque.'

'Oh.' Kortright bit his lip; then a thought struck him. 'Hey, Willard, is that what all this is about? A judgement on me for being insensitive with the talent? Because if it is, I promise on my mother's life—'

'No, it isn't,' Willard interrupted irritably. 'And besides, your mother died years ago. Can't you get it into that titanium-reinforced skull of yours, Kortright? You're *dead*. You're here because this is where people like you go when they die. Lyndon Kortright, this is your afterlife. Get used to it, pal, because this is where you live from now on. And if it wasn't for me getting down on my knees and pleading with Odin, you'd be somewhere a whole lot worse because, between you and me, Odin doesn't like you. *Capisce?*'

'Sure Odin likes me,' Kortright replied with a worried look on his face. 'He's a friend. Dammit, he's a client. Of course he likes me.'

'Lyndon, you got him the job, of course he hates you. That's why we've gotta think of some way—'

'Hold it.' Kortright held up his hand. 'You just said something interesting.'

'Everything I say is interesting, Lyndon. I'm a *god*, for Chrissakes. *Your* god. By rights, you should be writing all this down on a stone tablet.'

Kortright wasn't listening. 'I'm Odin's agent,' he repeated. 'I got him this job.'

'That we know. Dumbest thing you ever did, with hindsight.'

'So if I'm his agent,' Kortright went on, 'then he owes me commission. Ten per cent of everything he makes out of this Valhalla racket should be mine.' He blinked twice, then laughed. 'Finally, one of my clients is getting money, instead of all that incense and prayers and crap, and wouldn't you just know it, I'm dead and he reckons I can't collect. Well, we'll see about that.'

'Lyndon. Be careful what you ask for.'

Kortright shook his head. 'I don't work for him,' he said. 'Effectively we're partners. And this is no way to treat a partner.'

'Lyndon.' There was more urgency in Willard's voice than in the whole of the US Postal Service. 'I really suggest that we talk about something else. Tell me, how did you get into the agenting business in the first place? Was it what you always wanted to do right from when you were a little boy, or did you get a sort of road-to-Damascus vocation?'

Kortright growled, then yelped as the iodine he was dabbing on to his cut cheek made its presence felt. 'I'd have thought you'd have known that,' he said sourly, 'if you're really my own personal god. Y'know, I'm beginning to have my doubts about that. I don't think you're a god at all.'

Willard gave him a reproving look. 'Now then,' he said, 'I seem to remember something in the rule book about not taking names in vain.'

'Nah,' Kortright replied. 'You're getting names confused with heroin. Although in your case, I'd say a better comparison would be cocaine.'

'Really?' said Willard, uncomfortably. 'Why's that?'

'Because you're getting right up my nose. Now, do you think you could get lost for a while?'

'No,' Willard replied sadly, 'I'm omniscient, remember? And, as you say, I know exactly why you decided to be an agent. Money.'

Kortright nodded. 'No finer reason for doing anything in all of creation.' He screwed the top back on the iodine bottle. 'At least, that's the theory. I reckon it'd be a whole lot of fun finding out if the theory holds. Now then, like I was saying before you tried to change the subject: Odin. That sucker owes me a lot of money, and I'm gonna remind him about that.'

Willard made a disparaging gesture. 'Why bother?' he said. 'I mean, it's not as if there's anything here you could spend money on.'

'That's not the point,' Kortright replied. 'My guess is, faced with a choice between paying me what he owes me and finding some way for me to get out of here, and in return I forget about my commission from now onwards, I reckon I know which one he'll choose. So,' he added grimly, 'when he comes out here to tell me I'm due on stage, I'll tell him . . .'

'Just a moment.' Willard held up his hand. 'Who are we talking about, exactly?'

'Odin, of course. The producer. The guy holding the damn audition.'

'You think Odin is the producer?'

Kortright spread his arms. 'Who else? This is Valhalla, at least according to you it's Valhalla and you're supposed to be a god; this is Valhalla, he runs it, therefore he's gotta be Odin.'

'Hm.'

'You mean he isn't? Goddammit, then who is?'

'I didn't say he isn't,' Willard replied guardedly. 'I said "Hm". Look at it this way. If Odin's your client, surely you can recognise him when you see him.'

Kortright shook his head. 'What he looks like don't mean spit,' he said. 'He's a god. As you should know,' he added, 'better than anybody. Come on, tell me. Is that guy Odin or isn't he?'

'Um.'

'Oh for—' Kortright narrowed his eyes. 'I get it,' he said. 'You can't tell lies, can you? And you don't want to tell me the truth. So you aren't telling me anything. Am I right?'

'Mm.'

Kortright grabbed a towel and hurled it across the room. 'I don't know why I bother listening to you,' he said. 'First you get me killed, because you tell me that's the only way to find Carol. Fine; as a result, now I'm dead as well. Then you tell me this is Valhalla. I believe you, even though you don't show me no evidence or nothing. Then, when I figure out a way of maybe escaping from here, you try and talk me out of it; now you're trying to get me so confused about whether or not that geek of a producer is Odin that I won't have the nerve to ask him.' He leaned forward and put his hands threateningly on Willard's shoulders. 'In fact,' he said, 'you also told me you're a god – *my* god, dammit – and I believe that too, though I can't seem to call to mind any real hard evidence you gave me for that either. Maybe everything you've been telling me's a whole pack of bull. In which case—'

'Urggh,' the god broke in. 'Ggghhgh.'

'See? If you're a god, how come I can choke you with my bare hands? And if you ain't a god, then all that other trash you've been spouting's a lie too.' He gathered two handfuls of jacket collar and twisted. 'Where is this place? Who's in charge? If this is Valhalla, is Odin the producer? And where in fuck's name is Carol?'

'Ngk.'

'What? Oh, right.' Kortright relaxed his grip a little, allowing Willard to breathe. 'Well? I'm waiting.'

'Just let me – get my breath back.'

Kortright scowled horribly. 'See?' he said. 'I knew you weren't any kinda stinking god, you're just some jerk, right? A real god—'

He didn't finish what he was saying, because a flash of blinding blue light hit him in the chest, picked him up off his feet and slammed him against the wall like a squash ball. He seemed to hang for a moment, two feet or so off the ground, then dribbled down the wall like a raindrop on a window and drained away into an untidy heap of limbs on the floor.

'A real god,' Willard said, massaging his bruised neck, 'doesn't take that kinda shit from *anybody*. And that,' he added, flicking from his fingertips a big blue bogey of crackling fire that hit Kortright on the chin and slammed his head against the wall, 'is for calling me a jerk. Sheesh, why is it you humans can only understand one thing? No wonder what you guys wanted Heaven to be was Valhalla.'

'Sorry,' Kortright croaked in a tiny voice.

'That's better.'

'I found your arguments very convincing,' Kortright said. 'In fact, they're so neat I believe.'

'Good,' Willard said, folding his short, stubby arms across his chest. 'Now we're getting somewhere. All right, prove to me you believe.'

'Sure thing. What d'you want me to do?'

'Oh, I don't know.' Willard thought for a moment. 'How about a great leap of faith?' he said. 'That ought to settle this once and for all. Walk off this plank into this bottomless pit.'

Kortright looked down. He found that he was standing with his legs apart, each foot resting precariously on the lip of an impossibly deep-looking hole. Fall down that, he reckoned, and the next thing he'd see was a bunch of bewildered-looking guys standing upside down and wearing broad-rimmed hats with corks dangling off them, staring at him as he rose into the sky like an early Apollo rocket. 'That wasn't there before,' he commented.

'No,' Willard replied. 'Neat trick, huh?'

'Decidedly. Could you see your way clear to getting rid of it? I don't think it blends in too well with rest of the colour scheme.'

'Jump.'

When the Lord thy God says 'Jump', all you ask is 'How high?'

'But if I do that . . .'

'I'll save you,' Willard murmured. 'Promise. God's honour. Now jump.'

So Kortright jumped. When he landed the hole wasn't there any more. 'Ow,' he said, as the force of landing on the hard tiled floor of the dressing room jarred his left ankle.

'You do believe. That's all right, then. Right, I'd better make the most of being able to get a word in edgeways while I still can. Lyndon, you're a jerk.'

'I am? Well, if you say so.'

'Scumbag. Dirtball. Asshole.'

'If you say so, Lord,' Kortright replied humbly, keeping his feet absolutely still and groping for the edge of the dressing table. 'Here endeth the first lesson, huh?'

'You know why you're a scumball and a dirtbag and an ass-hole?'

'I don't need to know,' Kortright said, with utter sincerity. 'I just believe, is all.'

Willard shook his head. 'Because, after all this time, you still don't recognise me,' he said. 'You don't, do you?'

'Um. Well, in the sense that I recognise that you exist, you bet I do. Because, you see, I believe. I do believe in you, just like I believe in this extremely hard and unyielding floor.'

'Not in that sense,' Willard said harshly. 'I mean recognise like regular people do. Face rings a bell, that sort of thing.'

'Sorry. And I've got this really good memory for faces, too. I guess I must still be feeling a bit shook up after you slammed me against the wall.'

'Odd,' Willard mused. 'And not encouraging. I mean, how am I supposed to have faith in an agent who doesn't even recognise me when he sees me?' The scowl on his face melted into a smile. 'I had faith in you, Lyndon. I believed you could work miracles. I worshipped you. And look what you did to me.'

'Sure. What did I do?'

'What did you *do*?' Willard's voice became a shriek of rage, and Kortright tightened his grip on the dressing table. 'I'll tell you what you did, you bastard. You landed me with this god-damn lousy job, is what. "Trust me," you said, "I'll see you right, in no time at all you'll have your own pantheon, they'll be standing in line to see your second coming," you said. And what's this wonderful job you got me, Lyndon? I'm a fucking *janitor*. Looking after *dead people*. And the worst part – you know what the worst part of it is, Lyndon? You don't even know who I am.'

The world wobbled under Kortright's feet, but this time Willard was only indirectly responsible. 'Odin?' he whispered. 'That you?'

Willard nodded. 'Now he recognises me,' he jeered. 'You

know what? From now on I'm gonna have to call you Doubting Lyndon. Yes, you turd, it's me, Odin. Your *client*.'

'Oh.' Kortright tried to grin. 'So,' he said, 'got your own show and everything, huh? Glad to see you're doing so well.'

The blue lightning-flash that hit him this time was approximately three times as hard as its predecessor; any harder, and there'd have been a Kortright-shaped hole in the wall, in best Tom-and-Jerry fashion. 'Of course,' Kortright went on, as he struggled with the pain of breathing in, 'maybe round about now'd be the best time for you to re-evaluate your career direction. I mean, if you feel you've explored this phase in your professional life as far as you can go—'

'Faith!' Willard screamed. 'Trust! Belief! You betrayed me, Kortright, and now I'm gonna give you something you can really believe in; you and your damn bitch of a daughter.'

Kortright looked up sharply. 'Hey,' he said. 'Are you telling me you *killed* Carol, just to get back at me?'

There was a short silence while Willard/Odin considered his reply. 'Yes,' he said. 'You want to make something of it?'

'Dammit, Willard, you're a god. And gods don't do that kinda thing.'

Willard shook his head. 'Janitor gods do,' he replied. 'So long, Lyndon.'

The floor vanished, probably went to floor heaven, where good lino tiles go when they're all worn out, and Kortright fell into the hole. He fell for what seemed like a very long time; he closed his eyes (because seeing yourself go *splat* can cause deep-seated personality traumas, leading to self-doubt and a crippling loss of self-confidence) and waited not to see what would happen next. He hadn't read the script, but he had the feeling that when they next met, Mr Ground wasn't going to be his friend—

—And suddenly he wasn't falling any more; he was standing, out on his stage in front of his audience, who were staring at him as if he'd just been fished out of the Bay after a three-week underwater swim. He felt, in rapid succession, relief, joy and an excessively mature tomato hitting him in the face.

Valhalla, he thought. *Home*.

'Thanks,' said the Great Vincenzo through chattering teeth, as they helped him sit down and draped a blanket round his shoulders. 'If it hadn't been for you guys—'

The skipper of the *Market Forces* made a deprecating gesture, body language for *Forget it, no big deal*, and Vinnie smiled and nodded. The rest of the crew went back to what they'd been doing, technical stuff to do with the transportation of frozen fish in bulk. The captain, a tall, blond Viking-looking type, stayed behind.

'You are from Valhalla?' he asked.

Vinnie looked up at him. 'Excuse me?' he said.

'Valhalla Atlantic. You are survivor?'

Vinnie nodded. 'That's right,' he said. 'Say, do you know if anybody else made it? As far as I know, I'm the only one.'

The captain nodded. 'Radio from Reykjavik says look for survivors, but we find none except you. All the rest—' He drew a finger across his throat. 'Tragedy.'

'Right,' said Vinnie absently. In his mind he was already analysing his escape from the plane, examining the moves from a professional point of view. There was something odd about something.

'We go now back to Iceland,' the skipper went on. 'One day, maybe two. Meanwhile we radio, say you are safe. Your name?'

'Vincent Ehrlich.'

The skipper looked at him, then grinned. 'Same name as – how you say – great escaper. Escapeling. Escapist?'

'Escapologist.'

'*Ja*, escapologist. I am of his work a great admirer.' He paused and looked at Vinnie a little more closely. 'In fact,' he said, 'you are looking like him. Coincidence.'

Vinnie shook his head. 'Actually,' he said, 'I'm Vinnie Ehrlich the escapologist. I'm amazed you heard of me, though. Do you guys get any of the US stations on Iceland, then?'

'By—' The skipper described the shape of a satellite dish with his hands. 'We are greatly enjoying your show,' he said. 'Whenever we are in port, we are watching.'

'Tha—' Vinnie swallowed the rest of the word. 'What show?' he said.

'*The Great Vincenzo*,' the skipper said. 'On UPN. It is in Iceland very popular.'

'But that's—' Vinnie couldn't think what to say for a moment. 'That's not possible,' he said. 'We haven't even started filming the pilot yet.'

'Pilot? You film escape from aircraft? Crash of Valhalla Atlantic was part of your show?'

'Pilot episode. It's the sample programme, to see how well the show goes over.'

The captain looked puzzled. 'You mean for next series?'

'No, this one. The first one.' Vinnie narrowed his eyes. 'Hey, that's crazy. How can you have seen the show when we haven't even filmed it yet?'

'Excuse?' the captain said; but that was as far as it went. Suddenly the whole ship shuddered, like a wet dog shaking its coat, and the captain let out a yell of horror. 'Iceburgers,' he yelled. 'My God, the ship!'

Why the *Market Forces* sank so quickly, Vinnie didn't know, though he was dimly aware that the speed a ship sinks at is determined by its design. Whatever the technical details, this one went down faster than shares on a bad day on Wall Street. Vinnie had been in slower elevators.

There was no question of launching lifeboats. Even if there had been time, they were the only two people in the cabin, Vinnie and the skipper, and the skipper just stood there, wailing and cursing in what sounded to Vinnie like Klingon, though he guessed it was whatever they speak in Iceland. When he grabbed his shoulder and shook him, he pushed him away, gabbling something about Dennis Jones and going down with his ship; and by then it was too late anyway. When Vinnie managed to scramble his way across the sloping floor to the porthole, all he could see out of it was water.

Again, he thought. *Hm.*

He tried to open the door, but it was jammed; well, God knew how many billions of tons of water outside would do that. Calm professionalism took over. He left the captain kneeling and muttering what he assumed was a prayer, and jumped up in the air, trying to get his fingers into the mesh of the ventilation grid. So far, there wasn't any water in the cabin, which suggested that wherever the vent shaft led to – presumably one of those big U-bend things on the deck, like upended toilets – wasn't submerged yet. It'd have been nice to see a schematic, or have a rather better knowledge of ship design, but he couldn't and he didn't. There didn't seem to be any other way out, so at least there weren't any choices to agonise over.

'Here, you,' he said. 'Give me a leg up to the vent grid. I'll pull you up after me.'

The captain shook his head. 'No point,' he said, staring straight ahead. 'Better to be saying your prayers'; and he tugged at his bushy yellow beard with both hands. 'See you in Valholl, *ja*?'

Vinnie gave it one last try, and this time he made it. As his fingers hooked round the bars of the grille, he felt the retaining screws pull through the soft metal, and the grille gave way, revealing a square hole about one foot by eighteen inches. The grille was hanging lopsidedly. The screws having given way on the left side only, Vinnie pulled upwards, lifting his feet off the floor. With one hand clamped in the mesh, he reached up into the shaft with the other and found a handhold. *Been in worse fixes than this*, he lied to himself, as he started to climb. *Be out of here in no time.*

The handhold was a strip of steel trim joining two plates together; there were a series of them, standing just proud enough to provide something for his fingers to grip round, and strongly enough fixed to hold his weight. With a grunt he let go of the grille with his other hand just as the second set of screws pulled out of the frame and the grille came loose. He let go of it, allowing it to fall to the floor, and reached up for the next handhold.

In order to divert his mind from the impossibility of what he was somehow managing to do, as he climbed up the shaft Vinnie thought about what the skipper had told him about the TV show. Now that was truly strange. Nobody could make a television programme in their sleep, however much evidence there might seem to be to the contrary, and he knew for a fact that he had no memory of filming anything like what the skipper had described. At the very best estimate, they wouldn't even begin pre-production for another four months – realistically, six to eight – and the best-estimate release date was some time early in the new year. He tried to conjure up some slick explanation, but he couldn't. *Can't have heard the guy right*, he told himself, as he pulled his knee up as far as it would go and pawed at the side of the shaft in search of the strip of trim. *Translation error, I guess.*

Below him, the shaft was starting to fill with water. *Capillary action*, murmured the scientific advisers in the back of his mind; *the cabin must have filled with water, and it's being drawn up the shaft like Coke up a straw.* Since the only concrete advice the voice could come up with was *Climb faster*, he cut off its feed and turned his mind back to the apparent time paradox thing. What had the guy actually said? *The Great Vincenzo. It is in Iceland very popular.* How long after a show was made did it get released on foreign satellite? His agent would know, but he didn't. He tried to pull up the rest of what the skipper had said, but all he could remember was that last line, *See you in Valholl.*

Not if I see you first, fungus-face. The strain on his finger-joints was past all bearing, but he ignored that, too. By now he was able to brace his back against one wall of the shaft and force his way up by wriggling. *How many levels below deck am I?* he speculated, and decided it was probably better he didn't know. Ignorance allows optimism, in roughly the same way as oxygen allows you to keep breathing. The water, however, was nudging his feet, nuzzling him like a dog with its lead in its mouth. Whatever the outcome was to be, it would soon be over—

—And, dammit, it was: light, fresh air, and a slither from the bell mouth of the upside-down toilet on to a steeply inclined deck. He managed to grab the end of a rope just in time to stop himself sliding down the slope into the water. He really wasn't in the mood for another dead-weight climb, but what the hell, the show must go on. He hauled on the rope, feeling the rivets of the deck against his stomach and chest. *Eat my dust, Harry Houdini, looks like I've done it again*; he'd reached the end of the rope, and there were nice solid railings to pull himself up by, and a wonderfully convenient lifebelt to scriggle into before toppling over the side into the freezing cold North Atlantic.

Again.

As he hung in the water, he had a first-class view of the pointy end of the ship sliding under the water; a very quiet, peaceful way to go, just a slip and a *glop!* and that was it. Nothing to see now apart from a very substantial quantity of grey water under a grey, miserable sky.

Nothing apart from the helicopter that appeared out of nowhere, with a man dangling like a spider from a rope that fed out of the chopper's steel tummy. *Sheesh. Why am I not surprised?*

'See you in Valholl'? Guess I'm there already.

CHAPTER NINE

'To be kidding?' replied the fat, red-haired Viking mournfully. 'In a war to be getting frequently killed, off a duck's back the water. This . . .' He sighed, and shrugged his enormous shoulders. 'Peace is hell,' he said.

The Valhalla strike (more properly it was a fight-to-rule; however, when Carol had tried to explain the idea, the Vikings had so much trouble with a sentence in which the concepts *fighting* and *rules* were juxtaposed that she gave it up) was still holding, though only just. This was impressive, to say the least, considering the tactics Odin and the rest of the Valkyries had stooped to in their attempts to breach the picket line that divided the kitchens and Odin's office from the rest of the hall.

'Still,' Carol ventured, 'it could be worse.'

The Viking looked at her. 'To specify,' he replied. 'Please.'

'Well . . .' Actually, if you were the ghost (or whatever these people were; she still had no idea) of a long-dead hero who'd spent thousands of years joyously indulging himself in blood, booze and broads, it'd be hard to imagine how it could be worse, since the essentials of the strike were no blood, no booze and no broads; added to which there were the dastardly Management strike-breaking ploys. Some of them she'd anticipated: scantily-clad Valkyries prancing up and down the line waggling jugs of mead, double-headed battleaxes and untold square metres of cleavage, for example, and she'd warned them to expect it and they were being thoroughly – well, astonishingly enough, the word *mature* wasn't entirely inappropriate in this context, though it helped her to understand this sudden outbreak of restraint when one of the Vikings explained that like of horses the wee the mead, of one Valkyrie the bouncy bits to have seen all of the same likewise, and for toffee even to be fighting all girls were unable. Nevertheless—

'Hail, mariner!' It was Big Olga, most dogged and devoted of the Valkyries, back again with more mead, a bigger axe and – God alone knew where she got it from – more cleavage. All the other shield-maidens had packed it in for the night; fair enough, after a fourteen-hour shift of mead-proffering and hip-wiggling, but Olga was apparently back for another stint, grimly determined as an asbestos moth. You had to admire her steely tenacity, although the fact that she spoke her lines as if reciting some of the gloomier bits out of Ibsen made it easier to understand how the boys managed to resist her. 'Ho! But you are a strapping fellow,' she boomed, reminding Carol strongly of a Marine Corps drill sergeant bawling out a crummier-than-usual bunch of recruits. 'For a good time might you be seeking?' She swung the pitcher of mead at the Viking's head so fast that only his combat-honed reflexes made it possible for him to get his jaw out of the way in time. The swipe was, however, only a feint; as the Viking was swaying backwards, she brought her knee up into his groin with a crunch that was probably audible in Minneapolis. Wonderful coordination, Carol couldn't help thinking, but in her enthusiasm she was sending out something of a mixed message.

'Your time to be wasting, Olga,' the Viking whispered, as he sunk slowly to his knees. 'To be moved we shall not, shall not. Shame upon you likewise, unhappy of Odin the stooge.'

Olga grunted, kicked him in the head, and strode off. Carol helped the Viking up.

'For a thousand years,' he murmured, 'after the fair one I have pursued, vainly. Were it not that of principle this a matter is—' He looked down at his feet. 'Egil Halfdanson,' he said, in a rather bewildered voice, 'my toes why are you sucking?'

'Pardon,' replied the other Viking, licking his lips. 'But on your feet of mead was the Valkyrie spilling, and a long time it has been—'

The Valkyries, then, were a severe nuisance, but nothing they couldn't handle. Odin's approach was more subtle, and although before all this started Carol would have bet a year's tips that subtlety used against Vikings was about as effective as an emery board on a diamond, she couldn't deny that it was starting to get results—

('Again here is Warfather,' groaned the Viking to Carol's left, putting his hands in front of his eyes. 'Of this more with difficulty shall I endure.')

—Because all Odin did was stroll up and down in front of the picket line holding a two-foot-square mirror, not saying a word.

'To be departing entreat him,' said the red-haired Viking with a catch in his voice. 'That the day to see I should be dead, when not fighting in Valholl useless I stand here, like at a wedding—'

'Don't let him bug you,' Carol whispered. 'That's not what you should be seeing there. You know what I see when I look in that mirror?'

'Yes,' the Viking replied. 'You.'

'Apart from me. I see a bunch of guys who're slugging it out to the last drop of unshed blood, that's what I see. And you know what that makes you?'

'Wussies?'

'Heroes,' Carol replied firmly. '*Real* heroes. Think about it, guys. If you were fighting like Odin wants you to, would it hurt? Every time you got a leg or a hand chopped off, would it matter? Hell, no, it's all strictly temporary, it'll all get put right as soon as he pushes that old reset button. But this—' She gestured towards the line. 'Because of this, you people are really *suffering*. And if you don't suffer, it ain't proper heroism, is it?'

'A point she is having,' said a thin, lanky Viking. 'But Warfather also. And Warfather,' he went on, 'when our demands we are presenting, most definite he is, of fighting he cheats us not a whit. That Warfather should lie, hard to credit.'

That remark produced a rumble of agreement, deep and low as Mother Earth after eating too many onions. It made Carol nervous. She knew better than anybody that Odin was telling the truth; he couldn't give way to the Vikings' demands because he hadn't been cheating them to begin with. All in all, the situation was getting out of hand, and none of it looked to be getting her anywhere nearer to what she wanted. The thought of what it would be like spending the rest of forever here if the Vikings found out she'd been taking them all for a bunch of idiots wasn't a pleasant one.

'All right,' she said, 'tell you what I'll do. I'll go talk to Odin, one last time. Dammit, he's got to listen to reason sometime.'

'Why? A god he is. Reason he would not be acknowledging if in the bum it him was biting.'

Inside Odin's office, with the door firmly shut, Carol felt a little more relaxed. At least she didn't have to keep up the act here, and Odin was that much easier to understand than her loyal followers.

'It's pointless,' he said, after he'd poured them both a glass of orange juice (she hadn't been in the least surprised when he'd told her he was teetotal as well as a vegan). 'You've made your point, it's helped pass the time, now give it up. If you like, we'll cook up some load of bullshit about extended fighting hours, maybe even an extra hour's light-weapons drill between supper and lights out. That'll get us both off the hook, and then we can get back to normal.'

Carol shook her head. 'You know I can't do that,' she said. 'And you know what it'll take to break the strike. Let me go. It's that simple.'

Odin smiled at her, with something that could almost have been mistaken for affection. 'I'll say this for you,' he said, 'you've inherited your fair share of the Kortright negotiating skills. It's exactly what I'd expect Lin to do; never give in, bullshit to the very end, because the longer you refuse to give up, the further away the very end tends to get. There's a whole skyful of gods with thousands of temples and millions of worshippers who'd still be stacking shelves and working in gas stations if Lin Kortright ever admitted he was beaten.'

'Leave Dad out of this,' Carol said firmly. 'I know you've got some kind of crazy grudge against him, but that's nothing to do with me. Hell, if you didn't want the job you should never have taken it.'

'Really? Disobey my agent when he gave me a direct suggestion? Tell me, Ms Kortright, how would you define the term "professional suicide"? The core subject at kamikaze training college?'

Carol shrugged. 'But you're a god,' she said. 'What does it matter to you, anyway? In fact,' she added, wrinkling her nose, 'that's a question I've been wanting to ask one of you people ever since I was a little kid. If you're all gods, what do you need an agent for anyhow?'

Odin sat perfectly still. 'I don't quite follow, I'm afraid,' he said. 'Nobody just *becomes* a god, you know; just like you can't go marching on to the main lot at Paramount and announce that you've decided to star in a fifty-million-dollar movie. There's a limited number of openings for gods, so we apply, we audition, we get shortlisted, we sit by the phone for days on end not daring to move—'

'Why?' Carol interrupted. 'If you're omniscient, you'd know whether you'd gotten the job or not without having to wait for the phone to ring. And you have to be omniscient, otherwise you wouldn't be able to be a god. Dammit, if you've got what it takes to be a god, you can make them give you the job just by nodding your head or whatever it is you do when you're making magic; omnipotent, isn't that what they call it? If a guy says to you, "Thanks, we'll let you know", and next moment there's this hole in the floor where the guy used to be and a strong smell of sulphur, somehow I don't see how you'd have any trouble finding work.'

Odin rubbed his knuckles with the palm of his other hand, as if he had an itch or eczema or something. 'Poor Lin,' he said. 'He always hoped that one day you'd follow him into the business, you know. Really set his heart on it, he did. *Ode*, he'd say to me, *one of these days that little girl of mine'll be representing every major deity this side of Andromeda.* But if that's all you know about how these things work, all I can say is, he had a lucky escape.'

Carol carried on staring at him. 'You haven't answered my question,' she said. 'Why do gods need agents? And how come, if Dad gets ten per cent of everything you make, how come he isn't the biggest god of them all? I mean, ten per cent of every god in the world: that's a lot of ambrosia. And there's Dad, still living in a twelfth-storey apartment in Cleveland and driving a three-year-old Toyota. Doesn't add up, does it?'

Odin pursed his lips. 'Maybe he just likes Cleveland,' he said.

'Really?' Carol shook her head. 'Get real, will you? Cleveland only exists because Hell has a waiting list. Quit stalling; you're a god, you have to know the answer to this.'

Odin sighed, and massaged his temples with the tips of his fingers. 'Fine,' he said. 'You want to know, I'll tell you. Lin Kortright gets ten per cent of everything his clients get. What do gods get? Money?'

Carol thought for a moment. 'I guess not,' she replied. 'I mean, there's a hell of a lot of money floats around wherever there's a religion, but I never heard where the god saw any of it. Well, of course not,' she added. 'What would a god need money for?'

'What indeed?' Odin said, reaching in his pocket and producing a battered old pipe. Carol noticed that the bowl was attached to the stem with insulating tape. 'No, what gods get is worship. Belief. Faith. In other words, credit. And every last bit of credit we get, Lin gets ten per cent of.'

Carol bit her lip. 'When you say credit—'

'Belief.' Odin smiled. 'People believe in us. We believe in Lin Kortright; precisely one-tenth as firmly as all our worshippers believe in us. Now that's an awful lot of faith. You can't buy stuff with it, though. Not a hell of a lot you can do with it. What your father lives on isn't what he gets from us; it's the income from Kortright Civil Engineering Inc, the world leader in ecologically friendly landscape seismology.'

'What?'

'He has a company that moves mountains,' Odin explained. 'Using faith. Does a nice clean job, but it's slow and not all that precise, either, which is why most people who have mountains they want shifting tend to go for JCBs and dynamite; just as well, because even if he had queues a mile long outside his office door he'd only be able to do one or two jobs a year. I'm not sure of the exact figures, but it's something like five hundred kilocongregations to move one small tussock three inches to the right. It's a living, but that's all you can say for it. Enough to pay his business expenses and the rent on a dog kennel in the sky in the armpit of the State of Ohio, with just enough left over for the payments on the car and pizza once a month as a special treat. Oh, in the old days it was different; back a thousand years or so, he was raking in all the blood and lightly charred human entrails he could use, just from his South American clients. All it took was a little imagination and a touch of flair to see the possibilities for a fast-food chain in the Trobriand Islands—'

'Excuse me?'

'Cannibals,' Odin replied. 'Well, business is business, and if the guys are getting killed anyway, where's the big deal? All that's gone now, though; it's just faith and a bit of incense smoke now and again.'

Carol nodded. 'Figures,' she said. 'I always wondered where the smell in the bathroom came from. I assumed it was the drains.' She frowned. 'Trobriand-fried people, though; even by Dad's standards, that's *gross*.'

'It was also long before you were born,' Odin pointed out. 'Everything was different then. Have you any idea how old your father is?'

'No,' Carol admitted. 'Late fifties, I always thought.'

'You're not far off,' Odin said, 'in millions. And you know what keeps him alive?'

'Don't tell me. Faith.'

'That's right. All those gods out there needing him to be there for them, getting old and dying just isn't an option. You think it's bad that he never takes a holiday; the poor man can't even afford the time to die.'

For some reason, Carol thought *Valhalla*. 'Really?' she said.

'Of course. Every day, with every deal he makes, he gets that old blast of faith hitting him smack in the face and he's reborn, all his aches and pains and grey hairs leached out of him, ready to keep on doing his best for the people who're relying on him. And that,' Odin added, 'answers your first question, doesn't it?'

'Excuse me? I'm sorry,' Carol went on, 'but all this stuff you're telling me, I feel like I'm drowning in chicken soup.

There's too much of it and I can't digest it fast enough. Not to mention,' she added, 'the nasty taste it leaves in your mouth.'

'You don't like chicken soup, obviously.'

'How exactly does what you just told me answer my question?'

Odin leaned back in his chair and lit his pipe. 'Well now,' he said, 'you asked me what a god needs an agent for. And I'm saying the answer is pretty obvious. It's the same reason people need gods; because everybody, no matter who they are, needs *someone* to believe in.'

Carol thought about that for quite some time. 'I didn't see that one coming,' she said eventually. 'Then again, I guess I've never ever really thought about what Dad does. Guess I've never really, you know, *thought* about Dad at all. Well,' she added defensively, 'you don't, do you? It's like how you can live in a house for twenty years and never really think about the roof. Fathers are just, like, there; unless your parents split up or something, and your dad's a strange man who turns up twice a month to take you to the zoo and buy you a pizza. Funny, really; all I ever wanted to be was as unlike him as possible, and now you're telling me that he's the one thing even a god can have faith in. Except you, I guess,' she added. 'Because you hate him, don't you?'

'Oh yes.' Odin nodded emphatically. 'I believe in him all right. I have absolute and unquestioning faith in your father, because he was the one who made me take this fucking job. The only difference,' he went on, scowling, 'is that I believe in Lin Kortright in his aspect as a complete arsehole.'

Carol looked up at him sharply. 'You watch what you're saying,' she said. 'That happens to be my father you're talking about.'

Odin raised an eyebrow. 'I thought you just said you hated him too.'

'I said no such thing.'

'Pardon me.' Odin shook his head. 'You just said that your dearest wish was to be nothing like him.'

'That's different.' Carol clenched her hands and let them relax again. 'It's like I assumed that I ought to be different, because— well, he was always so goddamn *grown-up*, you know? Always coming home late and tired out, in a bad mood, never had any time for Mom and me. He never seemed interested in us, so I guess I decided not to be interested in him or any of the stuff he did. And he never talked about his work anyhow. Hell, until I was sixteen I thought he did sports personalities, not gods. It was only when I asked him if he could get me Carl Lewis's autograph and he said no, but he could get me a signed photograph of Quetzalcoatl if that was any use; and I said, "Who's Quetzalcoatl?" and he said, "Who's Carl Lewis?"'

Odin took his pipe out of his mouth and nodded. 'Lack of communication. Actually, I remember when he was trying to put together that Quetzalcoatl comeback tour— sorry, you were pouring your heart out, do go on.'

Carol glared at him. 'You don't understand,' she said. 'You hate him. Why should you care?'

'Oh, I care,' Odin replied. 'And I know that he cares more about you than anything else in the world, and you've caused him more unhappiness than anything else, come to that. Which is why,' he added sadly, getting to his feet and opening the door, 'you're here.'

Carol stared at him. 'You mean you had me killed just to get at Dad?'

'In a sense,' Odin said. 'I could confuse the issue by talking about a lot of things like allegory and poetic justice, but basically I chose you, as opposed to a whole lot of other stupid kids who should know better than to fritter their lives away in idiotic gestures but do it anyway, because you're Lin's daughter.'

'To hurt him.'

Odin nodded. 'Partly. But mostly to bring him here.'

'In your dreams,' Carol sneered, trying to ignore the stab of panic Odin's revelations had caused. 'He's way too smart to be caught like that.'

'Really? I imagine he'll be thoroughly delighted to hear you think so highly of him. Well, you'll be able to tell him yourself, of course; he'll be along in a day or two, once he's gone through immigration and general processing.'

'You mean—'

'Sorry, didn't I mention it? Me and my teabag memory. No, your father came in a while ago, been here some time, in fact. He actually came strolling in of his own free will, would you believe? Terrific gesture. Dramatic as two short planks.'

It took Carol a while to find any words at all. 'You really must hate us a whole bunch,' she said.

'Hate you?' Odin looked hurt and offended. 'I don't hate you, Carol,' he said. 'How could I? I've known you ever since you were born, watched you growing up and everything. You know what? This is the very same pair of trousers I'm wearing now that you puked up all over when you were twenty-one months old. That's an awful lot of history we share, Carol, and in all those years you've never done a single thing that's upset me or even annoyed me a little bit.' He breathed out through his nose, like a tired horse. 'And you see these shoes? They're the ones I bought specially for your sixth birthday party, the one where you had all your friends from school round and your dad hired a conjuror. At least, he told you it was a conjuror; what you actually got was the genuine article. How many kids do you know who had a god doing real magic at their sixth-birthday parties? Not that you'd have appreciated it even if you had known all those years ago; you'd have cried your eyes out because you wanted a proper human magician, same as all the other kids had at their parties.'

'I remember you now,' Carol said suddenly. 'You pulled a white rabbit out of my ear. And I was in floods of tears for a week because I really wanted a rabbit and Dad wouldn't let me keep it.'

'Ah,' Odin said. 'Well, we can do something about that.' He reached across and pulled a huge, fat white rabbit out of Carol's ear, then dropped it into her arms. It bit the top joint of her little finger. 'His name's Deathgrip,' he added. 'Docile enough for a wild rabbit but for heaven's sake keep it away from leads and flexes and phone cables. It'll be through anything plastic faster than the proverbial speeding bullet.'

Carol looked at him over the frantically scrabbling back legs of the rabbit. 'Get this thing off me,' she said.

'But it's what you've always wanted.'

'Not any more.' A spring-loaded paw caught her on the tip of her nose, making her eyes water. 'I changed my mind, somewhere around nineteen eighty-two. Please, take it back.'

Odin shook his head. 'Can't do that,' he said. 'Admin and all that. Once I've booked it out of the stores I can't book it back in again. If you've really and truly gone off the idea of having one as a pet, you could do worse than try it marinaded in red wine, with bacon and roast potatoes and something like a light Australian Riesling—'

Carol shuddered so much that she dropped the rabbit; it landed on all fours, hit the ground running and vanished into the space between the old-fashioned storage heater and the wall.

'I don't know,' Odin said, shaking his head, 'There's no pleasing some people. You don't like chicken soup, you don't like rabbit *à la mode paysanne de Provence*; what do you like? It's important that I know, now that you're here.'

Carol backed away. Unfortunately, Odin was very much between her and the open door. 'Why?' she asked. 'You just had me killed so you could trap my dad; what do you care?'

Odin shook his head wearily. 'You still don't get it, do you?' he said. 'This is *Valhalla*. Here, everything you've ever wanted, your every dream, comes true. You wanted a pet bunny, you got a pet bunny. You wanted a nice quiet, mind-less job waiting on tables in a bar – complete antithesis of what Daddy does for a living – you got it. You wanted to organise a strike – you finally succeeded. Most of all, your greatest wish, all your life, you wanted your dad to forget all about business and come and spend some – what's the phrase you Americans use? Quality time – some quality time with you. And now here you both are, with a whole *eternity* of quality time—'

Carol decided to take her chance. She put her head down and dashed for the door; would have made it nicely, too, if she hadn't tripped over Deathgrip the rabbit and gone sprawling on the floor, ending up heaped round Odin's feet like presents round a Christmas tree.

'A word of advice,' Odin said, reaching out a hand and help-ing her up. '*Always* look a gift horse in the mouth. That way, you can tell when they're about to reach out and bite off your ear. I'll let you know when your dad's cleared immigration.'

Carol gave him a long, cold look; in comparison, the ice ages were the one hot day in July that constitutes the average British summer. 'You wait and see,' she said. 'Once Dad gets here, you'll really have a strike on your hands. You ain't seen *nothing*.'

'You're very hostile,' Odin said. 'That's a pity, after all these years. Really, you make me wonder if I failed in my duty.'

Carol looked mystified. 'What duty?' she said. 'What're you talking about?'

'Didn't I mention that?' Odin smiled affectionately. 'I'm your godfather.'

Attila the Hun peered round the corner of the bicycle shed, then ducked back into cover. 'Get ready,' he hissed. 'They're coming.'

How long he'd been here, he had no idea. Time was pass-ing in lumps and clots, like the crap coming free from a blocked drain. Some mornings he woke up and found the sleeves of his pyjamas up around his elbows, the result of a sudden growing spurt. Nobody would tell him anything, but he had an idea he was now about eleven or twelve years old; nearer twelve than eleven, probably, but small and puny for his age. That figured, though; the Huns had always been shorter and wirier than the races they'd fought and annihilated, that was part of the thrill of the thing, the joyful triumph of the sensibly sized over a whole world of Tall Bastards.

'You all know what to do,' he said. It was a statement, not a request. Attila had hand-picked his gang, trained them, imbued them with his philosophies of life and waging war, to the point where he could almost rely on them. He looked at them now; seven grim, taciturn, determined freckled faces, his men, his magnificent seven samurai, and not one of them so much as a hair's breadth over four feet tall.

Alas, regardless of their fate, Terry Barrett's gang were walking confidently into the zone between the bike shed and the science block that Attila had mentally designated the Valley of Death. When he gave the signal, his advance party would dart out, hurl their missiles (carefully and painfully selected from the abundant raw material to be found every morning in the park just after dog-walking time) and take flight in the direction of the main school building. The Barrett gang would pursue, whereupon Attila would lead out the main body of his force to take them in flank and rear. It had worked against the Goths, it had worked against the Avars, it had worked against the Romans, and all those had been little more than dress rehearsals. When the bell finally rang for the end of dinner time, the balance of power in this sector of the playground would be changed irrevocably, for ever.

Like lambs to the slaughter; except that lambs are born with some vestigial trace of a survival instinct, which put them a long way ahead of Terry Barrett and his gang in the hierarchy of evolution. It was almost disappointing, in a way. As the trap closed, Attila couldn't help feeling that the clockwork precision with which his advance party wheeled and joined the mêlée as soon as the enemy had turned to face the ambush was wasted on these deadheads. A bunch of first-years could have taken them, maybe even *girls* . . .

'You! Pack it in.'

The magnificent seven froze, like mammoths in the Siberian ice. 'No!' Attila wanted to scream. 'Go on, what are you waiting for?' But no words came; those damned little-boy instincts had cut in again, triggered by the irrelevant sound of a teacher's voice. *The hell with teachers*, roared the inner Attila, *they're just more Tall Bastards, that's all; give me a baseball bat or a cricket stump and a kneecap to swing at, we'll soon see how tough they are. The bigger they are, the further they have to travel when they suddenly double up in unspeakable agony. But* . . .

'You,' said Mr Garrod. 'Wilson. I might have known. All right, the rest of you, detention.' (Not a cry of protest, not a howl of defiance, not even a whined 'But, sir!' from the lot of 'em, friend and foe alike. *Cowards!*) 'You, on the other hand,' Mr Garrod continued, 'are coming with me to see Mr Thompson.'

It's all right, urged the inner Attila, *Nature has condemned him to death, as She condemns us all. He'll get what's coming to him, sooner or later.* But the physical Attila felt a twinge in his bowels and bladder – it had taken him a long time to figure out what that was; he'd narrowed it down to a stomach upset or fear, and he hoped like hell it was a stomach upset – and somehow he couldn't lift his head and stare his tormentor in the eyes.

'Wait there,' he'd been ordered, and he duly took his seat on the bench outside Mr Thompson's office. Mr Garrod walked away and there was nothing to keep him there; no chains, no ropes, Mr Garrod hadn't even bothered with the elementary precaution of running a sharp knife across his Achilles tendon. Mr Garrod, it hardly needed to be said, wouldn't have lasted five minutes on the Steppes; unless, of course, Attila had had anything to do with it, in which case the poor bastard would probably have lasted five or six extremely uncomfortable days.

The door opened.

'You again.' He'd heard those words in this context so often he'd be forgiven for thinking it was his name (in which case, what would the 'U' stand for? Umberto?) But there was something unaccountably different about Mr Thompson today. Oh, for sure, he looked the same (another Tall Bastard; enough said); but there was somebody else looking down at him out of Mr Thompson's eyes, in the same way as somebody else peered at him whenever he looked in a mirror. 'Get in here,' said Mr Thompson's voice, 'and shut the door.'

As the door clicked shut behind him, he recognised the voice.

'You,' he said.

'Me.' Mr Thompson opened a drawer of the filing cabinet and pulled out a bottle. 'Kvass?' he offered. 'Pretty mild stuff, compared to what you're used to, but it's better than nothing.'

Attila nodded, and Mr Thompson filled a couple of tumblers. 'Never could get used to drinking it out of a glass,' Mr Thompson went on. 'In anything other than the skull of a defeated foe, it just doesn't taste the same.'

'You're Odin,' Attila said, pushing his glass across the desk for a refill. Mr Thompson emptied the bottle into it and pushed it back.

'Just for now,' he replied. 'Talking of which, remind me to drain all the alcohol out of this wimp's system before I go. He doesn't drink, you see, except for a half of shandy at Christmas, and the number one rule is, please leave your host's body as he'll expect to find it. Well, how are you enjoying Valhalla? Settling in all right, I hope.'

Attila stood up, intending to lean forward over the desk, but he could only just see over the edge. 'Odin, it sucks. You've got to get me out of here. All right, I was out of line running out on the paint-drying thing, I admit that, but enough's enough and I don't deserve this. Just take me back to my seat in the auditorium and we'll call it quits, okay?'

Odin looked at him for a moment and then laughed. 'Come on,' he said, 'you can do better than that. Where're the threats and bluster, diminishing into pitiful grovelling? I was expecting theatre, rhetoric, sawing the air, great impassioned speeches, not *Odin, it sucks, can I go home now?* Don't say you're going native on me, please.'

Attila scowled at him, but the stapler was in the way. 'All right,' he said. 'If I give you the full English breakfast, will it do me any good?'

'No,' Odin replied, 'but at least you'll have the satisfaction of having given it your best shot. Face it,' he went on, his patronising smile melting like snow on a hot exhaust, 'you're here for the duration now, and how you make out depends on what you do and who you turn yourself into. You aren't Attila the Hun any more; you're a short, fat, sensitive kid who gets his bum kicked in the playground and grows up to be a computer nerd or a *Star Trek* fan. Deal with it. All this pre-emptive bullying and beating the shit out of boys twice your size has got to stop, understood?'

Attila glowered at him, as if trying to barbecue him on the hoof. 'Why?' he said. 'It works. I can do it. And nobody pushes me around any more. What are you going to do about it, expel me from the school?'

Odin laughed; it was the sort of noise Attila had been able to make once upon a time, and it had nothing whatever to do with people telling jokes. 'So you reckon you can beat up on people who are bigger than you, do you? I'm warning you, Attila, things are different now. These days, there's always someone bigger than you, and the smaller you are, the harder you fall. Give it up, now, while you've got the chance. Get it into your thick nomadic skull, will you? The Romans *won*.'

Attila shook his head. 'Things change,' he said. 'People don't. I'm still me, you – you *tall* bastard. You can't take that—'

But Odin had gone, suddenly, like switching out a light. 'What did you just call me?' said Mr Thompson, in a voice of such utter incredulity that Attila wanted to giggle.

'Nothing, sir. Sorry, sir.'

'Yes, you did. Right, that's *triple* detention, and if I see you in here again before the end of term, I'm going to recommend suspension. Do you understand what that means?'

Oh, piss off, you fatuous git. 'Yes, sir. Sorry, sir.' *Dammit, why am I staring at my shoes? Why do I always stare at my shoes, like I've done something wrong? I haven't done anything wrong; because for men like me, like Attila the Scourge of God, words like Right and Wrong are utterly meaningless.*

'And do you understand,' Mr Thompson went on, 'why it's *wrong* to behave like that? Because if you don't understand—'

'I understand, sir. And I'm sorry, sir. Won't do it again.'

Mr Thompson looked at him for a long time; and because he was staring at his shoes, he couldn't look up and see who was looking at him from behind Mr Thompson's eyes this time. 'That's better,' he said, in a voice that made Attila want to be sick. 'This time, I really think you mean it.'

CHAPTER TEN

*G*andhi, thought Howard suddenly, as another smart missile belied its name by crashing into the ground and blowing itself up. *Bloody* Gandhi.

Ever since Odin had mentioned the name in passing, a few hundred deaths ago, it had been rattling around in the back of his mind like the loose jack handle in the boot of your car that you mistakenly believe is the big end going. Gandhi wasn't a subject he could claim to know a lot about; the last time the film had been on, it had clashed with *Xena: Warrior Princess*, and though his friend Dave had seen it, the only comment he'd had to make was that they'd got the number of buttons down the front of a Coldstream Guards second lieutenant's tropical dress uniform wrong, that being the sort of thing Dave took very seriously indeed. The bare facts, however, were buried somewhere in the cardboard box of useless data he'd been storing in the back of his mind since school, when to his disgust they'd had to do the twentieth century in History for A level, something that struck Howard (who regarded anything later than 1820 as out-of-date news rather than history) as a terrible waste of time.

Gandhi; wasn't he the bloke who overthrew British rule in India by entirely non-violent resistance? A curious notion, he'd always thought, akin to trying to put out a fire by hosing it down with petrol, but at the moment it had the overwhelming merit of being the one thing he hadn't tried yet.

The logic was simple. In Valhalla, people fight all day and come back to life in the morning, over and over again. Didn't it stand to reason, therefore, that if you didn't join in the fighting, they'd have to let you go? Would Valhalla tolerate a pacifist, or would it reject them, like a Lloyds Bank card in a NatWest ATM? It would be interesting to find out.

And so he did, twenty-seven seconds later, when a shell from a seven-inch naval gun (*Naval gun? But we're miles and miles from the sea*) left him very widely distributed and about a hundredth of a millimetre thick. When he next opened his eyes, he saw the same old landscape: barbed wire, burnt-out houses and shops, bodies slumped in doorways, the characteristic glossy brown-black of dried blood marking the pavement he was standing on. Either his next afterlife was set in Liverpool, or he was back where he'd started.

The Liverpool hypothesis was knocked on the head when he saw a tank lurch past, stop and move on (if this was Liverpool, someone would've stolen the tank's caterpillar tracks while it was standing still) and he was just about to file the Gandhi initiative under F for Failure when a thought occurred to him.

One non-violent man sitting in the middle of the road is an idiot. A thousand of them constitutes a Movement. All he had to do was persuade his fellow inmates to join him, and then maybe the scheme might work.

First, catch your Movement.

'Don't shoot!'

A stream of bullets passed overhead, so close he could feel

the blast of the shock wave. Tucking himself a little more tightly into the lee of the fallen-down wall he was hiding behind, he tried again. 'Don't shoot! I only want to talk to you.'

Once again, the bullets whizzed past, so close and so many that all he'd have needed to do to create the perfect colander was to hold his helmet a foot above his head. This was frustrating.

'Pack it in, will you?' he shouted. 'All I want to do is talk to you. I have this brilliant idea about stopping the fighting so we can all go home.'

His words must have touched a chord in the heart of his unseen assailant because, sure enough, he stopped shooting. Instead, he threw a grenade. Howard had just enough time to grab it and throw it back before it went off. There was a loud bang, and a moment later it started raining that warm, sticky red stuff. *Hell*, Howard thought. *So much for non-violence.*

So what? Gandhi wouldn't have given up so easily. A minor setback, such as blowing someone into taramasalata with a hand grenade, would have struck the great man as an interesting challenge, not the cue for total surrender. Beyond doubt, his first words of advice would have been something along the lines of *If at first you don't succeed, try, try again*, combined with a picturesque metaphor about omelettes and eggs.

He didn't have far to go before he came across another unseen sniper. This one was embedded in the ruins of a public lavatory that had at some previous stage in the day's programme taken a direct hit from a three-inch mortar, and the smell was quite repulsive. It didn't seem to be doing much for the sniper's mood, or his aim.

'Please,' Howard found himself saying, 'it won't take a minute, really. And then,' he added with a sigh, 'if I haven't convinced you that my idea's a good one, I'll hold still while you kill me. Now I can't say fairer than that, can I?'

The sniper held his fire, a very encouraging sign. Of course, it could just mean that he was swapping over rifle clips.

'Are you kidding?' said a faint, reedy voice from behind the evil-smelling rubble. 'What kind of moron do you take me for?'

Howard took a deep breath. 'It isn't like that at all,' he said. 'I mean it, really. Look, I'm going to get up from behind this rock and you aren't going to kill me; I'll have both hands up in the air where you can see them, and I'll throw out my weapons before I even start to move. Then I'll come on, really slow and easy. Simple as that.'

The sniper didn't say anything. Gradually, Howard eased forward, waiting for the rifle to start up again, until he was out in the open, too far to have any chance of getting out of the way if the enemy resumed hostilities. Still no response. He decided to push the risk all the way, and stood up.

'Hi there,' he said.

The other guy froze. He was in the middle of trying to unjam the mechanism of his weapon; there was an empty cartridge case stuck solid in the breech, refusing to budge. So much for the idea that the enemy had been listening to what Howard had to say. Still, as an exercise in creative serendipity it was worth seeing through to the end.

'It's all right,' he called out, as the other man scrabbled like clumsy lightning for a big axe that was lying half-submerged in the mud. 'I'm not going to hurt you, I promise. Look, no weapons of any kind. No sudden movements, I swear to God. Now then, I'm coming toward you.'

The other man, a long, thin, straggly type with a lantern jaw and a parsnip nose, stared at him and left the axe lying. 'Are you for real?' he said. 'You really aren't going to attack?'

Howard nodded. 'You got it,' he said. 'Non-violence. Peace on earth, goodwill towards men. Gandhi. I just want to talk, that's all.'

'Gandhi?'

'Gandhi.'

The other man's brow furrowed. 'Isn't that the name of a river in Northern India?' he asked.

'You're thinking of the Ganges,' Howard replied. 'Gandhi's the man who won his country's freedom by forswearing violence and relying on quiet persuasion and the power of example. That's what I want to talk to you about.'

'Not fighting?' The man looked at him as if he'd just suggested not breathing. 'Man, I don't think that's even possible.'

Howard made himself smile. 'It's worked so far, hasn't it? I persuaded you, and you haven't attacked me as a result. Now just think what'd happen if we each persuade two other guys, and they each persuade two guys, and they each persuade two guys— You get the idea? It's evolution in action, if you ask me.'

'Sounds more like pyramid selling to me.'

'That's okay,' Howard replied. 'Even if I had a pyramid, I wouldn't try to sell it to you.'

'But not fighting—' The enemy soldier looked confused to the point of panic. 'I don't know how you do that. I mean, what would you do instead?'

'Any number of things,' Howard replied confidently. 'The number of things you can do that don't involve fighting is so incredibly vast it'd take me forever just to list the category headings. My guess is, it's just been so long since you did anything except fight that you've forgotten how. Is that more or less right?'

The other man nodded. 'What the hell,' he said. 'I'll try anything once. What d'you think—?'

He didn't get any further than that; because Howard, who'd been gradually inching forward, had got close enough to the axe to be able to dive, grab hold of it and swing it round at shoulder height, burying the blade in the other man's head.

'Damn,' Howard said.

He let go of the axe and sat down dejectedly on the casing of an unexploded bomb. Goddamn rotten bloody instinct; he'd been this close to a breakthrough, almost close enough to convince himself that it was feasible. But then he'd seen the axe, just lying there in the mud with its handle sticking up, and it was as if someone had pulled the strings or pressed the remote control, jerking him into immediate and unexpected action. And in consequence, a man lay dead.

Yeah. Think about that.

As a humane and civilised alternative to butchery and slaughter, obviously a non-starter. Still, he'd invented the technique now, and there was no doubt about it, there was potential for a really neat and efficient way of taking out sentries and snipers. Pity to waste it. After all, a new way of making dynamite cheaper and better was no less valid just because you stumbled across it by accident while trying to invent a new breakfast cereal.

'Cheat,' said the corpse accusingly.

Howard's eyebrows closed ranks. 'All's fair in love and war,' he replied, rather half-heartedly. 'And I was utterly sincere at the time. It was just seeing the axe there, and thinking how nice it'd look between your eyes. Instinct, I guess. Or a programmed response, like— dammit, what's the name of the pudding person who did the dogs?'

'Pavlov,' replied the corpse. 'Now what kind of crummy excuse is that? "I was only obeying impulses." Slicing a person's skull like a boiled egg's hardly just a nervous tic, now is it?'

'In Valhalla,' Howard replied thoughtfully, 'it might just be. But I wouldn't worry about it if I were you. I mean, it'll all be all right in the morning, won't it?'

'True,' the corpse replied grudgingly. 'But according to the forecast it's going to be windy and wet with low pressure coming in from the north and east all day tomorrow, and today's supposed to be sunny and mild, with temperatures around twenty degrees centigrade (that's seventy degrees Fahrenheit).'

All Howard could think of to say to that was 'Oh well,' so he said it. Then he added, 'I expect you'll get your revenge in a day or so.'

'Doubt it,' the corpse grumbled. 'I haven't killed you for months, whereas this is the second time this week you've snuffed me. You know, a person could get a complex.'

Howard left him to welter irritably in his steaming gore and wandered off, not paying much attention to the shells and bullets that were buzzing all around like drowsy bees in summer. There was, he'd noticed, precious little correlation between the amount of care and attention he took and how long he lasted each day; if there was a statistical relationship, it was probably in the opposite direction – the less trouble taken, the longer he lasted. He was, in fact, musing on this very point when a shadowy figure slipped out of the ruins of an alleyway, crept up behind him, and—

Curioser and curioser. Sure, people creeping up behind you was as much a part of life here as crossing the road at a zebra crossing was back home. What up-creepers didn't do here was put their hands over your eyes and call out 'Guess who!' in a melodious feminine voice.

Some devilish new Ninja ploy? Perhaps, but he wasn't interested in the finer points of the martial arts. Quickly and efficiently he grabbed his assailant's arm, slung her over his shoulder and closed in for the kill, bayonet drawn—

'Lisa?'

'Nyuk,' replied Lisa From Internal Audit, wiping mud out of her mouth and eyes.

'Lisa? What in God's name are you doing here?'

He'd never found out her second name; he'd never had a pretext for asking. About all he knew of her backstory was that she was happily married to a large, volatile man who worked at the abattoir, and who by all accounts regarded his work as more of a vocation than a mere job. In consequence, Howard had always sought to keep a degree of distance between himself and Lisa From Internal Audit, a state of affairs that more or less suited him. True, she was a fascinating, not to say awesome sight, if you like six-foot white-blonde Aryans; but gorgeousness isn't everything, and his observations tended to suggest that she had the friendly, happy-go-lucky disposition of an unguarded chainsaw. Also – not that he was in any way prudish, but anyone that size and shape who came in to work wearing those sorts of clothes was likely to constitute a health hazard, and why people wasted their time and energy protesting about nuclear power and acid rain when there was Lisa From Internal Audit wandering around the place in what was either a very short skirt or a wideish belt, he couldn't say.

(Which reminded him; nothing he could remember in their working relationship had ever put them on the sort of terms where A creeps up behind B, puts her hands over his eyes and says 'Guess who!' in an alluringly girlish voice. Something like that would have stuck in his mind come what might, for all that his brains had spent more time out of his skull than in it over the last few months.)

'That wasn't very friendly,' she said, scrambling to her feet. 'I was just saying hello.'

Someone across the street fired at her with a high velocity rifle. She caught the bullet in her left hand without even looking, squashed it into a ball and threw it into the gutter. 'Hello,' Howard said. 'Lisa, what are you doing here? This is—' Even though he'd long since resigned himself to the fact that it was actually happening and not all a convenient dream to explain why he'd been out of the series for nine months, he couldn't quite bring himself to say the word *Valhalla*. He didn't have to.

'Valhalla,' she said. 'Yes, I know. Settling in all right, are you?'

'What do you mean, settling— *Get down!*' Even as he said the words, he realised that there simply wasn't enough time for her to react; he'd have to do it for her. He threw himself through the air, landing on top of her in the mud, while the space her head had been occupying a moment before was torn apart by the slipstream of a couple of hundred machine-gun bullets.

'This is cosy,' Lisa said. 'Though it'd be nice if you'd take your elbow out of my face.'

'What? Oh, sorry. There was someone shooting at us with a machine-gun, you see, so I—'

Lisa grinned at him. 'Nice try,' she said. 'Never heard that one before. Nonetheless—'

She drew back her left hand and gave him such a smack across the face that when he opened his eyes he fully expected to be looking directly at the small of his own back. 'Sexual harassment,' she went on. 'I could sue you for thousands.'

That was just about as much as Howard could take. He rolled over and slithered to his feet, somehow managing to ignore exactly what it was he'd just been slithering in. 'It was not,' he shouted. 'No way. Lisa, quite apart from I don't do that sort of thing, I wouldn't sexually harass *you* if you were the last woman in the world.'

Lisa looked at him, and suddenly he felt like a male black widow spider must feel when his girlfriend starts talking about honeymoon plans. 'You know,' she said, 'it's funny you should put it like that.'

'Huh? Like what?'

'The last woman in the world,' Lisa replied. 'You see, it so happens—'

Valkyries, Odin had explained; the choosers of the slain. And how can you make a choice unless you hold an audition first?

'Get this bum outa here,' said the usual voice. 'I don't know, goddamn time-wasters.'

'But *listen*,' Kortright yelled. 'Of *course* I can be Lin Kortright, I don't need any goddamn audition. I *am* Lin Kortright.'

Sniggering in the darkness. 'Guy says he's Lin-fucking-Kortright. Hey, buddy, if you're really Lin Kortright, where you been all these years? You been kidnapped by aliens, huh? You been up there in that spaceship with the little green guys and Elvis and JFK, talking to people back here on Planet Earth through their microwaves? Save it for the *National Enquirer*, pal, this is a serious audition.'

'You don't understand. I – am – Lin – *KORTRIGHT*!'

A sigh drifted out of the black void beyond the spotlight. 'Goddamn method actors,' it murmured. 'Hey, you. You sure you ain't really Dustin Hoffman?'

Kortright gritted his teeth and walked off the stage. All his life he'd been Lin Kortright; he'd been a wonderful Lin Kortright, the *definitive* Lin Kortright, he'd brought to the part a depth of feeling and compassion unequalled since Barrymore – no, wait. He *was* Lin Kortright.

Had been Lin Kortright.

Maybe, he reflected despairingly, *this is what it's like for Hamlet.* To judge by what he'd read, there was no way Hamlet would ever get to play Hamlet, except maybe in some crummy touring company driving round Arkansas in a beat-up old Volkswagen van. The real Hamlet had been some illiterate Viking princeling who didn't even have the balls to kill the bastard who iced his old man.

Is that it? I had my chance to be Lin Kortright and I blew it, and now the part's being played by Mel-fucking-Gibson? Puh-lease!

'Dad?'

All other considerations, including pain and fear of not being good enough to be himself, evaporated from his mind. 'Carol? Is that you? I can't see too good.'

'Dad? You look awful. Here.' And someone he couldn't

see took his arm and led him out of the line of fire. 'Dad, why were they being so rude to you?'

'Because I'm a lousy Lin Kortright,' Kortright replied.

'I always said you're better off sticking to character parts. What the hell were you doing up there in the first place?'

'It's a long story, honey.' With the heel of his hand he massaged his eyelids and cautiously opened his eyes. 'Carol, it's you,' he said. 'Really you. Are you all right?'

'Apart from being dead, you mean? Yeah, I'm fine. Dad, what are you doing down here? You aren't dead too, are you?'

Kortright nodded. 'I guess so. And hey, it ain't so bad.'

Carol looked dubious. 'It's terribly unhealthy,' she said.

'Probably no worse for you than smoking cigars,' Kortright replied. 'And that never did me no harm.'

'How do you know? Maybe that's what killed you.'

Kortright shook his head. 'Nah. I got in a fight in a bar.'

'In a *bar*.' Carol stared at him. 'Dad, you never ever go in bars. You were always telling me it isn't safe.'

'Yeah. Well, now maybe you'll believe me.'

He sat down on a wicker laundry basket, letting his feet swing against the side, waiting for the surge of relief, joy, whatever, to hit him. It was there inside him, burgeoning, getting ready; but there was some small thing, like a minor procedural glitch in a legal transaction or a speck of dust in a carburettor jet, that was holding everything back. He didn't know what it was, but he knew there was something.

'Carol,' he said, 'how did you get here? What happened to you?'

'Does it matter? I'm here now.'

'It matters.' He'd said the words almost before he'd acknowledged the thought in his own mind. 'I really want to know.'

'*Dad*.' She had on that pained expression, that 'Why have I got to tidy my room, I *like* it this way' face he'd known ever since she was a tiny baby. 'We haven't seen each other, called each other even, for *years*. Can't you think of anything more interesting to talk about than some nasty accident I had? I really don't want to discuss it, Dad, it upsets me. Okay?'

Valkyries. Be careful what you wish for. This is Valhalla, where all your dreams come true. 'Sure, honey,' he said. 'I'm just curious, that's all. Interested. I mean, dying is an important time in a person's life. What kind of a father would I be if I didn't give a damn?'

'Of course it's an important moment,' Carol said, and her voice was a little colder and more distant. 'I knew it had to be an important moment, because you weren't there. Same as you weren't there for any of the other important moments in my life. I expect,' she added bitterly, 'you were having to work late at the office again.'

On reflex and without thinking, Kortright said, 'Give me a break, honey. People rely on me, you know?'

'I know,' Carol said angrily. 'A whole bunch of *gods* rely on you. They believe in you, Dad. They're the only ones who do. I gave up trusting anything you told me when I was six years old.' She smiled ruefully. 'But there,' she said, 'I'm not a god.'

'You sure about that, honey?' Kortright murmured.

Carol stared at him. 'Dad, what in hell are you talking about?' she said.

'Don't "Dad" me,' Kortright answered, standing up. 'You aren't Carol, you're some goddamn lousy god who's playing games with my head, pretending to be my daughter.' He stopped, frowned, then snapped his fingers. 'Of course,' he said, 'how dumb can you get? You're Odin.'

Carol sagged, and stopped being Carol. 'How did you guess?' he asked.

'Easy,' Kortright said, half turning his back; then he spun round with remarkable agility for a man his size and shape and punched Odin on the point of the jaw, sending him sprawling on the ground. 'I knew you weren't Carol. Carol'd never have said anything hurtful and cruel, like you just said.

Not to mention the continuity error; Odin always comes out to meet me when I get off stage, but this time he isn't there and you are.' Odin tried to get up, but Kortright was standing on his hand. 'You asshole, Odin. And you're stupid, too. You really think I can be around gods ever since before there *were* gods, and not know one when I see one?'

'Get off my hand.'

'Oh yeah? Give me one good reason.'

'Because if you don't,' Odin said, 'I'll blow you into so many bits, people on five continents will inhale bits of you every time they breathe.'

Kortright scowled horribly but lifted his foot. 'Okay,' he said, 'so you're bigger than me. You know what that makes you?'

'A god.'

'A bully.'

Odin shrugged. 'Inevitably there's a degree of common ground between the two,' he said. 'Now then, don't get all uptight with me, I'm just trying to be nice. Granting you your heart's desire; it's all part of the Valhalla package. Of course, it isn't *real*, but then, what is? If only you'd given me a chance, I could have been Carol for you, I could have walked like her, talked like her – dammit, I had her backstory off pat, didn't I? Oh, and by the way,' he added, with a big grin, 'that stuff about the real Carol not saying hurtful stuff about her old man? Bullshit. You forget, I've had her here under close scrutiny, I've compiled an in-depth psychological study, character profiles, brain algorithm analyses, the lot. You got the right answer, Lyndon, but for the wrong reason.'

Kortright tried to grab him by the throat, but Odin was too quick; before Kortright's hand was anywhere near making contact, he'd moved ten feet out of the way and launched a bolt of sizzling blue light that picked Kortright up and dumped him in the corner of the room like a garbage sack flung into a skip.

'You should have taken what you were offered,' he said sadly, as Kortright struggled to get up. 'That way, you'd have had what you think you want, and I could have laughed myself stupid thinking about what a dumb-ass mistake you were making. Then I'd have had my heart's desire too, and we'd both have been in seventh heaven.'

Kortright growled, grabbed a three-legged stool and hurled it. The stool stopped a foot or so from Odin's nose, turned back, hovered for a moment directly over Kortright's head, turned into six pounds of mushroom-growers' delight, and dropped. While Kortright was still trying to maul the filthy stuff out of his eyes, Odin seized him by the collar and jerked him to his feet.

'Come along,' he said, 'you're on. Can't keep the producer waiting.'

Kortright had no choice but to stumble into the folds of the curtain, groping for the opening. Before he allowed himself to be pushed through, however, he rooted himself to the spot for a moment.

'Odin,' he said. 'Just answer me one thing. Those guys out there. The ones that hate me so bad.'

'The talent spotters. Yes?'

'Who are they?'

Odin smirked. 'I'd have thought you'd have worked that out for yourself by now. Take a close look. You'll see.'

And he did, in the short period of time before his vision blurred over with mashed rotten vegetable. They were all basically the same person; some of them at ages twenty, twenty-five and on up to thirty; some of them early forties, mid-forties, early fifties; some so old they were hardly recognisable, until you perceived the trend and looked carefully, in which case you could see the distinctive shape of the nose, ears and chin, stranded among the wrinkles and drooping folds of skin like the spires of Gothic churches sticking up out of a landscape of office blocks, traffic islands and shopping malls. They were all various ages and stages of one man.

Everyone's a critic, Kortright thought, gazing at them in disgust.

They were, of course, all Lin Kortright.

'If I were you, my friend,' said Vinnie to the pilot of the helicopter that had yanked him to safety from a watery grave a few minutes earlier, 'I'd find somewhere safe to put this thing down. Immediately.'

'Huh?'

'Or better still, break out the parachutes, a couple of those little inflatable rubber boats if you've got 'em, and let's bale out now, calmly and peacefully, instead of leaving it to the last minute and probably panicking and screwing everything up.'

'*Was? Ich kann du nicht hören.*'

'Because,' Vinnie went on, slower and louder, 'this helicopter is about to crash, any minute. When that happens I'll probably be all right – that seems to be the object of the exercise, me staying alive – but I wouldn't give much for your chances. Basically, I think you're probably one of those security guards with broad, smiling faces who beam down to the planet with the captain, say their three or four lines and then get eaten by the special-effects monster of the week. I put your life expectancy at— are you listening to me?'

'*Bitte? Ich kann Englisch nicht sprechen.*'

Vinnie slumped back in his seat, swearing under his breath. Dumb of him, really, to imagine that they wouldn't have covered that angle (whoever 'They' were); dumb of him to imagine that anything so simple and elementary as warning the pilot would work to break this horrendous loop he'd somehow managed to get into—

(*Bermuda Triangle? No, way too far north. The CIA? Unlikely.* Some kind of lousy practical joke by God seemed the only possible explanation; unless, of course, he was imagining it all, and the helicopter wasn't going to crash after all.)

'Forget it,' he sighed. 'And yes, I know you can't understand me, you poor goddamn extra, but I'll tell you this anyway. I'm sorry, really I am. You're gonna die, and it's just so that I can escape another horrible death, so in a way I guess it's my fault. No hard feelings, huh? Well?'

The pilot shrugged his shoulders; and then a whole galaxy of red lights started winking on the instrument panel in front of him, something started beeping frantically, and the helicopter shuddered and started to drop like a stone. Wearily, Vinnie unclipped the seat belt, rose unsteadily to his feet and wandered into the cargo bay. The door? Jammed solid, naturally. He put his weight against the handle, and it broke off. Now then, what did that leave? Well, there was another door in the nose of the chopper, or he could try smashing a hole in the perspex canopy; failing that, he'd have to cut his way out though the side of the fuselage, using the fire-axe fortuitously lying on the cargo-bay floor. Decision time; the helicopter was spiralling down anticlockwise around the vertical, like a sycamore seed, so he had to do something. If he faffed around with the door and the canopy and they turned out to be stuck too (no reason why they should be, but the same was eminently true of the cargo-bay door he'd just entirely failed to open) then he'd be in serious danger of running out of time. Better to start off with the last resort and bypass all that futile struggling with more obvious means of escape.

He picked up the axe and looked for something to hit. The walls looked depressingly solid, but once he'd levered off the trim, the remains of the door-locking mechanism struck him as rather more hopeful. Once he'd identified the bit of pressed steel that actually held the door shut, it was fairly straightforward work to cut through it with the axe, in spite of the frantic juddering of the helicopter and the pilot yelling at him in German. '*Nein, nein!*' the poor fool was screaming, as he finally got the door free and slid it back. No parachutes anywhere in sight, of course, but what the hell; it was just water down there, and they'd lost so much height while he was slashing away at the lock that it probably wouldn't be too far to fall. *Nuts*, he muttered to himself, and stepped out through the doorframe until he was standing on nothing.

When he hit the water, it was bitter cold. He went down a long way, but eventually he slowed down and was able to start swimming back up. When his head broke through the surface of the water, the first thing he did (apart from getting rid of some very stale air) was look round for any indication of where the helicopter had gone down – after all, the pilot might just have been another disposable stooge, but it'd be nice, just once, to save one of the poor bastards, rather than just leaving them to drown – but there was nothing: no burning oil on the surface of the water, no scattered flotsam, no churning white circle of foam; just an endless blue-grey expanse that met the grey sky at sloppily welded seams on the horizon. A pity; quite apart from the death of the pilot, some floating bits and bobs to cling on to would have gone down a treat.

Then he heard something – the drone of an engine. Treading water hard and doing his best to ignore the predatory chill of the icy water, he strained his neck back and looked up. The helicopter was still there; flying straight and level now, definitely the same one (he could clearly see the vandalised hold door he'd just thrown himself out of), circling round him in gradually decreasing circles. Hadn't crashed at all. *Just saved myself from an* entirely functional, non-crashing *helicopter that's now got the awkward job of rescuing me again. Bummer.*

The pilot must have spotted him, for the helicopter changed course, abandoning its methodical circling and heading straight towards him, coming down to within twenty feet of the surface. The power winch started to whine and he watched the cradle on the end of the long line dip into the water. *Embarrassing? You bet.* Fortunate the pilot couldn't speak English, really.

As he watched his rescuer coming in close, it occurred to him that the pilot was doing it differently this time: a steeper, faster descent, bringing him closer to the tops of the waves. Obviously the guy knew what he was doing, but to Vinnie's untrained eye it all looked just a tad hairy. Overshoot just a little, or wait a moment too long before throttling back and pulling up on the stick, and he could easily end up in the water; and with the cargo door wrenched open like that, if he did ditch in the sea, there was nothing to stop the water rushing in and flooding the chopper almost instantaneously, dragging it down to the bottom of the ocean before you could say—

Before you could say 'Oh, *shit*!'; and that wasn't just speculation, that was scientifically proven fact, because Vinnie made the experiment. He'd got as far as *oh* when the helicopter hit the water, but by the time he'd sounded the *t* of *shit*, it had completely vanished under the water, leaving behind a wake of ripples and a fast-growing oil slick.

'Bastard!' Vinnie yelled at the encircling sky, but if anybody heard, they didn't show any signs. Meanwhile, it was getting very hard to keep his leg moving, very hard indeed, and the only reason why he wasn't in agony from the pain was that he was numb from the waist down because of the cold. 'Hello, Death,' he said aloud, 'fancy meeting you here!' And he'd have added *Do you come here often?* if it wasn't such a fatuous question; nobody ever came here, because what with the cold and the isolation and the vast, incalculable quantity of water on all sides, Death hung out here all the time. 'Get out of that one, smartarse,' he said, and as he said it his mouth filled up with foul-tasting salt water, and he started to rise.

Error: bad command or file name. That should be *sink*, surely.

No, rise; because he was sitting astride the periscope of a surfacing submarine (he'd have realised it earlier, only because his legs were so numb he hadn't even noticed it) and the greatest threat to his life at the moment was falling off the periscope on to the steel decking of the conning tower. '*Noooo!*' he yelled, but the submarine either couldn't hear him or didn't care. Despairingly, he linked his arms round the periscope and slid down it, fireman's-pole fashion. 'Let me off! Go away! Go away or you're all going to die!'

Maybe they didn't hear. Maybe they didn't care.

Vinnie slithered to the decking and slumped like a discarded sock, mouthing obscenities at the relentless, ineluctable mercy of Heaven.

CHAPTER ELEVEN

'**D**ad?'
For a moment she was afraid it had been a dream;
that odd, recurring dream in which her father rescued her
from a burning ice-cream factory. (The fire wasn't the problem. The really nasty bit was the tsunami of melted ice cream
that cascaded down the corridors and threatened to engulf
her if she didn't keep running; a collector's item, her analyst
had told her, and indicative of either deeply repressed sexual
frustrations or too much Häagen-Dazs pecan toffee just
before going to bed.) But it wasn't. The hand on her shoulder
was his hand, and the cigar dropping ash on her face smelt
overpoweringly of her childhood.

'Dad!'

'All right, already,' he hissed. 'Keep the noise down. You
want to wake up Odin with your goddamn noise?'

Yes, definitely Dad. 'Sorry,' she mumbled. 'I knew you'd
come, I knew you wouldn't let them—'

'Carol.'

'Yes, Dad?'

'Shut the fuck up.'

'Yes, Dad.'

God, she hated it when he talked to her like that – still, that was the way he talked to her, same as he talked to everybody, even gods (especially gods) – but what she really needed right now was the reassurance that it was really him. Well, she'd got that, anyway, even if she did feel that old instinct to pull the cigar from between his lips and stub it out in his eye.

'Now listen up,' he said. 'Looks like everybody's asleep, so why don't we just walk over to the door, nice and quiet, and get the hell out of this dump? Agreed?'

She nodded. A small, anarchic part of her mind objected that it wasn't that easy and she'd found out herself by trial and error that, apart from the ones that opened on to the kitchens and Odin's office, the doors in Valhalla didn't go anywhere, just long narrow corridors that twisted and turned and smelt of moss until they brought you out on the other side of the hall from the one you'd just left. But things had to be different now. It stood to reason, because Dad was here and if anybody knew about getting out of Valhalla, he must do. He led and she followed.

The door was unbarred and unbolted, it swung open at the slightest touch from Dad's outstretched forefinger, and beyond it was (*Why am I not surprised?*) a gloomy, twisting tunnel that was dark and smelt of moss.

'All right,' she said, 'which is it, snakes and ladders or Monopoly?'

He ignored her. He was good at that. This was Dad all right. Dreams can have you sitting bolt upright in bed screaming, with the sweat running flash floods down your face and neck, but only your own flesh and blood can patronise you to the point of spontaneous combustion.

'Not a word, understood?' he growled, as if he was talking to the most stupid person in the world. 'We don't want anybody to hear us.'

Gee, Dad, really? I thought we wanted to make so much noise they'll hear us in Florida. Say, thanks awfully for telling me, I'd never have guessed if you hadn't. Carol waited until he'd vanished into the darkness of the tunnel, then followed, feeling her way with the tips of her fingers against the wall. The crazy thing was, she could feel half of herself yearning for him to trip over something with a ghastly ear-splitting crash, just so she could sneer at him for being the one who'd made the noise. With Dad, there had always been this supervening agenda, more important than anything they were actually supposed to be doing, this no-holds-barred fight to score points, to be right after all, to point out the other's shortcomings as loud and clear as possible.

It was definitely the same tunnel she'd been in before, the one that led nowhere; but this time it seemed to go on for ever, probably because he was edging along so painfully slowly. It was, of course, possible that somewhere in here there was a secret door only Dad knew about, opening on to a side spur that'd bring them out in the middle of Central Park. She had to believe in something like that, because she had to believe in him if she ever wanted to see home again. And she did, no question about that. If faith really could move mountains like Odin had told her, when it came to Dad he could have the Pyrenees doing line-dancing.

His mobile phone started to ring.

Down here in this tunnel, the sound was downright eerie, as well as loud enough to wake the dead. Before Carol could say anything, he'd pulled the phone out of his pocket and flipped up the aerial.

'Kortright,' he said.

Carol wanted to scream; not again, not *again*! Because this had happened all the time when she'd been a little girl: every picnic in the park, every trip to the zoo or the beach, every holiday, every carefully scheduled quality-time event when he was supposed to be giving her all his attention, that goddamn phone would ring and he'd be gone, leaving his body behind gabbling into that flimsy-looking foldaway mouthpiece. And every time she'd dance up and down in fury, making put-it-away gestures while he scowled at her and waved, *shoo, shoo!*

'Hades? Hades, my man, how ya doing? Say, buddy, this really isn't a good time for me, actually I'm just trying to— What? She's left you *again*? Hey, man, that's awful, I feel for you, really I do. Can I call you back, only— She said that, did she? Well, I told you, didn't I tell you? I said to you, Hades, that woman's gonna bring you nothing but unhappiness—'

Carol sat down on the cold, hard floor and folded her arms. What she hated most of all was the depth of feeling, the compassion, the understanding in his voice; it melted her heart to listen to him, and all the time she knew perfectly well that he was just trying to get the poor fool off the line, that he *didn't give a shit*, but even so there was more warmth and depth of caring in his voice than she'd ever heard when he'd been talking to her—

'Let her go, buddy,' he was saying. 'This time, say to her, honey, if you want to go, then go, it's time to move on— Yeah, well, you *think* you do, but really? Really really? Or just you *think* really, while deep down inside where it counts you're saying, screw you, you bitch— No, no, *I* don't think that, you know I don't. I think she's a really wonderful person, Hades, but a real mean bitch also. Yeah, what you might call a really multifaceted personality.'

She could hear footsteps, a long way off but definitely coming this way. He had his back to her now; it was time for the dance, where they walked round each other in circles, with her trying to get his attention and Dad turning his back on her, through a full 360 degrees, over and over. 'Dad, they're *coming*!' she mouthed; but he only glared horribly and stuck a finger in his other ear. 'You see, honey,' he'd explained to her so many times, patiently as if to a complete moron, 'when I'm on the phone and it's business, I gotta concentrate.'

And now here they were, trapped in a narrow tunnel with Odin and God knew what kind of amazingly horrible henchmen scampering up the line towards them, and here was Dad on a call, not giving a shit for the caller, not giving a shit for her, but *concentrating*—

'Forget it,' she said loudly. 'I'm going on alone.'

Kortright turned his back again. 'Hades, buddy,' he was saying, 'has it ever occurred to you, there may be just the faintest glimmer of a pattern emerging here? Like, the first day of April every fucking year, she leaves you, every October the first she comes back? No, no, I'm not saying it's significant exactly, I just thought I'd point it out, maybe leave you to draw your own conclusions— No, *no*, I didn't say that, I'm *not* calling your wife a whore, I'm just saying—'

His voice faded away as Carol hurried down the tunnel, her eyes streaming with tears that oughtn't to have been there at all. So why should it matter anyway? At least he had come for her, he'd actually bothered to show up. Possibly, just possibly, this was some extremely noble and courageous stratagem on his part – he was staying behind to hold them off, give her a chance to get away. *Yes, indeed; and be sure to keep your head down, or those low-flying pigs'll crash into the back of your neck.*

Here, in the dark, it was next to impossible to keep track of time or distance, particularly if your mind was on other things. One thing was certain, though; all the many times she'd tried running away on her own, she'd never got this far, and presumably the damn tunnel was going somewhere. The more distance she put between Valhalla and herself, the better it had to be. It was a long time now since she'd stopped hearing Dad's voice or the sound of any footsteps other than her own; all right, she thought, maybe he was an uncaring asshole who would rather talk on the phone to some jerk god than his own daughter, but he'd somehow managed to get the job done where she'd repeatedly failed. In the end wasn't that what counted, rather than the merely superficial expressions

of affection that could be faked as easily as, say, he faked all
that deep, heartfelt concern he was spewing down the line to
his pain-in-the-ass client? How many people could honestly
say that they had dads who could rescue them from the land
of the dead?

(Yes, there was always that, the feeling of being special that
he'd given her, right from her earliest memories. She'd never
understood it, of course, because children accept weird things
as normal, they don't ask, *Say, Dad, who was that strange guy
and why did he leave burn marks on the carpet everywhere he
walked? And why did he go out the window instead of the door,
and how come his dog's got three heads and Spot's only got one?*
But slowly, subliminally, she'd come to perceive the difference, though never seeing enough of it at any one time to
prompt her to comment or question; it had only ever been
small things, such as the fact that while all the other kids at
school tried to wait up on Christmas Eve for a glimpse of
Santa, in her house they all hid in the cellar with the door
bolted until they were absolutely certain he'd gone . . .)

Carol stopped. She could hear voices.

No, just one voice, dead ahead of her, round the next
corner—

'So she's got a major problem with how you earn your
living. So what? What're you gonna do, Hades my friend,
you're gonna throw up a career most guys in the business
would die for, just because some damn veggie tree-hugging
bimbo—'

She stopped dead in her tracks and listened. No footsteps;
not now that she was standing still. Slowly and carefully she
walked forward, taking care not to make a sound (she'd
always been good at that, ever since she was a little kid and
they'd played those creeping-up-on-Daddy games) until she
came round a sharp bend in the tunnel—

'You,' she said.

Odin smiled at her.

'Hades, my man,' he said, 'I gotta go. It's been great, speak to you soon. Bye.' He flipped back the mouthpiece, tapped back the aerial and put the phone back inside his jacket. 'Hello,' he said.

'It was you,' said Carol. 'Not him.'

Odin nodded. 'It's a wise child that knows her own father,' he said. 'Don't bother thanking me, by the way, it's all part of the service. You know, your heart's desire, what you really, really want most of all in the whole wide world.'

Carol glowered at him as if she was trying to melt him down to his socks with one ferocious glare. 'What the hell's that meant to mean?' she said.

'Simple.' Odin sat down on the floor and leaned his back against the tunnel wall. 'You wanted him to come, so I made it happen for you. Of course it wasn't the real Lin Kortright, but that doesn't matter.'

'What? You bastard, of course it matters. All that shit you just put me through—'

'I repeat,' Odin said, smiling sweetly. 'It wasn't the real Lin Kortright. I just took the version of Lin Kortright you keep in your head; a nicely defined, thoroughly realised character, but that isn't your father. That's Lin Kortright, Sacrificial Asshole; the thing you've created to take all the blame for you having made such an utter fuck-up of your life.'

Carol opened her mouth to say something, but she was all out of words, except for *bastard*, and she'd said that once already. She sat down too.

'No hurry,' Odin said. 'We can sit here as long as you like; after all, this is your Valhalla. But it's warmer back at the hall and the seats are a bit comfier. Not much, but a bit. Will you call the strike off now, please? It's actually causing me far less hassle than you think, but I have a tidy mind.'

'Screw you,' Carol said.

Odin sighed. 'I do hope that's just a figure of speech,' he said, 'because the charter says *Your every wish fulfilled*, but there are limits. Do you know why you're here, Carol? In Valhalla, I mean?'

Carol shrugged. 'I assume it's some kind of punishment,' she said. 'Like, I've led this truly bad life, all fucked up the way you just said, and this is to teach me a lesson or something. Is that it?'

Odin shook his head. 'That's not how it works,' he said. 'No punishment; after all, what exactly did you do wrong? You never got on particularly well with your father. Instead of going after a career, you got a job as a cocktail waitress. In spite of everything, you still had a space inside your head reserved for dreams. Excuse me if I'm being dense here, but where's the sin in any of that?'

Carol shook her head. 'All right,' she said. 'So if I didn't do anything wrong, why am I getting all this shit now?'

Odin smiled sadly. 'Because this is Valhalla,' he said. 'This is where you went when you died, to the afterlife you designed for yourself with such care and attention to detail. That's what an afterlife is, you see; it's your life, transferred from the small screen to the big screen – bigger budget, better special effects, same general idea.' He shook his head and stood up. 'Don't know about you,' he said, 'but I'm getting cold. I think I'll be heading back now. You come on when you're good and ready.'

He walked away down the tunnel, leaving her alone.

'I want to join the SAS,' said the voice.

The recruiting officer closed his newspaper and looked round the room. There didn't seem to be anybody there.

'I said,' repeated the voice, impatiently, 'I want to join the SAS. Bloody well wake up and give me the forms.'

There was something about the voice that commanded obedience. Slowly and methodically, the recruiting officer scanned the room. As an afterthought, when he'd found nothing in any of the places you'd expect, he looked in the shadowy overhang of the desk.

'Was that you?' he asked.

'Yes,' the very small person replied.

'Sorry, I didn't see you there.' The very small person scowled at him with such utter ferocity that he hurried back to his side of the desk. 'What was it you just said?'

The very small person breathed out through his nose. 'Look,' he said, 'obviously there's been a mistake. On the door it says Army Careers Office, but apparently you forgot to take it down when you took over the lease. I'd see to that if I were you.'

'No, really, that's what we are.'

'You sure about that?'

'Oh yes, definitely.'

'Well,' said the very small person, 'thank God we've got that sorted. Now then, let's see those forms.'

'Sorry, what forms?'

'The forms I need to fill in so I can join the SAS,' replied the very small person, and the sound of patience haemorrhaging out through his ears was distinctly audible. 'Come on, I know all about you people, can't do anything without filling out half a tree's worth of bits of paper. The sooner we make a start, the sooner I can get on to basic training.'

By standing on tiptoe, the recruiting officer could see down just far enough to make out the very small person's face. 'You want to join the SAS?' he said.

'That's right.'

'*You* want to join . . . ?'

There was a blur of movement, and before the recruiting officer had time to react in any way, the small person was standing on the desk with his hands full of the recruiting officer's collar. 'Yeah,' he said softly. 'Quick off the mark, aren't you?'

Frozen, like a rabbit caught in headlights, the recruiting officer stared blankly at the face that was almost touching his own. A scraggy, wizened-looking kid of no more than seventeen, but with the deep, hectoring voice of a sergeant major and the eyes of a barracuda. He'd have been profoundly intimidating if only he'd been eighteen inches taller.

'No,' the recruiting officer said, grabbing the kid's wrists firmly and pulling them away from his shirt. 'Now get down off my desk and bugger off.'

The barracuda eyes narrowed. 'What do you mean, "no"?'

'You don't understand "no"? Look it up, it's in the dictionary just after *nitrous* and *nix*. Now get out of my office. If you're still here in thirty seconds, I'll feed you to my daughter's hamster.'

'Why can't I join the SAS?' the kid demanded. 'Come on. One good reason.'

The recruiting officer smiled. 'All right,' he said. 'For starters, *nobody* just joins the SAS; you get selected after years of outstanding service, *if* you're really lucky *and* there happens to be a vacancy. Second, you're too young to join the regular army at all. But mostly,' he added, suddenly catching hold of the very small person with one hand, lifting him off the desk-top and throwing him across the room so that he bounced off the opposite wall and fell neatly and precisely into the wastepaper basket, 'because you're too – fucking – *small*. Does that go any way towards answering your question?'

'Too small?'

'Much too small. If you stood on a ladder you'd still be too small. If the country was suddenly invaded by field mice and we needed crack troops to crawl down mouse holes and slog it out hand-to-paw in underground tunnels you'd still be too small. You got that?' he said. 'Titch?' he added.

'All right,' said Attila. 'You've made your point. Now help me out of this damn bin.'

'Just so long as we understand each other,' the recruiting officer said, and he crossed the room and held out a hand to haul Attila up. When he was safely out again, Attila thanked the officer politely, twisted his arm effortlessly behind his

back and, using his own body mass, double-back-somer-
saulted him over his desk, leaving him squatting among the
shattered ruins of his chair.

'Thank you for explaining so clearly,' Attila said. 'I'll know
better next time.'

He stomped out of the recruiting office, reflecting bitterly
as he did so on the way this new life of his was being organ-
ised. Adolescence had swooped down on him like a seagull on
a half-eaten sandwich; he'd gone to bed eleven and woken up
seventeen, but without growing as much as a centimetre.
Since he'd been an undersized runt of an eleven-year-old,
this meant he had his work cut out just to avoid being trodden
on in the street; his chances of picking up where he'd left off
as the Scourge of God and unstoppable conqueror of the
entire world were now, as Odin had gleefully pointed out,
about the only thing on Earth smaller than he was. Yet the
urge to battle and prevail, to fly at the throats of his enemies
and never let go, was if anything stronger than it had been
back in the endless remembered summer of the fifth century
AD.

Flying at the ankles of his enemies didn't have quite the
same ring, somehow; neither did coming down like a Skye
terrier on the fold, or being the barbarian horde at the cat flap
of Rome. Trying to even the score by learning the latest
advanced combat skills and dirty tricks from the lads down at
Hereford might have helped a bit; if he was realistic, though,
he doubted it'd ever have made a significant difference. It was
all very well talking bravely about having the indomitable will
of a giant, but without a few more inches and pounds to back
it up, he might just as well try and intimidate the moon,
because the only way he was going to participate in the sack of
great cities was if some kind person gave him a lift on their
keychain.

He trudged disconsolately back down the High Street, his
by now highly developed navigational instincts keeping him

from getting shoved off the pavement and down between the bars of drain-covers. *Tall bastards*, he thought savagely. *Can't join 'em, can't beat 'em. I'd pack it in and give up if only I knew how it was done.*

'Attila?'

He stopped dead in his tracks, then turned round slowly. 'Joanie?'

The short, tubby little girl who'd spoken his name nodded and beamed at him. 'It is you, isn't it?' she said. 'Completely different body, but I'd know that brooding snarl anywhere. How on earth did you get here?'

'I could ask you the same thing,' he replied. 'Shouldn't you be up in the auditorium, watching the nice paint?'

Joan of Arc's eyes sparkled at him from under the little girl's thick eyebrows. 'I was,' she said. 'I was sitting there quite happily, keeping an eye on this little patch about the size of a saucer that I was sure was just about to reach that sort of gooey stage, you know what I mean – anyway, there I was, when all of a sudden I heard—'

'Don't tell me,' Attila interrupted. 'Voices. The same ones, or different?'

'Oh, the same ones, definitely,' Joan of Arc said firmly. 'At least, those are the only ones I ever listen to. *Arise*, they kept saying—'

'The only ones you ever . . . You mean there's, like, *lots*?'

'Dozens and dozens and dozens,' Joan confirmed. 'I'm only just starting to tell 'em apart; well, there's the police-car radio frequency, and Radio Belgrade, and a couple of Australian soap operas, they're quite easy to identify, and I'm pretty sure I've worked out who the funny little man is who keeps talking to me about hamburgers and there's a difference I'll enjoy.'

'You hear the voice of Ronald McDonald inside your mind?'

'All the time. Actually, he confuses me sometimes. I

remember once, we were besieging this castle in Normandy and nobody could understand why I kept ordering the artillerymen to bombard the walls with sesame seeds and dill pickle. Still, he's a bit more lively than the speaking clock.'

Attila nodded dumbly. 'Those aren't the ones that say *Arise*, I take it.'

'Oh no. Those are the angels, telling me to drive the English out of Provence. Talking of which, it's just as well I'm back, because . . .'

'I know,' Attila said, uttering up a silent prayer for the safety of Peter Mayle. 'But anyway, you heard the voices while you were watching the nice paint. Then what happened?'

Joan shrugged. 'I arose, of course; and, well, here I am. The trouble is,' she said, with a frown, 'people just don't seem to want to listen the way they used to. I mean, what's the big difference? I'm still me.'

Attila grimaced. 'Huh,' he said. 'So am I.'

'No, you aren't, silly, you're Attila the Hun.'

'Me, I meant to say, I'm still *me*. But do they listen? Do they follow me with their quivers on their back and their banners streaming in the wind? Do they buggery. Nobody wants to know. I tell you, I'm just about ready to give it away and try to find a nice, cosy little life somewhere being normal.'

Joan stared at him wide-eyed. 'But you can't do that,' she said, 'it'd be *wrong*. It'd be betraying your special gifts. It'd be like—' She thought for a moment. 'Well, it'd be just like me not taking any notice of my voices,' she declared. 'And I could never ever do that.'

Attila raised an eyebrow. 'You just said you did,' he queried. 'All the time, in fact.'

'My *angel* voices,' Joan explained patiently. 'My manifest destiny voices. I—' She broke off. 'Just a second,' she said, and her eyes rolled back in her head so far that Attila was sure she must be trying to read the label on the neck of her cardigan. 'Sorry,' she went on, 'that was them.'

'What, the angels?' Attila asked. She nodded. 'What did they say?'

'"We'll be right back after the break,"' Joan recited. 'I never did understand why they say that. It's always just before they urge me to go out and buy Fairy Liquid.'

Attila bit his lip. 'And do you?' he said.

'Oh yes. Look.' She held out her arms proudly. 'Hands that do dishes are as soft as my face. Talking of which, did you happen to notice a Tesco's near here? It's always cheaper in Tesco's.'

Attila thought for a moment. 'Back that way about a hundred and fifty yards. I'll come with you if you like.'

'Thanks,' Joan said, smiling prettily. 'I'd like that. So what have you been up to, then?'

Attila scowled. 'Growing up, mostly. Mug's game, if you ask me. What human life really needs is a big Fast Forward button to get you through the ads and previews. Excuse me if this sounds personal, but how in God's name did you manage to buy Fairy Liquid before it was actually invented?'

Joan gave him a soulful look. 'Faith finds a way, Attila,' she said. 'Faith always finds a way. Ooh look, here we are. Hang on while I get a trolley. If you like, you can ride in the little wire seat.'

A quarter of an hour later, as they emerged from the supermarket with a trolley overflowing with Fairy Liquid bottles, Attila asked, 'What are you going to do with all this stuff? We've got enough of it to turn the Atlantic Ocean into one big bubble bath.'

Joan of Arc bit her lip. 'That's a tricky one,' she said. 'The voices just say, *Buy mild, green Fairy Liquid,* and that's as far as they go. So usually I just find somewhere quiet and out of the way, dig a hole and bury it. It's in plastic bottles, so the wet can't get into it. One of these days I expect they'll tell me what I'm meant to do with it, and then I can dig it all up again.'

'I see. When the sacred soil of France has been purged of the defiling English, presumably. Though if it were me, for getting English stains off soil, I'd use something like Persil or Ariel rather than Fairy Liquid.'

'Oh, I buy those too,' Joan of Arc said cheerfully.

They lugged the trolley through the town centre and halfway round the ring road to the site of the new business park; there were always lots of deep holes and trenches on building sites, Joan explained, deep enough to stash a whole day's combined purchases. 'I always like to get there early,' she added, 'as soon as possible after the men have finished working, so as to get to the still-wet concrete before the mobsters do. You've no idea how frustrating it is to scoop out a trench in a bed of wet concrete, only to find someone's arms or legs sticking up out of it.'

'Some people have no consideration,' Attila agreed. 'So, apart from all this shopping and the stuff about the English, what else do the voices tell you? Anything about – oh, just to take an example at random – anything about how to get out of bodies?'

'Get out of bodies?'

'Yes, you know the sort of thing. Suppose I was trapped in a body I really didn't like and I wanted to hop out of it and find a more suitable one. Any hints or tips?'

Joan thought for a moment, then shook her head. 'I get Delia Smith sometimes,' she said, 'and once or twice I've had the cricket commentary, but nothing like what you're talking about. Sorry.'

'I don't think the cricket commentary'd be much help,' Attila replied sadly. 'They'd be able to tell me the last time it was done in a Test match, but not the actual technique for doing it. No, I need something a bit more practical and down-to-earth if I'm ever going to find a way of getting out of this *thing* I'm stuck in and back into something a bit more comfortable and me.'

'How about death?' Joan suggested.

'What did you just say?'

'I said,' Joan repeated, 'how about death? Death in battle, of course; some ghastly illness or being run over by a milk float wouldn't do you much good. But if you get killed in battle, or fighting at any rate, I don't think it has to be in an actual war, surely you'd find yourself back in the auditorium looking at the nice paint, and you could take it from there.'

Attila considered that. 'At least I'd be back where I started,' he said. 'Yes, that'd be all right. I could have a rest for a few hundred years, get my breath back and keep an eye on how the nice paint's coming along—'

'Must be nearly dry by now,' Joan speculated.

'Any minute now, I should imagine. Anyway, when I'm good and ready, I could break out again, only this time I'll make absolutely sure they don't try marooning me in some kid's body. After all, I'd know what to expect.'

'Quite. You know, that's not a bad plan. I might have a go at it myself. I'm getting nowhere fast, trying to get my message across around here.'

Attila nodded. 'Being in England must make it harder, for a start,' he agreed.

'Well, yes, it does rather. Go around urging people to drive the accursed English out of Sheffield and they just look at you.'

'All right,' Attila said, looking round the deserted building site. 'How does this grab you? We have a fight and kill each other, then we both go to Valhalla together. Saves dragging anybody else in.'

Joan nodded her head. 'Valid point,' she said. 'After all, if I picked a fight with a stranger I might make a mistake and kill him instead, and then wouldn't I feel silly.'

'Eliminate the variables, that's what I always say,' Attila agreed. 'Any preferences about what we fight with?'

Joan picked up a plasterer's hawk and let it fall. 'I wouldn't say we're exactly spoilt for choice,' she said. 'There's bricks, and my Fairy Liquid bottles – I suppose we could empty out a couple of those, fill them up with quick-drying cement; you'd have a couple of short, heavy bludgeons. Basically, though, it's just variations of the blunt objects theme; and,' she added, 'to tell you the truth, I can't say I care for the thought terribly much.'

'Crude,' Attila agreed. 'Messy.'

'No finesse. And, no offence, you'd have to stand on a ladder or something before you could reach any bit of me you could land a fatal blow on. All a bit hit-and-miss, really.'

Attila rubbed his beardless chin. 'I know,' he said. 'If we shinned up that scaffolding over there and had a fight on that platform and fell off—'

'We'd break our necks,' Joan exclaimed joyfully. 'Now that *is* a good idea.'

'Have to be careful, though. If we don't fall just right, we might survive.'

'Eeek.'

'Precisely.'

The scaffolding was rickety, to say the least, and Attila had to force himself to mount the first rung of the ladder that led to the top—

'Problem?' Joan called down.

'I'm stuck,' Attila replied, embarrassed.

'In what way stuck?'

'I can't reach the next rung.'

That was one of the things he liked about Joanie; either she didn't laugh at all or she kept it quiet so you didn't hear her. 'There's a bucket on a rope at the top,' she said. 'When I get up there I'll lower it down and haul you up, okay?'

'Thanks, Joanie, you're a pal.'

'Hey, what are friends for?'

The significance of that remark hit Attila like a meteorite the size of Port Talbot; because his usual answer to that question had always been 'Target practice?', accompanied by a cynical sneer. In other words, he'd never had a friend, in roughly the same way and for more or less the same reason that hammerhead sharks have difficulty finding a good dentist. He'd had a father (King Ruga, murdered in AD 434) and an elder brother (King Bleda, put to death in AD 443; in the Hunnish royal family, being king was a hereditary illness and invariably fatal) and a pet wolf called Deathfang (died after snatching a sausage marinaded in belladonna from Attila's plate just as he was about to bite into it, AD 444) and as far as warm, close relationships went, that was about it. Suddenly, after all this time, to discover that he had a friend—

Did he have a friend? He wasn't sure, not having any comparative data. But friendship, according to something he'd read once on a scrap of papyrus clenched in the dead grip of a severed Roman hand he'd found in his left boot one morning after a rather rowdy party, was one of the great pleasures of life, one of the things that made our stay on Earth worthwhile. A bit daft, surely, to quit a life that apparently contained it before giving it a whirl and seeing if it lived up to the extravagant claims on the packet.

'Hey,' he called out, looking up just as the bucket whizzed down and hit him on the head. 'What did you just say?'

'I said, "Look out, here comes the bucket."'

'No, before that.'

'I said, "What are friends for?"'

Attila took a deep breath. 'Target practice,' he said. This time it didn't sound right, somehow. Nevertheless, Joanie laughed.

'That's a good one,' she said. 'I'll remember that one. Provided having my brains splattered doesn't garble my memory, of course.'

'You liked my joke?' Attila asked.

'Yeah, not bad. Well, it's better than a lot of the ones I hear.'

'Don't tell me,' Attila said. 'You hear reruns of *The Two Ronnies* in your head sometimes.'

'Close,' Joanie replied. 'Actually, it's *George and Mildred*.'

'Dear God. I can see why suicide holds such a magnetic attraction for you.'

Not knowing quite what to do, Attila clambered into the bucket and gripped the sides tight with both hands. 'Careful!' he yelled, as it lurched alarmingly and left the ground.

'It's all right, I've got you,' Joanie called back. 'I won't let you fall.'

There was something in her tone of voice that reassured him completely. *Trust*, Attila realised, *I'm trusting someone. Two new experiences in one day. This is remarkable. Admittedly, I'm putting my life in the hands of someone who thinks TV commercials are the voice of God, but everybody's got to start somewhere.* 'That's okay,' he shouted. 'Steady as he goes.' *And she laughed at my joke without having to be threatened with being pulled apart by wild horses first*, he recalled. *Three new experiences.*

'There we are,' Joanie called out, hauling the bucket up to her level and tying off the rope while she helped Attila out of the basket. 'That wasn't so bad, was it?'

'No,' Attila admitted. 'Still, I'm glad I don't have to go back down again that way. It was a bit scary.'

'You thought so?' Joanie grinned. 'Me too. I'd never admit this to anyone, but I'm terrified of heights.'

Attila looked at her. 'You just admitted it to me,' he said.

'Did I? Oh, well, I suppose I did. But that's different. I mean, you're . . .'

'Yes?'

'Well.' Joanie's face flushed slightly pink, putting Attila in mind of the waters of the river Arno ten minutes after he'd stained them red with the blood of countless slaughtered Romans. 'It's just different, that's all. You see, I feel I can tell *you* things, because—'

'Yes?'

'Oh, just because, that's all. There's no need to make a big thing about it.'

He looked at her. *Maybe she's never had a friend before, either,* he considered. In fact, it was more than likely. Virgin warriors whose heads reverberate with the sound of invisible voices telling them how to get their tough whites looking like new even without the boil wash probably have as much difficulty forming meaningful long-term relationships as, say, Scourges of God. Shared interests and common experiences, the raw materials from which compatibility is formed; it was only to be expected that someone like himself, a man out of the ordinary, a man in a hundred million, should have difficulty finding someone who shared those interests and experiences, but now that he had found such a person—

(He looked at her out of the corner of his eye.)

—who also, by some extraordinary fluke fall of the dice, was a sensible height instead of being just another Tall Bastard, with birds nesting in her ears and snow on the top of her head all year round; was that Fate trying to tell him something?

'Joanie,' he said awkwardly.

'Yes?' she replied, not looking at him.

'Maybe—' It wasn't going to come easily, he knew that. He'd far rather stand off single-handedly against a hundred heavy infantrymen of the Fifteenth legion, with one hand tied behind his back and nothing to defend himself with but a wilted leek; he didn't, however, have that option. 'Maybe,' Attila the Hun said shyly, 'we oughtn't to fall off this tower. I mean, not just yet.'

'No?'

'No. Not until we've had a chance to— well, get to know each other a bit better.'

She looked up into his eyes. 'Oh, Attila,' she said, in a tone of voice that made him want to throw up, but in the nicest possible way. 'I think so too.'

'Gosh. You do?'

'Yes, I do.'

'Really?'

'Really.'

'*Really* really?'

'Really really.'

'Oh, Joanie!'

'Oh, Att!'

Whereupon, of course, they fell into each other's arms and embraced passionately; terribly sweet and heartwarming, but incredibly reckless on the top of a rickety scaffolding tower a very long way up from the ground—

'Oh, Att,' Joanie whispered. 'I do feel funny. It's as if the whole world's swaying backwards and forwards.'

'Isn't that wonderful? That's just how I feel too.'

'Oh, Att!'

'Oh, Jo—'

Thirty-two feet per second per second, straight down on to a stack of breeze-blocks.

CHAPTER TWELVE

'What do you mean,' Howard asked, 'the last woman in the world?'

Lisa From Internal Audit shrugged her broad shoulders. 'See any others, can you? In fact, have you seen a single one apart from me the whole time you've been here? Well?'

Not far away a machine-gun opened up, pounding the air with sound waves like a boxer jabbing a punchbag. Howard waited patiently for the noise to stop. 'No,' he replied, 'now you mention it, I don't think I have. But I wouldn't expect to, not in the middle of a battle.'

'Really? You're saying girls can't fight, are you? You want to try that out?'

Since Lisa From Internal Audit looked like she could have thrown the discus for East Germany back in the good old days before the Wall came tumbling down, Howard side-stepped that one. 'All right,' he said, dodging without even having to look as a fist-sized chunk of shrapnel whizzed past. 'Even if you really are the last woman in the world, how'd you *know* that? I mean, have you actually been round looking, or—?'

'Get down!'

The shell-burst reduced the building they'd been standing in front of to a cloud of brick dust, and left a hole you could have converted into a yachting marina (just add water). 'Thank you,' Howard said, scrambling out of the foxhole she'd shoved him into. 'You saved my life.'

'My pleasure,' replied Lisa From Internal Audit, smirking. 'Though there isn't really much point, is there?'

'Excuse me?'

'Not,' Lisa explained, standing up and picking inch-long slivers of broken glass out of her hair, 'when you're bound to get killed sooner or later today. I mean, it's a nice thought, but why bother? A snowman in Africa's got a better chance of getting life insurance than you have, don't you think?'

'Oh,' Howard replied. 'Well, it's the thought that counts, I suppose. All right, if it's so damn futile, why did you bother? You could have laddered a stocking, leaping around like that.'

Lisa shrugged. 'Instinct, I s'pose. I mean, it's human nature, isn't it? Protecting small, helpless creatures who aren't fit to take care of themselves.'

'Thank you so much. Next time, don't bother.'

'Oh, don't be like that,' Lisa said cheerfully. 'You got saved, didn't you? What have you got to complain about?'

(That was another thing about Lisa From Internal Audit that had always got up his nose; her habit of talking in rhetorical questions. Five minutes chatting with her was like taking an exam.)

'Sorry,' Howard said, nevertheless. 'And I was being careless back there. Honestly, after all the time I've been here you'd have thought I'd be able to hear incoming shells.'

She smiled at him. 'Most of the time you do seem to manage,' she said graciously. 'Maybe you got distracted. I mean, coming across an old friend in the middle of all this lot; wouldn't you say that was enough to take anybody's mind off what they're doing?'

There was something in the way she said that, taken together with the look in her eyes, that made Howard start to walk slowly backwards. But not for long—

'Careful!' This time, she floored him with a classic rugby tackle. 'Landmines,' she explained, scrambling up and sitting on his chest.

'Oh.'

'You don't believe me, do you?' She picked up a chunk of brick and lobbed it through the air. It landed about twelve yards away and vanished in a ball of orange fire and dust. 'They're only little ones, but still, big enough to spoil your appetite, wouldn't you say?'

Howard tried to shift a little, but he couldn't move. 'Thanks again,' he said. 'Twice in five minutes, and I thought you said there wasn't any point.'

Lisa pulled a face. 'Well, is there?' she said.

'Maybe there is,' Howard said. 'In the meantime, however, I'd be grateful if you could see your way clear to getting off me.'

Lisa pouted. 'Why? Going somewhere, are you? Not so long ago, you'd have given anything—'

Another shell exploded nearby and the shock wave sent her spinning, saving Howard from a lethal dose of cringing. 'Are you all right?' he called out half-heartedly.

'Fine,' she replied, standing up and brushing plaster dust off her skirt. 'Bright as a button. Well, actually I've chipped a nail, but not to worry.' She bounded back towards him, but thanks to his battle-sharpened reflexes he was able to get to his feet before she reached him. 'You're going to be a full-time job, I can see that,' she said.

'Full-time—' Howard's jaw dropped. 'Are you trying to say you're here as a— well, some sort of bodyguard?'

She nodded. 'I'd have preferred guardian angel, but body-guard'll do. Yes, why? Don't you want your body guarded?'

Howard backed away again. 'Like you were just saying,' he

said, 'there doesn't seem to be much point . . .' He didn't get to finish the sentence, because he backed into a shell crater and slid down the inside of the rim on his face.

'Hang on, I'll soon have you out of there.'

'No, no, really,' Howard assured her. 'I'm fine.'

'Up to your neck in mud in a bomb crater?'

'I like it here,' Howard said firmly. 'And it's, um, good cover.'

'That's true,' Lisa said. 'Hold on, I'll join you.' Whereupon she vaulted down after him, spraying him with more mud. 'Actually,' she went on, 'the word you're looking for is Valkyrie.'

'Is it?'

'Yes. Not bodyguard.' She crawled through the mud on her knees and leaned heavily on his shoulder. 'Another word for Valkyrie,' she said, 'is wish-maiden. You know, as in your dearest wish. Or heart's desire.'

'Is that so?' There was nowhere to back to in the bomb crater. 'Look, it's very kind of you, but shouldn't you be getting back to work before Mr Gibson sees you've gone?'

'I don't work there any more. Never liked it anyway.'

'Ah. Well, in that case, you really ought to be getting home. After all—' He ransacked his brain for the name of her evil, psychotic husband. 'Won't Vern be worried if you aren't there?'

'I've left him,' she replied crisply. 'Told him I'd got a better offer.'

For some reason, the thought of a slighted Vern with a big knife was infinitely more scary than any form of death he'd experienced in Valhalla; and the fact that he was now a self-taught but nonetheless highly proficient expert in marksmanship, knife-fighting and unarmed combat didn't seem the slightest bit relevant. Bullets and bombs might break his bones or even vaporise him completely, but Vern could do him a nasty injury. 'Wasn't that a bit sudden?' he suggested. 'I always thought you two got on like a house on fire.'

She shook her head. 'It was over years ago really,' she said. 'We only stayed together out of habit. And when this job came along—'

'As a Valkyrie, you mean?'

'That's right. I thought, being a Valkyrie, it's the sort of job where I'd have space to grow, you know, as a person. Besides, it was a chance for us to get to know each other better.'

'Really? Why would you want to do that?'

She laughed. 'Oh come on,' she said. 'Don't make me spell it out for you. Anybody whose idea of paradise is fighting all day, bashing people's faces in and blowing stuff up with bombs; obviously my kind of guy. Honestly, if only I'd known earlier, we wouldn't have had to wait so long before getting together.'

Wish-maiden, huh? How about if I wished she'd go away? Another shell ripped up an entire block of flats, showering them with fist-sized chunks of fast-flying plaster. Which was odd; the day's teatime bombardment wasn't due to start for at least another hour. This should have been the scheduled maintenance break, when whoever it was who did the actual bombing and shelling knocked off work for a breather and let the engineers crawl about with their oil cans and gauges. Could it be that his new bodyguard was actually attracting an increased level of shelling and bombing?

'Now look,' he said, as she put a hand on his shoulder. 'I really don't think this is the time or the place, they'll be starting the late-afternoon shift soon, which means there'll be bombs going off all round here.'

'We'd better stay put here, then.' Now the other hand. Grip like a vice.

'And also,' he said, 'according to a bloke I killed earlier, it's going to piss down with rain sometime around now. I really think I ought to be getting along.'

She shook her head. 'Not if there's going to be heavy shelling,' she said firmly, undoing the top button of his battle-dress. 'Bodyguard's orders.'

A part of his mind was saying, *Come on, is this really worse than getting blown to bits by three-inch mortars?* But the reply had to be 'Yes', because still, even after all this time (how much time? He had no idea), he couldn't quite believe that all the killing and getting killed was really real, whereas they didn't get any more real than Lisa From Internal Audit. Especially those piercing blue eyes; find a way of focusing them down to a tight beam and you could use them to cut solid chrome.

'Lisa . . .' She was trying to bite his ear. In the middle of a battle? Suddenly he wasn't convinced. 'No, stop that, I want to ask you something.'

'Well?'

'How did you get here?'

She scowled. 'Does it matter?' she said. 'I'm here now.'

'How did you get here?'

She sighed, let go of him, shook herself like a wet dog and turned into Odin. Howard jumped about six feet in the air; apart from that, he handled it remarkably well.

'I'll say this for you,' Odin said, straightening his tie. 'You're not as hopeless and pathetic as I thought you were. Or possibly you're more hopeless and pathetic than I could ever hope to imagine. Come on, own up. What put you off? Did you suspect all along that it couldn't possibly be true, or are you just terrified of girls?'

'The first one,' Howard said. 'Well, maybe a bit of both. What the hell was all that about?'

'Your heart's desire,' Odin replied. 'I refer you to that rich fantasy life you used to have when you were alive. Just as well it was rich, because it was the only thing even vaguely resembling a life you'd got. Wasn't it all fights to the death and steamy encounters with gorgeous women? And before you say anything, please bear in mind that I never ask a question I don't already know the answer to.'

Howard shrugged. 'All right,' he said, 'maybe once or twice

I might have wondered what it'd be like. I still say the punishment's a bit over the top.'

'Punishment?' Odin looked hurt. 'Who said anything about punishment? You only get punished if you do something wrong, surely. Do you think having fantasies about your female colleagues was wrong?'

Howard shook his head. 'I don't want to play word games,' he said. 'I think this must be punishment, because it's so horrible.'

'It'd be a neat way of doing it,' Odin agreed, 'punishing people for what they wish for by making their wishes come true. Maybe that's what Valhalla's for. Or maybe it's just a place you go to when you die. Personally I think it's the latter, but that's just my opinion. And I'm not even dead, so I'm hardly qualified to comment.'

'I should have known,' Howard said gloomily, looking away. 'I should have known when you caught those bullets in mid-air. So now what are you going to do?'

'This,' Odin replied. He snapped his fingers and vanished. A moment later, a bomb went off more or less exactly where he'd been standing, turning everything within a fifty-yard radius into fine white ash.

'Guys,' said Lin Kortright. 'Now just wait a doggone minute.'

The fifty or so Lin Kortrights who'd been listening to him audition for as long as he could remember started to mutter and hiss, as usual. One of them emptied his ashtray on the floor and aimed it, discus-fashion. It was, Kortright admitted, just the sort of thing he'd do if he was in their shoes. Which, of course, he was. Odd, that; he'd never really figured himself as a centipede.

'Whoa there, hold it,' he shouted. 'Guys, listen up. You gotta hear this, it's important.' They weren't listening. Well, they wouldn't, would they? Each and every one of them was him and they knew all his tricks and ploys, negotiating techniques, mind games, ways of unsettling an opponent while striking a deal; all his life, one thing had always been an unfailing source of comfort to Lin Kortright – the perfectly reasonable and justifiable belief that he could bullshit any life form composed of more than one cell. Now he had to face the unpleasant truth that the people out there were immune to anything he could throw at them—

(*Which explains why that sadistic creep Odin brought them here to decide whether I'm fit to be me; Jesus, what a nasty thing to do!*) Frantically, he thought, *If I were them (no, fuck it, if I weren't them, if they weren't me, whatever) what'd grab my attention? One thing and one thing only.*

'MONEY!' he said.

Fifty Lin Kortrights froze in the act of launching a variety of missiles.

'Money,' he repeated. 'So much money you just wouldn't believe. Plus,' he added, as inspiration lit up and kicked in, 'overall creative control, major awards and a percentage of the gross.' He'd got their attention; keeping it was going to be harder. 'And a chance to direct,' he added desperately. 'And executive-produce.'

A Kortright three rows back frowned thoughtfully. 'All of us?' he called out.

'You have my personal guarantee,' Lin Kortright replied. 'Trust me, you won't regret it.'

The fifty Kortrights gazed at him so hard that he could almost feel the flesh stripping off his bones. *Do I stare at people like that? I guess I must do. Man, I'm better than I thought.*

'Now you're starting to sound a bit more like Lin Kortright,' a Kortright said. 'Man, you sure took your own sweet time getting here; you wouldn't believe the bunch of deadheads and losers we've had in here auditioning to be you. Only make sure you aren't just stringing us along, wasting our time. Hey, I wouldn't want to be you if you are.'

'Tell us about the money, Lin,' said another.

Lin Kortright took a deep breath. 'There's this great deal,' he said. 'It's a multinational syndicate backed by Japanese corporate money – if I mention that Toshi Kawaguchi himself is on board, I trust I don't have to draw you a diagram – and they've developed this really cool thing called an anti-thanaton beam. It means you can, like, beam people backwards and forwards between life and death; and what does that immediately say to you, opportunities-wise? Yeah, obviously, tourism. Why wait till you're dead to enjoy luxurious twelve-star afterlives custom-created to meet your special needs and requirements? It's got the potential to be the biggest thing since *Star Trek*, and I got a slice of it; like, ten per cent if I can put together the right package.' He took a deep breath and prayed; who to, even he wasn't sure. 'Which is where you guys come in,' he added.

There was a brief silence.

'Come on, Lin, we know all this. We're you, remember?'

Lin Kortright shook his head. 'Not quite,' he replied. 'Because if you were really me – *this* me – and you'd just had this idea, you wouldn't be sitting here on your butts waiting for something to happen; you'd be out there pitching.' He grinned unpleasantly. 'And you surely wouldn't be sharing this incredible idea with a bunch of yourselves.'

The fifty Kortrights looked at each other. *He's back*, someone whispered.

'We know you, Lin,' said one of them. 'We know you're a bullshitter like there's never been. But we also know that, very occasionally, you do have the big idea. Hey, Lin, we trust you. We believe in you, even. Don't we, boys?'

The other forty-nine Kortrights nodded.

'Okay,' said Lin Kortright, 'here's the deal. We all go equal shares in this – hey, we're all Lin Kortrights together and there's gonna be enough to go round in any case – and in return, you help me get me – us – out of here. And Carol,' he added quickly. 'If she don't walk, the deal's off. Agreed?'

It took them five seconds to make up their minds. Five seconds can be a very long time.

'Deal,' said a Kortright.

'That's great,' Lin Kortright replied. 'And I know we aren't going to regret this. Okay, here's the idea. There's fifty-one of us, right?'

'We can count, thank you. Quit stalling and cut to the chase.'

'Fifty-one of us,' Kortright repeated. 'And there's one thing we now know about afterlives: if you happen to die in battle, you go to Valhalla and get what you've always wanted.'

'That's not true,' a Kortright interrupted. 'You died, you went to Valhalla. I don't remember us having this secret burning ambition to get up on a stage and pretend to be somebody else for money. And talking about money, where is it? If this was really the place where we got what we always wanted, this whole building would be stuffed so thick with rolls of thousand-dollar bills there'd be no room left for the air. I can't see no money, can you?'

Lin Kortright shook his head. 'You're missing the point,' he said. 'We aren't in it for the money. If you were the *real* Lin Kortright instead of some cheap Taiwanese copy, you'd have known that.' He smiled. 'Maybe I just had this voice at the back of my mind that kept nagging away, asking, *Who am I? What sort of guy, deep down, is Lin Kortright?* Well, I guess I finally got an answer to that, just like I'd always wanted.' He smiled thinly. 'Turns out Lin Kortright's a guy who thinks about nothing but deals and bullshit. Goes to show, guys; there's no crummier break than getting a straight answer to a simple question.'

The Kortright who'd raised the point waved his hand. 'Okay,' he said, 'I'll buy that for now. So there's fifty-one of us. So what?'

'Easy,' Lin Kortright said. 'Suppose you come to me and say you want a fortnight's vacation in Death, you want your afterlife like so – golden beaches, great surf, lots of hot chicks, cute boys in skintight rubber, whatever. I go away and I start wanting those things; wanting them real bad, like I really believe that was what I'd always longed for ever since I was a snot-nosed little kid. Then I pick a fight in a bar somewhere and get killed, and immediately there I am, in Valhalla, getting my heart's desire.'

'Like a tour guide?' a Kortright hazarded.

'You got it. Once I've gone to Valhalla and set up the afterlife according to the specifications, the customer beams in as well, has his vacation, beams out again. And me along with him, of course; all ready to start over again with the next customer. It's the ultimate in leisure experiences, and the joy of it is, once you've paid for the anti-thanaton emitter, each trip costs peanuts. Forget virtual reality, people; this is the future of luxury entertainment and leisure management, and we're in at the start; it's like being back in the nineteen-fifties and buying Honda shares at a buck for fifty.'

A soft buzz of conversation, like the sound of a million woodworms munching seasoned oak, filled the still air as the fifty Kortrights discussed the idea. It wasn't a lengthy discussion; fifty minds, as it were, with but a single thought.

'Okay, we're in,' said a Kortright who'd apparently emerged as spokesman. 'So what do we do now? First off, we've gotta get out of this place and make contact with the Kawaguchi people. You got any idea how we go about that?'

Kortright nodded. 'You all do what I tell you and it'll be fine, trust me,' he said.

'Trust you?' The spokesKortright snickered. 'Give me a break, man,' he said. 'I wouldn't trust you if you told me the sea is wet. I know you too well, remember. You're Lin Kortright.'

Kortright gave him a wounded look. 'Hey, pal,' he said, 'that was uncalled for. Hey, do you really think I'd lie to *myself*?'

'Why not?' The spokesKortright grinned like a piranha fish in a dentist's chair. 'Isn't that what you've done all your life?'

'This submarine,' Vinnie announced, 'is doomed.'

The guys in the chunky polo-neck sweaters stared at him and backed away, muttering in what was probably Russian. A pity; they'd been really nice to him, given him towels and hot potato soup and vodka, taken him to meet the captain (a great big cuddly teddy bear of a man with a beard so long and wide he'd never have to waste money on a duvet), shown him snapshots of their smiling wives and cute children . . .

'Doomed,' he repeated, enunciating clearly. 'You're all going to die. *I*'m not going to die, oh no, not me. *I* couldn't die if I soaked myself in gasoline, set light to myself and jumped off the Sears Tower into the reactor core of a nuclear power plant in the middle of meltdown. Dammit,' he added with a stifled sob. 'Hey, what are you guys staring at, anyhow? You never seen an immortal before?'

Cautiously, timidly, a submariner crept forward and cleared his throat nervously.

'Hello,' he said. 'I am speaking a small English.'

'You bet,' Vinnie replied with a disconcerting grin. 'And you wanna know something? Your English is very small, very small indeed, and it's never ever gonna get any better, not unless you're one hell of a quick study, 'cos any minute now you're going to die. Now then, what can I do you for?'

The submariner gazed at him out of eyes the size of soup bowls. 'We are to be dying?' he whispered. 'How is this to be?'

Vinnie shrugged wearily. 'Don't ask me,' he said. 'Could be any of a number of things. You could hit a submerged reef, or your engine blows up, or you spring a leak; hell, for all I know you could suddenly all go crazy and start killing each other. Does it matter? It's the being dead that counts, not how you get there. All you gotta do is die. Me, I've gotta figure a way of getting outa this goddamn underwater coffin.'

The submariner swallowed a couple of times, then retreated and conferred nervously with his fellows.

'Excuse,' he said. 'But if you are wanting to die, why will you be trying to escape?'

Vinnie laughed aloud. 'Because that's what I *do*, you poor fool,' he said. 'I escape from things. Shit, if I locked myself in the john right now and the sub blew up, I'd be thrown clear and float up to the surface in some kinda freak air bubble; but you know, that'd be so damn humiliating, bobbing up and down in the water in a Russian navy toilet with my pants round my knees . . . If I gotta keep surviving, then I might as well pretend to make an effort.'

Once again the submariner conferred with his colleagues. 'We are saying,' he pleaded, 'you are not to be talking like so; it is bad lucky.'

Vinnie shook his head. 'So sue me,' he said. 'And give my regards to Mr Jones. You'll be seeing him long before I do.'

The submariners shook their heads and went away, with deeply troubled faces. *Hell, I was just telling them what to expect*, Vinnie thought. *It was the least I could do.*

But an hour went by; then another one, and another one after that, and still the submarine showed no signs of hitting anything or getting blown up. Cruel, Vinnie couldn't help thinking, to toy with him like this, and not fair on the submarine guys either. Unless of course it was over; actually over, and the submarine *wasn't* going to sink or explode, and the next time he saw daylight it'd be through an open hatchway, as the submarine chugged into Archangel harbour, with crowds cheering and waving little flags . . .

Still nothing. No crash or groaning of horrendously over-stressed metal, just the ever-present subliminal vibration of the engines and the clank of boots on steel decking. Maybe it was over, then; in which case, what in Hell's name had it all been about? That was a scary thought, because it would imply, surely, that all those other guys, the ones in the plane and the ship and the helicopter, hadn't just been extras and eye-candy brought on to make the illusion convincing; they'd been real live (now ex-live) people who'd died while he'd gone on living. That thought made Vinnie feel very ill.

Ah c'mon; get on and sink, you bugger, before I go out of my mind. He could feel the tension nagging away at him, gnawing into him like bank charges sucking the blood out of a current account. Any more of this hanging about and there'd be only one thing he could possibly do; and he really didn't want to have to do it.

After four hours of sitting on his bunk staring at the bulkheads, he reached the point of no return. No more fooling around, no more mind games; obviously this time it was up to him. He swung his legs off the bunk, winced at the pins and needles in his left foot, and hobbled off down some sort of corridor towards the source of the engine noise.

How do you go about sinking a submarine? he asked himself. Somehow he'd got into his head the idea that there was a big hatch thing set into the hull, like a plug in a bathtub, and to sink the sub, all you had to do was pull the plug out and stand well back. But there was nothing of the kind to be seen; furthermore, the sub seemed to be pretty robustly put together, with steel plates and big rivets, nothing you could poke a finger through or puncture with a penknife blade. The engines might be a better way to go; chances were that if he wandered into the engine room and started turning handles and opening valves at random, sooner or later he'd connect with something lethal. Or maybe he'd stumble across the ship's armoury – it was a military vessel, after all, they'd be bound to have grenades and rockets and guns and stuff, something he could use to spring a big fat leak. Or what about the conning tower? If he opened that big lid thing, water'd come flooding in. Dammit, in every submarine movie he'd ever seen, the tricky part had been *not* sinking the frigging thing.

Nobody seemed to mind him wandering about; either they appeared not to notice him or they gave him cautious little smiles and waves, which was highly unnerving. Vinnie had never tried to murder anybody before, let alone a whole submarine crew who seemed for some reason to *like* him. It made the damn-fool games They were playing with him all the more thoughtless and cruel, and he made a solemn vow that one day, he'd make Them pay. All fine and splendid; but it wasn't getting the ship scuttled. Still no sign of anything obviously dangerous, not (being realistic) that he had any reason to believe he'd recognise it when he saw it. In fact, it was looking ominously like he was going to have to ask someone.

'Excuse me—' The utterly blank expression on the submariner's face reminded him: *these guys can't speak English.* Except for one, the guy he'd talked with earlier. Vinnie nodded his head positively. He'd search the ship (after all, it wasn't that big, so it shouldn't take long), find his interpreter and ask him how to go about committing acts of sabotage. And the sooner he made a start, the sooner he'd be able to accomplish his mission and get on to whatever it was he had to doom and then escape from next.

He found the small-English guy sitting hunched over some kind of instrument panel, staring into space and looking preoccupied. 'Hi,' he said. The small-English guy jumped in his seat, banged his knee of some projecting item of naval architecture, and stared at Vinnie in obvious apprehension.

'The ship?' he asked nervously. 'Is it that it sinks now?'

'No, dammit, that's the problem,' Vinnie replied. 'Which is why we need to talk. Just how do you sink one of these mothers? Hypothetically speaking, of course.'

The small-English guy stared at him and started shaking his head, like he was about to have a seizure or something. 'It's okay,' Vinnie said, trying to sound soothing and friendly; but the more soothing and friendly he tried to be, the more it seemed to freak the small-English guy out, until he made a horrified gurgling noise and jumped up, keeping the instrument console thing between Vinnie and himself.

'Look, this is crazy,' Vinnie said, still trying to appear relaxed and laid-back while circling predator-fashion round the console. 'Really, I'm not gonna hurt you; all I want to do is sabotage the goddamn ship. Now hold still, will you?'

He reached out. In retrospect, it was a mistake; he mistimed the grab and the small-English guy had plenty of time to avoid him and jump sideways, which he did. Unfortunately, he landed awkwardly, lost his footing and sat down on the console, causing red lights to flash and an alarm to go off. A computer voice started counting backwards in Russian, and the ship's PA system began making loud HOOP-HOOP noises. The small-English guy froze and stared at him in abject terror.

'Jeez,' Vinnie said, 'what's that goddamn racket? Can't you turn it off?'

The guy shook his head. 'Self-destruct,' he hissed. 'In two minute.'

'Huh? But—' *Yes. Well. Why fight it?* 'Never mind,' he said. 'So long, it was great meeting you guys. Thanks for the soup.' He turned and walked away, strolling, not running, towards the stairs that led to the bridge and the conning tower.

Ten minutes or so later, when his head burst out of the water like the first crocus of spring, he was still trying to work it out in his mind. No, he hadn't scuttled the ship, they'd done that themselves; but if he'd stayed where they'd put him and kept still and quiet, chances were the sub wouldn't have self-destructed. He opened his eyes and looked round, but he needn't have bothered. No survivors in little rubber boats, not even any wreckage or debris floating on the water. It had, of course, been a miracle that he'd got out alive, a freak concatenation of incredibly unlikely coincidences that he hadn't even bothered to take note of as they happened around him; he'd just assumed they'd be there, the way a surgeon expects the nurse to put the scalpel into his hand when he asks for it, and he hadn't been disappointed.

What next? Plane, ship, helicopter, submarine; it didn't leave much, unless it was a cycle that repeated itself endlessly, in which case the next rescue would presumably be another plane.

He looked up. No plane. No ship, for that matter, no helicopter, no submarine, not even a drifting log for him to cling to. *Come on, guys, whatever happened to continuity? Let's keep this gig slick. Bring on the next . . .*

Next to him, the sea suddenly and unexpectedly boiled. Startled, he trod water and tried to keep his eyes above the surface. Then something bobbed up out of the sea a few feet away.

'Ah, shit,' he complained, his voice heavy with disgust. 'No. No way. I am *not* getting in one of those buggers, and that's that, man, that's final. Hey, you just listen to me a goddamn minute here—'

If he said anything else, the noise of the wind and the sea blotted it out completely as the giant sperm whale that had just put its head above water opened its enormous jaws, swallowed Vinnie as if he were a dry roasted peanut, and dived again.

CHAPTER THIRTEEN

The strike was over, and the whole of the Valhalla campus echoed with the ring of steel on steel and bone, the gurgle of free-flowing mead, disjointed attempts at singing while profoundly drunk and the raucous melodies of Viking regurgitation—

(*Maybe*, Carol wondered, *this is also the Valhalla for mashed swede and macaroni; they get cooked, they get eaten, and by nightfall they're back again, ready to repeat the cycle—*)

—as if nothing had happened; which was fair enough, because very little had. The strike hadn't been broken as such, nor had there been any formal negotiated settlement. Instead, a day came when the Vikings had drifted back to their accustomed places and carried on.

'A horse once dead to be flogging . . .' one of them explained to Carol, who, for reasons of her own, no longer cared particularly much about the strike or anything to do with her surroundings. Nevertheless, enough of her residual personality remained to prompt her to argue the toss.

'But Odin's won,' she objected. 'You gave up, and he won. He screwed you.'

The Viking nodded in grudging acknowledgement. 'Of rats a bag is Odin, not to be being disputed. But nowhere at great velocity to be approaching is of futility the very essence.'

Carol shrugged. 'Whatever,' she said. 'It's up to you guys, basically. And if you can live – sorry, stay dead – with the fact that that jerk beat you—'

'With the smooth, occasionally a rough,' the Viking replied philosophically. 'And out of each other the shit to be beating to any extent, the injustices regardless, than nothing is better. Lo! To fighting I go. A time long it has been.'

Carol didn't reply and the Viking walked away, whistling out of tune and practising thrusts and parries with his sword. He looked happy enough, and that was ironic, since he was presumably just some kind of hallucination or hologram supplied with the scenario to make it seem more authentic. Maybe the unreal people were happy, but surely that wasn't the point. After all, you don't build a factory to give a secure, loving home to a bunch of machines.

'Feeling better now?'

'Where did you appear from?' Carol replied wearily. 'You've got this habit of suddenly being there which is really beginning to bug me.'

'Sorry,' Odin replied, without the slightest trace of remorse. 'Actually I'm everywhere at all times, it's all part of being a god. I'd have thought *you*'d have known that.'

Carol sighed. 'Don't start. And I don't believe you, either. I'll bet you there's all sorts of places you aren't.'

Odin shook his head. 'How I wish that was true,' he replied. 'But it isn't. Just think about that for a moment, will you? Have you any idea how big the universe is?'

'Oh please, spare me the Carl Sagan stuff.'

'No, really,' Odin said, with a degree of feeling that rather startled Carol. 'Think about it, just for a moment, before you walk away. Consider that it takes a particle of light two million years to go from the outer edge of this galaxy to the nearest point of the galaxy next door, and everything in between is empty. Nothing. Like Iowa, only worse. I'm out there. Dammit, I'm every bit as much out there as I am here. Ninety-nine-point-nine-nine-to-the-power-of-nine-nine-infinitely-recurring per cent of me hangs brooding in the interstellar void, nothing whatsoever to do, utterly cheesed off, while the remaining picopercent of me is here, rushed off my feet, hasn't even got time to stop for breakfast. That's what it's really like, being a god. No fun at all.'

Carol frowned. 'My heart bleeds,' she said. 'The rest of you should get a hobby or read a book or something, instead of taking it out on people like me who never did you any harm.'

'No sympathy, huh?'

'No sympathy. You need to get a grip of yourself, deal with it, the way we mortals have to deal with the thought of dying. Though,' she added venomously, 'if the rest of us knew *you* were here waiting for us, it'd certainly add a new dimension of terror to mortality.'

'Oh well,' Odin said, 'if you're just going to stand there being all hostile, then the hell with you.' He vanished, leaving nothing behind except a chocolate-bar wrapper and a very faint electromagnetic field. Carol sniffed disdainfully and walked away.

A few yards up the track, she came across two Vikings fighting. Neither of them was in good shape; blood was leaking out of both of them like oil from the crankcase of a Harley Davidson, and one of them looked like he'd been wagering his arms and legs in a Viking variant of strip poker and had just seen his opponent's full house while holding a pair of fours.

'Excuse me,' she said.

The somewhat dismembered Viking looked round at her, giving his opponent a chance to swing hard with his battleaxe and sever the poor fool's head from his neck. The head toppled forwards, bounced twice like a flabby beach ball and rolled up against Carol's foot.

'Sorry,' Carol said.

'Over spilt blood in crying no merit,' replied the head stoically. 'To be of assistance?'

'Nothing, really,' Carol said. 'I'm bored, is all.'

The head raised an eyebrow. 'To be bored?' it queried. 'In Valholl?'

'Yeah. Bored stiff. I mean, for God's sake, what is there to do around here?'

The Viking who still had his head on clicked his tongue. 'To be fighting, naturally,' he said.

'But I don't want to fight,' Carol objected. 'Sorry, but I don't go for all that macho-aggressive stuff. If I wanted to get hacked to death where I stand in the middle of a barren and inhospitable landscape, I'd go to LA.'

The Viking sniffed. 'Trying it you have been, to assume?' he asked.

'Well, no,' Carol replied. 'But what the hell, I haven't tried wasting away with diphtheria either, but I'm pretty sure I wouldn't enjoy it much.'

'To be trying,' the Viking said. 'Come! In haste! His weapons to be retrieving, whereupon at you to be having.'

'You mean, *I* fight *you*?' Carol shook her hair vigorously. 'Get real, will you? You're about ten times bigger than me and I'll bet you've been practising beating the shit out of people with swords and axes and stuff since you were in psychotics' pre-school.'

'Irrelevant,' the Viking said. 'In Valholl to be equal all warriors are.'

Carol scowled. 'Yeah, I heard that already. I thought that just meant we all get to vote at Residents' Association meetings.'

'In ability to be equal,' the Viking explained. 'This you are not knowing? For shame.'

Before Carol could reply, she heard a discreet cough at ankle level.

'To excuse,' said the head. 'To do and to see, things and people, with special reference to a dog hypothetical.'

'What? Oh, sorry.' Carol moved her feet to allow the head to roll past. 'Hey, mister. You forget something?'

'I believe not,' the head replied.

'Really? How about the rest of you?'

The head spun on the spot like a bowling ball at the end of its run. 'That you reminded me is good. Gratitude.'

Carol smiled. 'Don't tell me,' she said, 'you're so absent-minded you'd forget your own body if it wasn't usually sewn on.'

Once the head-and-body ensemble had cleared out of the way, Carol stooped down and looked at the magnificent garnet-encrusted hilt of the sword it had left lying on the ground. 'Just looking,' she pointed out, as the Viking reacted to her movement. 'So that's a sword, is it?'

'Verily.'

'Hmm.' Carol leaned a little closer. The hilt was surprisingly small. 'Mind if I just pick it up?' she asked. 'Without prejudice and all that crap?'

'My guest to be,' said the Viking politely.

It turned out to be even heavier than she'd expected, but the balance made up for most of it. There was an undoubted appeal about the thing, probably directly related to some sub-Freudian character defect ultimately caused by her lousy relationship with her schmuck of a father . . .

Yeah, it felt great. You could really damage something with one of these.

'Say,' she murmured to the Viking, her eyes still on the sword, 'how do you work these things? Is there a special knack to it, or do you just kind of lash out?'

'Of taste a matter.'

'Okay,' she said, and swung the sword in a gleaming arc,

until she felt an agonising judder running up her arm as far as her shoulder.

'Oops,' she said, looking down. 'Butterfingers.'

The Viking's head looked back at her. 'Of apology no need,' it said reassuringly. 'Of beginners, however, the luck.'

'What d'you mean? I thought that was a pretty good swing.'

'Respect,' said the head, 'but awful the style, and the footwork . . .'

'Here.' She bent down, picked up the head and popped it back on the Viking's shoulders. There was no click or fizz; but once the two had reunited there wasn't any trace of a join.

'Wow,' she said, 'nice trick. How do you guys do that? Velcro?'

'In Valholl, no problem.' The newly restored Viking stood up. 'Each day of lives nine to each of us vouchsafed is, hereinbefore I but times three having been slain, six to me remaining. To be fighting, and this time,' he added sternly, 'from cheating to desist.'

Well, why not? Last time around she'd died in her sleep, she hadn't even been there to feel what it was like. She'd felt cheated about that; it was like going to Europe and not being allowed out of the tour bus. Death in battle, *mano a mano* with a fierce and ruthless opponent, swordfighting – she'd always been a sucker for a good black-and-white-movie swordfight, the sort of affair where you know without having to look that before they're done someone'll have swung down from the top of the stairs on the chandelier, and the bad guy will have ruined a perfectly good lamp-stand by missing the hero's head with a haymaker and burying his blade in it. And if the Viking really was telling the truth and genuine blade skill counted for nothing here, she might even win.

'Okay,' she said, holding the sword at arm's length and trying to remember the way Errol Flynn stuck his backside out while taking guard in *The Prisoner of Zenda*. 'Let's do it.'

The Viking nodded and slashed at her. She thought, *Oh shit, parry!* and at once her arm moved, so that her sword blocked the blow. She felt the shock in her elbow, but the Viking's obviously superior strength hadn't counted for anything. *Cool*, she thought, and took a swing at him.

'Ack!' the Viking yelped involuntarily, as a red line appeared on his tricep. Carol blinked twice.

'Hey,' she said, 'did I just get you?'

'Ja,' the Viking grunted. 'To fight thus, where were you learning?'

'Wasn't me,' Carol replied. 'I mean, I don't know spit about swordfighting, 'cept for what I've seen in the movies. Does it hurt?'

'Not in Valholl. Urgh!'

He slashed at her again and, without even a conscious thought, she got out of the way (one step back, one left) and counter-attacked with a navel-level thrust. The Viking avoided it, but only by an inch or so after a standing jump. Before he could regain his balance, she feinted high and swept the blade down low. He stooped awkwardly to parry; she let her sword glide off his angled blade and recovered with another thrust. It scraped the inside edge of his elbow, and while he was yowling about that, she quickly stepped right and forward and swung hard at his unprotected head.

It reminded her a lot of the year when she'd won a coconut at the fair and her father had struggled to break it open for her. In particular it was the hollow, woody sound the coconut had made just before it finally gave up and shattered; exactly the same sound as the Viking's skull made when she hacked at it with the sword. The Viking looked at her without a word and dropped to the ground, motionless, as blood seeped through the crushed part of his skull in precisely the same way as the juice in the middle of the coconut had done. Uncanny similarity (unless this was all in her mind and she was using that memory to base this delusion on; that was a nice, comfortable theory and worked just fine except for one thing – it wasn't true).

'Of novices the good fortune,' the Viking said, sitting up. 'Down four, still to go five. This time, I the first blow to be striking, *ja*?'

'What? Oh, sure, *ja, ja*.' Carol relaxed, then took guard. She made a mess of it, because the Viking stepped neatly round her defence and sliced into her skull as if it were an apple.

Didn't feel a thing. Hey, don't say I missed it again, that'd really suck—

'Jesus,' the man was saying, and the scowl on his face showed that he really wasn't happy. 'What does a guy have to do to get a drink around here?'

Carol looked down at the tray in her hands, and below that the black and white tiled floor. 'Drink?'

'Yeah, before I grow a beard and die of old age. Shit, all I want's another bottle of Michelob.'

'Michelob?'

'You got it. What was so difficult, huh?'

She looked at him. He was about sixty-two, fat and white-bearded, wearing a baseball cap. He wasn't the Viking. He didn't appear to be Odin. The point was worth checking, though.

'Excuse me,' she said, 'but are you Odin?'

'Am I odeing what? And what's that mean anyhow, to ode? You got a cold or something?'

'That's fine,' Carol said. 'One Michelob, coming right up, soon as I've called my Dad.'

The man objected, but Carol was already standing at the bar, shovelling coins into the payphone. To her surprise, she found that she could remember her father's mobile number. Line engaged; but that was quite usual. She got the man his beer (Michelob; third shelf down, on the left, where it'd always been) then tried again.

'Dad?'

'No, it's me. Sorry. Would you like me to give him a message?'

Carol shuddered. 'Odin?'

'Large as death and twice as handsome. Do you want me to give your dad a message or not? Something cheesy, I'll bet: "Dad, I love you", or something of the sort.'

'Screw you.'

'That's not a very nice thing to say to your father.'

'That's not for him, that's for you.'

'Oh. Well in that case, same to you with Béarnaise sauce and a cocktail cherry. So long.'

The line went dead and she hung up. It was the bar, no doubt about it. Everything was as it should be, from the smell of the spilt beer to the inaudible drone of the TV in the corner showing reruns of the third season of *Cheers*. She looked round and saw Juanita, and Phil the owner, reading the *National Enquirer* behind the bar, and one or two customers she knew by sight; old barflies who were probably listed in the inventory along with the tables and glasses. She took half an inch of the skin of her forearm between thumb and index finger and tweaked hard: *Yes, ouch, check.* She walked to the door, up the stairs and out on to the street. The air was cold and smelt of New York, and when she had tried to go through the outside door and on to the sidewalk, no invisible barrier or force field had blocked her way. She was— it was incredible.

My life is a TV soap, and all that dying and Valhalla stuff was a TV soap dream. I'm alive.

Carol walked slowly back down the stairs. Phil the owner looked up at her, muttered 'Ferchrissakes,' and went back to reading his newspaper. The front page headline, she couldn't help but notice, read ELVIS NOT DEAD, SEEN BY TRUCKER IN DES MOINES. *Des Moines*, she thought; well, she'd guessed by now that Odin was a spiteful bastard, but what had Elvis Presley ever done to him?

She was back. It seemed a dreadful anticlimax to spend her first day back in the land of the living collecting empty glasses and wiping beer off tables, not to mention a waste of that wonderful and undervalued commodity, life; dammit, if she wanted to dole out beer to a pack of drunken bums, she need never have left Valhalla. Surely she ought to be *doing* something, achieving something, making a difference that would show the world that she was here. Her father had *died*, had *given his life* trying to get her home; and though he hadn't actually succeeded, surely she owed it to him to make an effort, instead of wasting her talents and abilities in this crummy dive. That way, her ordeal wouldn't have been in vain, if it prompted her to get out there and do what she was put on this Earth to do . . .

She looked round, but there was nobody standing behind her. Odd, that; she could have sworn someone was looking over her shoulder.

'Hey,' objected Phil, putting his paper down and lighting a cigarette. 'What are you just standing there for? I don't pay you to just stand.'

Carol could feel the cold fury flooding into her, like beer filling a glass. 'The hell with you,' she said, and she was about to hand in her notice, duly garnished with suggestions for some complex and biologically impossible exercises, when an unpleasant thought struck her.

'Phil?'

'Yeah? What?'

'Phil,' she repeated. 'Dammit, Phil, I know you from somewhere.'

The proprietor frowned. 'Sure you do, honey. You work in my bar, though for how much longer depends a lot on what you do in the next fifteen seconds.'

'No, no.' Carol shook her head as if trying to centrifuge her brains into her toes. 'I know you – something familiar—' She opened her eyes wide. '*You!*' she snarled.

'Huh?'

'It's you, you bastard!' She marched across to the bar and grabbed Phil by the collar. 'You *again*! How much longer are you going to play these goddamn games with me?'

Phil smiled at her; only, of course, he wasn't Phil. 'Oh, come now,' he said. 'Credit where it's due. It says in the prospectus *your every wish fulfilled*, and here you are, right back where you came from. Not to mention the sudden burning desire to make something out of your life – you always wished you had the drive and the energy, the motivation, to get a worthwhile job and fulfil your potential. So I made it happen. I'm so good to you I amaze myself,' said Odin smugly.

There were tears in Carol's eyes. 'It isn't real, is it? It's another of your damn tricks.'

Odin shrugged. 'Reality's such a subjective thing, don't you think? Anyway, I think it's real. It's real because this is where you *really* are, as opposed to where you thought you were. Can't get much more real than that, can you?'

'Valhalla?' Carol asked miserably.

Odin nodded. 'You were killed in battle by a Viking warrior,' he said. 'Where else would you be?'

'But at least it's a different Valhalla, isn't it?' she pleaded. 'I mean, there isn't all that smelly Norse crap and those dead warrior guys—'

'Dead warrior guys.' Odin grinned. 'Hey, Joe,' he called out to one of the customers. 'You were in Korea, weren't you?'

The customer glared blearily at him over the rim of his glass. 'Sure was, Phil.'

Odin dipped his head in thanks. 'And you, Lars, you were in 'Nam, right?'

'You bet, Phil. Right up to when that guy shot me.'

'Pete? Sven? Homer? You all got killed in the Gulf War, when that fuel tank blew up. That's right, isn't it?'

'Sure thing, Phil.'

Odin turned back to Carol. 'Dead warriors,' he said. 'And you know the last thought that passed through their minds, just before they finally blacked out for the last time? They thought, *Jesus, what I wouldn't give to be back in old Phil's place, back home in dear old NYC.* Or words to that effect. Their heart's desire, in fact. Plus, we have these really dinky barroom fights six times a day; you know the sort, the ones you see in movies where they break the balsa-wood chairs over each others' heads and nobody actually gets hurt?' He beamed with pride. 'Valhalla,' he said.

Carol made a little whinnying noise of pure misery. 'Oh, for God's sake,' she said pitifully. 'But this is even worse than that damn Norse joint. It's dark and dingy and smells of cigarette smoke.'

'It's where you wanted to be more than anywhere else,' Odin replied. 'Not that I'm disagreeing with you; I'm just stating a fact.'

It took Carol a moment or so to do it, but she pulled herself together; she shoved all her regret and heartbreak into black plastic sacks and slung them out of her mind. 'Okay,' she said, 'you win, this time. Now can we go back, please?'

Odin raised an eyebrow. 'Go back?' he queried. 'Go back where?'

Carol clicked her tongue. 'Valhalla,' she said. 'The Norse Valhalla. It's been so long since I was in this filthy smoke, I just can't take it any more.'

Odin looked at her. 'Sorry,' he said, 'maybe I haven't explained it properly. This *is* Valhalla. You came here when you died, and I'm afraid you're staying.'

'Staying? Here? But that's— I didn't die really, it was just one of those fake deaths, like all the Norse guys have, nine times a day? It wasn't real.'

Odin sighed. 'That word again. Of course it was *real*, you silly,' he said. 'He split your head open with an axe. What do you call that, a minor scalp wound?'

'It was a Valhalla fake death,' Carol insisted. 'Not real. I was dead already.'

'It was a perfectly genuine death,' Odin reiterated. 'They all are.'

Carol shook her head in disbelief. 'But that's crazy,' she said. 'All right, so when the Vikings zap each other, how come they always come back?'

Odin was drumming his fingertips on the bar top. 'They fight,' he said. 'They die in battle. They go to Valhalla. Sometimes, as you correctly pointed out, as often as nine times a day. Now, what part of that are you finding difficult to grasp?'

'But . . .' Carol gestured helplessly. 'You're telling me I'm stuck here for ever?'

Odin nodded. 'Or, at least, till the day you die in battle; and then you'll be here again, but in a different death. Now, I don't want to appear fussy, but all this chatting isn't getting the tables wiped, is it?'

A customer lurched to his feet. 'Hey, Phil,' he mumbled, 'go easy on the kid, will ya? You ride her too hard, you know that?'

'Oh Lord, is it that time already?' Odin didn't look round. 'Piss off, Norm,' he said. 'This is none of your business.'

The customer glowed with anger. 'Did you just tell me to piss off?'

'Yes.'

'Why, you—' He swung a massive fist, which Odin avoided easily; the blow continued unchecked until it connected with the jaw of another customer, who jumped up, grabbed his bar stool and smashed it into matchwood over Norm's head. Norm dropped to the floor without a word. Someone else caught hold of his assailant and threw him over the bar into a shelf of bottles; cue sound of breaking glass—

'Norm's dead,' Odin explained. 'For at least the next ten minutes. He really likes this place. In fact,' he added, as a glass whizzed by an inch from the tip of his nose and took out the big plate-glass mirror behind the bar, 'it's really heartening, the way so many of our regular customers keep on coming back here, time after time—'

It was dark.

Attila opened his mouth to whimper. He was scared of the dark. Sometimes, he was sure, there were *things* moving about in his room when it was dark, like the monster that lived under his bed—

Oh shit.

—Which was the main reason why he hated going to bed and made such a fuss when it was night-night time, though Mummy couldn't seem to grasp that. Mummy just thought he was being naughty and wilful, and the bitch of it was, he was too young to be able to explain what the problem was; and by the time he'd learned enough vocabulary and syntax to put his fears into words, he'd have grown up enough not to be scared of the dark any more. *Life sucks*, thought Attila the Hun.

Fuck a stoat. Not again.

'Mummy,' he called out, in a confused mixture of terror and boiling rage. 'Mum-*mee*!'

'Shuddup,' said a sleepy voice from the next room. 'Go 'sleep.'

'Mum-MEE!'

'Be quiet, you little toad, you'll wake your sister.'

'M—' He froze. *Sister? Don't have a sister. Never had a sister, none of the other times. (Other times? Times, plural? Oh God, dear God, how many times have I been here?)*

He peered round as the darkness thinned. His bed; the toy-box; Dobbin the rocking horse; the blackboard; the other bed.

Her bed.

'Joanie?' he whispered.

'Grmpf.'

'Joanie? Are you awake?'

'No. Go 'sleep.'

Joan of Arc, you dozy bitch, wake up and answer me. 'Joanie! Wake up. I want to ask you something.'

'Dz. Having nice dream. Talking to me. Go 'way.'

Gingerly, so as not to wake up the monster under his bed, Attila swung his feet over the edge and slid down till his feet touched the ground; then he groped round on the floor until his hand connected with something soft and furry. By the feel of it, Fern the fluffy pink rabbit; ideal. He fixed his eyes on the dark blur, and threw. Fern the fluffy pink rabbit hit Joanie solidly behind the ear, waking her up completely.

'Wa,' Joanie complained. 'Mummy, mummy, he threw rabbit at me!'

'Quiet,' Attila hissed urgently. 'Joanie, it's me. Me, Attila. Attila the *Hun*.'

'Wa— Huh?' Joanie sat bolt upright. 'Attila?' she said.

He crept across the floor, treading painfully on a Lego brick as he did so. 'That's right,' he said. 'You remember, don't you? We were on that scaffolding. We were—'

'Yes, all right,' Joanie muttered. 'I remember. What am I doing—?'

'It's what happens,' Attila replied. 'Over and over again, I think, I don't know. Usually, I think, we forget all about it. But this time I guess we remembered. Something to do with us being together, maybe.'

'I— Oh, just a tick.' Joanie cocked her head on one side, as if listening. 'No, it's just the funny man doing the shipping forecast. Sorry, what were you saying?'

'I wish you wouldn't keep doing that, it's so— Hey, Joanie, this is cool. This time, you're my sister. You never know, with the two of us we might be able to, you know, find a way out. We—'

The door opened and the room flooded with light. 'Get

back into bed this instant!' Mummy snarled, and before he knew what he was doing, Attila found himself back under his frilly blue junior duvet, cowering. *It's her*, he realised; *she's the one who suppresses the memories. When she's around we forget who we are.*

'O—', he said. 'Od—'

Mummy swung round and glared at him. 'Now what?' she snapped.

'Od—' There he was, dammit, behind her eyes, laughing. 'Oh dear,' he heard himself say. 'Sorry.'

'Oh, for pity's sake,' she hissed. 'You've not gone and wet your bed *again*?'

Attila felt his head nodding (and, come to think of it, the sheets *were* a bit on the moist side; *yech!*). Across the room, Joanie was sniggering. 'I said I'm sorry,' he protested – to his disgust he heard a catch in his voice, just a hair's breadth away from floods of tears. *I won't cry, dammit, not for you, not for anybody.* 'I d-didn't mean . . .' He could feel the disgusting things rolling down his cheeks, all warm and wet.

'Stop that snivelling at once,' Mummy ordered. 'Don't be such a baby.'

Oh sure. And whose fault is it if I am, you sadistic bastard?

When she'd gone and the room was dark again, he lay still, brooding. It was hard to stop himself remembering, now the floodgates had been opened and all those other times, those other loathsome, hateful childhoods came swirling back; those other nights he'd lain awake, not daring to move because of the monster under the bed. Well, there was just a chance this time, wasn't there? This time, at least, he knew what was happening to him, and he wasn't alone, either. Admittedly he'd have preferred Alexander the Great or Eric Bloodaxe or Robert Guiscard, someone a bit more practical and a bit less prone to breaking off in the middle of conversations to listen to the commercials in her head. But a loony ally was an improvement of several million per cent over no ally at all—

He froze. Something had moved, right at the very edge of his vision, in the dark space between the bed and the floor. Breathing very slowly, not moving a muscle, he waited. It seemed like hours, until he was sure he'd go crazy from trying to see out of the furthest limit of his peripheral vision; and then it was there again, that tiny little flicker of movement—

'*Gotcha!*'

It squirmed like hell, but he clung on, driving his nails into its loathsome scaly throat. He heard its claws scrabbling frantically on the carpet, he could feel the searing heat of its breath, and the terror surging through him like electricity. He knew it was strong, far too strong for him to cope with, but still he clung on and squeezed, and squeezed; until quite suddenly, after the most ferocious kick yet, it went limp between his hands and he knew that he'd won. At last, after so many lifetimes of terror—

Finally, you bastard. Finally!

He let go and rocked back on his heels, staring with fascinated horror at the bared yellow fangs, the huge black claws, the lolling green forked tongue. All those childhoods scarred by persecution and torment, and now he'd done it.

'Joanie!' he hissed. 'Joanie, wake up. I've killed it. I won!'

'Grmpf?'

'Look,' he insisted urgently. 'The monster that lives under my bed. I—'

Joanie groaned and stirred. 'Don't be silly,' she muttered. 'Isn't any monster. Go 'sleep.'

'But *Joanie*—'

'Go *'sleep*.'

He reached down to grab the corpse, drag it across the floor and drape it over her; but somehow it wasn't there any more. Just Fern the pink fluffy bunny, and a very distant echo of familiar, malicious laughter.

CHAPTER FOURTEEN

Howard woke up and glanced at his watch. 05:08 a.m., and it was broad daylight. At a wild guess, that suggested it was summer already. Or again. That was one of the problems about getting killed every day; you tended to lose track of time.

He listened; but all he could hear was the distant *whump!* of the long-range railway guns shelling West Bromwich. He yawned. Generally the main artillery batteries didn't start pounding Smethwick till just after six, so he had plenty of time for a shave and a leisurely breakfast this morning, if he felt like it. He looked up at the sky again; it was cloudless and blue, much too nice a day to be lounging around in muddy foxholes when he could be up and about. The shave, then, but hold the breakfast. After all, he'd be dead before he'd digested it, so where was the point in wasting time eating it?

Now then; yesterday, the comb. The day before that, the toothbrush. Today, either the teaspoon or the bar of soap. Tough choice.

Heads. The bar of soap. Right.

Good fieldwork, the great generals of history agree, is the foundation of victory. It had taken Howard a while to realise the importance of this fundamental rule, but he'd learned the lesson and taken it properly to heart. Now, thanks to hours of careful observation and reconnaissance, he had a pretty good idea of the daily routine of war-torn Smethwick. For example, at 07:15 precisely a six-man foot patrol would come around this corner at a brisk trot, which gave him a comfortable ten minutes to get busy with the soap.

At 07:14 he put the soap back in his pocket and strolled back to his cunningly hidden observation post behind the burned-out coach on the corner. A minute later, bang on time, the patrol bounced in, slid spectacularly on the soap and skidded down the road, straight into the brick wall Howard had selected for his trap. As they lay slumped and groaning, he pulled out a little notebook and made a note of the score. Six down before 08:00; already he was well ahead of schedule.

Howard could place exactly the moment when he'd decided to stop being a victim and try to make the best of being in Valhalla. It'd been at the end of a long day just before a booby-trapped door had blown him into his component atoms and pressed the reset button; he had been creeping carefully up a dark alley when he'd caught sight of his own reflection in a pool of water forming round a fractured main. His first reaction had been to whirl round and draw his knife to defend himself against the tough guy standing directly behind him, because the man reflected in the puddle hadn't looked anything like the Howard he had seen in his shaving mirror back in the old days. Where that Howard had been a sad, timid, droopy, spineless creature who looked like nothing so much as a recently deflated balloon, this new (and, it went without saying, improved) version had had a lot of things in his favour. Gone were the stumpy little arms and legs and the round pot-belly, the perpetually worried expression, the

beady hamster eyes. Instead, he had seen a man in the peak of
physical condition, with a look of supreme confidence bor-
dering on sheer ferocity shining out of those unwavering blue
eyes. That was what a sparse, simple diet and masses of fresh
air and exercise would do for you, over a period of (for all he
knew) years.

It had been quite a turning point. Instead of being a weedy
little guy fantasising about being a great and fearless warrior,
he was now a finely honed fighting machine, who'd learned
the tricks of the trade the hard way and who now feared death
about as much as the feathers between a duck's shoulders
feared the rain. Death, after all, was the least of one's problems in Valhalla.

In that puddle, he'd seen clearly the message that had been
eluding him all the time he'd been here, a message so obvious
that only a complete and utter loser (like Howard #1) could
possibly fail to see it. Eliminate the fear of death, the message
ran, and all your wildest dreams become attainable. It helped,
of course, that there were no cream doughnuts, televisions,
soft warm beds or deep, comfortable sofas here to lure a man
off the path of physical and mental fitness. But the important
thing had been that moment of total and sudden insight when
he realised that, thanks to this unique environment, he'd
finally become the thing he'd always daydreamed of being: the
perfect bare-essentials warrior. That simple but vital lesson
learned, he could slough off his dead-weight mortal self and
get down to enjoying himself. All due credit to him, of course,
for being able to appreciate a revelation when he saw one.
Ninety-nine people out of a hundred, encountering Truth on
the road to Damascus, jump out and start peering anxiously
at their dented bumpers or demanding the name of God's
insurers.

And now here he was, having the time of his life. Valhalla,
he'd come to appreciate, was many different things, but more
than anything else it was *fun*. It was the great playground that

his mundane, self-conscious childhood had missed out on, the supreme game of cowboys and Indians, every little boy's dream of a game of soldiers where nobody actually got hurt but all the bombs and bullets were *real*; as real as his skills, his muscles and his enjoyment of it all. It was the greatest shoot-'em-up game of all time (and to think that he'd once sincerely believed that *Doom II* was the ultimate in cool!) And it was his to play *for ever*. Unreal!

Howard pulled the soap out of his pocket, looked at it and smiled.

Needless to say, he'd quickly grown tired of the beginner's level; the one where you fought with guns and grenades and rocket launchers and other cissy stuff. For a week or so, he'd kept himself entertained by limiting himself to a knife, but that was still pretty damn easy – two or three hours, four at the most, and he'd killed everybody there was to kill; nothing else to do all day except wander round looking for a landmine to tread on so as to reset the game – so he'd abandoned the cold steel and taken to throttling his opponents with a bit of nylon rope instead. But Howard #2 and fourteen inches of cord soon proved to be more than a match for the feeble, slow-witted opposition and so he moved on to level four, limiting his offensive arsenal to small, innocuous household articles no more than six inches in length. So far he'd smothered his victims with absorbent paper tissues, ruptured their windpipes with the handles of spoons, cracked their skulls with walnuts fired from a sling improvised from a humble sock, slit their throats with the sharpened edges of ten-pence pieces after blinding them with pepper, strangled them with garrottes made from tightly twisted tea towels, splintered their bones with papier-mâché clubs constructed out of pulped-down copies of the *Independent On Sunday* (as if they weren't deadly enough already), shot them down in droves with straightened paper clips dipped in ingeniously derived spice-rack poisons and shot from a blowpipe fashioned from

Sellotape and the cardboard cores of toilet rolls . . . How can there be such a thing as a weapon, he'd learned, when anything can be adapted to the simple job of taking life? He'd hoped that at least soap might test his ingenuity and present some sort of a challenge, but it had turned out just as he'd expected: all the heavy metal in the world was no match for a bar of Imperial Leather in the hands of a man who was prepared to use it.

He who makes a weapon of himself gets rid of the pain of being a man.

Or words to that effect. Howard sauntered round the block and climbed the rickety ladder up the side of the old factory chimney, calculating as he went the skull-crunching terminal velocity of a bar of soap dropped from the very top.

After he'd successfully completed his experiment and cleaned the mess off what remained of the bar of soap, there wasn't a lot to do until 08:55, when it would be time to make another soap-slide and take out the St Nicholas's spire sniper on his way to work. He chose a well-appointed shell-hole, put his feet up on a chunk of shattered masonry and relaxed, turning over in his mind what he was going to do tomorrow. He'd just devised the six hundred and ninety-third way of killing someone with a tube of toothpaste when he became aware of a shadow falling across him.

'It's all right,' a voice said, before even Howard's superb reflexes could cut in, 'it's only me.'

Howard relaxed. 'Odin,' he said. 'How's things? Haven't seen you around for a day or so.'

Odin sat down beside him and screwed the top off his thermos flask. 'I've been catching up on the admin,' he replied. 'Paperwork. Red tape.'

Howard nodded. 'Red tape's pretty cool stuff,' he murmured sleepily, for the sun was warm. 'And not just as a garrotte. You can use it for tripwires, or twist it tightly to power a catapult. And as for paper – hey, don't get me started on paper. Give me a hundred sheets of A4 and I could take out half of Birmingham.'

Odin poured tea into the lid of the flask and handed it across. 'You're starting to get a feel for this, aren't you?' he said.

'You bet.' Howard took a sip of the tea. 'I guess this is what I was born to do. And to think, before I met you I'd never in my wildest dreams have imagined I had all this untapped potential inside me. I could have wasted my entire life and never known.'

'There now.' Odin smiled. 'And yet, when you first came here—'

Howard pulled a wry face. 'Don't remind me,' he said. 'Talk about gift-horses' teeth. Shows what a dumb, ungrateful little jerk I used to be, I suppose. Anyway, that was then, this is now.'

'Always pleased to hear from a satisfied client,' Odin said. 'Of course, there's some as would say the changes in you haven't all been improvements. For example, all this killing people and stuff. It could be argued it's a bit antisocial.'

Howard waved his hand dismissively. 'Balls,' he said. 'People have been killing each other for as long as there's been people to kill. It's— well, it's one of the chief ways we define our humanity.'

'Gosh,' Odin said. 'That's a good one, I must remember that. You don't mind if I quote you on that, do you?'

'Be my guest,' Howard replied indulgently. 'Mostly, though, I guess, it's finally finding that there's something I'm really good at, you know? I mean, *really* good at, like Olympic standard. I'd say I was Olympic standard, wouldn't you?'

'Gold medal standard, Howard, definitely gold medal standard. After all – soap. Now that's really something.'

Howard shrugged modestly. 'Soap,' he said, 'whatever. Next month I'm going to stop using things altogether, just rely on my bare hands. And teeth, of course. At least to begin with.'

'Ah,' Odin said. 'You're turning into quite a purist in your old age.'

'Minimalist, at any rate.'

'That's good,' Odin said approvingly. 'I like to see someone who's dedicated to improving himself.'

Howard grinned. 'Right,' he said. 'And it's more fun than the Open University; you don't have to write essays or go on study weekends.'

Odin emptied the last few drops out of the flask-lid and screwed it back. 'Nevertheless,' he said, 'all this killing, it's a bit— well, morbid, don't you think? And there's something at the back of my mind about Thou Shalt Not. Ring any bells with you?'

Howard shook his head. 'Strictly for wimps,' he replied. 'Wimps and losers. If it's neat quotations you're looking for, I suggest you pop round to your local library and ask if they've got anything by Charles Darwin. Now there was someone who knew about what happens to wimps and losers.'

'Really?' Odin stood up. 'Tell me what happens to them, Howard.'

Howard shrugged. 'They get what's coming to them,' he said. 'The snuff. The big zappo. Because the rule is, the guy who's left standing when the whistle blows is the winner. No silver medal in a knife-fight, Odin; that's what Charlie'll tell you.'

'I see,' Odin replied. 'I was under the impression it was all about evolving into higher, less primitive forms of existence. I guess I must have been confusing it with something else.'

'Probably. Sounds more like bad science fiction to me.'

'You may be right.' Odin put his flask back in his coat pocket. 'Actually, you might know the answer to this, since you're obviously well up on the subject. What's the opposite of evolution?'

Howard thought for a moment. 'It's not devolution,' he said, 'that's Scottish Assemblies and letting the Welsh have their own Channel Four. I dunno. Degradation? Decadence. De-something, at any rate. Can't say I've given it much thought, to be honest.'

'Oh well,' Odin said, 'I thought I'd ask. By the way.'

'Mmm?'

'You're sitting on a landmine. Have a nice day.'

'Wha—?'

One involuntary wriggle, and all that was left was a damp red patch in the mud where Howard had been sitting. Odin looked at it for a while and smiled. Then he felt in his pocket, took out a referee's whistle and blew it.

'Still standing,' he said, and walked away.

Howard, of course, didn't hear him, since he was in something of a state of flux, and an annoyed one at that. Somehow he got the feeling that he'd been made a fool of, though exactly how he wasn't quite sure. Grumpily, he settled down to wait for his body to piece itself back together again. *Toothpaste*, he thought—

—And found himself sitting on a bench.

It was a hard stone bench, in some sort of theatre or stadium. There were rows and rows of them, forming the shape of half a funnel, and sitting on them were thousands, possibly hundreds of thousands of people, all perfectly still and quiet, staring at a stage or podium far away in the distance.

Howard blinked and tried to focus. Hell, it was just a wall; a plain, blank wall with a sign on it saying *Caution – wet paint*. What on earth was he doing here? This wasn't Smethwick. More to the point, it wasn't Valhalla.

'Hey,' he said, 'what's the big idea? Where am I?'

A hundred thousand voices shushed him; but he didn't care. The old, unregenerate Howard would have curled up into a ball and dematerialised out of sheer embarrassment, but not Howard the Slayer. Any more of that out of them and they'd end up looking down the business end of a tube of Colgate.

'I said,' he shouted, 'what's the big idea? Where am I? This isn't Valhalla.'

The man next to him, whose face seemed oddly familiar (grey uniform, shiny black boots, funny little moustache) turned his head and gave him a contemptuous smile.

'Want to bet?' he said.

Lin, you're breaking up, this is a truly awful line. Lin?

'More kerosene,' barked Lin Kortright, 'quickly.'

Lin? Are you still there? Look, why don't you just send me a fax instead, because I'm kinda busy right now, and . . .

Frantically, Kortright grabbed the can from the other Kortright (#36, if anybody's interested) and sloshed kerosene on the fire. The flame jumped up.

'No, I'm here,' he shouted, 'don't hang up. Say, Merc, how'd you like to do an old buddy a fav—?'

As suddenly as it had spurted up, the flame died back, leaving the small potted fern only slightly singed. That had been #29's idea; wet the leaves first, then dowse it with kerosene. The oil burns on top of the water, the leaves underneath don't get scorched – *voilà*, burning bush; and toll-free during off-peak hours.

('Though I say it's damn cheapskate of the guy not to have an 0800 number,' objected #16. 'A regular god's gotta have a toll-free phone line.'

'Don't you believe it,' #7 pointed out. 'I read the other day where Quetzalcoatl has one of those numbers like the porno companies have, where he gets a buck a minute clear profit. And I always wondered why his invocations were so damn long-winded.')

Still here, Lin. Lin? Jesus, Lin, what's the matter with this line?

Lin Kortright (LK#1) sluiced the plant with more kerosene and snapped his lighter. It was out of gas.

'Here, mine's a Zippo,' said #32. 'Hey, since when did Lin Kortright carry anything but a Zippo?'

The fern ignited with an eyebrow-erasing *whoosh!* 'Is that better, Merc? I can hear you just fine.'

Yes, that's cool. Now then, what can I do for you?

'Merc,' Kortright said, 'just a quick favour, won't take more than a minute of your time. I died.'

Lin, I'm so sorry. Did it hurt? Hey, is this some sneaky way of telling me you haven't chased up those merchandising rights like I asked you?

'The deal's in the can, Merc, the Disney people said "Yes" and we're ready to roll. Now then, like I just said, I died. I was wondering, could you do something about that for me?'

There was a brief silence. *Do you mean died as in, like, ceased living?*

'Exactly right, Merc.'

Unreal. Hey, what's the angle? No, don't tell me, it's a corporate law thing, right? Someone in your organisation's trying to squeeze you out, so you die, inherit your own shares and bingo! Am I right?

'There or thereabouts, Merc. More thereabouts than there, but—'

Ah, I get you, it's that anti-trust thing, you know, the one where you set up a dummy corporation based in that transdimensional temporal anomaly out the other side of the Belisarius nebula—

Unbidden, #44 applied more kerosene, just in the nick of time. The sprinklers cut in, drenching the forty-nine Lin Kortrights who weren't sitting under a table with water.

'You got it, Merc,' said Lin Kortright, lying for the sake of a quiet death. 'Unfortunately, there's complications. Like, I can't get back. And I was just wondering . . .'

Way to go, Lin. I knew you'd find a way round that statute somehow. Maybe it's kind of a crazy thing to give your life for, but if it's what you sincerely believe in—

For some reason, that line gave Lin Kortright goose-bumps. 'I was just wondering,' he repeated, 'since I got you that gig as conductor of the souls of the dead to and from the underworld, maybe you could see your way clear to getting me out of here. If it's no bother, that is.'

Long silence. *Lin, you know I respect you a whole lot—*

('Oh shit,' muttered #27.)

—But you know better than anybody, I got too much at stake now, especially if this Disney thing comes off, I gotta be squeakier-clean than squeaky-clean, and bodysnatching—

'Would you call it bodysnatching?' Kortright asked mildly. 'I don't see it in quite that light myself, Merc. I see it more as—' He turned his head away from the fern, which was starting to pop and crackle as the kerosene burnt down. 'Quickly, guys,' he hissed. 'What the fuck do I see it as?'

'Social conscience,' whispered #37 immediately. 'Taking a stand on significant moral issues.'

'—Basic, fundamental profile-raising,' Kortright continued seamlessly. 'If you wanna play with the big boys, Merc, you gotta do causes and issues and all that shit, you gotta show you care. And let's face it, all the really cool issues got snapped up years ago. I told you back in '29, you shoulda done like I told you. Didn't I get you the ex officio chair of Save The Dinosaurs? Didn't I make it so you could have had Deities Against The Ice Age and Ban Catapult Testing Now, just by snapping your goddamn fingers? But no, you had to know best, and guess what, you missed out. Again. Your image is *dirt*, Merc, and we've got to do something about it *now*, unless you wanna be a glorified postal worker the rest of your career.'

I hear what you're saying, Lin. But how's helping dead guys escape from wherever the hell it is you've ended up going to make me look caring and concerned?

'Merc,' Kortright sighed, 'don't argue. I'm your agent, Merc, you're supposed to have faith in my judgement. You do trust me, don't you, Merc?'

The longest silence so far, during which #44 poured out the last of the kerosene.

Of course I trust you, Lin. Who else can I trust if I don't trust you? All right, you just tell me where you are and I'll come and get you.

Kortright just had time to tell him before the flame finally sputtered away, leaving the fern looking like a used-matchstick tree. 'Deus ex machina, huh?' said #39, breathing out slowly through his nose. 'I always liked deus ex machina. High profile, good money and they only need you for the last week of filming, so it doesn't bitch up the schedules.'

Lin Kortright let his breath out in a rush. 'We did it,' he said.

#41 nodded. 'Assuming we can trust the little bastard,' he added. 'Me, I wouldn't trust him as far as I could sneeze him out of a blocked nose.'

'It's not as if we have a choice,' Kortright replied soberly. 'Oh sure, left to myself I wouldn't trust *any* god to tell me the time if I was standing under the clock at Grand Central. But you know what they say; when you're drowning in boiling shit and a guy throws you a rope, does it *really* matter if he's a lawyer?'

#41 shook his head. 'Oh, I'd trust Mercury not to double-cross me,' he said. 'I just don't trust him to be able to find the place on his own, is all. Remember that time he had to go warn the people of Atlantis that their island was about to sink, and instead he went and caused that panic in Georgia?'

Against all the odds, however, Mercury did show up just under an hour later—

'No way,' he said.

Kortright frowned. 'Merc,' he said, 'Merc, look at me. This is Lin Kortright here, remember.'

Mercury shook his head. 'No, it's not,' he said. 'It's fifty-one fucking Lin Kortrights. What'm I supposed to do with fifty-one Lin Kortrights, smuggle you guys past Security under my coat?'

The look of shocked disappointment on Lin Kortright's face was a masterpiece. 'Hey, Merc,' he said, 'you don't think I'd bring you all this way just to rescue one guy, do you? Give me some credit, please. One guy is just a guy, but fifty-one guys is a *minority*.'

Obviously, Mercury hadn't looked at it in that light, because he limited his next protest to a muted 'Yeah, but Lin—' which in context was as good as saying 'Yeah, let's do it.' Kortright nodded his approval. 'Rescuing a minority, Merc, that's box-office. It's more than that, it's pure Hollywood. The only bummer is, Charlton Heston's too old to play you.'

Mercury frowned. 'What, you mean chess or something? Like a pro-celebrity tournament?'

'Play you in the movie,' Kortright said patiently. 'Which reminds me; on the way out of here, we gotta find a sea. You've gotta part a sea, or we might as well not bother.'

As it turned out, the side door Mercury sneaked them out of turned out to open into the land of the living in the exact geographical centre of Mongolia, which meant that parting a sea would have taken them several thousand miles out of their way. Mercury, who'd set his heart on the stunt as soon as Kortright suggested it, wasn't happy; it didn't say anything anywhere, he argued, about it having to be an *existing* sea, and by the looks of this place it could use a little extra water anyway. So Kortright let him have his sea, which he parted quite beautifully just before it vanished into the burning sand of the Gobi desert in a huge cloud of steam, without leaving so much as an eggcupful of moisture behind. Making a mental note to hire Mercury a whole new team of writers as soon as he got back to his office, Kortright led the way across the blinding white dunes to a lonely, sun-bleached bus stop beside the drift-covered road.

'Thanks, Merc,' he said, 'you done good. There'll be no stopping you now.'

Mercury smiled happily. 'It was your idea,' he said. 'You know what? Together, we make a great team.'

Lin Kortright thought of the steam cloud dispersing on the stiff desert breeze. All that water had to have come from somewhere; please God he'd at least had the common sense to take it from a major ocean, where nobody but a few oceanographers would notice, rather than scooping out the Mediterranean and leaving Sicily and North Africa staring at each other in horror over a vast, bone-dry canyon. 'It's like I always say, Merc,' he replied. 'People who need people need people they can trust.'

'Sure. It's a shame about Heston, though. Maybe I should just pop back and rescue him too.'

Kortright shook his head. 'We'll get Harrison Ford instead,' he said. 'Or Tom Hanks. If he's not too busy,' he added.

'That'd be cool, Lin. Hey, you never know, maybe this'll even help me get on *Xena*.'

Lin Kortright pursed his lips. To the gods, he knew, all things are possible; there's possible, however, and there's miracles.

'Leave that one with me, Merc,' he said. 'I'll see what I can do.'

It was only when the bus pulled up, and the other fifty Lin Kortrights were turning out their pockets trying to put together the equivalent of sixty-two cents for the fare, that he realised that he'd forgotten something.

Something important.

Dammit, wasn't that always the way? As soon as it came to business, his mind filled up with the deal like a lavatory cistern filling with water after the chain's been pulled, and everything else was immediately submerged. All that stuff about Mercury and his goddamn sea, and he'd forgotten Carol.

Shit, he thought. *That doesn't look good.*

Still, he argued, as the bus creaked painfully away from the stop, laden down with fifty-one Lin Kortrights, forty-six ancient nomad women on their way to the autumn sales at Ulan Bator and seven goats, *I'm definitely going back for her. Or at least, I'm definitely going to get her out of there. As soon as I've clinched the deal with Kawaguchi and the anti-thanaton beam syndicate, I'm definitely going to see to it that she gets out of there. Till then, she'll just have to have a little faith.*

It was roomy, no doubt about that; and quiet, too. And the decor was soothing, in a monotonous way, provided you liked pink. The smell, though, was downright offensive.

'Hello?' Vinnie called out, but the only reply was his own voice, echoing back from the high, vaulted roof. Waste of time shouting, in any case; if they were going to come when he called, they'd have done so by now. It was obvious they knew he was here.

The fact he'd been in the belly of the whale for (as far as he could tell) three days now suggested at least that the pattern had been broken; the whale hadn't sunk or sprung a leak or collided with an iceberg, and here he still was. It hadn't made the slightest effort to digest him, either; and that, together with the fact that it had swallowed him at all (whales don't eat people) implied that this wasn't a standard production-line whale, but more of a specialised – even custom – job. He was pretty sure of this now, since his observations over the last few days had revealed quite a few tell-tale clues that confirmed the hypothesis. Like, for example, the electric light.

It was just one solitary dim lamp, a sixty-watt bulb, maybe even a forty, dangling a foot or so from the apex of the stomach's vast ceiling. Vinnie wouldn't have noticed it at all if he hadn't been looking carefully; the bulb and the flex were pink, just like everything else, and it was so far up that at first sight it was indistinguishable from the scores of other small, bulbous pink dangly bits that were bobbling about up there. If he hadn't asked himself the question 'How come I can see so well inside a fish's stomach?' he'd never even have thought to look.

Once he'd seen it, however, it changed his perception of the whole situation. He didn't know a lot about whales, but he was prepared to bet money that no other whale in history, not even Moby Dick, had had electricity laid on inside its digestive system. It was a hint, a clue; and, once he'd noticed it, a fairly insulting one at that. Whoever was responsible just didn't care about subtlety, or appearances, or even plausibility.

Another dead give-away was the fresh water, which came cascading down from the mouth of the gullet, fifty or so feet above the stomach floor, three times a day as regular as clockwork. That argued a built-in desalination facility somewhere on the premises, along with a pretty sophisticated timing system. A lot of trouble to go to, sure; but whoever it was who had taken that trouble had stopped short of providing anything so useful as a bottle or a pot to store water in. If Vinnie wanted to drink, he had to slurp it up as it came sloshing down the walls, and if he missed out, he stayed thirsty. Likewise there was more than enough food – twice a day it avalanched shrimps, alive-alive-o, served on the full shell but without knife, fork or any other refinement; certainly no garlic marinade and twist of lemon. The eight inches or so of seawater that lay permanently on the floor was actually agreeably warm, the temperature of a bath after you've been in it for a quarter of an hour and are just thinking of getting out. Oh, it would have been perfectly possible to live here indefinitely. Horribly possible, in fact.

Vinnie checked his watch; it was time for the bowel to open. High spot of his day, this.

It hadn't taken him more than a minute to write off the gullet port, which was where he'd come in from, as a possible means of escape. Even after he'd recognised the futility of it, he'd still wasted quite a few hours fruitlessly trying to climb the soft, slithery stomach lining in an effort to reach it. Pointless, of course; there was no way in the world to get a grip on the walls without something to dig in with, and since his nails were too short and he'd carelessly come out without his ice axe and crampons, that was an end of it. That only left the hole in the other end of the stomach, the waste-extraction port.

There would be no difficulty reaching it; almost the only thing he had to worry about in here, in fact, was not reaching it. The sinewy diaphragm that opened twice a day sat in the stomach floor like a manhole cover or the plug in a bath, and the floor sloped down at a gentle gradient so that the day's garbage could slide effortlessly down into the pool that covered the opening. It would only take a little carelessness to end up in that pool, but that wouldn't be a good idea at all. In his time, Vinnie had had his share of heartburn and indigestion, so he'd already had a pretty shrewd idea of the effects of concentrated stomach acid. Being methodically minded, however, he'd experimented by throwing in handfuls of prawn shell and watching them dissolve almost as soon as they touched the surface. It wasn't a spectacle that he found encouraging, professionally speaking.

He'd explored other possibilities, of course, all of which centred around the basic idea of getting the whale to throw up. He'd tried tickling, pinching, jumping up and down, kicking the sides, even hurling himself at them like a violent man in a padded cell. He'd tried overloading the acid pool, shovelling armful after armful of shrimps into it until even the ferocious acid couldn't dissolve them fast enough to stop the pool getting clogged. Waste of time. This fish had a stronger stomach even than his uncle Woody, and that was saying something.

The gurgling noise was starting, and Vinnie instinctively covered his ears. For the short time it took for the bowel to open and the contents of the pool to drain, the noise level was unbearable; yet another defence to frustrate escape attempts, he couldn't help thinking. But he forced himself to put his hands down again, just in case there might be some clue he'd missed. He felt his eardrums pop.

The only chance he'd seen was the moment after the acid sump had drained, when the bowel diaphragm was closing. Actually, that was an abuse of the word *chance*; the moment lasted no more than a second and a half, the hole was almost certainly too small for him to wriggle through, and it stood to reason that, even if he succeeded, all that would happen would be that he'd slide down the bowel to join up with all that corrosive acid at the first kink or U-bend, even if the contraction of the bowel itself didn't crush him to death first. If he was crazy enough to go down there, he was a dead man, no two ways about it. The fact had to be faced. Until such time as his host either let him go or killed him, Vinnie was stuck here, with the damp and the raw shrimps and the smell. Escape was, finally, not an option.

No question about that. Vinnie was, after all, a professional. He knew about these things.

So, when the gurgling noise started to die down and the last bucketful of prawn tissue dissolved in neat hydrochloric acid was slipping away down the plughole, he shouldn't have taken a deep breath, dug his nails into the palms of his hands and started to run. Absolutely not. The whole point of being a professional was that you didn't take the no-chance options.

As Vinnie hit the diaphragm and felt it closing around him, he couldn't help thinking, in spite of all the other claims on his mental bandwidth, of an old man with no teeth trying to eat a jelly baby. There was (he reflected, while he drove his arms and legs against the soft pink wall that was trying to crush him into something the size and shape of a golf club) that same degree of inappropriate futility: a whale, trying to shit an undigested escapologist. He couldn't see the point, really. He wasn't having a good time and he doubted very much that the whale was enjoying the experience; yet all the evidence seemed to suggest that this was what he was meant to be doing – otherwise why the electric light, the fresh water and the minuscule, one-in-a-million chance of escape? *Well,* (he thought, as the diaphragm suddenly let go and he found himself desperately bracing himself with his outstretched arms and legs against the walls of the pitch-dark slimy chute to keep himself from dropping into the seething cauldron of acid below) *I really hope you're watching and you haven't just popped out for a cup of coffee and a doughnut, because I'm buggered if I'm doing this again.*

As far as active participation in the escape bid went, that was all for now, apart from the sinew-bursting strain of pressing his elbows and knees against the walls to slow his descent. There really wasn't anything more he could do; rather a waste, in fact, of his professional skills and abilities, because any fool with the stamina to keep pushing with his arms and legs could be doing this, it certainly didn't require the talents of one of the world's greatest exponents of the art of escapology. Turds, after all, do this sort of thing every day, without any of the hours of study and practice he'd put in over the years. In fact, he couldn't help thinking, they almost certainly did it a whole lot better than he did. Mind you, they had advantages that he didn't share, like a complete absence of bones, skin or nerve endings.

Who are you, and why are you doing this to me? It was, oddly enough, the first time Vinnie had ever asked that question, the one that everybody else seems to be asking at least once every day of their lives, and he'd hoped to be able to carry on avoiding it for a good few years yet, in the same way that he'd always managed to avoid death by getting out of its way whenever he felt it was getting a bit too up close and personal. *What do you want to do when you grow up, Vinnie?* they'd kept asking him when he was a kid. *Here's all human knowledge, look; which bit of it do you most want to learn?* He'd never had to think twice about answering that one. *I want to learn how to get out of the way. When I grow up, I want to be somewhere else.* And it had worked, too. He'd learned the secret that the immortals guard so jealously, that the only way to live forever is not to die, and every day since, either in front of the audience and the TV cameras or in the seclusion of his workshop where he practised so carefully, he hadn't died and hadn't died and hadn't died. Even now, when his life had narrowed down to being a particle of fast-moving whaleshit being shot down a smelly tube in total darkness, he still had it.

He shot out of the whale's backside like a torpedo.

How he reached the surface he never knew, because the G-forces and the shock of hitting the water at a speed of several hundred feet a second wiped his mind out and put him cosily to sleep. The next thing he saw was the sky; and then, as he rolled painfully on to his side, sand and rocks and sea and a green hillside sweeping down to meet him like a reception committee.

'I'm alive,' Vinnie said aloud. 'Well.'

He stood up, looked around for his clothes (no chance; they were probably still somewhere inside the whale, what rags and tatters were left of them) and started to walk slowly up the hill; at the top of which was a small, quaint, unspoilt little Cornish fishing village, where a rosy-cheeked policeman arrested him, charged him with indecent exposure and locked him up in a cell.

'But wait,' Vinnie protested as the door slammed shut. 'I've just escaped . . .'

'Oh yeah?' the policeman replied as he turned the key. 'Well then, let's see you get out of this one.'

CHAPTER FIFTEEN

'Thank you,' said Mr Kawaguchi, with a slight nod of his head. 'You've done well.'

Odin smiled. 'My pleasure,' he said. 'Really,' he added.

'The data you accumulated for us on the rate of decay of the human soul in the period immediately after death has proved invaluable,' Mr Kawaguchi continued. 'The third sample, for instance—'

Odin nodded. 'Howard. Sad case, that. I guess you could say death brought out the worst in him.'

'That's just the sort of information we needed,' Mr Kawaguchi confirmed. 'Now that we have statistical evidence about how rapidly a— let's say, a somewhat flawed human personality takes to break down into actual psychotic disorder . . .'

'Inadequate's the word I'd use,' Odin said. 'Not flawed.'

'Really? Aren't you being a little severe in your judgement? His only flaw, if you can call it that, was a preference for the world of his imagination as against reality.'

'Inadequate,' Odin said. 'After all, nobody ever said I had to *like* the little bastards.'

'Whatever,' Mr Kawaguchi said. 'With this information, we've been able to build in safety protocols that ought to make it possible for us to safeguard even our most— hm, *sensitive* clients against lasting psychological damage. Likewise, samples one and two, the father and daughter – an inspired selection, if I may say so.'

'Thank you.'

'By observing how long it took for the bond of natural love and affection between parent and child to disintegrate under the stresses of the death environment, and cross-referencing that against the results from sample four, the megalomaniac with the will to endure for ever—'

'Please,' Odin interrupted. 'I'd be careful with that data if I were you. I did warn you, Attila's a rather atypical specimen.'

'Oh, we've taken the standard deviation into account,' Mr Kawaguchi said, with a wave of his hand. 'That wasn't difficult. The net result is that we've been able to extrapolate vital algorithms to predict the erosion curve of human individuality in the face of eternal nothingness; our researchers can now place the point at which the One is assimilated into the Whole to within ninety-six decimal places.'

'That many,' Odin said. 'Fancy. Is that enough?'

Mr Kawaguchi shrugged. 'It's as exact as we can get. This is, after all, the prototype; we simply don't know how precise we need to be, at least not yet. There is one thing I don't understand, though. The last sample.'

'Joan of Arc? Well, Attila's had a crush on her for ages, and I just wanted to see how many times love could transcend death. My starting bet was forty-six, but that was a huge over-estimate.'

'No, I didn't mean her,' Mr Kawaguchi said. 'The escapologist; the Great Vincenzo, Vinnie – Vinnie—' He frowned. 'His surname escapes me for the moment. Why did you include him? After all, he never actually died.'

Odin's brow creased. 'Who?'

'The escapologist,' Mr Kawaguchi repeated. 'The man who kept on cheating certain death. First you crashed his plane, then his boat sank, then his helicopter, then the submarine, finally that whale—'

Odin closed his eyes for a moment, accessing the part of his omnipresence that had been there and seen it all. 'Him? That was nothing to do with me.'

'Oh.' Mr Kawaguchi's eyebrows flickered. 'You mean to say that all those extraordinary experiences were just coincidence?'

Odin shrugged. 'As far as I know, yes. Wasn't me, anyway. I suppose it could have been some other god.'

'One of the ones who move in mysterious ways, you mean?'

Odin smiled. 'That's just showing off. No, what I mean is, if it was some *other* all-embracing divine plan, I wouldn't know anything about it. At any rate, he wasn't part of the experiment. Like you said, he didn't die.'

'Ah.' Mr Kawaguchi tapped his fingers on the desk. 'I took it that you were giving me data on the resilience of the human spirit, the determination to survive at all costs, the indomitable nature of Man that defies every . . . But obviously not.'

Odin shook his head. 'Please,' he said. 'Who needs to know about the lab rat that happens to be allergic to the cheese?'

'I see,' Mr Kawaguchi said. 'Anyway,' he said, 'your contribution to this project has made the difference between success and failure. Thank you.'

'Any time. And you'll agree,' Odin went on, 'you'd never have got data like this if you'd stuck with Kortright.'

'Oh, most definitely not. A human, even one as dedicated as Mr Kortright, could never have achieved so much.' While he'd been talking, Mr Kawaguchi had been making out a cheque. It had taken him ever such a long time to write in all those noughts. '*Your* insight, however . . .'

Odin held up a hand. 'Strictly speaking, I was really only doing my job.'

'Oh? You take such pains over all your clients?'

'Of course,' Odin replied. 'For me, you see, it's never been just a job.'

Mr Kawaguchi looked at him over the edge of his spectacles. 'Really?' he said. 'I was under the impression that you weren't happy in your work.'

'Oh, I'm not,' Odin replied, folding the cheque neatly in two and stowing it in his shirt pocket. 'I hate every moment of it. But that's never stopped me doing it to the very best of my ability. And since I'm a god—'

'Quite,' agreed Mr Kawaguchi. 'Although a more inquisitive man than myself might be tempted to ask why an omnipotent should persist in a job he finds repugnant.'

Odin shook his head. 'Doesn't work like that,' he said. 'It's a matter of killing time, you see. If you're immortal, you've got to have something to pass the time, or else you go crazy.'

'A job, in other words.'

'That's it. But, on the other hand, there's only so many jobs a god can do.'

Mr Kawaguchi picked up the tiny scale replica of a *wakisashi* battle sword that lay on his desk, unsheathed it and tested the edge against the ball of his thumb. 'You mean you're overqualified?' he hazarded.

'Partly,' Odin replied. 'Mostly, though, it comes down to fragility. The world's just too— I suppose *breakable* is the key word here. Setting a god to do mortal work's like passing a three-phase industrial power supply through a torch bulb. So we can only do work that's suitable; which is another way of saying that the only thing a god can do is be a god. And unfortunately, what with the spread of the Big Four religions and the trend towards global secularisation and loss of faith in anything much, there's too many gods chasing too few godheads. You have to take what you can get, or what your agent can get for you.'

'I see,' Mr Kawaguchi said. 'How unfortunate. However, I foresee that our new venture might go some way towards alleviating the problem.'

'You bet,' Odin replied. 'If you go creating artificial afterlives for everybody who can afford one, there's going to be a hell of a lot more opportunities for the divine community, especially in the post-death sector. Really, the way I see it, you and I are doing godkind a favour.'

Mr Kawaguchi inclined his head graciously. 'We do our best,' he said. 'At Kawaguchi we make a point in our employment-creation strategies of positive discrimination in favour of underdeveloped local minorities, such as yourselves. We see it as a moral obligation.'

'"Underdeveloped local minorities",' Odin repeated slowly, 'I see. Isn't that a bit patronising? Just a little?'

'Perhaps. We prefer to think of it as the caring, sharing face of global domination.'

'Playing god, in other words.' Odin's lips twitched into a thin smile. 'Well, I have no problem at all with that,' he said. 'It's not as if we're really fit to look after ourselves, after all.'

Mr Kawaguchi's face didn't move. 'Your words,' he said. 'Not mine. Nevertheless,' he continued, 'there is an argument for saying that an extension of our management techniques into areas traditionally dealt with by individual gods or small, family-based pantheons might well provide a more efficient and effective service in the medium-to-long term. Obviously,' he went on impassively, 'we can never replace you with humans; nor would we wish to do so. But we might help take some of the weight off your shoulders by providing you with an overarching managerial structure that would allow you to concentrate on your specialities rather than the mundane task of day-to-day administration.'

'Right,' Odin said, pulling a face. 'In other words, you're going to ease us out and pension us off. And what will the robin do then, poor thing?'

Mr Kawaguchi steepled his long, slender fingers. 'In any event,' he said, 'such a project, even if feasible, would lie a long way in the future. We're probably looking at a timescale of centuries.'

'Sure. It's a pity that you won't live to see it,' Odin said ruefully. 'And that I will.' He stood up. 'Anyhow, it's been a real pleasure doing business with you, and if you've got any further questions, please don't hesitate. You know where I am.'

'You're everywhere,' Mr Kawaguchi replied. 'You're a god.'

'Exactly. Makes me easy to get hold of in a hurry. So long.'

'One last question, if I may.' Mr Kawaguchi picked up a pencil and balanced it on the palm of his hand, achieving an unlikely equilibrium. 'Do you feel any guilt about having stolen Mr Kortright's original idea and cut him out of the deal he helped set up in the first place?'

Odin thought for a moment. 'No,' he said. 'Why?'

'And what about killing him and his daughter? Do you feel any pangs of conscience about that, I wonder?'

'None whatsoever.'

'And now that you've achieved your objective, do you intend to bring them back to life and allow them to return to normal?'

Odin shook his head. 'No way,' he said. 'And besides, I couldn't even if I wanted to; I mean, death's death – you can't just cure it with penicillin. You're the only one who can do that; you and your anti-thanaton beam.'

'Assuming it works,' said Mr Kawaguchi. 'Personally, I would have preferred it if we'd run some tests first, just in case there are some last-minute glitches. Of course, the theory is sound enough, but we obviously can't anticipate the unanticipated.'

'Ah,' said Odin, thoughtfully. 'You mean, things outside the knowledge of mere human technology? Seemingly random and inexplicable factors you simply can't understand?'

'Precisely. Acts of God. Good day to you, Odin-san.'

Odin shrugged and walked away, being careful to concentrate his mind on the cheque nestling safely in his pocket. In a way, gods were a bit like the old-time landed gentry: all the social status, all the beautiful old houses and priceless heirlooms and faithful family retainers, but a perennial shortage of actual folding money, a shortage that could be awkward in today's crassly materialistic world, sometimes reducing them to the indignity of opening their houses to the public. It was certainly more comfortable to think about the money than to allow his mind to dwell on what might happen if the anti-thanaton beam didn't quite work as it should; and that he was the god who'd made it possible by cooperating so closely with mortals. As he'd told Mr Kawaguchi, he wasn't the least bit bothered about stealing Lin Kortright's idea or causing the deaths of Kortright and his daughter; moral scruples don't bother gods in the same way oceans don't catch colds. It was more a fundamental unease about the thought of mortals interfering with such matters. The thought of mortals meddling with things they didn't understand wasn't a problem; the problem would be if they *did* understand them.

Your worst nightmare, if you're a god: *humanus ex machina*.

The satellite was a tiny speck of dandruff on Infinity's black velvet shoulders, a minuscule blinking light, like an aggravating facial tic. In all the places they were, the gods looked round and noticed it out of the corners of their all-seeing eyes. Imagine it, if you will, reflected in the divine iris, impudently winking the eye of God against His wishes.

And, a fraction of a second after it came online and began emitting a concentrated stream of anti-thanaton particles that raced (so much faster than light; what, after all, can move as fast as death?) to every corner of the universe simultaneously, moving even faster than the infinite universe could expand, every god (except one) in the cosmos grabbed his phone in blind panic and tried to call his agent—

'Hm,' said Mr Kawaguchi, raising one eyebrow as he read the message on his computer screen. 'Unfortunate.'

'Dad?' Carol dropped a glass, which shattered. '*Dad?* Is that you? What the hell are you doing here?'

The customer, who'd been a long-dead Korean War casualty a moment ago but who now appeared to be her father, lifted his empty glass. 'Trying to get a beer,' he said. 'But without any success. What kind of service d'you call this?'

'Dad, you're *alive*!' With a degree of athleticism she'd never displayed before in this life, Carol vaulted over the bar from a standstill—

(*Couldn't have done that last time I was here*, she thought. *Goes to show. Death is good for you.*)

—and hugged him with all her strength. 'Dad, I was so worried, I thought you were— hey.' She stopped squeezing. 'If you're alive and I'm here as well, guess I must be alive too. Well, what d'you know?'

'Would you let go of me, please?' Lin Kortright asked feebly. 'I'd hate to come back to life just to be loved to death.'

'Sorry.' Carol let go. 'But what happened? How did we—?'

'The anti-thanaton beam,' Kortright said disgustedly. 'That bastard, that little shit Odin stole my idea, and—' He pulled himself up short with an effort. 'They finished working on the anti-thanaton beam and switched it on, but it seems like they screwed it up somehow, because it started abolishing death. You know, destroying it. If they hadn't shut if off in time, there'd have been no death left at all.' He shuddered. 'Hey, it's enough to make you want to smash up all the technology you can lay your hands on and go live in the Arizona desert. Anyway, one of the things it did was pull the two of us back to life. I guess we'd died before our time or something screwy like that.'

'Excuse me.'

Kortright looked round at the plump, gormless-looking young man on the bar stool next to him. 'Yeah, what is it? Say, are you English?'

The man nodded. 'Not my fault,' he said. 'Excuse me, but— well, this isn't Smethwick, is it?'

Carol shook her head. 'I think it's New York,' she said. 'I really, *really* hope it is, anyhow.'

'But wherever it is, it ain't where you just said,' Kortright added. 'Why?'

'Oh, nothing,' the man replied. 'I, um, I think I'll be going now.'

Kortright put out a hand and stopped him. 'Just a second,' he said. 'Who are you?'

'I don't know,' the man confessed. 'I have an idea that I'm either Howard something-or-other, or else I'm Conan the Barbarian.'

'Right.'

'Or Rambo,' the little man added. 'I'm afraid I'm still a bit confused about the details. I don't think I've been very well recently, to tell you the truth.'

'Sure. Why don't you go sleep it off somewhere quiet?'

'I might just do that,' the man replied sheepishly, and got up to leave. Before he could do so, a figure appeared in the doorway.

'Odin,' Kortright stated, accurately.

'It's all right,' Odin replied, 'I'm not here officially. I just stopped by to put the fear of gods into you, that's all.'

Carol, who was visibly restraining her glass-throwing hand, scowled at him. 'Won't work, buster,' she said. 'Because we're here and we're alive and we ain't going back, so screw you.'

Odin nodded. 'It's okay,' he said. 'You got off on a technicality. It happens.'

Kortright curled his lip. 'A technicality, huh?'

Odin shrugged. 'Well, it all sounded pretty technical to me. But I'm not bothered about it, really. After all, I'll have you all again, sooner or later. Sooner than you think, actually.'

Carol shook her head. 'Not unless we die in battle,' she said.

'Ah.' Odin smiled. 'But what's human life, if not an unending battle against the arbitrary and gratuitous cruelty of the gods? See you later, alligator.'

'Maybe,' Carol replied. 'Maybe not. Maybe I might just find out how to build one of these anti-thanaton beams for myself, and fry your immortal ass. You think I can't do it? You forget, I got a degree in electronic engineering.'

'I don't forget,' Odin said sweetly. 'You did, but not me. So glad I've managed to bring a shred of purpose back into your otherwise wasted existence. You've lost weight too,' he added. 'So've you, Lin, it suits you. And Howard— well, you can't win 'em all, and in your case I'd hate to think I'd succeeded. Enjoy the rest of your lives, people.' He glanced at his watch. 'Forty years; I think I've just got enough time to run a few errands and have my hair cut, and then it'll be time to check you all in again. By my timescale, at least,' he added unpleasantly. 'So long, perpetual losers.'

'Kortright Associates, can I help you?'

'Yeah,' growled the voice at the other end of the line. 'Since when did *I* answer the goddamn phones?'

'Since there were fifty-one of you, I guess. I mean, we've gotta find something for all of us to do.'

'Not that. Gives the wrong impression. What the hell kind of agent answers his own calls? And how can you say you're not there or you're in a meeting?'

'Good point. Did you just call to yell at us, or was there anything?'

'You called me, remember? Left a message on my answering machine. Nearly gave me a heart attack, hearing myself talking to me like that. Then I guessed it must be you.'

'Not you. Us.'

'Whatever. So, I gather you've decided to come and work for me. Nice of you to tell me.'

'Actually, no.'

'No? So what're you doing in my office, answering my phone?'

'No, you don't understand. We don't work *for* you. We *are* you.'

The voice at the end of the line was silent for a moment. 'You want that I should make you all partners? Are you crazy?'

'With respect, you're the one who's talking to himself, and they do say that's a sure sign of . . .'

'Answer my question, dammit. Are you trying to muscle in on my business?'

' "Muscle in" isn't really accurate. You see, it's our business now. Well, it always was, of course. But you're right, there isn't room for fifty-one partners in a business this size.'

'Glad you agree.'

'And that's why – with the utmost regret, of course—'

'Huh?'

'Not that we don't really appreciate your very substantial contribution to the success of this enterprise; nevertheless . . .'

'Hey, just you hang on a minute, you can't squeeze me out of my own goddamn business.'

'So what're you gonna do? Sue yourself?'

'Hey . . .'

The line went dead.

Attila opened his eyes. He hadn't remembered closing them.

'Ah, *shit*,' he said.

The auditorium. In the far distance, the wall. All around him, row upon row of silent men and women, concentrating like mad. Next to him, Joanie, also concentrating like mad. This was . . .

This was better than being three again. Or seven. Or thirteen. Or seventeen. Hell, spending the rest of eternity on his head in a lake of burning tar would be better than being seventeen again. Nevertheless, he didn't feel good about it. When the strange green light from the sky had washed over him, just as he was falling off the scaffolding for the who-knew-how-many'th time, and he'd hit the ground head first and *not died*, he'd allowed himself the luxury of hoping that his situation had significantly improved, instead of just going back to an earlier version of Reset.

'Sh,' said the man next to him. 'It's just getting to the exciting bit.'

'Oh sure,' he replied; but in spite of his ennui, a tiny flicker of the old glamour crept over him. And it wouldn't do any harm to take just one peek.

He raised his binoculars.

'Hey,' he said.

'Shh!'

'Yes, but—'

'*Shhh!*'

He took another look, just to make sure. He was right.

The paint was dry.

'Hey', he yelled at the top of his voice, 'everyone, listen! It's dried. The paint has dried!'

'*Shhhh!*'

'But it's *dry*,' Attila protested. 'Look at it, for pity's sake. No glistening sheen. No slight variations in colour. I'm telling you, the paint is no longer wet . . .'

They'd stopped listening. Some of them (Joanie included) had their hands over their ears, others were just blocking his words out of their minds. That was crazy.

'Oh, for crying out loud,' said Attila the Hun; and he jumped up, ran down the aisle and started to climb the wall.

At first they were all too stunned to react at all. Then they started shouting, screaming, cursing, throwing telescopes and tripods and thermos flasks and notebooks and video cameras and shoes and items of jewellery and apple-cores and moisture meters and even a few thin, sharp-edged copper coins. Attila ignored them as best he could, and went on climbing. When he was finally astride the top of the wall, he held up his hands and spread them wide.

'Look,' he called out, 'no paint.'

A folding stool hit him in the chest. He wobbled for a moment but managed to keep his balance. There were ten men in black uniforms with big shiny boots heading straight towards him down the main aisle.

'Look at me,' he howled. 'Look at my hands. Look at my clothes. If the paint was even the slightest bit wet, wouldn't it have come off on me? It's dry, goddammit, dry.'

'That's him,' someone in the front row said, and pointed. The leader of the shiny-boots nodded and advanced towards him, drawing a big heavy metal flashlight from his belt as he came.

When Attila came round again, he found that he was back in the auditorium; but this time he was right out on the far left side, and his feet and hands were chained to the floor. Worse, his head was wedged in some kind of stiff plastic collar that stopped him from looking anywhere but straight ahead. There was sticking plaster over his mouth, too.

'Mmm,' he said emphatically. 'Mm mmmm mm m. Mm.'

'Sh,' replied his neighbour, eyes fixed on the wall.

'Mmmm. Mmmm. Mm. *Mmmm!*'

His neighbour lowered his binoculars, turned his head and fixed him with a murderous glare. 'All right,' he said, 'I'll explain this just the one time, so listen up. The paint is *wet*. Any minute now it'll start to dry, but at the moment it's still wet. Now, if the paint's wet, the guards will come and take off the gag and the chains. If it isn't, they won't, and you'll have to suffer the misery of sitting there for the rest of eternity watching a *dry* wall. Now then,' he went on, 'who in his right mind'd want to sit forever watching *dry* paint? There wouldn't be any point, would there?'

'Mm,' Attila conceded grudgingly. 'Mmmm mm m.'

''Course I'm right,' the neighbour said. 'Now then, it's up to you; one *Mm* for yes, two for no. Is the paint wet or dry?'

'Mm.'

'Sorry, I don't think I quite heard you. Is the paint wet or dry?'

'*MMM!*'

And sure enough, when he looked at it through the specially calibrated telescope they were kind enough to bring specially for him, he could see quite clearly that the paint was wet; well, not wet exactly. More sort of just ever so slightly getting tacky at the edges, which meant that the fun would start at any moment. Definitely not dry, though. Not dry at all.

Some time later, Attila became aware of an annoying itch, threatening to spoil his concentration. Without taking his eye away from the eyepiece of the telescope, he reached back to scratch; but it wasn't any part of his head or body that was itching, it was his mind.

Hey, he ordered. *Cut that out.*

The itch apologised. It hated having to disturb him at a time like this, what with the paint being just about to start getting gooey on top, but could he by any chance remember who he was? Only they were filling out some forms at Subconscious Central, and it seemed that nobody could remember the name . . .

Name?

What we're called. Our name. You know.

Attila scratched his head. *Sorry, can't help you there. Didn't even know we had one.*

Oh, replied the itch, dying away. *Maybe you're right and we've been imagining things. Which wouldn't be all that unusual, since of course we're your imagination.*

My what?

Your imagination. It's kind of a . . . Sort of . . . Well, you've got one. Had one. Once.

Attila shook his head and was about to tell the itch off for distracting him when suddenly everybody else in the auditorium was on their feet, yelling and screaming and cheering and hugging each other and singing—

'What?' Attila asked, bewildered. Nobody took any notice.

The celebrations went on for a very long time. Finally everybody quietened down and started to file out of the auditorium in an orderly fashion; except for Attila, of course, because the shiny-boots had forgotten to take off the last of the chains, the one that connected his ankle to his seat. He ought to have mentioned it at the time, he knew, but he'd been so caught up in watching the nice paint that he hadn't even noticed that the chain was still there until some time after they'd gone. Still, he was able to grab the sleeve of one of the others as he shuffled by down the aisle.

'What's going on?' he asked. 'Why's everybody leaving?'

The woman whose sleeve he was holding (was the face familiar? Joan something? He couldn't remember) prised his fingers loose and let his hand drop. 'It's over,' she said. 'The paint dried.'

'Huh?'

'It dried, quite suddenly, just like that.' She snapped her fingers. 'Oh no, don't say you missed it.'

'I—' Attila opened and closed his mouth a few times like a goldfish. 'I suppose I must have done.'

The woman shrugged. 'Your own silly fault,' she said, 'for letting your attention wander.'

Then she walked by, and left him alone

'Visitor for you,' said the prison warder.

Vinnie awoke and propped himself up on his elbow. 'For me?' he repeated blearily.

The slide in the door ground shut and the door itself swung open. A tall, straight-backed man Vinnie had never seen before in his life walked in, and the door slammed shut behind him.

'Hello,' the man said. 'You still here?'

'What?' Vinnie had to think for a moment. 'Oh, you mean I haven't escaped. Hey, where's the point? It's not as though I've done a murder. I've got a week to go and then I'm out of here on parole. If I escape, all that's down the toilet. No, I'm staying put.'

The man raised an eyebrow. 'Oh,' he said. 'You surprise me. Especially since you've got this nice cell that just happens to overlook the blind spot in the perimeter fence, where by some weird coincidence there's a weak point in the wire you could just squeeze through, no problem. Just the bars on the window between you and freedom, in fact.'

Vinnie shook his head. 'Not me,' he said. 'You must be thinking of someone else.'

'I suppose I must have been,' the man replied. 'Sorry I bothered you.'

'That's okay.'

The man turned to call the warder, then he looked back over his shoulder. 'Still,' he said, 'you might as well have this. I don't happen to like Victoria sponge myself.'

From under his arm he produced a round Tupperware box. He put it carefully on the floor, then banged on the door. 'So long,' he said

'Ciao.'

When he'd gone, Vinnie opened the box and lifted out the cake. He looked at it for a moment, then plunged his fingers down into the icing until he felt metal. He grinned, then pulled out the file.

Nah, he thought. *It'd be a really dumb thing to do.*

The file seemed to be looking at him through its covering of crumbs and sticky goo. It made his fingers itch.

The smart thing to do is stay put, keep still, do the time, let Justice run its course. And besides, I don't do that stuff any more.

He ran the edge of the file over the ball of his thumb. Nice sharp, clean teeth. Then he looked at the window; first at the bars, then at the clear blue sky beyond.

On the other hand, Vinnie thought, *what the hell is the good of freedom if they give it to you? Only kind of freedom worth having is what you take for yourself.*

First, however, he ate the cake. After all, he might be on the run for a very long time.

ONLY HUMAN

Tom Holt

Something is about to go wrong. Very wrong.

But what can you expect when the Supreme Being
decides to get away from it all for a few days, leaving
his naturally inquisitive son to look after the cosmic
balance of things?

A minor hiccup with a human soul and a welding
machine soon leads to a violent belch and before you
know it the human condition – not to mention the
lemming condition – is tumbling down the
slippery slope to chaos.

There's only one hope for mankind.
And that's being optimistic.

Only Human is a wildly imaginative comic fantasy from
one of Britain's sharpest, funniest writers.

WISH YOU WERE HERE

Tom Holt

It was a busy day on Lake Chicopee. But it was a mixed bunch of sightseers and tourists that had the strange local residents rubbing their hands with delight.

There was Calvin Dieb, the lawyer setting up a property deal, who'd lost his car keys.

There was Linda Lachuk, the tabloid journalist who could smell that big, sensational story.

There was Janice DeWeese, who was just on a walking holiday but who longed for love.

And finally, but most promising of all, there was Wesley Higgins, the young man from Birmingham, England, who was there because he knew the legend of the ghost of Okeewana. All he had to do was immerse himself in the waters of the lake and he would find his heart's desire. Well, it seemed like a good idea at the time.

OPEN SESAME

Tom Holt

Something was wrong! Just as the boiling water was about to be poured on his head and the man with the red book appeared and his life flashed before his eyes, Akram the Terrible, the most feared thief in Baghdad, knew that this had happened before. Many times. And he was damned if he was going to let it happen again. Just because he was a character in a story didn't mean that it always had to end this way.

Meanwhile, back in Southampton, it's a bit of a shock for Michelle when she puts on her Aunt Fatima's ring and the computer and the telephone start to bitch at her. But that's nothing compared to the story that the kitchen appliances have to tell her . . .

Once again, Tom Holt, the funniest and most original of all comic fantasy writers, is taking the myth.

'Tom Holt stands out on his own . . . If you haven't read any Tom Holt, go out and buy one now. At least one. But don't blame me for any laughter-induced injuries'
Vector

NOTHING BUT BLUE SKIES

Tom Holt

There are very many reasons why British summers are either non-existent or, alternatively, held on a Thursday. Many of these reasons are either scientific, dull, or both – but all of them are wrong, especially the scientific ones.

The real reason why it rains perpetually from January 1st to December 31st (incl.) is, of course, irritable Chinese Water Dragons.

Karen is one such legendary creature. Ancient, noble, near-indestructible and, for a number of wildly improbable reasons, working as an estate-agent, Karen is irritable quite a lot of the time.

Hence Wimbledon.

She becomes positively incensed, however, when she discovers that her father, the Adjutant General to the Dragon King of the North-West, has been kidnapped by a mob of angry weathermen. An increasingly angry Karen heads out on a quest, or, at least, a hobby, to rescue her father from their evil clutches.

And some people start building Arks . . .

Other Orbit titles available by post:

☐	Snow White and the Seven Samurai	Tom Holt	£6.99
☐	Only Human	Tom Holt	£5.99
☐	Wish You Were Here	Tom Holt	£5.99
☐	Open Sesame	Tom Holt	£5.99
☐	Paint Your Dragon	Tom Holt	£5.99
☐	My Hero	Tom Holt	£5.99
☐	Odds and Gods	Tom Holt	£5.99
☐	Here Comes the Sun	Tom Holt	£5.99
☐	Expecting Someone Taller	Tom Holt	£5.99

The prices shown above are correct at time of going to press. However, the publishers reserve the right to increase prices on covers from those previously advertised without prior notice.

orbit

ORBIT BOOKS
Cash Sales Department, P.O. Box 11, Falmouth, Cornwall, TR10 9EN
Tel: +44 (0) 1326 569777, Fax: +44 (0) 1326 569555
Email: books@barni.avel.co.uk

POST AND PACKING:
Payments can be made as follows: cheque, postal order (payable to Orbit Books) or by credit cards. Do not send cash or currency.

U.K. Orders under £10	£1.50
U.K. Orders over £10	**FREE OF CHARGE**
E.E.C. & Overseas	25% of order value

Name (Block Letters) _____

Address _____

_____

Post/zip code: _____

☐ Please keep me in touch with future Orbit publications

☐ I enclose my remittance £_____

☐ I wish to pay by Visa/Access/Mastercard/Eurocard

Card Expiry Date

_____